The Criminal's Cure

Nicole Knight

ISBN 979-8-9990250-0-5

Cover design by Cover design by Beautiful Covers by Ivy

All editing and formatting done by Desert Ink Editorial

CONTENT WARNING

This book deals with heavy themes of violence, drug use, violence against children, organized crime, and murder. Please take care of yourself if any of these elements may be triggering for you.

CONTENTS

Chapter One

ROMAN

I'VE DONE A LOT of scary shit in my lifetime.

Jumped out of an airplane. Swam with great whites. Free climbed over part of the Grand Canyon. And that doesn't even include the amount of danger I've faced as head of one of the most powerful Cosa Nostra families based out of the city of Sin. I'm an adrenaline junkie at heart, and luckily, my lifestyle provides no shortage of opportunities to indulge in.

Yet, nothing prepares a man for the sheer panic he faces watching his six-year-old son teeter across a rickety, old jungle gym. The thing is a death trap. I can literally hear the screws on it rattle from here. If it had been any other day, I probably would have ignored Ty's begging and distracted him with another activity—preferably one that wasn't quite as heart attack inducing as this.

Today isn't any other day, though.

Today marks exactly six months since Talia died. Six months since I lost my wife and Ty lost his mom. Six months since the unthinkable happened and our entire world was turned upside down.

Ty doesn't understand the significance of the day, but the looming anniversary has been heavy on my mind for days. Still, when he came bounding into my room this morning asking to go to the park, I couldn't say no. He could have asked me to book a flight to Mykonos or dye my hair every color of the rainbow, and I probably would have done it. After all he's been through, I can't stand to disappoint him.

"Look Dad!" he calls from the top of the climbing structure, waving his arms wildly.

My stomach lurches, but I try not to let him see me cringe. "That's great, bud. You're kind of high up, though. Why don't you keep your hands on the bar, okay?"

The words sound so foreign coming out of my mouth. I never pictured myself being such an overprotective father, but things have changed drastically over the last few months.

Talia's death wasn't an accident, it was cold-blooded murder. I was away on business and an intruder broke into our home. In her last act on Earth, she locked Ty in our bedroom closest, shielding him from any danger as she was beaten within an inch of her life just on the other side of the door.

I can't bring myself to imagine the things he must have heard, and the fact that I wasn't there to protect either of them will haunt me until my dying day. Not to mention her killers are still on the loose.

You'd think as the head of a major crime organization with every imaginable resource at my fingertips, hunting them would be easy, but it's proved to be anything but. The lack of success is driving me insane, and it consumes my every thought. Finding them and making them pay is the only tangible thing I can control, and it's my top priority—out of both vengeance and necessity.

Ty isn't safe while they're still out there, and I'll be damned before I'll let my son get in harm's way because of my job again.

I wipe a bead of sweat off my brow and glance up at Ty. His shoulders are already red in the blistering Las Vegas sun, and I realize I forgot to put sunscreen on him.

Damn it.

This is the kind of thing I'm not good at. I can take Ty on all kinds of adventures, teach him how to play sports, roughhouse—but it's the day-to-day things that escape my mind. Like the fact that I need to plan twenty extra minutes to get him to school each morning just to wait in the drop-off line. Or that it isn't a good idea to let him watch zombie movies with me because he'll wake up with nightmares. Or where we keep the children's Tylenol, and once I find the damn stuff, how much do I give a six-year-old?

It's in the tiny moments that we miss Talia the most. She was an incredible mother, and she made everything run so seamlessly behind the scenes that I'm not sure I'll ever fully recover.

Talia wasn't the love of my life, by any means. She was a good friend, and her father worked under mine for years. Assuming my father's role demanded a wife, and Talia was the logical choice. For what she and I lacked in passion, we made up for in collaboration. We worked well together, and we got along, and that's more than I can say for the vast majority of arranged marriages.

"Five more minutes, Ty!" I've probably increased his skin cancer risk enough for one day, and it's about time for lunch.

"Do we have to?" he whines as my phone rings.

A trusted New York contact's name appears, instantly grabbing my attention. I ignore Ty's protest and answer.

"Leo?"

"Roman, hey. Is this a good time?"

"Yeah man, what's up?" I shove my fingers through my hair, pulse racing. The news he has could change everything, and I'm almost jittery with anticipation. Or maybe it's just too much coffee. Either way, I stand, pacing a few yards away from the playground.

"I'm not positive about any of this, so I don't want you to get your hopes up, but we might have a lead. I met with a supplier yesterday who spent some time out West. He was in Vegas a few months ago working with Los Chavos, a new group in La Eme, and some young kid was running his mouth about a job they did."

La Eme? A Mexican Mafia hit? That doesn't seem right.

"Our supplier was asking me about it because the kid mentioned that they went after an Italian Mafia Don. Thought we might have some inside information."

"You think I'm dealing with a street gang?"

"Honestly, I don't know what to make of it. The only reason I'm calling you about it is that they had specific details that weren't made public. Like that you were out of town. And that your son was there, specifically locked in the closet."

The hairs on the back of my neck rise as a blinding rage hits me. He's right. That fact was never released. Only someone who had been there that day would have known Ty was home.

I swallow, taking a deep breath as I weigh what all this means.

"It could be nothing, but you need to be careful, Roman." His voice is flat. "If this really is La Eme, then they're—"

A rapid burst of gunshots cut through the air. Tires screech as bullets spray across the area to the pulse of a machine gun and park goers scream and run for cover.

Above it all, I hear Ty.

"Daddy!" I turn at his panicked shriek. He's halfway between me and the playground, confusion and panic flashing in his eyes.

Dropping my phone, I lunge toward him, but I'm not quick enough. His body jolts and his eyes widen. A crimson stain expands across the bottom of his t-shirt.. All the wind is sucked out of me like I've been shot myself.

Time seems to slow, and my progress toward him feels like moving through concrete. Terrified parents shove their children out of the way, taking cover wherever they can. Others have been hit, and the playground quickly turns into pure madness.

The air stills, and the shooting ends as quickly as it started, but the carnage has just begun. I should take down the make and model of the car. I should run to my truck to follow as they flee, but I don't because every natural instinct has me turning toward my son. Nothing else matters.

When I finally break free of the crowd and get to Ty, I find a woman leaning over him. Her hands are on his chest, applying pressure to the wound to stop as much bleeding as she can. She reaches up, pressing two fingers underneath his chin as she checks for a pulse, and we both breathe a sigh of relief when she finds one.

"Come on buddy, stay with me," she whispers, pushing a wisp of blonde hair out of his eyes. I'm frozen with fear, hardly able to look at him lying here as my heart stabs with pain. This can't be happening. Not again. I can't lose my son.

I need to do something. I've dealt with gunshot wounds before, but my mind can't seem to process it, and the helplessness is eating me alive.

I fall to my knees next to Ty and the woman notices me for the first time.

"Is this your son?" she asks, glancing up at me. Her tone is even, almost calm, as she keeps her hand on Ty's wound. I hear her words, but a verbal response feels like an insurmountable task right now, so I just nod.

"I'm a doctor at St. Luke's. He's going to be okay, but I need you to call an ambulance. We need to get him to the hospital."

Her mention of the hospital jerks me back to reality. She wants me to call an ambulance, but I can't do that. St. Luke's is where Talia died. I can't take him there. I can't take him to *any* hospital; that will only make us easier targets. I need another plan and fast.

I finally find my voice. "No. No hospitals."

"Are you crazy? We need to get him to a hospital so he doesn't bleed out. The bullet is still inside of him." The woman looks at me as if I'm speaking another language.

Fuck. She's right.

Sirens fill the air and any time I have is quickly disappearing. We can't stay here, but if I don't get Ty help, then he could die. With police and hospitals clearly out of the question, I need an alternative.

All of a sudden, it hits me.

"You said you're a doctor, right?"

"Yes, but—"

Without thinking, I pull the gun out of my waistband, pointing it in her direction.

"Wh-what are you doing?" the woman stutters, eyes wide as she pulls back.

"You're coming with us," I growl, keeping the gun on her with one hand while I scoop Ty up into the other. The car isn't far away and I edge her toward it with a jab of my pistol to her ribs.

She moves compliantly, but not without a soul searing glare in her eyes. "You can't do this."

"Shut up!" I try to control my breathing and get a hold of myself. Ty's life depends on me...and her.

Ty stirs slightly in my arms, a quiet moan escaping his lips. "Daddy..."

"It's okay, buddy. I've got you. Everything is going to be fine."

"We have to get him to a hospital. He's going to die!" She tries one more time to change my mind, but there's no point.

Ignoring her, I open the car door and lay Ty on the seat. "He's not going to die. You're going to keep him alive. And if you don't..." I narrow my eyes on her. "I'll kill you."

CHAPTER TWO

THIS IS THE EXACT reason I never run in the park.

Well, maybe not the exact reason, but only because I never could have dreamed this up in my wildest imagination.

"You know this is illegal, right?"

Good one, Maddie. Like the guy who carried a gun in his pants for an afternoon at the park cares about what's legal.

My captor seems to agree because he chuckles, locking eyes with me in the rearview mirror as he weaves in and out of traffic. He's quiet, and oddly calm for the absolute hysteria that just ensued. He's either completely heartless, or he's used to this kind of thing—neither option feels all that comforting. If he's heartless, he won't think twice about killing some random woman, regardless of whether or not I can save his son. And if he's used to drive-by shootings and evading the police, then that means he's dangerous. *More* than dangerous.

Crime is pretty prevalent in Las Vegas. The city pretty much runs on all the illegal activity that happens behind the scenes. This man looks like he's right in the center of it, and now, so am I.

"What's his name?" I ask. Regardless of what an asshole his father is, I can't just let this little boy die.

"Ty. He's six. No prior medical issues and he's O negative blood type." He rattles off his son's stats like he's trained for something like this, but there's a thinly veiled urgency and fear in his voice. No matter how prepared you might be for disaster, you never know what it'll feel like in the moment, and just for a second, I feel bad for him.

Then I catch sight of the gun in his lap and remember how I got here, and the sympathy vanishes.

Ty fades in and out of consciousness. The bleeding has mostly stopped, but with a gaping wound in his stomach, there are at least a thousand other things to worry about. Blood loss. Infection. Internal damage from the bullet still lodged inside. I see the sliver of brass, so I know it isn't all that deep, but that's not to say it'll be easy to get to or that it hasn't already caused irreparable damage.

"Look, we really need to get him to a hospital," I urge. Maybe now the gravity has had time to set in, he'll understand how important it is. "The bullet is still inside of him and—"

"Then get it out," he snaps, white knuckles gripping the steering wheel. That's the only hint he's nervous.

"In a moving car?" I almost laugh. "You really are out of your mind if you think I can do that. Especially with driving like yours."

"Just keep him stable. We're almost there." Where exactly is *there*? If it's not an emergency room, it won't make much difference, and I don't need him to tell me to know that it won't be. Wherever we're headed, I won't have the supplies or the support or anything that I need to give his son a fighting chance, and I need to figure something out quickly.

"Damn it!" He slams the wheel with his hands, wrenching back to check on Ty. "We're in a traffic jam. You're going to have to do it here."

Panic strangles me. Does he think I'm some kind of magician? It wouldn't be the first time I removed a bullet, but the procedure is risky in the best of circumstances. It could break off and splinter, or dislodging it could make the bleeding even worse. I have no tools, no medication, and I've been jostled around so much that I'm already car sick. What's going to happen if I've got a blade in my hands?

I don't even have a scalpel, so that doesn't matter.

When I don't immediately start to move, his poisonous eyes bore into me and I hear the click of his gun. There's no more time to stall. I'm out of options—either I figure this out, or he kills me.

By now, my adrenaline has worn off and the reality of my situation sets in.

"I don't think I can do this," I murmur, hot tears bubbling in my eyes. "I've never done a procedure like this on my own."

The man swallows, squeezing his eyes shut as he lowers his gun. When he opens them again, I'm surprised to see them clouded with emotion. Fear, uncertainty, desperation. He chews on his lip, staring down at his son. "Please," he begs. "You're my only shot."

A bit of that sympathy creeps up again, and I feel myself softening. Maybe it's wishful thinking, or maybe I'm just delusional from the stress, but behind his tough as nails exterior, I see a father who is absolutely terrified of losing his son.

Am I actually about to do this? Am I actually going to help the man who refused any type of real medical care for his son? A man who has been nothing but hideous to me despite my efforts to help...

I have just enough of a bleeding heart to agree.

"I'm going to need something sharp. I have to make the opening bigger." I take a deep breath, barking out orders as If I'm actually in the operating room.

"There's a latch behind the passenger seat. Everything you need should be in there," he deadpans, void of all emotion once again.

As I flip the hook and peel back the leather of the seat, I'm speechless. A bottle of vodka, a knife, some towels, gauze, painkillers, and a few other things fall out.

"O-okay," I stutter, sifting through his supplies. The preparation floors me, and I glance up at him in the rearview mirror.

He holds me stare as a smirk curls at his lips. "For emergencies."

"What kind of emergencies require you to have a makeshift wound kit in your car?" Yeah, he's definitely involved in some highly illegal shit. You don't do this kind of thing if you're a teacher or an accountant.

"Less talking, more working." He clenches his jaw, eyes on the road as he makes a turn.

"Can you try to keep the car as steady as possible?"

"I'll do my best," he says. "And you do yours."

I don't need to be told twice, so I grab a towel and slip it underneath Ty.

"He won't feel any of this, right?" He looks back again.

I shake my head. "Not while he's unconscious. But he keeps coming in and out, so I'm going to have to do this fast."

He doesn't answer, but the engine purrs as he floors it, speeding to our final destination.

Taking the bottle of vodka, I twist the cap and pour it over Ty's wound to clean it as best I can. It's not perfect, but it'll help. I take another towel and dab at it. With practiced hands, I clean the knife off as well, then press the blade into Ty's skin, elongating the wound so I have a bit of room to work. More of the bullet is in view now, and I reach for the tweezers. Sucking in a sharp breath, I tighten them around the base and tug on it gently to be sure there isn't a rush of bleeding. If there is, I'll have to leave it in until I come up with a new plan. With the nearly translucent hue to Ty's face, I can tell he's already lost too much blood, so I can't risk it.

Thankfully, the bullet slides cleanly, and I pull it the rest of the way out. It comes out completely intact, and I breathe a sigh of relief. No fragments, no splintering. No heavy gush of blood that would indicate internal damage.

"I got it. I got it out," I say as much to him as to myself. I can't believe I actually did that. My first solo surgery and it was in the backseat of a car barreling ninety miles an hour down the highway. Holy shit.

"Why is he bleeding so much?" the man growls, his brow furrowed with rage.

There's a slow trickle of blood coming out of the wound, and I press another towel to it. "It's okay. The bullet came out clean and this amount of blood is totally normal. If there was anymore, then—"

He gets out of the car, slamming the door behind him. Until right now, I didn't even notice we'd stopped. The door to the backseat opens up, and he scoops Ty into his arms, snatching the towel out of my hands and pressing it to his wound. "Let's go."

"Where are we?" He completely ignores me as we get to the door of a huge warehouse type building. Its metal siding rattles in the wind, and there isn't a single window aside from a few aptly placed sky lights on the slanted roof.

"Here." He thrusts the towel back at me. "Keep pressure on it."

I fight the urge to laugh. I'm the professional and now he's ordering me around? You'd think that after I just saved his son's life, he'd show at least the slightest bit of appreciation, but I'm quickly realizing that this guy lacks even the most basic self-awareness.

He fumbles with a set of keys, and eventually he flips the lock, bursting through the door with a loud and attention-drawing bang. Two men sit at the front of the warehouse playing cards, and they look up at us when we walk in.

"Jesus, Roman. What is going on?" The taller of the bunch rushes toward us, clearing a spot off on the table for Roman to set Ty down.

"Drive-by at the park," he says flatly as he lays his son back. Taking the towel from me again, he holds it to the wound.

"Ty was hit?" The other guy's face turns sheet white, and he scrambles for a medkit.

Roman nods. "Once in the stomach. I think he's stable now, though."

"What the fuck is all this blood from then?"

"The bullet was blocking his blood flow," I jump in to explain. "When I took it out, all the backed-up blood was free, so it just seems like he's bleeding a lot. He's going to be okay, really."

All three men stare at me, noticing that I'm here for the first time.

"Who is she?" The tall guy nods his head towards me.

"She's a doctor," Roman says. "She volunteered to help Ty."

"Volunteered?" I scoff. This man either lives in a completely alternate universe than the rest of us, or he's on some very good drugs. Either way, I can't bite my tongue. "More like you forced me into your car at gunpoint."

His friend rubbed the bridge of his nose. "Please tell me she's kidding."

Roman shrugs as if he couldn't care less about any of this.

"Roman!" the guy barks again.

He groans, throwing his hands in the air in exasperation. "Well, what did you expect me to do, Joe? It wasn't like I could take him to the hospital. It was Los Chavos, I know it."

Of course he knows who the shooter was. He was probably the target, which only makes me more suspicious of him. All I wanted to do was help the poor little boy, and now I've ensnared myself in some brooding criminal war.

"La Eme?" his other friend snarls. "Here in Vegas?"

"Enough." Joe shuts them down with a venomous stare. "We're not talking about this in front of her. What is she still doing here, anyway?"

Ty's body jolts, halting the conversation. He coughs and a few drops of blood appear on his lip.

Damn it. There must have been more internal damage than I initially thought.

"Help him!" Roman's voice booms off of the walls as he shoves me toward his son.

I bit my lip, trying to figure out what to do next. Taking out the bullet was one thing, but this is completely different. He needs x-rays and an ultrasound and a tube in his chest, and I can't do any of that on my own. Especially not here.

"Please let me call the ambulance," I beg. "They'll take care of him, I promise."

"No. How many times do I have to fucking say it? No hospitals. No ambulances."

"The bullet is out now, and you could probably pass it off as some other wound. You wouldn't even have to tell them it was a gunshot. We can say he got impaled by something in the park, or that there was a car accident. They'll take good care of him, I promise."

Roman whips out his gun again, pressing the cool metal to my temple and cocking it back. The click sends a chill winding through my trembling body, and I squeeze my eyes shut.

This is where I'm going to die. I just know it. Right here on the floor of this warehouse. In just my sports bra and shorts, still gross and sweaty from my run. But what do I care? It's not like anyone is going to find my body. No one knows where I am or who I'm with. Hell, I don't even know that—I was a little too distracted trying to take a bullet out of a child to see the street signs while we drove. Now no one is going to know what happened to me at all.

"Jesus, Roman. Get a hold of yourself." Joe attempts to calm him, but I doubt it will work. We've obviously established that Roman isn't the kind of man who takes kindly to opinions he didn't ask for.

"Not until she helps Ty." He strides forward until he towers mere inches in front of me, so close it's like we're sharing the same breath.

I can't even bring myself to look up at him, the heat from his glare so intense that I think it might be enough to kill me itself.

Holding my hands up, I take a breath. "Fine. He needs a chest tube. The bullet probably pierced one of his organs and we need to get the blood out."

"Do it," Roman sneers.

Rummaging through their med kits, I don't find much I can use at all. Clearly, they aren't equipped for this kind of emergency or injury, yet here we are. On the table, I see a straw. It's flimsy and completely unsanitary, but it's the best thing I've got and it might get the job done until I can convince Roman to get his son to a hospital.

"I need the vodka and the first aid kit from the car."

"Get her what she needs," Roman directs the other guy, who takes off to get my supplies.

I move towards Ty, nudging Roman out of the way. To my surprise, he doesn't put up much of a fight and lets me through. My hands tremble as traitorous thoughts echo in my head. *I shouldn't do this. I can't do this. We've got to get to a hospital.*

He's left me with no other choice, though. Finally, his friend comes back inside and hands me the alcohol and the kit. I pour vodka over the straw, praying that it'll be enough, and then I feel around Ty's chest and abdomen. Right at the center of his chest, there's a pressure buildup; I can see the swell forming just below his ribcage. It isn't the worst-case scenario, but it isn't exactly ideal either.

Judging by the location, the bullet could've pierced his lungs, or at least grazed one. I make a small incision over the area like I've done countless times before and blood streams out quickly. After pouring more alcohol over the wound, I work the straw in between folds. When I get it inserted about halfway, I set it in place, holding my breath and hoping it will start drawing out the blood.

Everyone is on edge as we wait. *Come on, Ty.*

When a small drop of blood appears at the top of the drain, I almost think my eyes are playing tricks on me, but it's followed by several more. A steady trickle begins and the pressure in Ty's chest deflates. He's breathing on his own.

Roman looks up at me. "He's okay?"

"For now." I nod. "But this won't hold forever. He's going to need a real chest tube, and medication, and somebody to monitor him. You *really* need to take him to the hospital."

"You have supplies to do all of that at the hospital?" Roman arches an eyebrow at me.

Of course, we do. It's a hospital.

I ignore the idiocy in his response as relief floods me. Have I finally gotten through to him?

Suddenly, he turns to Joe.

"Take her to the hospital so she can get the supplies she needs and bring her back here."

Joe nods.

My eyes widened in horror. "Are you crazy? Even with the right supplies, this is nowhere to do the level of care he needs. It's probably crawling with diseases." Judging by the cockroaches on the floor and all the fast food containers scattered around, that isn't an exaggeration. "You can't do this. This is kidnapping. It's child endangerment. Your son needs a doctor."

Roman stands, stalking towards me with the authority and candor of a man who isn't used to someone questioning him. "I've had about enough of that smart mouth of yours. He has a doctor. You. And if you want to live, I suggest you do what I say. Go to your precious hospital, get the supplies you need, then come back and fix Ty. If anything happens to him, or you so much as utter a word of this to anyone at the hospital, I will put so much lead in you that you'll sink to the bottom of the Hoover dam. Are we clear?"

I open my mouth to speak, but nothing comes out, the words dying in my throat. My knees threaten to give out on me at any moment and my whole body quakes..

He takes a punishing hold on my arm, fingers digging into my bicep so hard that I almost whimper. "I said, are we clear?"

All I can do is nod. I'm in way over my head here.

CHAPTER THREE

I'M GOING TO JAIL.

Either that, or I'm going to die. There's just no other way that this can work out. A few hours ago, the worst thing I'd ever done was get a speeding ticket and now I'm about to rob a hospital. Somehow, it's not the felony charge or potential jail sentence that scares me the most. It's the cold, vicious criminal who's only redeeming quality is that he cares about his son.

At least I think he does. I don't have more than a few small glimpses of his vulnerability to go off of, but why else would he be making me do all of this? For some reason, I want to give him the benefit of the doubt when it comes to his love and concern for Ty. Whether he deserves it is something else entirely.

It doesn't take a genius to figure out what Roman and his friends are into. The guns, the matching tattoos, the avoidance of police...Not to mention how they knew the attack was on them or how no one even batted an eye when they heard Roman kidnapped me at gunpoint. It all screams gang, and there is no shortage of that in Las Vegas.

They give me exactly five minutes to clean myself up before we leave. Joe hands me an oversized sweatshirt and a pair of leggings to change into, and

I can't bring myself to think about who they belong to. One of their wives? Girlfriends? Or the most likely option—they belong to another woman they've abducted. I frantically wash all the blood from my body, paranoid that I'm going to miss a spot and blow the entire thing. Letting my blonde hair out of its ponytail, I drag my fingers through it in an attempt to make myself look presentable.

The drive with Joe to the hospital is quiet, my hands trembling and sweaty. With each turn he takes, my heart pounds in my chest and the closer we get, the harder it is for me to breathe. By the time he pulls into the parking lot, I've almost worked myself into a full-blown panic attack.

"In and out." Joe's voice jerks me back to reality.

"Wh-what?"

"Breathe. In and out. You're so nervous that you've been holding your breath. You're going to make yourself pass out." That's actually not a bad idea. If I pass out in the emergency room, someone would have to check me out and at the very least, I could buy myself some time.

"Here." With a smirk, he hands me a water bottle. He's getting more amusement out of this than he should be, which doesn't make me feel any better. "You've got to calm yourself down. If you walk in there like this, you'll have everyone in that hospital suspicious of you."

I swallow, staring at the big red Emergency Room sign. "Maybe I *want* to tip them off."

"No, I think that's about the last thing you want to do. At least if you value your life," he says, cutting the engine. "Roman doesn't make empty threats. And no offense, Doc, but a sweet little thing like you wouldn't last twenty-four hours under his torture."

Torture.

Wild ideas of what exactly he means by that flash through my mind making my stomach knot. "What kind of people are you?"

"The less you know, the better." Joe checks his rearview mirror as a couple passes by. "Even if you do save Ty, Roman can't let you go if you know too much."

The idea of him letting me go seems like a pipe dream, but I have no choice but to play along. Roman hasn't shown the slightest bit of remorse or retreat, but Joe is different. I wouldn't jump straight to nice, but he's not *quite* as hostile as his boss and he hasn't held a gun to my head.

"How do you want to play this?" he asks, unbuckling his seat belt. "You want to say I'm your boyfriend? Cousin? How well do you know these people?"

I can hardly hear him speak over the hammering in my chest. "Can't I just go in and get you the supplies, and then you let me go? I promise I'll get you everything you need for Ty. Please, just let me go."

My pleas fall on deaf ears. Joe is completely unmoved by my suggestion, and my stomach sinks.

"You know that's not going to happen." He sighs, the smallest hint of sympathy in his voice. "And just in case you get any wild ideas about running, you should know that he has eyes on us right now. And he's got men combing through every single detail of your past. Where you live, where you work. Where your family lives and works. Friends, boyfriends...there'd be nowhere for you to hide."

There's no winning this game. Even if I follow his rules. Even if I save Ty. Even if this plan goes absolutely perfect.

"He's going to kill me even if I save Ty, isn't he?" I nearly choke on the words, panic pulsing through me again.

"Let's just get through this." His avoidance is all the answer I need.

I take a deep breath. *Come on, Maddie. You can do this. Just walk in there, lie to your coworkers, and steal thousands of dollars' worth of medical supplies. Easy.*

Maybe if I reframe this a little, I won't feel so terrible. I took an oath, right? To help those in need? Ty is certainly in need, and if I focus on that, I can get through this.

Or maybe, I'm just as delusional as Roman is.

Regardless, it's showtime. I force myself out of the car before I can change my mind and Joe follows close behind me.

I'm not even two stops in the door before I run into Dr. Bauer, the head of trauma surgery at the hospital and my boss.

"Madison! Thank goodness. I've been trying to get a hold of you all morning. There was a shooting at the park and we've got eight victims. I need you in a trauma bay immediately."

Anxiety prickles through my core at the mention of the shooting. With every spare thought consumed by Ty, I never considered the other victims. "I'm so sorry, Dr. Bauer. I can't. I'm not working today. I'm just here to get a few things out of my locker."

Dr. Bauer stares at me in disbelief. "What do you mean, you can't? I know you're not in, but it's all hands on deck."

Before I can come up with a good enough excuse, Joe interrupts from behind me.

"Dr. Bauer?" Joe sticks his hand out. "I'm Maddie's cousin, Joe. We had a death in the family and have to go out of town immediately. That's why she can't come in today."

I bite back a laugh at the way he calls me Maddie, like he's known me my entire life, but I have to give him credit for committing to the act. The sympathy on Dr. Bauer's face tells me he bought it.

"Oh, I'm so sorry to hear that. Take all the time you need, Madison. And please give my regards to your parents."

He rushes away without waiting for a response.

Joe grabs my arm and pulls me to the side. "Your parents? I thought you said you didn't know these people very well." To be fair, I didn't say anything when he asked me about it in the car because I was still spiraling on his casual mention of torture.

"Do I need to be worried about him talking to your family?"

"Relax." I shake my head. "My dad's in medicine. He and Dr. Bauer are acquaintances, but they don't talk regularly."

"You better hope they don't, because that's a loose end I can take care of real quick."

The threat is a harsh reminder of what's at stake here, and just how callous these people are. Now, I've put Dr. Bauer's life in danger, too.

"Wait here," I tell him, ready to get this over with. The longer we're here, the greater the risk becomes of putting even more people in harm's way, and I can't stand the thought of it.

I duck inside a supply closet at the end of the hallway. Luckily, it's fully stocked, and I start stuffing bandages and tubing and a few things into the bag that Joe gave me. It's not perfect, but it will have to do.

Oh shit.

My knees nearly buckle when I realize that I'm going to have to get the rest of what I need from the pharmacy. Playing grab-and-go in the supply closet is one thing, but smuggling drugs out of here is going to be a lot more difficult.

Come on, Maddie. Think.

Joe is waiting for me when I come out of the closet, nowhere near where I told him to stay. "Are we good?"

Biting into my lip, I shake my head. "We've got a problem."

"What kind of problem?" Joe narrows his eyes at me in a way that makes my heart stop.

"Ty needs medication. He needs antibiotics and sedatives and lidocaine...those are all things that have to be checked out and thoroughly documented."

Joe clenches his jaw, whipping out his phone. "You take the long way to the pharmacy, and leave the rest to me."

"Okay." I don't trust Joe as far as I can throw him, but right now, we're teammates and I need him if I want to make it out of this.

The pharmacy is just down the hall, and I recognize the technician right away.

"Hi Dr. Taylor. Need something for one of the shooting victims?" She smiles brightly, completely unaware that she's about to participate in a crime.

"Yes," I say. "I need two bags of amoxicillin and two of oxycodone. And can you throw in a vial of lidocaine? And an order of Midazolam."

"Got it. What's the patient's ID number?" She pulls something up on her computer, my pulse skyrocketing with every click of her keyboard.

"Um..."

"Perfect." She rolls her eyes. "The entire system is down on the busiest day we've had all month."

She hands me a pen and a piece of paper. "Here. Write the ID number down while I go get your stuff. I'll have to enter it later this week."

I glance back at Joe, who sits patiently in the waiting area. He shoots me a cocky wink when our eyes meet. Did he honestly just hack into the entire hospital database? Before I can really think about all the ramifications of that, the tech comes back with my things and I walk towards Joe.

If it's possible, I'm even more nervous than before.

"Everything okay?" he asks.

I nod. "Let's just get out of here."

Joe swings his arm around my shoulder as we walk out of the emergency room. "We make a pretty good team, Mads."

"Don't call me that," I say, squirming out from under him.

Joe chuckles. "I have to say, you have more guts than I gave you credit for. You might survive Roman Molanari yet."

CHAPTER FOUR

ROMAN

MADISON MARIE TAYLOR. TWENTY-SEVEN years old. Born and raised in St. Louis, Missouri. Graduated med school last year, and took a residency in trauma surgery at St. Luke's.

Medicine seems to be somewhat of a family tradition for the Taylors. Her dad is ranked as the top trauma surgeon in all of St. Louis, and she's got two older brothers, who both followed in his footsteps.

She spends her off days volunteering at the local animal shelter, can run a marathon in four hours and twenty-two minutes, is allergic to coconut, and when she was seven, she nearly drowned in her backyard pool. Those are just some highlights from the file that Dante put together on her in the last hour. It's basically all useless, but her handiwork has held up and Ty's been restful since she and Joe left. Reading up on Madison has given me something to do so I don't go insane.

I thumb through a few of the pictures that Dante printed, stopping on one in particular. It's a snapshot of her at a wedding, in a long black dress that fits her like it was sewn right onto her body. Deep brown eyes, honey dipped curls draping over her shoulder, and a pair of rosy lips that frame a sparkling smile.

Setting the picture down and closing the file, I rub my jaw. I sure hope she's a good doctor, because it would be a fucking shame to kill a woman who looks like that.

"You're sure about this. Roman? There are plenty of hospitals that we could take him to. It doesn't have to be—" The file on Madison kept Dante occupied too, but now that he's finished, he's getting antsy.

"We're not going to a hospital. He'll be much more comfortable here, and I can control the situation." Not to mention the security.

Joe and Dante might not understand why I'm so adamant about this, but that's because neither of them lost their wives to a medical error. Perhaps the worst part of Talia's death is that it was completely preventable. They got her to the hospital in time, and she could've survived her injuries, but there was a mistake made with her medication.

As unreasonable as it might be, letting a random doctor we met in the park operate on Ty feels less risky than wheeling him into the same hospital, with the same doctors, who killed his mother six months ago.

"Right." Dante paces in front of me, raking his fingers through his hair. "And what do you plan to do with the girl once all of this is over? It's not like we can just let her go."

He's got a point. It was a mistake to talk about the attack so freely in front of her—now she knows too much. I can't just let her go, at least not without a high-level of security on her at all times to be sure she doesn't go to the police. It's going to be expensive, but I'd spend all the money in the world to keep Ty safe.

"Depends."

"On?" Dante presses.

"On whatever I fucking decide, Dante."

Why can't he just let this go? I don't pay him for his opinions or expertise—that's Joe's department. Dante is only here because he's six-foot-eight, two hundred eighty pounds of pure muscle with a temper that could rival the hulk. And because, as much as he irritates me, he's one of my best friends.

Dante, Joe, and I grew up together. When I took over the business for my father, it was an obvious choice to bring them with me. Honestly, I'm not giving Dante enough credit. He's one of the most feared and lethal enforcers in the entire Cosa Nostra, and I'm lucky he's on my team.

He's probably only pressing me because he knows whatever happens to Madison will fall on him.

I walk over to the couch, kneeling next to Ty. While they were at the hospital, Dante and I moved Ty to my house, where I knew he'd be the most comfortable. He's nestled on the couch underneath a blanket his grandmother made for him, peaceful and sleeping for the time being. There's a bit of blood on his chin, and I wipe it away with my thumb as my chest tightens.

I swore nothing like this would ever happen to him. I can only imagine what Talia would say if she was here, and none of it would be good.

When we first got married, Talia understood what our marriage meant, and she was content with the life I could give her. It wasn't until after Ty was born that things shifted. She wanted out, and she begged me for years to let all of this go, to take them far away from the danger and violence. It wasn't that simple, though.

You don't just leave something like the Mafia, especially when you're at the helm of the entire organization. It would have been even more dangerous for us to be out on our own, alone and unprotected. Here, at least we have an army of men willing to die to protect us and keep us safe.

Something changed inside of me the day Ty was born, too. I held him in my arms, and suddenly, everything became about protecting him and giving him the best life possible. I fully believed that meant staying here, and I still do, but I'll be damned if there isn't the slightest piece of me that still wonders where we would have ended up. What I'd be doing now. If Talia would still be alive.

It's a fleeting thought, though. I'm good at this shit. I've been in charge for six years, and have already nearly tripled our profits and production. The problem is, the better you are at this job, the more danger you attract. Everyone wants a piece of you. Everyone's gunning for you.

And yet, I still wholeheartedly believe that Ty is safest here. I just need to find some way to fix the current situation.

Fixing things usually comes easy to me, but the only way I know how to fix this is to use more violence. I'm all Ty has left now, and putting myself in danger isn't a wise choice. Once I know he's healthy and safe, I can start working on a plan of revenge. For both him and his mother.

"You moved him?" I didn't even hear them come inside, but Madison is already yelling at me. *Jesus Christ.*

"Yeah. You mentioned more than once that the warehouse wasn't up to your hygiene standards, so I figured you'd want something a little nicer." I stand, turning to face her tiny frame. She has to tilt her head up to make eye contact with me, and when she does, she looks at me like I'm an absolute idiot.

"You could have ruptured the drain by jostling him around like that," she snaps. "He could have bled out and this all would have been for nothing."

I stiffen. Even if she is right, I don't like the way she's speaking to me. "Well, if the drain came out, wouldn't that mean that you placed it wrong?"

"Actually, no—" She crosses her arms over her chest, a pointed scowl that surprises me. Going toe to toe with a crime boss isn't for the faint of heart, and she's got to know what's going on by now.

"Enough," Joe hisses. "He's here now, so let's just do what we have to do."

Madison doesn't move and neither do I. I'm not quite ready to let it go, but Ty's voice draws us both back to reality.

"Daddy?" He's hoarse and disoriented, but the sound is music to my ears. He has enough strength to speak, and that's a good sign.

"I'm right here, buddy." I kneel next to him, taking his little hand in mine. My voice breaks, the emotion of the day finally catching up to me. "How are you feeling?"

"My chest hurts." His tiny features twist into a frown as tears bubble in his eyes. His breathing is a little labored, but he gets more and more alert, a bit of color coming back to his cheeks.

"I bet it does. I can help with that." Madison smiles brightly, sitting next to Ty on the couch. "My name is Maddie and I'm a doctor. It's my job to help you feel better. Is it okay if I take a look at you?"

Ty nods, and I ease back, giving her a bit of space to work.

"You were at the park." Ty recognizes her.

"That's right. I was," Madison says as she gets her supplies together. "I'm impressed that you remember that. You were really brave back there. I definitely would have cried."

"Crying is for babies. That's what Daddy says."

Madison flinches, but she doesn't look the least bit surprised that I'd say something like that.

"Buddy, I didn't mean—" The explanation dies on my lips because she interrupts me.

"I think you're brave, regardless. In fact, I might need a little help to give you your medicine. Think you can handle that?"

"Yeah!" Ty is enthusiastic about the idea. She's good with him, and I feel a pang of guilt about how things transpired. I would do anything for my son, but a less abrasive approach might have been better.

She pulls out a canister of cream from her bag. "This is magic lotion. You put it on your body and you can't feel anything. Want to try?"

Ty swipes his finger across the top, loading it with the ointment. He rubs it on his arm and waits a couple of seconds before looking up at her in amazement. "It worked!"

"I told you it would! Now, how about putting some right here?" She points to a spot on the inside of his elbow and Ty spreads it across his skin.

"Perfect." She grins. "Now, I'm going to put something called an IV in your arm. It's a special tube that lets me give you medicine so your body can heal."

Madison takes a needle out and preps it. "Okay, Ty, take a deep breath for me."

Ty sucks in. "Great. Now let it out slowly." He follows her instructions, pursing his lips to release the air in a measured exhale just as she presses the tip of the needle into his arm.

"That's it. You're doing great, Ty."

I watch, but Madison is so quick with her work that I barely make out what she's doing. Soon, she's got the entire thing placed and Ty hardly even notices.

"Joe, can you get me something tall I can hang this on?"

He nods, and rushes off, returning with the coat rack from the entryway. "Will this work?"

"That's perfect." She takes it from him, winding the tubing up and draping it over a hook. Withdrawing a bag of some kind of liquid from her supplies, she attaches it to the IV. Soon, it's pumping into him.

"What's that?" I ask.

"It's an antibiotic and pain killer combo. It'll help kill any infection he might have before it gets too far and help manage his pain the next few days. And this is more sedative..." She hooks another one up. "It'll help with the pain when I take the drain out and hopefully keep him quiet for a few days."

"How are you doing, Ty?" she asks, flashing him a smile.

"Good."

"Good," she says, moving down to the drain in his stomach. "Now comes the tricky part. I had this in your stomach to help relieve some of the pressure, but now we can take it out."

"Is it going to hurt?" Ty asks, frowning in fear.

"It might a little, but we're going to do it really fast. And your dad is going to hold your hand the whole time and you can squeeze as hard as you want."

Ty cracks a small smile. "What if I squeeze so hard I break his fingers?"

"Even better." Madison winks at Ty and then glances up at me. "Come right over here." She gestures to a spot up by Ty's head and I carefully sit.

"Alright, little man, let's see what you've got." I offer him my hand and he eagerly takes it.

"Okay, I need you to take a big, deep breath in. You don't know how to count to ten, do you?"

"Of course I do. I can count to a hundred," Ty snaps back, giving Madison exactly the reaction she was looking for.

She laughs. "Great. How about backwards?"

Ty looks at me, not as confident in his response this time. I shrug. "I bet you can. Why don't we do it together?"

"Okay," he agrees.

"Great. You tell me when you're ready." Madison uses a wipe to blot around the wound and the base of the straw. It's not drawing any more blood out, and I can't tell if that's a good thing or not.

For a minute, I wonder if I really did do something to mess it up when we moved him.

Ty hesitates for a second, and then finally gives her the go ahead.

"Here we go, Ty. Remember to count. One hundred...ninety-nine..." she instructs, getting right to work.

"Ninety-eight." His voice is shaky, and he fights hard not to cry as Madison tugs at the straw.

I give his hand a tight squeeze and count with him. "Ninety-seven...ninety -six...ninety-five...ninety-four..."

Ty is tough as nails as she slides the straw out, his whole body tightening. He lets out the smallest whimper when the last bit releases and she puts a piece of gauze over the incision. There's a bit of blood, but nothing like before, and I pretend not to see the relief flood Madison's faces.

"You're doing great, buddy. Almost there."

"One more big breath in for me." Her voice is so gentle it's almost calming me down, and I'm a bit in awe of her. She's obviously very good at what she does, and she has Ty completely comfortable; unphased by all of this.

Ty takes a deep breath.

"Good. Ninety-three...ninety-two...ninety-one." We all finish the last numbers together.

Madison smiles, snapping her gloves off empathically for effect. "All done!"

"That's it?" Ty and I both say at the same time.

"Yep! You did great! And now all you have to do is lie here while your body starts to heal and watch all the movies and eat all the ice cream you want. Doctor's orders."

"Hear that buddy? You're going to be feeling better in no time!" Hopefully, I sound more confident than I am. No stitches? No more tubing? She doesn't seem like the type of person who would risk a child's life just to get back at me, but it feels like there should be more.

"Why don't we get started on that now?" Joe comes into the room and turns the TV on. He plops on the couch next to Ty, who dissolves into giggles. Joe is like an uncle to Ty, and the two are best of friends. We never would have survived the last few months if it hadn't been for Joe and his wife, Sarah.

He smirks up at me and I let out a sharp laugh. "What? She said doctor's orders."

With Ty occupied, I help Madison clean up.

"You're welcome." There's a familiar bite in her voice, all the gentleness and warmth she'd given to Ty completely gone.

"What?"

"I said you're welcome. Usually, when someone willingly goes out of their way to help you, you would say thank you."

It's both odd and refreshing that she isn't afraid of me. Despite me holding a gun to her head and kidnapping her this afternoon, she's as feisty and argumentative as ever. There isn't a person in my life I'd let get away with speaking to me the way she is, but I've got to admire the audacity.

I clench my jaw. "I wouldn't exactly say you did it willingly."

"Yeah, forcibly kidnapping someone kind of takes that option away." She glares. "Speaking of which, I need to get going. Keep him on the IV for the next forty-eight hours and if everything looks good after that, you can take it out. I would suggest hiring someone to take care of his wounds and rehab. They're going to need to be dressed constantly for a while, and once he's feeling up to it, he'll need to build his strength up slowly."

"You're not going anywhere. At least not until I figure out what to do with you." I might have gotten a little ahead of myself with this one. It isn't like me to act without all the details seamlessly ironed out, so I'll blame the desperation. I didn't think about what I would do with her after the fact, just that I needed her right then.

"What are you talking about? You said if I saved him, you'd let me go."

"What I said was if you saved him, I wouldn't kill you."

Madison's face turns white, teeth sinking into her lip. "Roman, please. I swear, I won't tell anyone about this. Just please let me go."

Her pleas have me feeling things far past the logistical benefits of keeping her here, but I shove the thought away. Jesus, what's wrong with me?

"Dante, can you show Madison to a room upstairs?"

"Roman, you can't do this!" she insists, growing more flustered by the second.

I let out a sharp laugh. "Madison, if you haven't figured it out by now, I can do just about anything I want. I appreciate what you did for Ty, but I'm sure you can understand that letting you walk out of here isn't an option. Not with what you've seen today."

"So what? You're going to keep me here forever?"

"Dante, upstairs. Now."

"You're out of your mind if you think I'm going to stay here as some kind of prisoner," she hisses, jerking away from Dante. He finally gets hold of her and leads her up the staircase. I watch until they disappear down the hallway, listening to her protests the entire way.

"What the hell are you doing, Roman?" I didn't even realize Joe was next to me until now.

I wish I could tell him. Every logical part of me knows I should let her go. Ty is stable, and every second she's still here only digs me into a deeper hole. By now, people might be looking for her or noticing that she's gone. It would be easy for me to put a man on her to be sure she stays quiet, so what exactly am I doing?

Then something strikes me. Madison proved her worth as a doctor today, and I could use someone like that around here, especially with Ty recovering. Having her around permanently is more enticing than it should be.

"I'm going to offer her a job."

CHAPTER FIVE

I'M A RUNNER.

Distance running is my specialty, but I can be pretty fast when I need to be. I could probably make it at least a few miles away before anyone even noticed I was gone, if I could just somehow make it outside.

Dante dumped me off in a second story guest room, so it's not as simple as just climbing out. There are no trees close by, or even a bush I could aim to land on. I could tie a few bed sheets together and try to shimmy down, but I'm doubtful that would actually work in real life. It seems like just a movie thing. I could jump, but that alone could break my leg, or worse, and then any chance I have of running would be gone.

God, what am I even saying? Even if I made it out, I don't have the slightest idea where I am. Somewhere within an hour of the hospital, but that doesn't give me much to go on.

This place is like a fortress. From the bedroom window, I have an expansive view of the property, and in other circumstances, I might think it was pretty. Thick towering trees line the area and there's even a little pond with a paddle boat tied to a dock just down the way. Right underneath my window is a huge pool with crystal clear water and a few errant floating toys and dive sticks scattered around. The driveway is lined with intricate, colorful cobblestone that looks like something out of a Spanish village, which matches the stonework and stucco on the eves of the house. It wasn't like I got a proper tour, but from what I saw so far, I can tell it's enormous. At the end of the road, a massive wrought iron gate sits closed. Probably locked tight. Even if it wasn't, there are four guards posted with heavy artillery strapped to their chests, and I doubt I'd make it far.

Not to mention that, with connections like Roman's, I'd probably have to hide out somewhere in the wilderness to avoid him. To be fair, a cave out in the middle of nowhere sounds more appealing than my current situation. At least, I know what I'm dealing with out there.

Inside these walls, it's a whole different ball game. I know virtually nothing about organized crime, but I've heard enough to know that I'm in major trouble here. Roman is the kind of man nightmares are made of, and I have no idea what he's capable of. My anger towards him has slowly morphed into fear as the gravity of my situation sets in. Any hope I had of him coming to his senses and letting me go is long gone.

It's all part of his game.

Maybe someone will come looking for me when I don't show up for work tomorrow. *Wait.* They won't because Joe bought some time and told them I was going to be out of town. And I just spoke with my mom yesterday, so she won't be suspicious for at least a few more days. My stomach turns at the thought of what a man like Roman Molanari could do to me in that amount of time.

I glance at the window, weighing my chances once again. Maybe if I took a running start and dove out the window, I could make it to the pool, letting water break my fall. At this point, I'm dying either way, so I might as well give it a shot.

I try to twist the lock, but it's so tight I can't maneuver it. Right now, it's my only option, so I grip it with all my strength and try again.

"I wouldn't do that if I were you." Roman's voice sends a chill down my spine. He caught me red handed unlatching the window. I didn't hear the door open, but suddenly he's only steps away from me.

"Do what?" I swallow, my throat tight. "It's stuffy in here. I needed some fresh air."

He stands close to me, and I realize it's the first time I've truly looked at him since all of this began. It's his eyes that I notice first—piercing, icy blues that look like they're staring straight into the depths of my soul. His sharp jawline is flecked with facial hair, and his full lips press together in an arrogant smirk. A black t-shirt stretches across his thick, broad shoulders, and he fills out every inch of his larger-than-life frame. Rippling muscles, an impressive collection of tattoos, and an ego that barely fits in this room.

Roman is gorgeous in an intimidating sort of way, and when he arches an eyebrow in my direction with a taunting look on his face, I almost forgot what a smug asshole he's been.

Almost.

He chuckles, striding toward me so slowly that the anticipation is painful. We're close. Uncomfortably close. Intimately close.

"Do you think I'm stupid, Madison? That you're the first person who's tried to open the window and escape?"

When I don't answer, he continues.

"Let me save you the trouble. It doesn't end well. Even if you were to get it open, I've got two snipers on the roof, plus perimeter security that would make the White House look like an easy target. You wouldn't make it ten yards without a bullet to your head."

I have to fight to keep myself collected so he doesn't see how rattled I truly am. I don't want to give him the satisfaction.

"What do you want from me?" I ask.

"I came up here to offer you a proposition. And I guess an apology."

"An apology?" Honestly, I'm shocked he even knows the word.

"Yes." He chews the inside of his cheek. "I guess I haven't been as friendly to you as I could have been, especially since you saved Ty's life. And if you took it that way, I'm sorry." The way he trips over the words is a dead giveaway that he isn't used to apologizing.

A sharp laugh escapes my lips.

"Something funny to you?"

"That's not how you apologize to someone." I cross my arms over my chest, refusing to back down. Now that I know nothing I do will sway his decision to let me go, I won't let him walk all over me.

"Excuse me?"

"You can't say that you're sorry for the way I took something. Apologies are about taking responsibility for something you did, and all you did was pass the blame off to me for how I interpreted it."

He scoffs. "You've got a lot of nerve for a woman bargaining for her life."

"And you've got a lot of nerve for a man who needs me and my medical degree to take care of his son."

Roman stiffens. "I guess that brings me to my next point."

"The proposition."

He nods. Fantastic. Now what is he going to make me do?

"You've got $200,000 in school loan debt."

"Do I even want to know how you found that out?"

He ignores me. "I want you to live here and work for me for the next six months. Rehabbing Ty and dealing with any other potential...emergencies that might come up. You'd need to stay here, but obviously your room and board would be covered in addition to any payment. If you agree, I'll make sure that your debt disappears and you have your pick off positions at St. Luke's once that six months is up."

I can hardly believe what I'm hearing. *Potential emergencies.* Is he serious? He wants me to patch up his guys after more issues like today? I don't know if my nerves can handle another day like this one.

Still, the amount of money he's talking about is sickening, and in such a short time frame. It's life changing, and I've eaten just enough Top Ramen the last few weeks to entertain it.

"You have that kind of pull at St. Luke's, but you won't take your son there?"

"St. Luke's and I have a history." He clenches his jaw. "None of that matters, though. Trust me, they'll do whatever I want."

I don't know what's crazier—his offer or the fact that I'm actually considering it.

"What exactly would this entail?" I ask cautiously.

"Exactly what I said. My team has unique needs that come up from time to time. I need someone who is good under pressure, understands discretion, and has enough medical knowledge to make do."

I didn't go to medical school to *make do*. I went to be a trauma surgeon. To save lives. But the idea of having my loans paid for is too attractive to ignore. Wanting to prove myself to my parents, I've been adamant about putting myself through medical school and now I'm drowning under bills.

It's not like Roman would be paying me for sex or as some sort of escort. I'd still technically be using my degree and have a legitimate job, but how exactly would I explain this to my parents? To my friends?

"I also need someone that I can trust with Ty. Regardless of how I acted today, I appreciate what you've done for him. Not just removing the bullet, but the way you were with him earlier. You really put him at ease. He's comfortable with you, and if I have to find someone else, it'll be like starting from the beginning. You and I both know that wasting time isn't in his best interest."

Jesus, what is wrong with me? Am I actually considering this? Less than five hours ago, the man kidnapped me and held me here against my will. The more time I spend with Roman, the more entangled in his web I get—a deceitful, unlawful, dangerous web. At best, the things he's involved in are illegal. At worst, they'll cost me my life.

Although, I'm still not sure that isn't my fate, regardless. "What happens if I don't agree?"

Roman stiffens, eyeing me carefully. If I had to guess, he was expecting me to jump at the offer without any hesitation, and I've caught him off guard. "If you don't want to, you can leave here tonight and we'll go our separate ways. But I will have constant eyes on you to be sure that you're not going to the police about anything that happened today. And you can forget about getting a permanent position at St. Luke's."

"You're serious?" I ask. "How did your compromise turn into blackmail?"

"I told you. My top priority is the safety of my son, and I will stop at nothing to make sure of that." His face hardens. "You know my terms. When you've made your decision, I'll be downstairs." He hesitates, then adds, "I sent someone to your apartment to get you a change of clothes. I didn't think you'd want to wear those all day."

The door slams sharply behind him and I jump. I can't help but laugh. It's like he truly believes that sending someone to my house to get me clothes is a thoughtful gesture, not an insane invasion of privacy and gross show of force. Deep down, he wants me to know that he can do whatever he wants, whenever he wants.

I should expect nothing less from what he is showing me so far. The man is infuriating, but he's smart. He knows that the money and positioning is too good for me to refuse.

He presented it as a choice, but is it really one?

I don't think so.

Chapter Six

ROMAN

My ENTIRE JOB IS based on my ability to read people. To pick up on their cues. Read between the lines and anticipate their every word and move.

So saying I was a little thrown off when Madison didn't graciously jump at my offer is an understatement. Usually, my encounters with women go one of two ways. They're either paralyzed with fear of me, or falling all over themselves trying to impress me. Either way, it's pretty easy to get them to do whatever the hell I want, but Madison is different. She has no business getting to me like she does.

With those big doe eyes and hotter-than-sin body, she's as irritating as she is gorgeous, but it's her personality that's got me by the balls. The wit, the stubbornness, the brilliance. She's clearly not my biggest fan, but I'd be lying if I said I didn't like the challenge. And besides, sometimes hate sets the stage for some mean sexual tension.

Maybe it's the emotion of the day getting to me, or maybe I just haven't gotten laid in a while, but regardless, I'm already thinking things I know I shouldn't.

Madison Taylor is in my head, and it's a fucking problem.

I don't like feeling out of control, so I turn to what I know for a distraction.

"What do we know so far?" Ty is fast asleep on the couch by the time I get back into the living room. Joe and Dante sit next to him, totally entranced by the new Smurfs movie.

At the sound of my voice, they both bolt up in a pathetic attempt to make me think they weren't slacking off. I gesture to the kitchen, wanting to have this conversation away from Ty.

"Dante has a call in to Chief Howes to see if we can get our hands on some of the evidence. These guys knew exactly what they were doing. It was such a public place that it's almost impossible for us to investigate ourselves."

"Isn't that what I pay Howes for?" I growl. The guy has been on our payroll for the last five years, and his only job is to give me what I need when I need it and keep the force off my ass.

Joe lets out a heavy breath. "I don't think I need to remind you of all the red tape there is with this. It was a park in the middle of summer. There were hundreds of witnesses and three people were killed. Not to mention we don't have anything concrete to prove that they were targeting you specifically, or if it was completely random."

I bite back my laughter. A coincidence? Is he serious? "My kid gets hit on the anniversary of his mother's death and you're going to go with *coincidence*?"

"We just need to be careful, Roman. Let's see what Howes comes back with, and will explore other avenues in the meantime."

"Look into La Eme. See if you can find any local groups they've got that we don't know about. I was on the..." A visceral memory hits me when I think about that phone call with Leo, and my chest tightens with guilt. I was distracted when Ty got hit, and that will haunt me forever.

"What?" Joe looks at me, confused why I trailed off mid-sentence.

"Leo thinks that La Eme carried out the attack on Talia. I was talking to him when the shooting started."

"If they came after Talia, then I think it's safe to assume that this was them, too," Dante says.

"We're not doing anything based on assumptions," I remind him. "Get me something I can use."

Joe doesn't look convinced, but he doesn't have to be. I'm the one that calls the shots around here. I know that Joe and the rest of my men are perfectly capable of finding these guys and making them pay with everything they've got. It isn't about that, though. This is personal, and I want whoever it is for myself.

"Is Madison staying?" Dante asks.

"She's still thinking about it."

"For the record, I still don't think this is a good idea," Joe quips.

"And I still don't care."

Joe chuckles, his eyes trained on me. "She's a first-year resident with close to zero experience, Roman. The only reason she's still here is because she's smoking hot."

Without hesitation, I pull my gun out and aim it squarely at Joe. "Would you to just get the fuck to work? You're on my last nerve."

"Okay, okay." Joe chuckles, not phased in the slightest. "Let's go, Dante. I think we've had enough gunshot wounds for one day."

"Maybe," Dante snickers. "But at least now Roman has a naughty nurse to fix us if he ever does actually shoot."

"Now!" I bellow, raking my fingers through my hair. Dante and Joe are my best friends, closer to me than my own brother, but I'm not in any mood to joke around. The possibility of losing Ty today was too much, and my nerves are absolutely fried.

Ty wrestles in the other room, and I go to him, Dante and Joe following close behind.

"Hey bud." I smile. The dark leather creaks as I sit next to him. He already looks better after a little rest and some meds.

"How are you feeling, munchkin?" Joe ruffles Ty's hair.

"Hungry." Ty beams, loving all the attention. He seems so much better, and maybe I'll talk to Maddie about taking out the IV when she comes down. *If* she comes down.

"That's my guy." Joe laughs. "I'll bring Sarah by to see you tomorrow. Think you might be up for that?"

After Talia died, Joe's wife became my default babysitter. I don't like to leave him very often, but when I absolutely have to, she's about the only person I trust. Plus, Ty adores her and they've gotten pretty close over the last few months.

"Good deal." Joe grins and then turns to me. "I'll be at the office for the next few hours, but call me if you need anything. Do you want me to have Sarah bring something over for dinner?"

"No, we'll be fine. Thanks, though. Let me know if you hear from Howes."

"You'll be my first call." Joe raises his hand to his forehead in a sarcastic salute, and the two leave.

"How does a hamburger sound?" I asked Ty.

"And fries?" He raises an eyebrow at me. At six, the kid is already a negotiator and I don't know if I should be proud or scared.

"I think I can manage that. Why don't you lay back down and I'll go make us some?"

"Deal." Ty snuggles back into the couch and I pull the blanket over him.

I don't have a lot in my cooking arsenal, but burgers are my specialty. The last time I made them though was for Talia's birthday. Both of our families came over, and despite her and I having a gruesome fight earlier in the day about getting Ty away from the Mafia, we put on brave faces for the party. The memory stings worse tonight than ever before.

I don't want to think about it anymore today, so I try to distract myself while I cook. The problem is, the only thing that works is thinking about Madison, and that gets me just as riled up, but for an entirely different reason.

What the hell is taking so long? Any normal person would have jumped at the chance I handed her, but she's made me wait all afternoon. I should go up there and demand an answer from her, but before I get the chance, I hear something behind me.

"Ahem." She clears her throat, a flicker of apprehension in her eyes.

"Hey."

"I've thought about it, and I'll take your deal." Her shoulders slump a bit this evening, and she isn't glaring at me quite as viciously as she was earlier. The air isn't friendly, but it isn't all out combative, so I consider that progress. We've got some work to do if we're going to have a relationship—professional or otherwise.

"Great," I say all too quickly.

"But I've got some conditions."

I rub my chin, trying to pinpoint when exactly I let her think that this was a negotiation. Compromise isn't really in my nature, but I want her to take the job.

"Which are?"

"My work at the hospital has to come first. I've worked too hard to slack on it now. I know *emergencies* usually come up without warning, but that has to be my priority."

"Sure." I nod. "I'll work around your schedule as best I can." It's not like I want to keep her cooped up here like some kind of Beauty and the Beast shit. I'll have to send someone to watch over things when she's at the hospital, though, just in case.

"And if you're serious about this, you need to promise me you'll defer to me for medical care. Especially Ty's. You're paying me because I know what I'm doing, and you can't argue with me every step of the way."

A protest dies on my lips, because she's right. I'll have to get used to taking orders instead of just dishing them out.

"Anything else?"

"Yes, actually. I don't know what kind of world you live in where abducting someone is okay, but that's not the way this is going to be. If I'm staying, I want to come and go as I please." She crosses her arms over her chest, and the move pushes her perfect tits up in a punishing way. It's better than when she was running around in her running shorts and low cut tank, but she's got the kind of body that looks good in anything.

I force my gaze up, bracing myself against the counter's edge. "Today didn't play out how I wanted to by any means, but I was desperate and I'm sorry. You can come and go as you want, but safety is my top priority. This position is in my most trusted circle of advisers, so security is non-negotiable. Whether you're at work, home, or out, I'll have someone with you. Most times, you won't even know they're there, but this is as much for your protection as it is for ours."

Madison's eyes darken with the potential of what getting involved with my group actually means for her. I hold my hand out to her. "We've got a deal?"

"Yes." She swallows, shaking my hand. A spark surges through my body at the connection, rocking me more than it should. She must feel something, too, because she holds on for a few seconds longer than necessary before pulling away, flustered and on edge.

"Are you hungry?" I ask, attempting to diffuse the awkwardness between us. "I'm making burgers for Ty and I and I can easily throw another on the grill."

"Ty can't eat that. He's been through a lot today, and he needs to be on a liquid diet the next few days."

"You've got to be kidding me. The kid is sitting up and..."

Madison's face sharpens. She doesn't have to say a word for me to know what she's thinking.

Defer to her.

"Fine." I sigh, handing her the plate I made for Ty. "I hope you're not a vegetarian because someone is going to have to eat all this food. And Ty definitely won't be happy with his new nurse."

"*Doctor,*" she corrects. "I'm his new *doctor.*"

She takes the plate as a taunting smirk flares on her full, pink lips.

"Right. Sorry." I turn to the freezer for two reasons—to get some fruit out for Ty's smoothie and to cool myself off before things get too far.

If the doctor keeps looking at me the way she is, we're going to have some serious issues.

CHAPTER SEVEN

Madison

MAYBE I HIT MY head in all the commotion of the day. Or maybe I have an undiagnosed brain tumor. I've seen it before, how a tumor alters the way a person would normally think and they make all kinds of rash or out-of-character decisions. It's got to be something like that because nothing short of a traumatic brain injury or a tumor justifies what I agreed to.

I wake up in a panic the next morning, not recognizing the bed I'm in as I stare at the ceiling fan spinning above me. Briefly, I consider I might still be dreaming and not awake at all, but then pieces come back.

The shooting. Roman kidnapping me. Me stupidly agreeing to work for him. God, what was I thinking?

Unfortunately, I know exactly what I was thinking. I was thinking about the rent that's due in ten days and how I'll pay it out of my negative account. I was thinking about the hundreds of thousands of dollars in student loan debt that I haven't touched. I was thinking how nice it would be to have my pick of cushy jobs at St. Luke's once all this is through. I was thinking how good it would feel to do this all on my own, without having to grovel back to my parents for help. And I was thinking that Roman Molanari isn't exactly the worst thing I can spend my days looking at.

And so I signed a deal with the devil.

That may be an exaggeration because after our less than stellar introduction, Roman settled down quite a bit. He made me dinner, and we actually had a conversation without either of us wanting to gauge the other's eyes out. Afterwards, he set me up in a luxurious guest room suite. The bathroom alone is bigger than my entire apartment, and it's got three enormous windows that overlook a beautiful lake and flower garden. It's the bed that really does it for me, though. After months on my paper-thin mattress, this one feels like I'm sleeping on clouds, and the blankets are so buttery soft and cozy that I'm positive I've never had a better night's sleep in my life.

And maybe it's the sleep that has me thinking so clearly today. Beyond all the money and fancy things, I know I got played. He's a master manipulator, and he offered a deal that I couldn't refuse. Roman knew what he was doing, and he got exactly what he wanted. Part of me doesn't want to give him the satisfaction, but it's not like I'm getting screwed here. If I can just get through these next six months, my life will be drastically different.

Since Joe's family death story got me out of work, I spend the next few days getting used to things at Roman's. His men help me move my things, and I turn my apartment keys in to my landlord.

His request that I stay there seems extreme, but I don't complain. The bed alone is worth putting up with his cocky and overbearing personality.

By the time Wednesday rolls around, I have to go back to work.

The morning is uneventful. I tend to Ty's wounds, giving Roman a quick lesson on how to dress them himself, and then leave for the day. He's doing so much better, but his pent-up energy from being cooped up makes it difficult to keep him quiet and still.

The drive from Roman's to the hospital is quick, and soon, I'm sitting in the parking lot, heart thundering in my chest as I gather the courage to go inside and pretend like I didn't steal thousands of dollars in supplies and medication a few days ago. If anyone finds out about that, I'll lose everything. My job, my license. All of this with Roman will be for nothing, and I'll be done before I even begin.

I can already see the disappointment on my dad's face if I get kicked out of the trauma surgery program here. Following in his footsteps has been my dream since I was a little girl, but it's also been his, and sometimes that pressure is suffocating.

It's just one more reason this deal with Roman has to work. I can't fail, and without the money, I'm dangerously close.

When I step into the emergency department, I almost expect security to tackle me and haul me off to jail right there. When that doesn't happen, I relax a bit, but I'm still on edge. I remember Joe telling me that my body language could give me away, so I do my best to control my breathing, the picture of composure as I walk down the hallway.

"Madison?" Dr. Bauer stops me. "I wasn't expecting to see you so soon. How are you doing?"

"I'm doing okay. Thanks, Dr. Bauer. I'm ready to be back at work."

"Glad to hear it," he says. "You let me know if you need any more time. And by the way, one of the pharmacy techs was looking for you this morning."

All the blood in my veins runs cold. Oh, God. I'm sure she knows I made the entire thing up.

"And there are a few patients in the ER I would like for you to see this morning. Why don't you get settled and come find me?" he calls over his shoulder as he walks towards the lobby.

I pressed my lips into a firm smile. "Sounds great."

Stalking into the staff lounge, I throw my things into my locker and plop onto a chair with a heavy breath.

I can do this. I can do this.

The day actually goes by much quicker than I expect, and once I am seeing patients, it's the only thing on my mind. Somehow, I avoid the pharmacy tech, and at least buy myself a little time. When my shift ends, I'm exhausted, but oddly relaxed as I gather my things from the lounge.

"Maddie!" someone calls as I'm walking out.

My stomach drops when I see the pharmacy technician.

"I'm so glad I caught you."

"Hey Quinn." I smile nervously. "Dr. Bauer said you were looking for me. I'm sorry I didn't make it over there. We were crazy busy, and I didn't think you would still be here."

"No worries! I just wanted to double check on the patient number you gave me the other day. Once the system came back up, I looked, but I couldn't find the patient."

"Oh, that's strange." Not really, considering I made it up off the top of my head. This is a disaster. "I'm rushing out right now, and won't be back until Saturday, but I can come by then and fix it for you."

"That's perfect! See you then!"

I hurry out of the lounge and make my way to the parking garage. At least I've got some time to figure this out.

When I get to Roman's, I use the code he gave me to get through the gate.

I park my car and head inside, cringing as I take in the disaster that the house has somehow turned into. This morning, it was nice and neat and put together, but it seems over the course of the day, a hurricane ripped through. There's laundry and dirty dishes strewn all over the place and it smells like a frat house.

Joe sprawls out in the recliner, and Ty is sitting up on the couch, playing some sort of video game.

"Ty, I need it now," Roman calls from somewhere in the house.

Ty looks down at a shirt and starts to tug at it, squirming to get it over his head.

I wince at the way he moves because his wounds could easily open again.

"Here little man." Joe notices the struggle, too, and pauses the game to help him get it off.

Ty takes it and throws it back over his shoulder, and the dirty T-shirt comes flying toward me. Roman catches it right before it hits me.

"Hey!" he snaps, pointing a finger at Ty. "What have I told you about throwing things in the house?"

The sternness in his voice sends a shudder through me, but it's not fear I'm feeling. It's something different.

Ty groans, rolling his eyes. "Sorry."

"Don't say sorry to me. You almost hit Madison."

"Maddie!" Ty's eyes light up. "You came back."

"How are you feeling, buddy?" I set my bag down and walk over to the couch. He looks so much better with the color returning to his face and the flare of excitement in his eyes. He's completely off of his IVs and getting stronger by the minute. After what he's been through, it feels like a miracle.

"Good. My dad won't let me play basketball with uncle Joe, though." He glares back towards Roman.

"Sounds like he's taking good care of you, then." I smile.

Roman looks surprised by the compliment, and to be honest, so am I. I went into this with next to no faith in him, but he's really turned things around in regards to taking care of Ty. The history with St. Luke's he mentioned still piques my interest, but I'm not about to pry.

"It's time to lie back down, anyway, Ty," Roman says. "You've been sitting up playing for a while."

"Aw, come on, Dad! Does he have to?" Joe mocks, teasing Roman.

"Yeah, come on, Dad!" Ty echoes.

"One more game, but that's it," Roman cautions them. The sentence is barely out of his mouth before they have another round started.

Roman turns to me. "Sorry about the mess. Between laundry and trying to keep him still, I've barely had time to breathe today."

I have to stifle a laugh. He sounds like such a househusband, completely out of his element. He's not as scary or domineering with a dishrag over his shoulder, but I doubt he wants to hear that.

"It's okay," I say. "Should I get Ty something to eat while he's occupied?"

He and Joe battle back-and-forth on the couch as their cars race on screen.

"At least Joe is good for something," Roman says, letting out a sharp laugh. "That would be great. I'm almost done in here."

Ty is still on a restricted diet, so I take him some yogurt and applesauce. Once Joe leaves, he eats a little, but he's exhausted, and soon he's fast asleep on the couch.

Roman notices when he comes back out, and lifts Ty into his arms with an effortless one-armed swoop. The seams of his t-shirt stretch over his swollen muscles and an elaborate sleeve of tattoos peek out from underneath the fabric, trailing down to his flexed forearm. My eyes trace each line, but I can't make out what it is and, unfortunately, his clothing covers most of it. So, I'm left to imagine.

Wait a second. Am I honestly fantasizing about this guy right now? Part of me is ashamed, but there's another part—a tiny part—that isn't so easily deterred.

Thankfully, something brings me back to my senses, and I look away before he sees me staring. The smug grin on his lips tells me I've been caught, though.

A gentleman might have let me off the hook, but Roman Molanari is no gentleman.

"Like what you see?" His chuckle nearly strangles me and I feel like I might die on the spot.

As if he didn't already have such a high opinion of himself, now he's caught me checking him out and I'll never hear the end of it.

That cave in the wilderness sounds better and better.

"Just wondering what you have against wearing clothes that actually fit you. Is everything you own so tight?"

Roman smirks. "I'm going to take him to his room. I'll be right back."

I nod, desperate for this entire interaction to end. Once I hear Ty's door shut, I rush up the stairs and down the hall to my own room. Standing in front of the bathroom mirror, I splash some cold water on my face. I can't risk another interaction with Roman going like that one did. Quickly, I change out of my scrubs and my stomach growls.

Getting something to eat means I might run into Roman again, and I don't know if my ego can handle that, but I'm starving.

When I get into the kitchen, I find Roman settled at the end of the island. A bottle of wine sits on the counter, a hefty glass already poured beside it, but Roman isn't enjoying it. His head is in his hands, and he lets out a slow, emotional breath.

The floor creaks as I walk in, giving myself away, and he glances up, but says nothing. "I'm going to make something to eat," I say, breaking the silence. "Want anything?"

He shakes his head and then gestures to the wine. "Someone recently told me my clothes are fitting a little tight, so this is dinner tonight."

"Mmm." I press my lips together. "As your doctor, I highly advise against that, and you promised to follow my orders. You need some actual food."

"Whatever you say, Doc." He chuckles.

There isn't much to work with in here, but I find some tortillas and cheese and a little grilled chicken I can throw together for quesadillas.

"Sorry, I obviously didn't have time to make it to the grocery store. You'd think after six months I'd be better at this whole single parent thing." He shakes his head and his thick dark brows furrow. "I'll be sure and get there tomorrow."

I've wondered about Ty's mom since I got here, but Roman has offered very little in that department. In fact, that is the first time he's even vaguely mentioned her.

"You don't have to buy me food, Roman. That wasn't part of the deal." I sprinkle some cheese onto the tortillas and toss them into the skillet.

"Neither was you making me dinner, but here we are." He tilts his head with a grin as he stands to take another wine glass out of the cabinet. "How was work?"

"It was okay. Busy." I bit my lip, already anxious about how I'm going to explain the mystery patient when I go back in. "Nothing I can't handle."

His face twists as he hands me a glass of wine. "What happened?"

"It's really nothing, Roman." I turn to grab some plates, but he catches my wrist.

"Don't lie to me, Madison. Is someone at St. Luke's giving you a hard time?"

I jerk my arm out of his grasp, reeling away. "The only one making things difficult for me is you. When I took the medicine for Ty, I had to come up with a fake patient number to give to the pharmacist. Joe did something to the computer so she couldn't look right then, but when she went in later to log everything, obviously, she couldn't find the person. I just have to figure something else out."

He's quiet for a minute and then whips out his phone. "What was the number?"

"Why does that—"

"The number, Madison." He clenches his jaw, brow pinching with irritation.

"I don't remember. It should be on the labels."

"Consider it taken care of. I'll have the patient in the system before I go to sleep tonight." Roman takes a bite of his food, so casually that it's almost like he didn't just tell me he'd hack into the hospital database and falsify all kinds of records.

"You can do that?"

Roman snorts, as if it should be obvious. "Of course I can. Don't worry about it anymore. Now can we eat? I'm starving."

I should ask more questions.

I should, but I don't.

CHAPTER EIGHT

"MADISON." MY BODY SHAKES as someone calls my name. "Madison, hey, wake up."

When I open my eyes, it's pitch black. I take a second to adjust, blinking at Roman's imposing frame in the shadows, standing next to my bed.

"What the hell are you doing?" I scramble up, backing away from him as I clutch the bedsheets. Panic grips my chest, and it tightens so much that I have to fight to catch my breath.

"It's okay." He holds his hands up. "It's just me."

As if that's reassuring.

"I didn't mean to scare you. You were sleeping pretty hard."

"Yes, because it's the middle of the night." I groan, glancing at the clock. I feel like I barely fell asleep, and I probably did since I got stuck at the hospital so late. The house was quiet when I got back, everyone tucked into their beds, so the last thing I expected was to see Roman standing in my bedroom. "What is going on?"

"I need you," he says, pausing a beat longer than necessary, no doubt to let my mind wander with his words.

"One of my men got hurt tonight."

That jolts me awake. So far, I haven't had to fulfill the other part of my job description for Roman, but it looks like that's about to change. His lack of detail has my mind swirling with possibilities as I climb out of bed. At this time of night, I know it won't be good.

Roman grabs my sweatshirt off the chair in the corner, tossing it to me. "Better get dressed. We're going to the warehouse."

"What about Ty?" I ask.

"Joe's here in case he needs anything."

Roman steps outside so I can change. A soft knock comes practically seconds later. He must be anxious. "Madison? Ready?"

"All set." I follow him into the hallway, down the stairs, and out to the garage. He opens the door to his truck for me, and soon we're on our way.

"What happened?" I ask as I pull my hair up into a high ponytail. It's not the hairnet I'd wear in the operating room, but it'll do.

"Don't know much yet. He was on a job tonight and there was some sort of altercation."

"What kind of job?" The question is out of my mouth before I really even know what I'm saying.

Roman eyes me carefully. "You really want to know?"

"No, actually. I don't think I do." I think we'll all be better off if I just adopt an ignorance-is-bliss policy for the next six months. A don't ask, don't tell type thing. Curiosity churns inside of me, but the more I know, the more trouble I'll wind up in.

He chuckles. "Didn't think so."

I do at least have to know what I'm working with, so I keep the questions focused on my work. "Is it a gunshot wound?"

Roman shakes his head. "Just a stab wound."

Just. Every time I feel even the slightest bit normal around Roman, I get slapped in the face with a harsh dose of reality. A few hours ago, we were making quesadillas and talking about the weather, and now he's whisking me away in the middle of the night, minimizing a stab wound his buddy got while committing a crime.

The warehouse isn't far, and we're there quickly. More men than I would have imagined at this time of night are gathered around a table at the center of the room, almost like it's a party. It's noisy and crowded and I can barely see the injured man sitting front and center.

He's got the attention of every man in the group as he sips from his highball glass, regaling them all with the details of his night.

"And the motherfucker pulls out his knife. Gets me straight across, just above my knee, but I pull my gun and blow his brains all over the damn dock."

The other guys erupt into laughter and cheers. There are guns and empty alcohol bottles strewn all across the tables, and no one bats an eye.

Great. Roman pulled me out of bed in the middle of the night to wrangle a bunch of drunk idiots and stitch up a knife wound on a guy who's a very explicit story teller.

Roman stiffens next to me, completely put off and unimpressed by the story. Almost offended.

"Enough!" The scowl on his face shuts up every man in the room, and he demands their attention. "This is Dr. Taylor, and she'll be working with us for the next few months. She's here to check on Russ, and if any of you so much as glance at her with anything other than utter respect and appreciation, then you'll be meeting a similar fate as Russ's buyer tonight. And cool it with the language in front of her. Everybody clear?"

They all nod, most afraid to move a muscle without his permission. Everyone is quiet, and a few scramble up to clean up a bit of the mess. There is no question who is in charge, and the way he commands the room and orders around men twice his age is as hot as it is unnerving.

"Good. Now get back to work. It sounds like we've got cleanup to do."

Roman doesn't elaborate on what he means by *cleanup*, but based on Russ's story, I've got a good idea. The group disperses and Roman leads me to the table.

There's a cart full of supplies ready for use. "Everything you need should be right here, but if there's something missing, then let me know and we can get it for you."

I'm not sure I want to know where these hospital grade materials came from, but as long as I didn't have to steal it, it's not my business.

"Dr. Taylor, this is Russ." He gestures to the glassy eyed man.

Russ gets a sloppy, drunk smile on his face and straightens in the chair. "Nice to meet you, Dr. Taylor."

"Nice to meet you, too."

"When Roman said he was hiring a new doctor, I pictured an old, fat guy, but you're a delightful surprise."

Irritation flickers in Roman's eyes. "Enough with the small talk. It's the middle of the night and we're all tired. Just show her your fucking leg so we can get out of here."

"You got it, boss." Russ stands up, struggling to work his jeans up over his knee as Roman steps a few feet away to talk to Dante. Even at a distance, I still feel the weight of his stare on me as I work.

"Why don't we put this away for now, too?" I suggest, sliding the whiskey out of his reach as he sits back down.

"Aw come on. It's a cheap painkiller."

"It's also thinning out your blood, which will make it harder for me to stop the bleeding and stitch you up."

"Oh, beauty *and* brains. Yes, ma'am." He chuckles, leaning back in the chair as I put on some gloves. He props his leg up on the table so I have a better view.

For the most part, the cut has stopped bleeding, but it's nasty. Dirty, jagged, and about five inches long, right across the inside of Russ's knee. "How did you say you got this?"

"The guy I was delivering to tonight," Russ says. "Didn't like the price, I guess. Guy's lucky he got any piece of me at all before I put the bullet through his head. Chicks dig scars, anyway, right?"

He shoots me a skeevy wink that makes my skin crawl.

I know next to nothing about the type of things these guys are into, but I know wounds, and his story doesn't add up. Blades usually cut clean, especially if Russ was swiped the way he said he was. The wound is so jagged it looks more like the skin tore.

"Do you still have the knife?" I ask.

Russ tosses it up onto the counter, and the shiny metal glistens in the harsh factory lighting. It's clean, not a single drop of blood on it, which doesn't make sense for how grimy and dirty the wound is..

I don't know that I even want to involve myself, and the wound will be easy enough to treat without knowing how it really happened. I glance up at Roman, but he's still deeply engrossed in his conversation with Dante, and I let the thought die.

"I know a place where we can get some good drinks after this..." Russ slurs. "What do you think?"

Roman steps closer, still listening to Dante, but not too far to eavesdrop on us and he doesn't look happy.

"What I think is, if you put half as much energy into your job tonight as you are into hitting on me, then we might not be in this situation." I look up at him.

Out of the corner of my eye, I see Roman smirk, relaxing back into his conversation with Dante, content with the way I handled myself.

Russ lets out a gruff sigh and tilts his head back. "How long do you think this is going to take?"

"Not long," I say, reaching for saline and some gauze to clean the wound out. Once it's flushed, I cut back some of the dead skin and start to stitch him up. It takes about ten minutes, and then I put a bandage over the top for the time being.

Russ hasn't said much, but he has to get in one last shot.

"Don't be afraid to check me out a little higher, Doc. I think I'm having some residual pain—"

Without warning, Roman's next to us. His hands violently cinch around the man's neck and he sputters for air.

"What the fuck did I say about disrespecting Dr. Taylor, Russ?" Roman growls. "Huh?"

"Jesus, Roman. It was a joke." He rubs at his throat once Roman lets him loose.

"Well, it wasn't fucking funny. You've been giving her a hard time the entire time she's been working on you. Dr. Taylor is here in the middle of the night to take care of your sorry ass because you're so incompetent at your job that you went and got yourself knifed. Not to mention you left your DNA all over a crime scene...the cops would haul you to jail if you had to go into the hospital. So I'd suggest you keep the jokes to yourself from now on, yeah?"

"Yeah, absolutely. Sorry Dr. Taylor."

Roman's reaction rattles me, and I stand in shock for a second. Russ is obnoxious, but even I know he's just playing around. What the hell just happened?

"It's okay," I finally say, my voice shaking. Quickly, I turn my back to the two men to avoid the tension and clean things up.

I purposely tune out the conversation that they have, and after a few minutes, Roman and I are both ready to go.

"Sorry about Russ," he says once we get in the truck. "Some of these guys aren't used to having women around and they forget how to act. I'll be sure anyone you treat is the pillar of respect from now on."

"Like you?" It's hard to hide the snark in my voice. It's funny to listen to Roman talk about respect when a few days ago he forcibly kidnapped me. Granted, things have been different since, but that's the pot calling the kettle black, if I've ever heard it.

"Fair." Roman chuckles, arm draped over the steering wheel as he winds through the dark roads. "Although, I will say it's kind of impressive the way you hold your own like you do. I don't think Russ has ever been spoken to like you did tonight, and it serves him right."

"I'm used to it." I shrug.

"How so?"

"Well, trauma surgery is a pretty male-dominated field. My dad is the head of trauma for an entire network of hospitals in St. Louis. And I've got two older brothers. I grew up around arrogant men who think the rules don't apply to them."

"I guess that's why you and I get along so well." Roman's mouth slants into a taunting smirk.

"I'm not sure I'd say we get along."

"Ouch." He chuckles, glancing at me out of the corner of his eye. "And here I thought you and I had a budding friendship, Doc."

CHAPTER NINE

ROMAN

"Well, I could certainly use a drink after that. How about you?" I ask, holding the door for Madison as we come in from the garage.

Usually, after there's some kind of issue or complication on a job, I can't sleep. I'm up for hours unable to turn my brain off, but tonight, my nightcap has more to do with the fact that I want more time with Madison. I enjoy talking to her when we're not at each other's throats, and tonight, it almost felt like we were a team.

She's tough, and she's good at what she does, and even though I don't want to admit that this could be more than business, the line is starting to blur.

She's lived here for two weeks, and it's almost too easy how seamlessly we've settled into a routine. I'd forgotten how good it feels to have another adult to come home to. To share some of the household tasks with. To talk to someone who doesn't eat, sleep, and breathe the Italian Mafia the way most of my friends and family do. Madison is like a much needed breath of fresh air in this house.

"It's two in the morning," she says, looking up at the clock as if that's going to make any difference to me.

I don't respond as I open the liquor cabinet and get a bottle of Macallan 1824 from the back. It's a special occasion scotch, but tonight is as good of night as any. I reach for a second glass and raise my eyebrow at her.

When she sits at the island instead of continuing to protest, I get my answer.

I pour two glasses, sliding one across the counter to her. "It's a nice night. Why don't we go out to the patio?"

"Sounds great." Madison follows me out the back door and finds a cozy spot on the couch as I flip on the fire table.

The sky is full of stars, and the moonlight reflects in her eyes as I sit across from her. She's so fucking gorgeous with that sleepy smile that part of me wishes I could whisk her upstairs for an entirely different kind of nightcap. Maybe that would get her out of my system and I could finally concentrate on all the other shit I've got happening. That would never happen, though. Once would never be enough with Madison, and I know that for a fact.

"How was work?" I ask, stretching my arm along the back of the couch, careful not to touch her.

Madison lets out a sharp laugh, her head dipping back as her long honey curls fall behind her and graze my forearm. The move sends a wave of her perfume in my direction that's every bit as intoxicating as the whiskey I'm drinking.

"What's so funny?"

"You woke me up in the middle of the night to go stitch up your friend that killed a man in a drug deal, and now you want to make small talk about my day at work as if none of that happened."

Scratching my chin, I chuckle. "Well, I guess when you say it like that, it sounds a little strange."

"More than a little." Madison shifts her weight. "You're going to have to level with me here, Roman. I know you're some kind of gang leader, but I need the specifics. I need to know exactly what I got myself involved in."

"You're sure?" I swallow, staring into the flames. "Because if you don't like what you hear, you can't just walk away. The more you know, the deeper you're involved."

"How much deeper can I get? I just listened to a man admit to murder and you plot a coverup."

She's got a point there. She's practically my employee, and even at the end of six months, I won't be able to let her go without some hefty non-disclosures and surveillance. "I'm not a gang leader."

She arches an eyebrow at me, waiting for more.

"What I do is...bigger. It's more intricate and sophisticated."

She already knows the gist of what I do, so putting words to it shouldn't be this hard. I still struggle, though, like somehow slapping a label on it will make her run, but she doesn't back down.

"How so?"

Running my fingers through my hair, I lean back. "My family runs a section of the Italian Mafia. I inherited the position from my father, just like he did from his."

Madison doesn't answer for a second. She looks at me like she's trying to decide if I'm telling her the truth, eyes narrow and apprehensive.

"Like *The Godfather*?"

I snort. "Well, a lot of that was sensationalized for the movie, but more or less, yeah. Like *The Godfather*."

"And you run the whole thing?"

"There are parts of the group throughout the whole country, but I run everything here in Vegas. I own an import and export line that sends gun parts all over the world."

"Just the parts?" she asks, a cautious curiosity flickering in her eyes.

"Yeah." I nod. "Parts aren't traceable. Parts are legal."

"I didn't expect the Mafia to care about what's legal," she quips. For as smart as she is, that streak of stubbornness always catches me off guard. I just told her I run part of the Mafia and have access to everything that entails, and she still gives me a hard time. I don't know what it says about me that I actually enjoy it.

"If you've got a legitimate business, it's easier to hide the less...legal things."

Madison presses her lips together, eyes darting away as her fingers trace the top of her glass. She wants to ask, and when she looks up at me through those thick, dark lashes, my heart races. She's got no fucking clue what she does to me.

"What *less legal* things do you do?"

"Never drugs. That shit gets messy, and too many people get hurt," I say. "We're mostly in big ticket gambling and counterfeiting. It's easy to do in a place like Vegas. Obviously, issues come up, and we have to handle them in some unconventional ways, but it's like any other business. I look at profit margins and target demographics and potential investors. All of that stuff. At the end of the day, it's about making money and monopolizing the area."

When Madison finally speaks, I barely hear her over the flicker of the fire. "Okay."

I expect her to say more, and when she doesn't, I burst out laughing. "I tell you I run a section of an international crime organization and all you say is okay?"

Madison bites her lip, pulling a smile as she does. "I don't know what to say. I knew from the beginning that your job was dangerous and highly illegal, so Mafia leader tracks."

"It's called a Don. I'm a Mafia Don."

"*A Mafia Don*," she repeats. "I guess I understand why you didn't tell me that before I agreed to work for you."

"Would it have changed your answer?"

She considers her answer and then shakes her head. "No. As long as you're paying off my debt with real money and none of your counterfeiting bullshit."

"You've got my word. Your money will all be legal." I chuckle. Her answer surprises me a little. I've had Madison pegged as a quintessential good girl. Sensible. Responsible. A rule follower. But if the idea of the Mafia doesn't send her running, maybe I've been wrong.

Maybe there's a little more mystique and adventure underneath all of that common sense and restraint. Maybe there's a girl desperate for a little wild and crazy, and maybe I'm just the guy to give it to her.

How do you follow something like that up? Roman just gave me the rundown of his job as the head of a major criminal organization and he lounges back on the couch so casually, you'd think we were talking about the weather. He even tried to pass it off like he's a regular CEO, as if I haven't witnessed firsthand how wrong that is. Mention of the Mafia alone should have been enough for me to end this right where we're at. To get my things, move out, and forget, I ever knew the name Roman Molanari. I'm still sitting here, though, and it's not because he slapped a pair of cement boots on me. It's because I'm intrigued—and probably delusional.

At this point, I've been up for almost twenty-hours, and I can barely keep my eyes open as we talk, but I'm not ready for the night to end. This almost feels normal, and I like *normal* with Roman—when we're not arguing or butting heads or dealing with some sort of criminal crisis, that is. He's easy to talk to when he isn't ordering me around, but even that doesn't bother me like it should. In fact, I kind of like it.

I don't know how long we've been out here, but it's long enough that the ice in our glasses is completely melted, and tiny droplets of condensation drip down the side from the heat. Between the fire and what's building between us, it's intense.

Roman relaxes back, legs spread wide, one arm draped across his lap and the other dangerously close to my leg. There's plenty of room, and either of us could scoot over, but we don't.

When I look up at him, he captures my gaze with a pair of stunning crystal eyes that make my stomach flutter.

"Do you like it?" I glance away. Those are the kind of eyes that a girl could lose herself in. And if I'm not careful, I will.

"What? Being in the Mafia?"

I nod. "You said you inherited the position from your father, which usually means you were just given it and didn't have a choice. Would you have chosen it if you had an option?"

A strange look washes over him as if he's never considered the idea. He swallows, scratching his stubbled chin. "It's been a tough year. I don't know if I have a good answer for that."

Roman's body clenches, his fingers gripping so tightly to the glass in his hand I'm afraid he might crush it. My question struck a nerve, and I wish I hadn't asked because it shifts the mood. He doesn't say anymore and the subject dies.

A few minutes of silence pass between us, and when he turns to look at me, whatever pained emotion was there before is gone. It's like he flipped a switch, turning off any bit of vulnerability or candor he had and taking back the reins.

"I think I still owe you a proper apology." Roman slants his eyes up toward me. Heat ripples through my core when he looks at me that way, and I completely lose my train of thought.

"A proper apology? I didn't know I'd ever hear those words out of Roman Molanari."

"Well, keep interrupting me and you might not." He chuckles, that strong jawline flinching. "I just want you to know that I'm sorry about how things started between us. Like I said, it's been a tough year and I've been under a lot of stress."

Part of me wants to ask about the *tough year*, but I'm a little nervous, too.

"Apology accepted. I probably would have done the same if I were in your shoes."

"Somehow, I find that hard to believe."

"Okay, maybe not the exact same." I blush, tucking my knees up into my chest and turning toward him. "But I can understand being willing to do anything for someone you love."

Silence sits between us for a few seconds. "He's been through a lot."

"Does he ever see his mom?"

"Uh..." He draws in a deep, hesitant breath and clenches his jaw. "She's...Ty's mom...she died several months ago."

Roman's words gut me. There's never been another woman around and he doesn't wear a ring, so I assumed they were divorced or she left. It never occurred to me she was dead, but it all makes sense. Ty's injury probably brought back all kinds of emotion from losing his wife, and his reaction at the time is now even more understandable.

"Oh Roman, I'm so sorry. I can't imagine how hard that is on both of you."

"It is." He nods. "We're just trying to get our footing, which is why things are kind of hectic. She...She did absolutely everything for us. It's been an adjustment."

"You don't have to justify that to me. It's honestly impressive you handle things the way you do. Ty's lucky to have you."

"I wouldn't go that far. I couldn't keep either one of them safe." His eyes darken, and he takes another sip of his whiskey. He balls his fists at his side. "Talia was murdered, and it was my fault. I was out of town and the men who attacked her...they were trying to send a message to me."

Murdered. It's one thing to lose a mother and wife, but to lose her in such a traumatic way feels almost impossible to get through. Poor Ty. Poor Roman. His face fades at the weight of what he told me, and I can't imagine carrying that around.

"And you think the same thing happened with Ty..."

"It would be a huge fucking coincidence if it was random," he says, rage pulsing through him. "And I don't believe in coincidences. I just have to prove it."

Reaching over, I set my hand on top of his, gently sweeping my thumb across it. "I'm so sorry, Roman. I'm sure it's probably hard to talk about, but I'm here if you ever need to."

He glances down at our intertwined hands, and a look I can't quite make out flashes through his eyes—a thirst, a craving.

Neither one of us moves, but we both consider it. Consider crossing the line. Consider what it could mean. Consider how dangerous the game we're playing right now is.

Roman and I are from two vastly different worlds, and it takes thirty seconds of conversation to figure that out. All of my life, I've done the right thing. The good thing. The sensible thing. And even sitting here with Roman feels like the opposite of that. The man could wreak absolute havoc on my life with the snap of his fingers, which he's already proven, but somehow that only adds to the thrill. Between the alcohol and lack of sleep, part of me thinks a little shakeup to my world is exactly what I need.

He's got me curious, and that's a slippery slope.

But reality grips me just in time. There is no world in which Roman and I work. Where I come out of this unscathed. Where we can just fool around for a few months and hope for the best. Right now, there is a very thin, very professional line between us, and crossing it is about the worst thing we can do, so instead of giving in, I pull back.

I let go of Roman's hand and stand. "I should probably get to sleep. I was up early, and have to be tomorrow, too."

"Me, too." He clears his throat, eyes darting away.

Desperate for a little space between us, I take our glasses and rush into the kitchen while he turns the lights down and puts the fire out. After a few minutes, he joins me inside.

"Sorry to drag you out like that tonight. I'd like to say it won't happen again, but most emergencies like this happen at night."

"No worries. It's part of my job."

My voice hitches on that last part, a reminder to both of us. Attraction, chemistry, temptation aside...I'm here because it's my *job*. Because Roman is paying me.

And in a few months, I'll be gone.

Chapter Ten

Madison

"You're up early." Roman's deep voice vibrates from behind me as he walks into the kitchen. I turn around, but he doesn't look at me at first. When he does, I almost wish he hadn't. I haven't even had my coffee yet, and I shouldn't have to test my restraint so early in the morning after such little sleep.

Roman is a sight to behold in his freshly pressed suit and jet black tie. The stubble that scattered his jawline last night is gone, and as he pushes his sleeve up to fasten a shining gold Rolex on his wrist, he shows off his flexed forearms. His brow furrows, and he bites into his lip as he concentrates on flipping the clasp of his watch strap. When he gets it, he looks up at me with a smile that makes my stomach flip.

God, please tell me I don't look as flustered as I am.

The tension between us has been growing for days, and after last night, my head is about to explode. I shouldn't feel the way I do about the man. Not after he kidnapped me. Not after he blackmailed me into staying. Certainly not after he poured his heart out to me last night about his late wife.

It broke me to hear the anguish in his voice as he told me about her. There's something so devastating about seeing a man like Roman show his emotions the way he did, and no matter how strong the connection or draw is between us, it isn't the time. *Six months*. He's probably not even ready for a rebound, let alone anything else. I have enough self-respect not to put myself in that situation, but more than that, I don't think he's ready.

"Good morning. I've been up for a while. I didn't sleep very well." Between the adrenaline and the emotion of the night, my brain refused to shut off.

I turn my back to him again, reaching for a coffee cup in the cabinet. As luck would have it, there aren't any on the shelf I can reach, so I tilt up onto my tiptoes. My fingertips brush against the ceramic mugs, but I can't quite get a hold on one.

Without so much as a warning, Roman slips behind me. He's got one hand on the counter, so close to me it grazes my hip, and with the other, he reaches over me to grab two mugs from the shelf. His body brushes against mine for a brief few seconds, and I can feel his bulge through his pants. Sparks spread across every inch of me, heat rushing to my core as I freeze in place. As much as I want to fight it, there is no denying how attracted to him I am anymore.

I want Roman, and whatever consequences might come from that.

Right when I think he might lean in, he pulls away with a satisfied smirk on his face as he fills both mugs. "Not comfortable in your room?"

"No," I say, taking a shallow breath. The moment between us was both an eternity and a flash. "The room is great. In fact, I may take the mattress with me when I leave."

Roman chuckles, handing me a mug. "We can negotiate that."

Our tastes in coffee are almost as different as our personalities. I need fancy creamers and syrups to stomach the taste, but Roman takes his as black as the tattoos on his skin. I almost cringe as I watch him chug it, but I look away before he can catch me staring.

"I actually couldn't sleep because I had something on my mind that I wanted to talk to you about."

"Oh, yeah?" Roman moves around the kitchen, pulling out cereal and milk and a few other things. In my time here, I haven't ever seen him have anything for breakfast besides coffee, but Ty will be up soon.

"The guy from last night—"

"Russ?" He glances over his shoulder, sitting down at the kitchen island.

I nod. "Last night, when he was talking about how he got injured..."

Suddenly, I have second thoughts about telling Roman. What if I'm wrong? What if I tell him and he does something to the guy, and it's all a big misunderstanding?

Roman narrows his eyes at me. He isn't going to let me off the hook that easily. "Yeah?"

"Well, I guess...I mean, I could be wrong. And I don't really want to get involved. Stitching up cuts is one thing, but—"

"Spit it out, Madison."

"He said the guy didn't like the price and so he lunged at him, right?"

"You don't believe it?"

I shake my head. "The cut. It just didn't look like a knife wound to me. Usually, they're clean and straight, but it was jagged. Almost like it was torn on something. And his story doesn't make much sense. Don't you think if you were going to stab someone, you wouldn't risk being off balance by bending down so far?"

Roman doesn't answer at first, sweeping his thumb across his full lips.

"And why not go for something more vital? If the guy was in front of him like he said, he could have easily stabbed him in the stomach or the chest or the neck. But he goes for a place that's virtually harmless? It could be nothing...but it just doesn't add up to me."

He's quiet, and for a minute, I wonder if I've made a huge mistake.

ROMAN

Fuck, I could listen to her talk like this all day.

Part of Madison's appeal is that she's so far removed from my world, but hearing her talk like she's right in the thick of it does things to me I'm almost ashamed to admit. And I don't get ashamed by much.

It's got me out of sorts in the best way, but I have to shut that feeling down. I've got too much to do today to let my mind already start wandering to her.

Not to mention what she's saying actually makes perfect sense. She's right. I didn't read much into the story because I had no reason to question Russ. I still don't, except the word of a woman I barely know against a guy who's been with me for years.

"I don't know. It just...I thought you should know."

"No, you're right. It doesn't make sense." My fingers tighten around my coffee cup. I have enough threats from outside, but if I've got guys on my team lying to me, that's something else entirely. "I'll look into it."

"Will you let me know what you find out?" She swallows, pressing her mug to her lips and fidgeting with a stack of papers on the counter. "If he's innocent and—"

"No one is innocent in my world, Madison," I cut her off. "But one thing I can promise you is that I don't rush into things. Before I act on something, I know every related fact and outcome. If Russ is telling the truth, then no harm, no foul."

"And if he isn't?"

"You sure ask a lot of questions for someone who doesn't want to be involved."

"You're right." She shakes her head, holding up her hand. "I don't want to know."

Madison moves around the kitchen, getting herself breakfast and packing a lunch for work. With the conversation halted, I glance through my phone and notice a message from Sarah, Joe's wife. When I have things come up at work that I can't move, she is usually my go-to, but she's sick and won't make it this afternoon like I planned on.

"Damn it," I groan, rubbing my forehead. Most days, I could bring Ty with me, but I have a meeting with an arms dealer and I don't want him anywhere near that. And since my circle of trusted babysitters is virtually nonexistent, I don't have many options.

"What's wrong?" Madison asks.

"Ty's babysitter canceled and I have a really important meeting this afternoon." I let out a heavy breath. Canceling so suddenly isn't a good look, and this is a connection that we really need. I can always hear the lecture I'm going to get from Joe.

"What time is it at?" she asks.

"Uh, two o'clock." I glance at my watch and gather my things off of the counter. I've got about a hundred other things that need my attention before then, too. I could postpone my inspection at the dock this morning, but that would put us behind a couple of days and...

"I can do it."

"Wh-what?" My mind is so focused on restructuring my day that I almost miss what she says completely.

"I said I can do it. I just have a staff meeting this morning and I can be back about noon, if that gives you enough time."

Rubbing my chin, I think about her offer. She'd really be coming in clutch, and I already know Ty loves her. I don't like to leave him with many people, but she's about as responsible as they come.

"Really?"

"Sure." She shrugs. "Just a couple of hours, right?"

"Three tops. I'll be home by five."

"Then it's no problem at all," she says. "We'll have a good time."

"Madison, you're really saving my life here. I can't tell you how much I appreciate it."

She shrugs again, shooting me a smirk that almost levels me. "Saving lives is kind of my specialty, remember? And by the way, you can call me Maddie. Most people do."

Getting on nickname basis feels like a microscopic step in the right direction, but I'll take what I can get.

"Well, then, thank you, Maddie. I owe you big time."

"Something tells me I might like having a favor to cash in with the Italian Mafia." She winks, giving me a small wave as she takes her coffee and starts towards the stairs. "I have to go get ready now. I'll see you at about noon."

"See you then."

CHAPTER ELEVEN

ROMAN

JOE IS TALKING. HIS mouth is moving and words are coming out, but he might as well be speaking another language with what I'm retaining. The investor's content expression suggests things are going smoothly, yet my attention has been monopolized by a certain blonde doctor who has no fucking clue the power she holds over me.

We sat there for hours last night, just talking and sitting under the stars. The drinks came easily, and the conversation even easier. I opened up about parts of my life that I haven't shared with anyone, and Maddie took it all in stride. The fact that she barely flinched when I told her I was in the Mafia was still a little baffling, but a welcome surprise. All my cards are on the table now, and she isn't running scared.

That should be a relief, but it isn't, because my life would be a lot easier if she had run. If Maddie was turned off by what she heard and put her walls up, I wouldn't have to fight so hard to restrain myself. To stay away from her. To keep things professional.

I wouldn't have to stare at the rosy flush in her cheeks and fuck-me look in her eye like I didn't want to do just that. I wouldn't have to wake up with an excruciating hard on that even a cold shower can't touch. I wouldn't have to lie awake in my room all night fantasizing about what could have happened while she's right on the other side of the wall.

Jesus, I need to get laid. There's no shortage of options in a city like this when I'm looking for a nameless, no strings fuck. Tourists looking for a good *What Happens in Vegas* story, bachelorette parties throwing themselves at you for VIP access, even some of the local dancers and cocktail servers take little persuasion. The opportunities are endless, but none of that sounds the least bit appealing right now.

It all pales compared to what's waiting for me at home, which, ironically, is one thing that's staunchly forbidden. The line between us couldn't be harder, and honestly, I'm pretty damn proud of myself for walking away from it last night. That resistance took an ungodly amount of strength, though, and I can almost feel that resolve fading.

Last night on its own was enough to rattle me, but this morning was the final nail in my coffin. It's not just my physical attraction towards her that has me by the balls; I'm obsessed with everything about her. She's considerate and generous and wickedly smart. As of late, personality isn't the first thing I look for in a woman, but it's what really seals the deal for me with Maddie. She's a knockout in every way, and if I know what's good for me, I'll stay away.

There will be no one time with Maddie. No casual. No temporary. I'm already wound too tightly for that. The only problem is, I don't know how to do anything else. The only exception to my rule was Talia, but nothing about that relationship was real. We both saw other people on the side, and apart from when we were trying to have a baby, we never slept together.

Commitment and the long term aren't in my DNA, so I already know that I'll fuck things up big with Maddie. Somehow, someway, she'll wind up hurt. Even worse than my less than stellar loyalty record, my world eats good girls like her up. She's too pure for the darkness and danger I'd bring into her life, and that's not something I want on my conscience, no matter how much I want her. It's stupid and reckless to even consider anything else.

I've made it this far. Only five more months to go. How hard can that be?

The thought makes me snort out loud, and both Joe and our investor shoot me confused looks. Fuck, I've got to pull myself together.

I used to be good at compartmentalizing. I kept my home life at home, and work had my full attention when I was here. Today, though, that feels next to impossible. Maddie saved my ass by stepping in to watch Ty so I could take care of things.

Except, I'm not really taking care of things. I'm sitting here fantasizing about where I'd rather be and what I'd rather be doing.

Maddie is at the top of that list. It's like the more my brain tells me no, the more I want her. And if last night and this morning are any indication, she wants me, too.

When I brushed up against her to grab the coffee mugs this morning, the heat between us was hotter than a Vegas summer. The way she pressed against me. The tilt of her hips into mine. The longer-than-necessary linger. The morning could have easily taken a different turn, and I wish more than anything it had. I've been relatively well behaved for now, but anymore chance encounters like that, and I can't make any promises.

Jesus. Just like that and I'm down the rabbit hole again. Luckily, the meeting looks like it's wrapping up.

Joe and the investor stand up, and I follow suit.

"Thanks for meeting with us today, Roman. I feel like we've made some good progress and hopefully we'll be working with each other soon."

"Absolutely." Damn it, I don't even know his name. "We'll talk things over and be in touch soon."

Joe eyes me like he knows I don't have any fucking idea what we've spent the last hour talking about. "I'll see you out, Raymond."

Raymond.

We shake hands, and Joe leads him to the lobby.

Important meetings like this are always conducted at our office instead of at the warehouse. It's more of a commute than I'm used to, but it's worth it for the view. From the twentieth floor, we've got an incredible vantage point of both the Strip and the mountains. To the outside world, it looks like a standard shipping company, but this conference room has witnessed vile, gruesome conversations that most people could never dream up.

A few minutes later, Joe is back, and he lets the door slam behind him.

"Did Raymond get off okay?"

Joe snorts. "Do you care? You hardly said two words to the man during that meeting, and don't even pretend like you weren't daydreaming about your new plaything."

"Maddie isn't my new plaything." I clench my jaw. How dare he talk about her that way? "She's working for me. An employee. That's it."

"Maddie?" He eyes me.

"Forget about it, okay?" I brush him off, bracing myself against the polished oak conference table. "If I'm distracted, it's because I'm worried that shit is falling through the cracks here while I'm trying to chase down the men who shot a park up to go after my son."

Joe stiffens, but he doesn't take offense to my claim that he's letting things slip because we both know I'm deflecting. The last thing Joe is is sloppy. Perceptive is much more his style. "We're solid," he says. "But I had some guys look into Russ after your text this morning."

"And?"

"And she's right." Joe clicks his tongue, obviously a little surprised. "I didn't want to believe it, but one of the car ports had a surveillance camera put up a while ago. Russ knew about it, and conveniently, all the footage was deleted. I spent all morning recovering it."

Joe pulls out his iPad and slides it in front of me. The footage is grainy, but I can clearly see Russ in the alleyway. He's alone, which is odd because he was supposed to be meeting a client to deliver. Russ glances around the area and then he breaks the lock on our unit and starts piling gun parts out. A second later, another person pulls up like he knows Russ. The two talk and start loading pallets of my product into the car. Hundreds of thousands of dollars of product. The motherfucker was stealing from us.

I glance up at Joe, who nods at the screen. Great, there's more.

After they get a good amount loaded, a fight breaks out between the two partners and the other man shoves Russ down. He cuts his leg on the side of the garage, tearing it on some shredded metal, just like Maddie said. Russ pulls his gun out and shoots the guy point blank.

"What the fuck did I just watch?" I toss the screen onto the table, rubbing my temples.

"You watched a man who has been with us for the last ten years try to steal almost a half mil in product, shoot his partner dead over some kind of disagreement, and fabricate a story where he's the victim so we wouldn't now."

"Did you bring him in?"

Joe nods. "He sang like a fucking canary. Admitted the entire thing. And it's not the first time. He's been swiping a few parts here and there to sell on his own. So small that no one would know the difference."

"Jesus Christ." I rake my fingers through my hair. There aren't a lot of hard and fast rules in this business, but stealing from the hand that feeds you? Yeah, that breaks every fucking one of them.

"How do you want me to play this? He's locked up now. We can do it quickly and quietly if you want, or..."

"Or make an example out of him."

Joe nods. "You make the call."

With all the turmoil over the last few months, a show of force might not be the worst thing. Especially when the act of betrayal is so personal and so blatant. I won't tolerate this behavior from any of my men; it's best to just nip it right in the bud.

It's easier to make a call like this when it's someone you don't know. A rival. An enemy. I guess that's what Russ has made himself into, though.

"Let him rot for a few days and then we'll make a show of it." I grit my teeth. "I don't want this happening again."

"You got it." Joe nods. "I'll set it up."

Joe and I finish things up at the office and I head home.

The house looks nothing like it did when I left. Laundry put away. Toys picked up. Jesus, the floors even look clean enough to eat off of. Maddie is a magician, and I have no idea how she balances things like she does. On days I'm alone with Ty, I get nothing done, and the house looks like a war zone, and I've had much more practice than she has. I almost feel guilty for all the slack she picks up.

Maybe I'll take Maddie and Ty out for a nice dinner tonight. A thank you, not only for all the help she's been, but for picking up on Russ's made-up story. She's proving herself to be a valuable asset on every front.

"Hello?" I call, winding my way through the house. There's no sign of them in the living room or the kitchen and a twinge of panic sparks in my stomach until I glance out the patio doors.

Maddie has her back to me, sitting on the edge of the pool as Ty floats in the water on a giant tube and shoots a super soaker into the air. Even through the thick glass, I can hear them laughing; the sound is music to my ears. Any bit of tension I brought home quickly vanishes, and I inch the door open, joining them.

Neither of them notices me at first, and as I get closer, my heart pounds in my chest. Maddie's got a sheer lacy cover up on, and I can see the shadows of a barely there black bikini underneath. The small tease is enough to send me into overdrive as I walk toward her. It's hard enough to hide my attraction under normal circumstances, but it's damn impossible when she's got her long tanned legs dangled in the water like she does—painted pink toes splashing around, coverup draped on her bare thighs threatening to inch higher with every little kick she does.

I stifle a moan, imagining the masterpiece I'd unwrap if I could rip that delicate fabric right off of her, and finally put all of that chemistry between us to rest. And if Ty wasn't around, I might have.

"No way you can do a backflip..." Ty smirks as he floats by her.

"Yes way! My brother taught me when I was about your age." Maddie laughs, tilting her head to the side.

"Prove it," he taunts, egging her on.

Ty notices me out of the corner of his eye and waves wildly, his tube teetering back and forth. "Daddy!"

Maddie whips her head around, startled by the interruption. Her blonde curls are tucked back with a pair of sunglasses and there's a blinding smile on her face. She's got no clue how beautiful she is, and that kind of humble confidence is hard to come by these days.

"Hey Bud." I grin, waving as I pull a lounge chair up next to the edge of the pool a foot or two away from Maddie.

I love seeing him active again. It's been a tough few weeks of recovery. When you're used to a kid who is usually bouncing off the walls and regularly risking his life in his latest dangerous hobby, it's hard to see them so down. Today, he looks like his old self and that's a welcome relief.

"Hey." Maddie turns her smile to me, a flush in her cheeks. "I wasn't expecting you home so soon. How long have you been here?"

"Long enough to hear you promise my son a little backflip demonstration."

Maddie laughs, shaking her head. "I didn't promise a demonstration...I promised I could *do* one."

"Prove it!!!" Ty calls.

"It's been a long time, buddy. Maybe another day."

"I double dare you," he taunts. The kid sure likes his trash talk.

She glances up as if she's looking for some backup, but she won't get it from me. Ty wants to see Maddie's cool trick, but I'm in favor of it for an entirely different reason. If she's getting in the water, that means she's taking her cover-up off and I can steal a glimpse of her body.

"That's not something you just casually mention in conversation." I shrug. "I think Ty's right. Better put your money where your mouth is."

"Yeah! Come on, Maddie!"

"Fine." Maddie stands, inching the cover-up over her head and tossing it at my feet. "One time."

"Yeah!" Ty cheers as she makes her way over to the diving board. He maneuvers his tube to the side of the pool.

Jesus Christ. Maybe this was a bad idea. Every bit of her is fucking delicious. The dangerous curves, the sway of her hips, the determined look in her eye. I'm into a bit of torture, but it isn't even fair at this point.

She takes a band off of her wrist and ties her golden honey hair into a ponytail. As she walks out to the edge, she flashes a playful smile at us. "I'm only going to do this once. Understand?"

I can't help but laugh, and Ty nods enthusiastically.

Maddie turns, edging her heels to the end of the board. With a bend of her knees, she jumps and launches herself into the air, her smoke-show body spinning into a backflip so precise and perfect that it looks like it could win gold in the Olympics. I shouldn't be the least bit surprised, because the girl doesn't seem to do anything halfway.

Ty looks back at me with shock and amazement when she hits the water with barely a splash. "That was so cool! She really did it!"

"Yeah, it was awesome!" I agree.

Maddie surfaces and swims to the edge.

"I told you I could do it."

"That was so cool, Maddie! Do you think you can teach me?" Ty beams. He thinks Maddie is a superhero, and I can't blame him.

"Sure! Let's give your chest another week to heal and we can start practicing." She grins, lifting herself out of the pool.

Ty is thrilled with her answer, and starts paddling around the pool again.

I reach for the towel on the lounge chair and offer it to Maddie, mostly for my own benefit. Seeing her wet has my mind wandering into some treacherous places, and I'm still aching from the erection she gave me this morning. If I have to look at her like this much longer, I'll be in some serious pain again.

Maddie takes the towel, standing only inches away from me as water droplets race down her body. She shakes her hair out, propping her foot up on my chair and rubbing the towel up and down those long, toned legs to dry off. I have to turn away to keep any semblance of composure. She has to know what she's doing to me, and judging by the way she keeps at it, she likes it. When she wraps the towel around her body and covers up, I can finally breathe again.

"What did you think?" she asks, demanding my attention back.

"That was *very* impressive." My mouth is so dry I can hardly speak. "I didn't think you were actually going to do it."

Maddie sits on the other side of the chair. Now I'm positive she knows what she's doing, because there are empty chairs on either side of me, yet she chose to set her nearly naked body mere inches from me. If the sun hits it just right, the thin material is practically see through.

Fuck me. Keeping this professional was hard enough, but with her putting the full court press on, it's next level. Her confidence only makes her sexier to me. No man should be expected to have the amount of restraint I do.

"Well, he dared me." She shrugs. "I've got two older brothers and I know you never back down from a dare. Especially a double dare."

I chuckle, rolling my sleeves up a bit. Whether it's the weather or Maddie, I'm about to work myself into a heat stroke.

Although maybe that wouldn't be such a bad idea, because if I'm unconscious, Maddie will have to give me mouth-to-mouth, in a purely professional way.

"Thanks for hanging out with him this afternoon," I say. "It looks like he's had the time of his life."

"He's a good kid. Did your meeting go okay?"

I nod. "Went fine. But, uh, I wanted to tell you...I had Joe look into Russ's story a little more."

Maddie raises a curious eyebrow.

"You were right. He was stealing from us and tried to cover the whole thing up."

"Really?"

"Yep. There's surveillance of the whole thing. He cut his leg on the door of my storage unit while he was loading shit up."

"Wow." She bites her lip. "I'm really sorry."

"You have nothing to be sorry for." I shake my head. "In fact, without you, I would have been down a lot of money before I knew what was happening. Let me take you to dinner tonight to thank you. You, me, and Ty."

"Oh." Maddie's face falls a little, and she tenses. "That's really sweet of you, but you don't need to do that."

"I want to. Plus, you stepped in for Ty today. Dinner is the least I can do."

"Well, the thing is, I've got dinner plans with somebody..."

Her words hit me like a fucking freight train. She's going out with somebody? Did I misread all of this? After all the sexual tension, the banter, the signals and she's got a boyfriend?

Suddenly I feel like an absolute fool. It never occurred to me to ask her, and now I've had myself so tightly wound over a girl who is even more unreachable than I thought.

A twinge of jealousy twists through me, and all that does is make me angry. I shouldn't feel as jealous as I do. I shouldn't feel as possessive as I do. I shouldn't feel a lot of the things towards Maddie that I do. And it needs to stop. She's every color of forbidden, and I need to get a hold of myself before I have a real mess on my hands. Before I forget the entire basis of our relationship.

A job. A contract.

"No problem. Come on, Ty. It's time to go inside."

"Ten more minutes!"

"No, now!" I call, clenching my jaw. "Maddie has a date and I have to get some work done."

"Roman, it's not—"

"You better go get ready," I cut her off. "I'm sure you're even more behind schedule now that we made you get into the pool. Have a good time. We'll see you tomorrow."

Maddie narrows her eyes at me, her confusion quickly turning to anger. "You know, you can't..."

"Bye Maddie!" Ty climbs out of the pool before she can finish.

She swallows whatever she was about to say to me and turns to him. "Bye buddy. I'll see you later."

I turn in frustration, heading for the house, before I can make an even bigger ass of myself.

Chapter Twelve

Madison

"So, KIND OF LIKE a private doctor?" Jake glances up at me as he scans the menu. We've been to this restaurant at least a dozen times during his visits, and it hasn't changed, but he always pretends he might try something else.

"Yeah, I guess so." I chew the inside of my cheek, staring at the ice melting in my margarita. It sounded good at first, but adding tequila to my already raging emotions isn't the best idea.

No one in the world has ever gotten to me the way Roman does. Never made me angrier. Never frustrated me more. Never turned me on quite like he does. And aside from a few incidental touches and pointed looks, we haven't done a damn thing.

I wanted to avoid the topic of him entirely tonight, but I should have known that Jake would want the rundown of my new job. I left out the finer details, because my brother is about the last person I want to know that I'm working for—and am insanely attracted to—a vicious mobster.

It's about as out of character as I could get, and honestly, he might try to have me committed if he knew the truth.

"Hmm." He presses his lips together, setting the menu down. "I think I'll get the salmon this time."

Like always.

Predictability must be a family trait. Me, Jake, and even our brother, Lucas, are all exactly the same in that department.

None of us went through any bout of teenage rebellion, but that was probably because we never had the time to. Growing up in the shadows of my father, one of the most notable trauma surgeons in the entire world, and then two equally talented and driven brothers, was anything but easy.

I idolized my dad as a child and wanted to be exactly like him. Unlike other girls, I preferred a white coat and scalpel to princess dresses and fairy wands, wanting to be a trauma surgeon just like him. His dream was my dream.

My brothers and I were constantly competing over who had the highest grades, the most scholarly awards, the best offers from colleges and med schools. It always felt like a race, and like I was born already behind. Medicine is fairly male dominated already, but trauma surgery is its own beast. I could probably count the number of notable female trauma surgeons on one hand, so the odds have always been stacked against me.

Even as kids, my brothers got more opportunities than I did. They got to go to work with my dad, observe surgery, and meet the doctors. I was always "too young" or the injury was "too gruesome" for me to see. And in college, it was even worse. Because my dad was a John Hopkins alumni, my brothers inherited two legacy spots there. I had to fight for a spot with thousands of other hopefuls, and work ten times harder for the same things that my brothers were handed.

Somewhere along the line, it stopped being about a dream for me, and more about proving myself to my family and anyone else who doubted me.

The server comes and Jake and I order, and we suffer through a little small talk. Usually, I love when he comes to visit, but my mind is consumed with Roman tonight.

His reaction when I told him I had plans threw me off. He's been leading me on for days without making any kind of move, and the moment he thinks I'm seeing another guy, jealousy consumes him.

Even if this was a date, he has no right to react like that. Nothing turns me off faster than the half in, half out thing that Roman and I have been doing. It's stupid and childish, and one of us needs to put an end to it. One way or another.

I probably enjoyed his reaction more than I should have. Having the upper hand for a change is nice, especially when it makes Roman as uncomfortable as he usually makes others. Not to mention the look of simmering jealousy in his eyes sent a shockwave through my core. He's strung me along like a damn yo-yo the last few weeks, and I'm clinging to the slightest bit of confirmation that he feels the same way I do.

"So, how many patients do you see a day there? Can't be many if it's just for this man's staff."

"It's not," I agree. "I've really only seen two patients in the few weeks I've been working for him. But it's good money, and I'm so busy at the hospital that it's nice to have a quiet, boring job to bring in some extra income."

Quiet and boring is almost laughable in regards to what I'm doing.

Jake gives me a funny look and shrugs. "Suit yourself. You know you could come home to St. Louis and have your pick of departments..."

"Except for Trauma."

My father gave spots to my brothers even though I desperately wanted one, and now there's no room there for me. Neither one of them cared one way or another, but I did.

"Right." Jake takes a drink of his beer. "But general surgery has a great spot open. It pays well. You get consistent hours. You're closer to home."

Now that sounds *boring and quiet.*

Living in Las Vegas has brought me out of my shell, even before meeting Roman. I like it here. I like who I am here. And going home feels like giving in to yet another thing my family wants.

"I've got some time left on my contract, but who knows after that?"

My answer satisfies him for now, and we get through the rest of the meal enjoyably. He tells me about a new girlfriend and we swap stories about crazy cases we've seen lately. By the time dinner is over, we're both completely stuffed and my cheeks hurt from laughing so much. The very worst part about all the competition between us is that it's strained the normal brother-sister relationship. Times like this, I miss it even more.

"What did you say the name of this guy you're working for is? Maybe Dad knows him."

I almost laugh out loud. There is no way my dad and Roman would have ever crossed paths, but Jake's tech savvy and even a simple Google search of Roman paints a pretty clear picture.

"Uh, I don't think he'd know him," I say. "We're—"

I'm cut off by the ring of my phone. As I fish through my purse, Roman's name flashes on the screen. My gut instinct is to throw it into the Koi pond a few feet away from us, but I can't do that. He's paying me to be available to him at all hours, no matter how angry I am or how childish he's being.

"Hello?"

"Maddie, hey." His voice is short. "We had another incident tonight. Can you meet me at the warehouse?"

My stomach sinks. Incident is ominous. I wish he'd just tell me what was going on so I could prepare. "Um, sure. I'm about thirty minutes away."

"That will work. Get here as soon as you can."

The line cuts.

"Everything okay?" Jake arches an eyebrow at me as he signs for the bill.

"That was my boss. I'm so sorry, but they've had an emergency and I have to go." I gather my jacket and purse.

"No worries at all." He stands, setting his napkin on the table. "I have an early flight tomorrow. We'll see you in a few weeks, right? For Dad's party?"

"Uh, yeah, I'll be there. Thank you for dinner." I give him a quick kiss on the cheek and wave as I head out.

Parking in Las Vegas is notoriously terrible, and my car is several blocks away. Roman's tone was urgent, and I can only imagine what kind of mess is waiting for me. If history is any indication, it's something terrible and someone's life is in danger, so I take a cab instead of wasting time getting to my car.

It's a quick drive to the warehouse, and I hurry inside. Unlike the first night, there is no clear victim. There are about ten men casually milling about; no one seems hurt.

"Hey Doc!" one of them calls.

"Nice outfit!"

The dress and heels I wore to dinner feel vastly out of place, and I wish I had my sweater. "Is Roman here?"

Behind me, he clears his throat. Leaning against the doorframe, he has his thick forearms crossed over his chest and a gruff expression. He's in a pair of gym shorts and a gray t-shirt, which seems odd, considering that even when he woke me up in the middle of the night, he put on a dress shirt and slacks just to come here. "Hey Maddie."

"Hey, who is hurt?"

"Right this way." Roman nods behind him and walks that way. I follow, confused by how nonchalant everyone seems to act. With someone hurt, you'd think there would be a little more urgency.

"What happened?"

Roman leads me into a gym at the back of the warehouse. "We were playing a little pickup game and one of the guys got hurt."

My whole body stiffens, anger flaring as it becomes clear what's happening here. Did Roman honestly just make up an emergency to get me out of what he thought was a date? "You called me here for a basketball injury?"

"I hired you to treat my men, Dr. Taylor. I don't remember specifying what injuries would qualify." Roman smirks, eyeing me as I enter the room. "Sammy, let Dr. Taylor have a look at your leg."

Sammy comes forward and doesn't look hurt in the slightest. No blood. No broken bones. No dizziness. In fact, he practically skips to the chair in front of me. As twisted as it is, I want him to be hurt, because it means Roman isn't the self-centered asshole he's coming off as.

"Oh sure, boss." Sammy grins, sticking his leg out. "It's sore back here." He points to the back of his thigh.

Fuming, I suck in a sharp breath and bend down. "Can you describe the pain?"

"Comes and goes." He shrugs. "A little twinge when I jump, but not too bad."

I fight the urge to roll my eyes. A sore hamstring? Roman is used to manipulating people and getting what he wants, but that won't be the case with me. I can play games too.

"Actually, can you climb up onto this table so I can get a little better look? Lay flat on your stomach."

Sammy does as I ask, and Roman's eyes bore into me as I run my hand along the back of Sammy's bare leg.

"Hmm. Might just need to be rubbed out a bit," I say, inching his basketball shorts up high onto his thigh. I press the heel of my hand into the muscle and Sammy nearly comes off the table.

"Holy shit, Doc. That feels so good."

Every muscle in Roman's body tightens as I smirk, not taking my eyes off of him as I continue to rub out Sammy's leg. He's furious, steam practically coming out of his ears as he watches. "Good. How about this?"

I press again, running my hand all the way from the outside of his hip down to his knee. Up and down and up and down. "Mmm. How's that?"

"So fucking good." Sammy groans.

"Good." I smile. "The hamstring starts all the way up here..." I dig my hands into the muscle of his butt. "So it's important to get it really, really deep."

Sammy groans again and Roman's face twists into a look of rage like I've never seen before. For a minute, I wonder if I went too far, but I realize that's a thought that's never crossed Roman's mind with me, so I pile on.

"Are you sure that feels okay? I might need to get a better angle. Is it okay if I climb up here and straddle—"

"He's had enough." Roman grabs his shoulder, ripping Sammy right off the table. "What's the diagnosis?"

"A sore hamstring." I press my lips together. "And a boss with a disgusting jealous streak."

Roman arches an eyebrow at me. I was trying to curtail my anger until we had a little more privacy, but that wink does me in and I can't hold back.

"Sammy, you can ice and take some ibuprofen; it should help. And you, Roman, there isn't much you can do for that obnoxious ego besides going to hell."

I turn on my heels, bursting out of the gym. Our confrontation draws the attention of all his men, and they all watch as I storm toward the front door.

A stiff breeze hits me as the door slams behind me, and I let out a heavy sigh. God, that man is unbelievable. This is all just a game to him and I'm a pawn. He's proved it over and over again, and it's time I start to believe him.

The door flies open behind me, and the air turns cold. Roman's face is harsh enough to stop my heart, and I step back, my heels hitting the red brick of the warehouse. A wicked smile curls on his lips as he moves forward, slowly closing the distance between us. With each step, my chest gets tighter, and it's harder and harder to breathe.

Soon, he hovers just inches above me, the bergamot in his cologne filling my lungs. He's got one hand on the wall next to me, pinning me against the brick with his body. I can't bring myself to look up, but Roman's rough finger settles on my chin. He tilts it until I have no choice but to meet his eyes and it makes me dizzy. Dizzy with fear. Dizzy with lust. I can't make out which.

"What the fuck do you think you're doing?"

My lips curl into an innocent frown. "Treating your men. Isn't that what you hired me for?"

Roman is seething. The vein on his neck bulges as he cages me in, letting out a harsh breath.

"You think I'm going to let you walk out of here after speaking to me that way in front of my men? After that little tantrum? I'm paying you to be available at any fucking second, for any medical reason I deem necessary. Isn't that right?" Roman's gravelly voice rakes over me like hot coals, a burn that excites me as much as it hurts.

There's a strange glint in his eyes, and I'm not sure if he's about to kill me or to kiss me.

When he doesn't do either, I'm even more flustered.

"Where is your car?" His voice is tight as he looks around the lot.

"It's...still downtown," I whisper. "I was in the middle of dinner when you called and I thought it was an emergency, so I didn't want to waste time by rushing back to my car a few blocks away."

"You took a cab at night by yourself?"

"You didn't give me much choice, Roman." I roll my eyes. "Like I said, I thought it was an emergency. Not a silly basketball mishap."

Roman clenches his jaw, sighing heavily. "Wait for me in my truck. I need five minutes inside and I'll drive you home."

He stalks back inside, leaving no room for argument. For a minute, I'm frozen, the authority in his voice turning my insides into putty. I shouldn't let him get to me the way he does, especially tonight. The slam of the door makes me jump and kicks me back into gear. Roman's truck is parked right in front of the warehouse and I climb into the passenger side. It's so quiet out here I can hear my panicked heartbeat ringing in my ears as I wait.

Chapter Thirteen

MAYBE CALLING MADDIE TO the warehouse in the middle of her date wasn't my best idea. In fact, as we drive home and the two whiskeys I had start to wear off, I realize it might have been my worst.

It was dumb and immature, and Maddie's more than pissed. She's livid, actually. The look on her face is so harrowing it could spook the most hardened of criminals. And the worst part is, she looks so goddamn beautiful. Whoever she was out with was important enough for her to impress, and even though my raging jealousy started this, it bites at me again.

Fuck, this girl has my number. The way she can so effortlessly get under my skin is downright impressive, and she's a hell of a lot ballsier than I gave her credit for. I almost lost my shit when I saw her rubbing on Sammy that way. It took an exorbitant amount of strength not to tear her off of him and rip Sammy to shreds right then. But as usual, I'm the one to blame, and for a split second, I kick myself for not faking the injury myself.

Maddie hasn't said a single word since I got in the truck, and neither have I, mostly because I've been trying to find the words to tell her that I'm sorry. Apologizing isn't something I do often—a trait I got from my father. He used to say that a man's got to stand behind his actions, even when he's wrong. Even with four divorces under his belt, he still maintains that. I'm not nearly as stuck in my ways, but it's still hard for me to admit when I'm wrong and I just can't seem to stop fucking up with Madison Taylor. Kind of like a car crash. I can see it happening, but I can't do a damn thing to stop it. Maybe I'm trying to push her away subconsciously because I know how this ends.

Maybe I want her to hate me.

If tonight's any indication, I'm doing a damn good job of it. I pull into the garage, and we're about to walk inside when she finally speaks.

"You were right earlier." She doesn't even face me, and she's so quiet I barely even hear her.

"Huh?" Maddie's words completely catch me off guard.

"You said that you were paying me to be available for all medical emergencies that come up with your men, and you're right. But we both know that wasn't what tonight was about."

"What do you think it was about, then?" I clench my jaw.

"You're jealous." Her painted red lips press into a firm, defiant line as she crosses her arms over her chest. "You called me to the warehouse for a bogus injury to assert your dominance because you thought I was on a date."

Well, she hit the nail on the fucking head there. I grip the doorknob so hard that it almost pulls off as I let us inside.

"Maybe Sammy's injury could have waited until tomorrow," I concede, tossing my keys onto the counter.

"Maybe?" Maddie hisses, whipping her head around to face me.

"I'm sorry, okay?" My words lack any level of sincerity, because I'm really not. The thought of Maddie out with another guy looking as insatiable as she does enrages me, and truth be told, I'm glad I did it. That's not what she wants to hear, though, and I was married long enough to know that a man can end most fights by just telling the woman what she wants to hear.

It's shitty relationship advice, but right now, all I want to do is get away from her before she sees how hard my dick is. Angry Maddie is hot and there is no way around that. Add the low cut dress and high heels she's wearing and I'm basically a lost cause.

"I shouldn't have interfered."

"Yeah, you're damn right you shouldn't have. You don't own me. You don't get to say who I spend my time with, or what I do." She's got her hands perched on her hips, and she stares me down.

I shake my head, eyes trained on the floor. She's right, and there isn't even anything I can say to defend myself.

"I know that you're used to people bending over backwards to do whatever you ask, but if there's any chance of us working together cohesively these next few months, you need to understand that that's not how it's going to be with me."

I snort. *God, that smart little mouth.* There's something so sexy about the cheekiness in her voice. That sass and attitude only turn me on, but the sharp scowl on her face makes it clear that's not her intention. Maddie is nearly the first woman I've met who doesn't throw herself at me, or as she said, *bends over backwards to do what I ask.* I'm drawn to a challenge, but deep down, there's nothing more attractive than a woman who can hold her own and call me on my shit.

"No?" I arch my eyebrow, closing the distance between us with two strides as she backs her way against the kitchen counter. We're so close now that I can almost taste the tequila on her breath. "It won't be like that with you?"

The moonlight pours in from the windows, illuminating her provocative silhouette. This fucking dress...manipulation is a game I'm usually pretty good at, which is why I know Maddie knew exactly what she was doing by putting it on tonight. It's so tight that it almost looks painted on, black satin pushing her tits up and hugging every temptatious curve she's got. Thank God Ty's staying at Joe's tonight.

"N-no..." Maddie stutters, stiffening as she tries to hold her ground. "It won't."

"Really?" I wrap one arm around her waist, setting on her lower back as I pull her in. With my other hand, I grip the nape of her neck, strands of that golden honey hair tangling in my fingers. "I bet if I let this hand slip lower..." My hand falls from her lower back to her ass. "If I kissed you right now..." Tracing her jawline with the other hand, my thumb sweeps across her lower lip and then drops to the hem of her dress. "Or if my fingers find their way right up under your dress, inching higher and higher until I reach the band of your panties and then slide my fingers inside..."

Maddie gulps, a red hot blush covering her cheeks as her petite frame presses into my body.

I smirk, tracing up her bare thigh high enough to elicit a sweet little moan out of those impossibly full lips, but not so high to make my head explode. A furious heat builds inside of me, so intense that it's blinding. "I bet I'd have you bending forwards, backwards, and every way in between."

She lets out a flustered breath, hovering between frustration and infatuation.

When she finally finds the composure to speak, I'm the one reeling.

"That's a bet I'll take."

ROMAN NEEDS NO ENCOURAGEMENT.

The second those words are off of my lips, he crashes into me in a kiss that leaves nothing to the imagination. It's slow and dramatic and raw and a release of all the pent up tension and passion that's been building between us for weeks. Initially sweet and gentle at first, building until it hits an overwhelming intensity. Dominant isn't even a strong enough word. Roman's kiss is straight up possessive. It reaches every part of my body—gripping my heart, stealing my breath, weakening my knees as his fingers tug at my hair. Any faded objections still floating in my mind are silenced by the kiss.

I've never been kissed like this, and I already know I never will be again.

His tongue coaxes my lips apart and then slips inside. I cling to him desperately as he ravishes every part of me, my fingers digging into his firm, muscled shoulders.

When he pulls back, his teeth scrape against my bottom lip with a sharpness that makes my body throb and riddles me with longing. Every nerve inside of me is on high alert, anticipating whatever is going to happen next. Roman has me feeling things I never even knew existed and the last thing I want is for him to stop.

Luckily, he doesn't. A strong arm slips underneath me and lifts me onto the counter. He positions himself between my legs, cupping my chin with a look in his eyes that makes my core quiver. He gives me another frenzied kiss, a broad hand resting on my bare thigh. When he backs away, nose brushing against mine, I'm breathless and absolutely desperate to feel it again.

"Please, Roman."

Please? I'm begging now? One kiss and all self-respect I've got flies out the window?

He seems to like the sound of it, a taunting, playful smile on his lips. Roman drags his lips along my collarbone and then presses one soft kiss just underneath my ear. "Backwards, forwards, and every way in between."

"What?"

An uncertainty settles in his eyes and he pulls back, leaving a cool, hollow space where his body just was. "I told you I could get you to bend anyway I wanted, and I did."

There's a sinking feeling in my stomach as his words sink in. Was this just another game to him? Was he playing with me this whole time? The high I felt just seconds ago comes crashing down, knocking the wind right out of me.

"Roman, what is—"

"You should get some sleep, Maddie. See you in the morning."

I'm too stunned to speak as he disappears up the stairs. What an absolute asshole. Just when I think he might have a single redeeming quality in him, he goes and proves me wrong.

Chapter Fourteen

ROMAN

If there's one thing about me, it's that I stand by my actions—right or wrong.

I don't have a lot of regrets. I rarely second guess myself. But ever since what happened with Maddie the other night, that's all I've been doing. I've replayed those moments over and over again in my mind, and each time I do, it only gets worse.

To be honest, I'm sure if I'm more upset with myself for kissing her or for walking away. The line between us is so blurry now I wouldn't know how to make it right if I tried. Luckily, she hasn't given me the chance, making a damn near art of avoiding me the last couple of days.

To save myself from judgement, I haven't told Joe or Dante what happened, although I'm sure they've heard about what went down at the warehouse through the grapevine. At least calling Maddie out of her date wasn't the worst thing I did that night.

I need something to take the edge off, and lucky for me, I have one waiting down in my tombs. Russ will make the perfect target for the pent-up anger I've got. I wanted to let him sweat it out a bit more, but I need the release now.

Dante and Joe are waiting for me when I get to the lock-up area. They have Russ sitting at the center of the room behind a table. He's blindfolded, hands locked into cuffs in front of him on the surface. At the sound of my footsteps, he jolts, jerking against the restraints.

"Roman! Is that you?" His voice is shaky. "Roman?"

I ignore him, striding toward Joe and Dante.

"How's it going?"

Joe shrugs. "Still not taking any accountability. Swears it's a big misunderstanding."

I laugh out loud at the idea. It takes a prideful asshole to stare at the footage we have and still try to deny what he did.

"How do you want to handle this?" Dante asks.

"I'll take care of it." I say. This betrayal feels personal. Russ has been on my side for years. I've defended him. I've provided for him. And when I was at my most vulnerable, he turned on me.

I survey the variety of tools that they've laid out for me. Hammers. Drills Pliers. Blades of all different sizes and shapes. I'm feeling rather creative this afternoon, and I can think of ways to use all of these on that lying, stealing bastard. The hammer particularly catches my eye.

It makes a scraping sound on the metal table as I pick it up. I take slow, deliberate steps toward Russ, who is still squealing.

"Roman! You've got to listen to me, man. I didn't do it!"

"Oh, Russ. We're so fucking far past that." I chuckle, closing the distance between us.

"I swear, I was going to give it all back."

Reaching forward, I rip the blindfold from his eyes and he squints as he gets his bearings.

"You know, Russ, I believe that. I really do. You've always been loyal. Hardworking. And I've appreciated that."

"Yeah, yeah..." He says, trying to catch his breath. "I have. You're right."

Hope flickers across his face, but when he sees the look on mine, it quickly fades.

"What I don't appreciate, though, is you taking advantage of me when I was down." I glare, hardening as I stare at him.

"Roman, that's not... I didn't..."

"I was at my lowest, Russ. Lost my wife... almost lost my kid... You knew I was distracted and off of my game, and instead of picking up the slack like the rest of my guys, you decided to steal from me."

He opens his mouth like he has something to say, but nothing comes out. Before he can, I rear the hammer back and bring it down across his thumb.

"Ahhhh!" he cries out in pain, reeling back, but the cuffs won't let him.

I raise it again, this time hitting his index finger. Slowly I work all along his right hand, snapping each finger one by one. Once I'm done there, I move to the left. Russ shrieks as his bones shatter with the force.

"Jesus, Roman! Fuck!" He yells.

"It'll be hard to steal from anyone again with your fingers broken, won't it?" I snarl.

"I'm sorry. I really am," he pleads, but it falls on deaf ears. Broken fingers or not, he's not going to have the opportunity to steal from anyone ever again.

I take the hammer back, swing with all my force toward him. Blood splatters when it hits his jaw. Another uppercut to his chin and I hear the bone crack.

It doesn't take long for Russ to lose his spirit, collapsing against the table and taking each blow with little fight. When he's unable to hold himself up anymore, Joe and Dante cut him loose and drag him back to his cell.

I sink down into one of the chairs, catching my breath as I rake my fingers through my hair. Usually, this kind of thing would bring me some relief, help me blow off a little steam. Somehow, today, though, it's done the opposite. If I thought this would help clear my mind of Maddie, I was dead wrong.

All I can think about now is what she'd think of what I just did.

CHAPTER FIFTEEN

ROMAN AND I HAVE somehow gone an entire week without being alone in the same room—I'm not sure if I'm avoiding him, if he's avoiding me, or if our paths just haven't crossed, but somehow we've made it an entire week without being alone in the same room. Considering his bedroom is one very thin wall away from mine, that's a big feat.

We've had dinner a few nights, but only with Ty or Joe and Dante as a buffer, and even then, we haven't spoken a word to each other. I can't stop replaying what happened the other night in my mind and it's driving me absolutely crazy. Of all the twisted things Roman has done, this one somehow takes the cake. What kind of person demands I leave in the middle of my date just to kiss me like he was leaving for war, all to prove a point?

Not even Roman Molanari could be that selfish and out of touch. I refuse to believe it.

Not after the way he kissed me. Not after the things he said. Not after the spark I felt between us. You can't fake that kind of passion, and I know something else is going on.

But as time passes and he doesn't even attempt to talk to me or apologize, I wonder if I'm giving him too much credit.

Maybe he really is that much of an asshole.

It's late when I get home from work, and the house is quiet. Between my busy week at the hospital and the effort I've put into avoiding Roman, I'm exhausted, and all I want to do is take a hot shower and go to bed.

Stopping in the kitchen for a glass of wine, I flip on the light. My heart almost stops when I see Roman standing at the fridge. The door is open, and he scans the shelves for something to eat. He glances up when I walk in, nodding toward me with a careless grunt.

"Hey."

"Hi," I say, moving toward the cabinet. The last thing I want to do is have this conversation tonight. I don't say a word as I grab a glass out and open a bottle of wine that's on the counter. I pour myself a big glass and spin around, hoping to make my getaway, but Roman stands right in my way.

"You're in a hurry," he says.

"I didn't think you'd notice with the way you've been avoiding me lately."

Roman tilts his head, confusion creasing his face. "The other night? Remind me what happened?"

He can't play dumb for long, though, because a smirk teases at the corner of his lips.

"You're an asshole." I roll my eyes, brushing past him.

"I don't know what you're so upset about," he calls after me. "We made a bet. I proved my point, and you lost."

"Goodnight Roman."

I can hear him chuckle behind me and it only infuriates me more.

Only when I'm in the safety of my bedroom can I finally breathe. The bed looks so inviting, but I resist the urge to sit down because I know I'll never get back up, so I force myself into the bathroom to shower and brush my teeth. All I want is for this day to end.

The bathroom in my guest suite is about as big as my entire apartment was. In fact, just the shower itself might be. Three shower heads—one overhead and

one on each side—provide a powerful, massaging spray. Natural stone tiles cover
the walls and floor, and with the press of a button, I can make the whole thing
fill up with steam that smells like a lavender field. It's a dream, and just as good
as any spa I've been to.

I flip the faucet on and let it warm up while I peel my clothes off and toss
them into the corner. It isn't just Roman that has my mind all over the place,
it's dinner with my brother. He mentioned my dad's party, which I completely
forgot about and, truthfully, wasn't really planning to attend. In my rush to
leave, though, I committed, and now I have to figure out how to backtrack out
of that one.

Not to mention, I'm expecting a call as soon as Jake tells him about my new
job. At best, he'll be curious. At worst, he'll be skeptical and demand more
information.

I open the foggy glass door, ready to step inside, when a furry creature
crouched in the corner of the shower catches my eye. A spider the size of a
grapefruit sits back on its haunches, trying to avoid the water spray.

"Aaaaaaaah!" a shrill, half-cry, half-scream escapes my mouth as I clamor
away, desperately flailing for a towel. It's almost like it taunts me as I lean against
the vanity. Spiders don't normally scare me, but I've never seen one so big. It's
at least six inches long, and I'm frozen, afraid to move.

As I try to figure out what to do, the bathroom door bursts open, and Roman
stands in the doorway. He's disheveled, shirtless, and there's a vicious look in his
eyes that chills me to my bones.

"What? What's wrong?" His head swivels around the room as he looks for a
threat, gun drawn.

"There..." I can't even put a sentence together. "In the shower..."

Gun drawn, Roman cautiously peers around the edge of the shower, as if he
expects an intruder. Seconds later, he bursts into deep laughter, so amused that
he bends over, hands on his knees, as he tries to catch his breath.

"Are you serious? You screamed like that because of a spider? I thought
someone was being murdered."

I glare at him. "That thing could easily murder me! Have you seen the size of it?"

"That thing"—Roman shoots me a taunting smirk—"is a camel spider. It isn't even venomous."

"I don't care. I still want it out." My voice almost sounds like a whine. I'm not sure how much I trust Roman's knowledge of spiders, because it certainly looks deadly.

"Okay, Princess." He chuckles, raking his fingers through his dark, messy hair. When he glances back, he does a double take, gaze falling the entire length of my body. His teeth sink into his lower lip, and a low, almost inaudible groan escapes his lips.

After days of radio silence, he's choosing now to pay attention? To check me out? What is his...*oh, damn it.* Then, it hits me. I don't have any clothes on. In my haste to grab a towel, I reached for the closest thing, which apparently was a hand towel. I'm standing in front of Roman, almost completely naked, and the thick bulge in his shorts tells me he's very well aware of it.

God, could this get any more awkward?

My cheeks flush, and in a rare gentlemanly gesture, Roman grabs my robe off of the hook and tosses it to me. "I'll take care of the spider. You can use my shower in the meantime."

Slipping the robe around my body, I hurry out of the bathroom without a word, too distraught to even thank him. I need space and a clear mind, so despite the strangeness of using Roman's shower, I go to his room.

I'm not sure what I expected, but this definitely isn't it. Roman's room looks virtually untouched. It's sterile and harsh, like no one even lives here at all. Aside from a large mirror over his dresser, the dark gray walls are bare. Almost an entire wall is windows, but he's got the shades pulled down so tightly that you can hardly tell. The bed is enormous, almost twice as big as a typical king size, and it's neatly made. It's hard to imagine a woman ever living in this space. He must have changed it after Talia died.

Across the room, there is a set of double doors and I go through them to the bathroom. It's every bit as luxurious as I expect. The shower is twice the size of mine, with five shower heads, and there's a clawfoot jetted bathtub in the corner next to a window. A switch next to the door activates the heated tiles beneath my feet. Just like in his room, everything has its place and there isn't a single thing out on the counter. His woodsy cologne, still lingering in the air, is the only hint he's been in here.

Wanting to avoid another spider incident, I check the shower immediately, and then turn on the water. I don't see anything, but I can't shake the feeling of creepy crawlies all over me while I'm in there. So much for a long, hot shower. I dry off quickly, slipping my robe back on and heading out to Roman's room.

He's sitting on his bed with his laptop on his lap. Could he at least put a damn shirt on? I can't help but think he's doing it on purpose, especially after the way he's been acting.

"That was fast." He catches my gaze.

I clear my throat, walking towards him. "Yeah, I couldn't get the spider out of my head, so it wasn't quite as enjoyable as I hoped. Did you kill it?"

The sympathy in his smile is more sincere than I expect. "Your spider friend has been relocated and won't be bothering you anymore."

I don't like the sound of relocated as much as dead, but I'm certainly not going to be the one to handle it. "And you're sure it wasn't poisonous?"

As I sit on the bed a safe distance away from him, I pull my robe around me even tighter. I can't afford another wardrobe malfunction around him right now.

"Positive. We get camel spiders all the time. All they'll do is give you a nasty bite."

"I'd like to avoid that, too."

Roman chuckles, shutting his computer and setting it to the side. "Well, you don't need to worry about it anymore. I made a pass through your room to be sure there weren't any others, but I'll call the exterminator tomorrow if it will make you feel better."

"Wow." I arch an eyebrow. "That's uncharacteristically chivalrous of you."

That strikes a nerve with Roman, and he drops his head, rubbing his chin like he does when he's trying to craft the perfect response. Finally, he looks up with a softness in his face.

"I'm sorry about how I acted earlier. How I've been acting all week. I really fucked up."

"Another apology? That must be a record for you," I quip.

"Yeah, well, I guess you're making me do a lot of things I'm not used to."

"I am?"

He nods. "You were right the other night. The second I heard you were going out with another guy, I went out of my mind with jealousy. All I could think about was that bastard sitting across from you all night doing all the things I wish I could. I was thinking about the way you'd tuck your hair behind your ear when he made you laugh, or the blush you'd get in your cheeks when he offered to buy you another drink. How he'd get to hold your hand, kiss those lips, probably even more once he took you home. I know it doesn't make any sense and I don't have any right to feel like that, but I did and..."

I realize that Roman still thinks I was on a date, and I can't let him ramble on any longer without knowing the truth.

"Roman, I wasn't on a date," I cut him off.

"What?" He snaps his head up like he thinks he misheard.

"My brother was in town." I sigh. "You didn't give me a chance to explain. Otherwise, I would've told you that."

"Jesus, Maddie, really?" He shakes his head, letting out a sharp breath. "I don't even know what to say."

"I don't either. I don't know how you can say you feel that way about me, and then still string me along and play all your stupid games like I'm some kind of toy to you."

He swallows, wringing his hands out. "Maddie, I didn't cut things off the other night just to mess with you. I like getting you riled up, yeah, but only when I intend to do something about it."

"So what was it, then?"

"That was me panicking. It was me realizing that we were about to cross a line that we can't come back from. You and I are a bad idea. There's no way we work out. I'm only going to drag you into my darkness if we even try." He tugs at the end of his hair, words catching in his throat. There's a bit of emotion there that takes me by surprise. "People around me get hurt, Maddie. You've seen that firsthand. And I know myself—one time, one taste of you would never be enough. So I guess I thought if I made you hate me, it would push you away. Because that's where it's safe, Maddie. Away from here. Away from me."

I take a deep breath, giving his words a second to settle.

"I don't need you to protect me, Roman. It's sweet and all, but I can take care of myself and I can make my own choices." Reaching for his hand, I intertwine our fingers. "Maybe I don't want *safe*, Roman. Maybe I want passion and impulse and even a bit of your darkness."

His fingers grip my neck, pulling me in until our foreheads rest against each other. The cool, minty taste of his breath gives me chills as he brushes a kiss across my lips. "I'm not good for you, Madison. I've been trying like hell to stay away because I know this is a bad idea."

"Why don't you let me be the judge of that?"

Chapter Sixteen

ROMAN

When Maddie smiles at me, it's an invitation. Permission. Approval.

And it's exactly what I've been waiting for.

Sweeping an arm underneath her, I lay her back against the bed. Her golden curls splay out onto the comforter as I hover over her. A fierce craving settles into my already pulsing cock as she looks up at me with those big doe eyes. I want to take my time with her and savor every second, but after being so tempted the last few weeks, my impatient body has other plans.

My mouth crashes into hers with a rough, possessive kiss. I've been on edge ever since the kiss the other night, and the taste of her offers the slightest sense of relief. It's short-lived, though, because all I want is more. *So much more.*

Maddie locks eyes with me, a treacherous smirk playing on her lips while she tugs at the wrap on her robe. With a flick of her wrist, the whole thing comes undone and pools around her naked body, and my heart slams into my chest.

Holy fuck.

Out of respect for her, I tried my best not to look when she was cowering in the bathroom, but now that she's willing and bare beneath me, I devour every inch of her naked body. A low groan rumbles through my chest as my hands trace her vicious curves, each one so flawlessly crafted that it almost hurts. Down her shoulder, across the swell of those perky tits, over her ribcage, and all the way to the dimple of her hips. I settle there, dropping my gaze to the valley between her thighs.

When Maddie lets her knee fall open, my breath snags at the peak of that hot, wet pussy. I can already imagine it stretching around my cock as I'm deep inside of her, but I don't want to get too far ahead of myself. I've waited too fucking long to rush through this.

"So fucking beautiful," I growl, burying my face in the nape of her neck. The smell of my shower gel lingers on her skin like a possessive mark, and it awakens something primal inside of me. I kiss along her collarbone, dragging my teeth across the sensitive skin as her candy lips bow and she lets out a tiny gasp.

Maddie weaves her arms around my neck, tugging at my hair as I nip and suck at her neck. The noises that she's making drive me fucking wild, and our bodies grind together. I still have my shorts on, but the fabric is a thin barrier between us and I'm dying to feel her skin against mine.

"You're sure?" I whisper. "Because if we do this, I don't know if I'll ever be able to let you go."

"I'm sure." She nods, a rosy blush on her cheeks as she looks up at me. Her eyes pool with desire, desperate and needy and practically begging me to take her.

I roll to the side and work my shorts off, straddling her again once I'm completely naked. Maddie's breath shallows out as I watch her eyes travel over me, mercilessly checking me out. Her eyes start at my mouth, then fall to my chest, then my abs, and finally settle on my cock that stands at perfect attention. Instinctively, she clenches her thighs in a cute little show of resistance that I know won't last long. As stubborn as ever, she doesn't want me to see how wet she is. How hot I've already made her.

A flicker of panic pulses through her eyes as what we're about to do sinks in. It's not like I know Maddie's full list of sexual partners, but I can already tell this isn't something she does very often. For all of her confidence and bravado, she's a little nervous.

Leaning forward, I press a kiss to the corner of her mouth to calm any self-consciousness she feels. "You're in charge here, Maddie. You tell me if it's too much. Or if you need a break. Or if we need to stop. Got it?"

Her teeth sink into her lower lip as she nods. "I'm good, Roman. I promise." With her assurance, I pick up where I left off.

NOTHING IN THE WORLD could prepare me for the way Roman Molanari looks at me. There's an intensity and fire that sears straight into my soul, and his touch is even more extreme. His fingers leave a trail of lightning as he traces along my body—through my hair, down my ribcage, across my chest. With a hand on either side of my shoulders, he cages me against the bed and I feel so small as his strong, broad body towers above me.

God, he's so *hot*.

My chest tightens as I soak in the sight of him. The thick, muscled shoulders, the firm, rippling abs, the larger-than-life erection that presses against my thigh. I can't stop myself from looking because every inch of Roman looks like it was sculpted from pure granite. When he catches me staring, he smiles, and it steals my breath. He's so far above anything I'm used to, it makes me anxious, but one reassuring kiss is all it takes to quiet my nerves.

"Fuck, Maddie," Roman groans. "Do you have any idea how long I've thought about this? How long I've imagined what those sweet lips taste like? How they'd feel on mine? How it would sound to hear them cry out my name?"

He moves slowly, purposefully, down my body as if he's following a map, touching me and kissing me with a gentleness that he's never shown me before. One that melts me.

"You're all I've been able to think about these last few weeks, Maddie. Touching you, kissing you, burying myself inside of you..."

He drags his fingers up my thigh, edging them further and further apart until I feel the slightest brush against my core. It's almost enough to unravel me right then and there, but he's only just beginning. If I know anything about Roman, he's not going to make this easy on me.

Sucking in a sharp breath, I arch into him as he traces my entrance. Just that small touch makes me dizzy as I cling to his broad, steadying shoulders.

"You've thought about it too, haven't you?" His voice vibrates against my ear as his tongue swipes just below against the sweet spot on my neck. My core throbs, desperate for him. Aching for him. "Tell me about it, baby. Tell me what you pictured when you thought about us together..."

"Roman, I..." Words completely fail me as he teases me, fingers sliding into my wet, slick folds but not yet close enough to satisfy me. I'd never expect torture to feel so damn good.

"Was it this?" Roman puts a finger inside of me. He twists it around, drumming it against my raging body.

"Oh God, Roman." My voice is so whiny, so needy, that I barely recognize it.

Then he slips another in. And another. "Did you think about my fingers inside of you while you begged for more? Or how wet this sweet, perfect pussy would get with each stroke?"

The more I squirm, the bigger his smile gets, and the more intense his stare is. His deep brown eyes hold mine captive as he plays me like a damn puppet. Finally, I close my eyes, but he strokes my cheek.

"Uh huh, right here, baby."

His thumb rolls against me as he pulses in and out. It's slow at first, but his pace builds until it's frenzied. Disorienting. Almost punishing. His touch demands my satisfaction, but then, just as quickly, it's gone. His touch leaves a cool emptiness inside me, taking my breath away. What the hell? He's not doing this again, is he? He's not going to—

Before I can even finish the thought, Roman flips me onto my stomach. Pushing his hands up my legs, he edges my knees open and I shiver as the warmth of his breath blows over me. And then I feel the flick of his tongue. "Or was it this? Did you think about this, baby?"

"Mmm," I moan, gripping the sheets as if my life depends on it, heart pounding in my chest.

Pinning me to the bed, Roman holds me exactly in place so he can ravish me as he desires. He laps against me, his tongue drawing circles against my slick flesh, and then diving inside of me.

Oh, my god.

My entire body coils up; the sensation more than I've ever experienced. It's overwhelming, and for a moment I tense. Roman is just as receptive as he is thorough, though, and he picks up on it immediately. He digs his fingers into the muscle of my ass, stroking and massaging until I start to relax.

"That's my girl. Easy."

He kisses the inside of my thighs, giving me an opportunity to pump the brakes if I want to. When I don't, his kisses move farther until I'm at the mercy of that magic tongue again.

My chest presses into the bed as he works me over, broad hands planted on the back of my thighs. Reaching my arms up, I clutch the sheets, desperate for something to brace myself as the feathery strokes of his tongue consume me.

By the time he comes up for air, I'm wound so tightly that a breeze in the right direction could make me explode, and I have to catch my breath. I hear Roman fumble toward the nightstand and the crinkle of a condom wrapper as he tears into it.

As I turn over, he pulls me to the side of the bed, my hips teetering at the edge. He slides his palm underneath me, lifting my leg and raking his fingers all the way down from my thigh as he rests my ankle on his shoulder.

"God, Maddie. You're so beautiful."

The gravel in his voice makes my stomach flutter and his hips settle over me. My pounding heart echoes in my ears as he presses into me. Slow at first, and then, inch by inch, he fills me to the absolute brim.

"Ah!" I cry out, my body stretching to accommodate his swollen length.

Roman eases up, bringing a strand of hair from my cheek as our eyes meet. "Okay?"

"I'm...good." I'm so breathless that it's a struggle to even speak. "So good. Please don't stop."

At my insistence, he starts to rock against me, our bodies finding their own synchronic rhythm. Blood rushes through my veins, a sensation that goes straight to my head and wipes out any thoughts or emotion besides this right here.

Besides his body intertwined with mine. Besides his urgent, powerful hold on my hips. Besides the sheer ecstasy I feel as he slides in and out of me.

When I reach to touch him, Roman catches both of my wrists in a firm hold, pinning them above my head. The heel of his palms press into each of mine as he drives deeper, his pace slowing but the intensity only ramping up.

"Mmm," I moan, arching my back as I pull against him, and the resistance floods me with a furious, flaming desire. He breaches every one of my defenses, and I let him. Let him devour me. Let him claim me. Let him hold me like he owns me...and in this moment, he does.

Another one of his intoxicating kisses robs me of my senses, and I realize that I'm fully under his control. My body trembles as I surrender, letting myself submit to his prowess. I don't expect it to hit me like it does, but being at his mercy sends an intense craving coiling through me—one I can almost taste as he brings me to the edge.

Roman's only focus is on my pleasure, his warm, lustful kisses littering my body as he bucks against me. My eyes shut and I stuck in a sharp breath, my orgasm hitting me in drugged waves with his last thrust.

"Ohhhh god, Roman..." I whine, digging my nails into the back of his hand as he holds me in place. The resistance makes my release all the more intense and a blistering heat grips me as my body clenches around him, giving him the final push to his own climax.

"Fuck, Maddie," he hisses as that hypnotic wave crashes into him. Burying his face into my neck, he groans, and we collapse against each other onto the bed.

For a moment, we're quiet; the only sound is our labored breathing as we lie there. Still too high on him to consider the consequences of what we've just done, I reach for his hand. He takes it, pulling me on top of him.

"You're so fucking perfect, Maddie. You know that?" The rasp in his voice makes my body tingle, as if I have anything left to give. "I could do that forever."

Forever.

"Me too," I whisper, my head falling back onto his forearm.

Neither one of us thinks about what that word actually means, but for now, it's the truth. I could live inside these last few moments with Roman and the contentment I feel for eternity.

Chapter Seventeen

As I lay on Roman's shoulder, fingertips tracing the endless lines of his tattoos as his chest rises and falls with each breath, my mind is almost blank. Nothing else matters, nothing else exists, except for us, in this moment together. I don't want to think about what happens next, or what this means moving forward, because, right now, everything is perfect and I'm not ready for that to fade.

I don't exactly have a long line of experience to compare it to, but sex with Roman is like nothing I've ever experienced before. He knew just how hard to push me, when to pull back, and exactly where to touch to drive me wild, like he designed my sweet spots himself. It was almost irritating how fast he mastered me, but he was patient and intentional and took every cue I gave, so by the end, he knew what I wanted even before I did.

It was everything I expected, yet nothing like it at all, and as we lay here, it only gets better. I half expected Roman to kick me out and send me back to my room the moment it was over, but he did the opposite. His strong arms have held me for almost an hour, his fingers gently caressing my back and shoulders. We lie tangled beneath the sheets, naked bodies pressed together like we were designed for each other.

As tired as I am, I don't want to breathe too hard for the risk of ruining the moment, because I know what comes as soon as it's over. Instead, we lay in the quiet, both lost in our own thoughts.

This thing between us is almost more than I can handle. One minute he's infuriating me, and the next, I'm absolutely positive I'll never be able to live without his touch. It's disorienting in the best and worst of ways, and I know that what we just did is only going to complicate things.

Not only are we completely incompatible on paper, he's my boss. I left my lease and I'm counting on the money he's paying me to get me out of debt. And we just slept together.

Roman leans close, and he presses a kiss to my forehead. "Are you okay? You haven't said much."

"I'm great." I smile up at him. "Just taking it all in. That was...it was incredible."

He grins, catching my mouth in his. "For me, too. I don't know why the fuck we waited so long."

"Probably because we've got ourselves a little bit of a mess now." My stomach knots as I sit up, covering my body with his bedsheet. The elation of the moment slowly dwindles, replaced with gripping reality.

"Maddie, there is no mess." Roman props himself up. "I meant what I said earlier. You're in control here. If you want this to be a one-time thing and we never speak about it again, then we'll do that. No questions asked."

It's probably the most logical answer, but each word he says is like a twisting knife in my chest. His face is unreadable, giving no clues to how he's feeling until he finally speaks again.

"But you should know that's not what I want." He swallows, resting his palm on my cheek, his thumb sweeping across it.

"It's not?"

"Of course it's not." He's almost offended that I asked. "Is that what you thought?"

I don't answer, biting my lip as I try to make sense of what I'm feeling. "I don't really know what to think, Roman. You've been playing a game with me since the moment I got here...and I can't say that I haven't been laying here thinking what happens now that you got what you wanted."

Roman's eyes widen, and he lets out a heavy breath. "Maddie...I'm a fucking asshole. You're right, I've acted like a dick the last few weeks and I'm sorry, but it's only because you've made me absolutely insane since the moment you got here. That's not an excuse. I'm just telling you like it is. But don't for a second think that you are some kind of game or conquest for me. It's the exact opposite, actually. I've started to get feelings for you in the last few weeks that I haven't felt for someone in a very, very long time. Probably never."

He pauses, rubbing his chin. "And that scares me. I don't like being out of control or unprepared, and that's why I've been acting like I have. You kind of made me lose my mind." He lets out a sharp laugh. "Maddie, I think you're brilliant. You're witty and you're passionate and you're fucking gorgeous. I'm done pretending that I'm not attracted to you. I'm all in on this. I want to see how things go between us, but I'll also respect how you feel about it, so you've just got to tell me. We'll work it out however we need to."

His words catch me off guard. I didn't expect that kind of honesty from him, and I realize it's the one thing I've been craving from him for weeks. The truth. To know how he feels. For us to be on level playing fields.

While dating Roman sounds exhilarating, I'm not sure I completely trust him yet. He says all the right things, but it still makes me nervous. Despite my reservations, I'm willing to give it a shot. Roman and I are captivated by each other; our chemistry is undeniable. Not to mention the white hot attraction between us. He's about the last person in the world that I'd imagine ending up with, but there's something even more special about how unexpected this is.

"I want to see what happens, too," I say. "I don't want it to be a one-time thing, but I think we should take this slow. So that we can really get to know each other."

The sincerity in his smile makes my heart skip.

"I was hoping you'd say that." His muscled arm snakes around my neck and he pulls me in. His lips are rough on mine, but everything in his kiss is reassuring. "We'll take this as slow as you want."

When he backs off, I can't surpass a yawn. I don't even know what time it is, but it's late and I've been up since five.

"You should get some sleep," he offers. "You work in the morning, right?"

"Bright and early at 6AM." I nod. "I guess I should head back to my room."

"Stay with me," he pleas, tugging at my hand.

"I thought you wanted me to get some sleep." I cock my eyebrow at him. As tempting as another round sounds, I'm not sure my mind or body could take it without a little rest.

Roman rolls his eyes. "I meant stay here to sleep, Madison. I'm not a complete animal."

I consider protesting, but curling up in that big comfy bed wrapped in Roman's protective arms all night is more enticing than I can resist, so I climb back in next to him.

"Mmm, this feels nice." I sigh, snuggling into his chest as he covers us both up with the down comforter.

Roman grunts. "Okay, you definitely need to stop making those noises if we're just going to sleep."

"Maybe I should put my robe back on," I say, reaching for it.

"That's definitely not happening." He jerks me back and wraps his arm around my waist, bracketing me against him as our bodies curved together like lock and key. My head rests on his thick forearm as he runs his fingers through my hair.

"You know, it's highly unprofessional to be sleeping with my boss," I tease.

"You're right. What the fuck are we going to do about that?" He chuckles, continuing his massage down to my neck. "I've got it! Maddie, you're fired."

"Be serious, Roman." I giggle, rolling over to face him.

"I am serious." He shrugs. "If we're dating, there is no way in hell I'm going to have you around my guys. Watching them constantly looking at you was tough enough before you were mine."

The way he calls me his should offend me, like some sort of possession, but I like how it sounds and a smile pulls at my lips.

"Problem solved."

"But what about—"

Roman puts his finger to my lips. "You held up your end of the deal and treated my guys when I asked. I'll still hold up mine and pay your loans off."

"And my lease? I canceled that a few weeks ago."

"So? You have a room here." Roman placates me with answers, but we both know my objections are futile.

"Right, because *living* with you is taking things slow."

"That's a good point. But you're down the hall so far it's as if you were in a separate apartment. Besides, who is going to kill the spiders if you move out?" He smirks as if he's throwing the ultimate trump card.

"That's a *very* good point."

"Close those pretty eyes of yours now, Maddie. One of us has to work in the morning. And now that you've lost this job, you better hang on tight to your other one."

"Just don't tell them that you fired me if they call for references." Bantering back and forth with him feels so natural as we lay here.

"Oh, don't worry about that. I'll give you a glowing reference. Fantastic oral skills, very vocal, willing to try any position..."

"You forgot that I take direction well."

Roman grins, brushing my hair out of my eyes. "Very well. And that stamina. Wow."

"I'll be sure to keep you in mind if I ever decide to apply for a job as a stripper," I quip, pressing my lips together.

"Now there's a job where you can sleep with your boss. As long as it's me, that is."

"Goodnight, Roman."

He leans in, slanting his mouth to mine in a kiss before I roll over. "Goodnight, Maddie."

His body engulfs me again, pulling me in tight against his chest. I feel his heart beating against my back, and our breath syncs until we find the same rhythm and drift off to sleep.

Chapter Eighteen

ROMAN

We've barely been asleep four hours when Maddie drags herself out of my arms and back to her bedroom to get ready for work. I'm absolutely spent, but without her here, my bed feels cold and lonely, and I can't fall back asleep. Instead, I head downstairs and make her a cup of coffee before she heads out.

The sweet goodbye kiss we share is enough to light up my entire fucking nervous system again, so any chance I had of getting sleep is obliterated. I've still got a few hours before Ty wakes up, so I opt for a workout to release all of this pent up energy.

I'm still reeling from the way last night unfolded. After weeks of trying to deny myself and force Maddie away, I almost was successful. Even I was surprised at how much of an asshole I was. I mean, kissing her that way and then leaving her hanging? Yeah, not one of my finer moments.

Although, considering the absolute agony my dick has been in for the last few days, I definitely served my punishment. That one might have backfired on me more than I intended, because teasing Maddie is a double-edged sword. Getting her riled up turns me on just as much, and trying to fight that is hopeless. It was stupid of me to push her away to begin with. Maddie knows who I am. She knows what she's in for. And she's right—that's a decision she can make for herself.

And thank God, she decided to give it a shot.

Last night was the best sex I've ever had. Physically, it rocked me to my absolute core, the rush and sensation better and more intense than anything I've ever even dreamed of. Maddie is a fucking goddess, and having that salacious body in my arms took me higher than any drug or substance ever could. What surprised me most, though, was the connection between us. I expected the spark and the chemistry, but the emotional part was new to me. The way I wanted to please her. To take care of her. To make her feel better than she's ever felt before. Her release was just as important to me as my own, and watching her eyes roll back in ecstasy was incredible.

I loved Talia deeply, but never romantically, and we never had any kind of physical attraction. If this is what sex feels like with someone you have a genuine connection with, I'm in serious trouble—or Maddie is depending on how you look at it—because I want to do that all day, every day.

After a few rounds with the punching bag, I call it quits and head back upstairs. I take a shower, but it doesn't help get my mind off of Maddie because all I do is picture her in there.

Maybe it's my hero complex, but I could almost kiss that spider for the opening it gave me last night. I've been craving Maddie for weeks, but seeing her nearly naked body crouched in the corner in fear of that spider, and needing me to save her, flipped a switch inside of me. I loved being needed, especially by her. She has such a strong personality that she's rarely vulnerable enough to take any kind of help from someone else, but last night was different.

And I'm so glad it was.

By the time Ty wakes up, I feel like I've lived an entire day. I've worked out, showered, and gotten a good chunk of work done. It's like Maddie rejuvenated me, and I'm on top of the world.

He scowls, slinking into a chair at the kitchen table with a serious case of bed head. "Where's Maddie?"

"Hey, bud." I ruffle his hair as I sit next to him. "She's at work. How did you sleep?"

Ty groans, tossing his head back dramatically in ignoring my question. "I thought she was gonna be here. She promised she was going to teach me how to do a backflip into the pool."

I raise an eyebrow carefully. "Well, let's do something to take your mind off of it until she gets home? Maybe go to the park?"

His whole body tenses, frozen in place as his cheeks turn ashen. "How about something else?"

And that's when I realize what I just suggested. *The park.* He was nearly killed there just a few weeks ago. Fuck.

The park used to be one of his favorite places in the world. It was a sort of solace for him after Talia died, but now it's tainted with its own painful memories. Ty's been doing so well lately that it didn't even occur to me he might still be harboring some trauma, and now I feel like a fucking idiot. Of course he is. Why didn't I see it sooner? And more importantly, how can I help him?

"Sure. We can do something else," I say, changing the subject. "What about the mall? I was thinking we could get you some new clothes before you start back to school."

Ty hasn't been back since the shooting, and we're both a little leery of it. It's nerve-wracking to send him off when I still don't have a handle on what's going on or who's after us, but I know it's the best thing for him. He needs that stability, and his teacher has been absolutely wonderful in the wake of what happened with Talia. I know he misses his friends, but I'm expecting it to be a hard adjustment, so I've been trying to think of ways to make it easier.

A new wardrobe is one of my ideas. Specifically, the new Jordans he's been asking about. It's extravagant for a six-year-old, but these are kind of extenuating circumstances.

"Sure. That sounds fun," he says quietly.

"Good. How about some breakfast first? Cereal? Toast?"

"Maddie's been making me pancakes."

"Every day?"

Ty nods. Well, damn. How can I compete with that?

"Tell you what, I'll get Maddie's recipe and learn how to make them, but how about Lucky Charms for today?"

He grins enthusiastically as I pour him a bowl. He wastes no time diving into it.

Once he finishes and we're ready to go, Ty and I head to the mall. We haven't been out since the shooting, and truthfully, one of the first times we've done anything like this since Talia died. I've tried to be the father he needs, but juggling so much has proven difficult. I've been so focused on the logistics and making sure we survive, that I've kind of overlooked the fact that what Ty needs most of all is my time. But with the way he is enjoying himself today, I know I need to make it more of a priority.

After we get a few outfits and secure the coveted pair of shoes, we head home. In the backseat, Ty's non-stop chatter about the game he's been playing with Joe fills the car as we're stopped at the light. When I look out the window, I see the glass towers of the hospital just a few blocks west of where we're at and my mind immediately travels to Maddie. The thought of her inside those walls somewhere causes my mind to drift. I picture her in her scrubs, wondering if she's thinking about me, still sore from last night.

Jesus, what the hell is wrong with me? I've never lusted over anyone like this before.

"Hey!" Ty calls from the back. "That's where Maddie works."

"It is." I nod.

"Can we take her lunch on our way home?"

His suggestion makes my stomach drop. I haven't set foot in that hospital since Talia died, and even though I could definitely go for seeing Maddie, I don't know if I can.

"Uh, I don't know if that will work today, buddy. We're running late getting home anyway and..."

"Please, Dad," he begs, the excitement in his voice cutting me. "Please!"

Jesus, he's a tough kid to resist.

"Sure," I agree before I really even know what I'm doing. My pulse skyrockets as I turn toward the hospital. It's so loud I can hear it in my ears, almost like I'm about to have a panic attack.

"Yeah! Let's get her sushi. She *loves* sushi."

"Is that what she said?" I tap my thumb on the steering wheel, taking a few slow breaths to calm myself down. *I can do this. It's just a building.*

Ty nods. "She likes sushi and something called calamari that is like little teeny octopuses. Can you believe it, Dad? She eats octopus!! She told me one time she even caught one and ate it! Blehhh!"

"Disgusting." I laugh at the way his nose scrunches up in the rearview mirror, and don't bother to get into the difference between an octopus and a squid with him. The mistake makes it even more adorable. "You really like to spend time with her, don't you?"

"She's really fun, and really smart," Ty adds, playing with one of the Lego sets we picked up. He couldn't even wait until we got home to tear into it. "Like really, really smart. Don't make her leave like my other nannies, okay, Dad?"

He catches me totally off guard and I burst out laughing. "Why would you say that?"

"Because they all start to like you, and then they have to leave." He narrows his eyes at me like that's my fault. We have gone through a string of less than stellar babysitters, and his assumption isn't that far off, so Talia had sent them all packing.

"I'll do my best," I assured him. "But Maddie isn't your nanny, she's like...a friend."

"She's a doctor, Dad. A *surgeon*." Ty doesn't find this nearly as funny as I do, so I bite back my laughter.

"You're right. But she's still our friend, right?"

"Like a girlfriend?" He eyes me carefully.

"Well, no. Not exactly, no."

Suddenly I feel very harshly judged by my six-year-old.

"Do you want her to be?" A small smirk tugged at his lips.

He knows exactly what he's doing. God, this kid is too smart for his own good.

"I don't know, bud. That's adult stuff. I don't want you to worry about it, okay?"

Thankfully, Ty drops the subject as I whip into the parking lot of a sushi restaurant across from the hospital.

Even though I want more with Maddie, it's way too soon to be having that discussion with Ty. Although he doesn't seem to be all that put off by the idea.

CHAPTER NINETEEN

"ALMOST DONE." I SQUINT, looping the last stitch through and setting my utensils down. Derek gives me a goofy smile as he inspects his finger.

"Looks good as new, Dr. Taylor. Even better than before." He grins, waving his hand around in the air.

This is the third stitch job I've done on him in as many weeks. Derek's a carpenter and it's truly a wonder he's made it as long as he has because the man is more accident prone than a bull in a china shop. Clumsy doesn't even begin to describe it.

Last week, it was a nail gun, and the week before that a wet saw. And he got his latest injury when he tried to hoist a beam up onto the table saw all by himself. At his age, working in the shop alone is dangerous in any capacity, and he's glaring proof of that. I've never actually seen any of his work, but with the amount of blood this guy loses in the workshop, I'm a little curious.

"I don't know about that." I smirk, snapping my gloves off and tossing them into the trash can. "Try to stay away from the table saw for a few weeks, okay? As much as I enjoy our time together, if you come in here again, I may just insist you find a new job."

"If you would just agree to go to dinner with me, Dr. Taylor, then I wouldn't have to injure myself to spend some time with you." He winks.

"Ah, charming and handy. What more could I want?" I giggle, rolling my eyes as I fill out the rest of his chart. Derek's a massive flirt, but he never means it. Not only is he about forty years older than me, he's got a wife at home who usually comes with him when he visits. Not today, though, because she had already warned him that working alone was a stupid idea.

"So what? Same routine?" Derek asks, grabbing his flannel and hat and following me out into the hallway.

"Yep. Keep it dry and clean, and let me know if it's getting tender or red in the next few days."

"You got it." He pats my shoulder. "See you soon, Dr. Taylor."

"Don't make it too soon, Derek." I wave, watching as he makes his way to the check-out desk at the other end of the ER.

It's been a busy morning, but most of my patients have been like Derek. Quick and easy. It's nice, but days like today are not why I went into medicine.

I duck into the staff lounge for a quick break, and I wince when I catch sight of the clock. Only noon? I barely slept two hours last night by the time Roman and I settled in, and I'm dragging.

I've got six hours left on shift, but it's not nearly enough to make me regret a single second of last night. My body still aches from the things he did to me, and every once in a while, I catch myself daydreaming about it. It's hard to focus when all I can think about is how good his body looked with the moonlight dripping in through the curtains and how his strong hands felt on my body. I'm so lost in flashbacks that I can almost hear his voice.

Wait a second.

I really *am* hearing his voice. Is he here? Is something wrong with Ty?

I jet up, poking my head out of the door

Sure enough, Ty and Roman are standing in the emergency room lobby talking with Dr. Bauer.

"It's been a long time, Roman. How are you doing?" Dr. Bauer says. His body is stiff as he sticks his hand out.

Roman doesn't shake it, and his jaw hardens. "Fine, thanks."

They know each other? Did I miss that? Roman's hatred of hospitals flickers through my mind, and I have about a thousand questions. Is it because of Dr. Bauer? Did something happen between the two of them?

Dr. Bauer isn't just my boss; he's been my mentor since I arrived here as a brand new resident, fresh out of school. He's taken me under his wing and I can't imagine him doing anything to upset Roman.

"I'm here to see one of your..."

"Maddie!" Ty shrieks happily, racing towards me. He slams into my legs, wrapping his arms around them in a tight hug, nearly knocking me right off my feet.

"Woah! Slow down, buddy." I laugh, bending to his level. "What are you guys doing here? Is everything okay?"

"We wanted to bring you lunch!" Ty beams, looking back towards Roman.

Roman gives me a guilty smile, holding up a paper bag with a shrug. "Ty's idea."

"You two know each other?" A strange look washes over Dr. Bauer as he glances back and forth between Roman and I.

"They're friends, definitely not boyfriend and girlfriend." Ty smirks up at Roman, who chuckles, but looks like he wants to crawl underneath a rock after being outed by his son.

I can't help but laugh. Ty's interjection is distraction enough to break up the tension that looms for everyone—almost everyone.

"Oh." Dr. Bauer presses his lips into an awkward smile. "Well, have a great lunch. Madison, Come by my office when you're done, will you?"

"Absolutely, Dr. Bauer. I'll see you then."

He nods back, scurrying off like he can't get away from Roman fast enough. There's a strange air between the two of them and it's got me so curious.

"Come on, Maddie! Let's eat!" Ty squeals, grabbing my hand and pulling me towards the front doors. He runs a few steps ahead of Roman and me to a picnic bench that overlooks a pond.

"Definitely not boyfriend and girlfriend, huh?" I raise an eyebrow at Roman as we walk. His pinky grazes mine, and then he catches my hand in his. The touch makes my heart swell.

Despite his declarations last night, I still almost expected Roman to wake up with a change of heart, so I was pleasantly surprised when he got up just to make me coffee and kiss me goodbye before I left for work. And holding my hand in public is even better.

"I swear, that kid has a mind of his own." He lets out a heavy laugh as we sit down. "He put me on the spot this morning and I didn't know what to say."

"I'm just giving you a hard time. I don't care what we call this as long as we keep doing it."

His face breaks into a wide smile as he leans in, pressing a quick kiss to my lips. "Oh, we're going to keep doing it, alright. And make no mistake, I want you to be my girlfriend. I just promised we'd take this slow, and I need to be careful with Ty. He's...it might be hard for him to understand right now."

The sweet, conscientious side of Roman is new to me, but I have no complaints. I could get used to it.

"How has your day been?" Roman asks as he pulls takeout containers from the bag. Whatever it is, it smells incredible.

"It's been busy. Nothing too crazy, but a few frequent flyers."

"Frequent flyers?" He raises an eyebrow.

"That's what we call people who come in all the time. Sometimes with legitimate reasons, sometimes without. I saw a man this morning that I've stitched up three times in the last month."

"Wow." Roman chuckles, crossing his ankle over his knee as he leans back. "Well, I'm sure it can get crazy here. Probably nice to have quiet shifts."

I shrug, chewing on my lip. "I kind of like the crazy."

"Really?"

"Yeah." I sigh, trying to hide the defeat in my voice. This wasn't exactly what I had in mind when I went into medicine. "It's what I went to school for to begin with. Trauma surgery."

"And that's not what you do here?" he wonders.

"Not exactly." I swallow, wondering how much of this I should get into with Roman right now. "There are only a few hospitals in the country that let you fast track into trauma. Most of the time, you go through a general surgery residency, like what I'm doing here."

"Where can you fast-track?"

"There are programs in LA, New York City, and St. Louis."

Roman arches a curious eyebrow at me. I'm ready to drop the topic before I overshare all of my family issues, but he presses. "Aren't you from St. Louis? Why didn't you do it there if it's what you want?"

I don't know if he's really listening or if he just plays the interested date part well, so I give him the short answer.

"My dad runs the program in St. Louis and he won't give me one."

"Because he doesn't want to show favoritism?"

"Because he's kind of a sexist prick who doesn't think women should be in the field, including his own daughter." I don't even mean to say it out loud, and the moment I do, I cover my mouth. Did I really just admit that out loud?

Right away, I realize it's not a part he's playing. He's furious, completely offended on my behalf, and it's kind of sweet. "Seriously? That's bullshit."

"Yeah." I bit my lip. "And what's even worse is that he sent me here under the pretense that Dr. Bauer would let me in on more critical care cases than most other hospitals, but he rarely even has me in surgery. Most days, I just work as a general practitioner."

I may have some friends and like the city, but I'm counting down the days until I can get out of here. At least, I was until I met Roman.

"Jesus, Maddie. That sucks." His face creases with a frown. "I'm sorry."

"It's okay," I say. "Any experience is good experience, I guess."

I've heard those words a thousand times from my father over the years, and they leave a sour taste in my mouth.

"I could talk to him. Bauer." Roman darts his eyes away. "Get him to put you on some bigger cases."

"What's the deal between the two of you, anyway? You're friends?"

Roman scoffs. "We're absolutely not friends. He just owes me, and if you want me to talk to him..."

"No." I shake my head. "Thank you, but I don't need you to get involved and pull strings for me. I'll figure it out."

"Okay," he says. "But if you change your mind, just say the word. I've got a friend in New York, too, who could—"

"Roman." I shut him down because I want a job one hundred percent on my own merit. Not because of him. Not because of my dad. I want to earn it.

"Right, sorry." A deep laugh passes through his lips and it's a sound I could listen to all day. Roman is serious so often that seeing him genuinely laugh or smile feels special.

"So what's for lunch?"

"Sushi!" Ty chimes in. He's completely out of breath from his run, and plops himself down next to me. "No octopuses, though."

"Octopi," Roman corrects with a laugh.

Ty's face immediately scrunches up in disgust. "No, I don't want it in a pie, either."

Roman and I share a laugh that goes over Ty's head, and we eat. Ty tells me about all the new clothes he got and promises to show me his Lego set when I get home, but soon, he's off running again. A flock of geese fly off, honking as he chases them down toward the water.

"Wow," I say. "He's really getting his stamina back."

"Yeah," Roman agrees. "He's doing really well."

"You think so? You think he's handling all of this okay?" I chew on my lip hesitantly.

Roman's eyes shift to Ty, and he's quiet for a moment, as if he isn't sure how to answer. "I...I really don't know. I thought he was, but this morning I asked him if he wanted to go to the park and he immediately shut down. Wanted nothing to do with it. It used to be his favorite place in the whole world."

"Well, that could take time, Roman. He's still learning how to process things," I tell him, tracking Ty as he races across the field again. "He'll come back to it in his own time. Kids are so resilient."

"Yes, they are." His eyes meet mine across the table, lips curling into a smile. "Come here. You've got a little soy sauce there."

He wipes his finger across my lip, the simple touch sending a harsh, prickly heat through my body, making my cheeks flush. I cross one leg over the other before my body gets carried away. It's almost embarrassing how easily he gets to me. How much he can make me feel with a little brush of his skin on mine.

He lets his hand fall onto mine, intertwining our fingers. "Hey, I was thinking...If we're going to try this, like for real, I should take you out on a date."

The idea of a date with Roman gives me butterflies. It's one thing to continue what we're doing behind closed doors, but being with him in public makes me even more confident that he really wants this. "Yeah, we have gone about things a little backward, haven't we?"

"Usually sleeping together and moving into my house comes *after* a first date, but I'm not complaining."

"What did you have in mind?" I ask him.

"A surprise, actually." He smirks. "How does Friday night sound?"

"I'll have to check my schedule. Maybe I can pencil you in."

Roman isn't even slightly amused. "Madison, I'm taking you on a date Friday night. Be ready at 7PM."

"You know, for my definitely-not-boyfriend, you sure are bossy."

"Trust me, you haven't even seen how bossy I can be."

"You mean you get worse?" My eyes widen playfully.

"I can show you, if you'd like." Under the table, his hand lands on my knee, fingertips grazing my thigh. Even beneath my scrubs, his touch is fiery. "Ty seems occupied here. We can go find a supply closet or something."

For a fleeting second, I consider his offer. Ugh, what am I thinking?

Truthfully, I know exactly what I'm thinking. I'm thinking that Roman's sculpted body is hidden underneath that tight white t-shirt and it makes me weak when I picture it. I'm thinking that the sex we had last night won't be near as hot as sex we have in a closet with the threat of someone catching us. I'm thinking that I have six long hours to make it through before I can go home and cash in on all the promises he's made.

God, I've got to get out of here before I let myself get carried away.

"As tempting as that offer sounds, I have patients to see...but I might be persuaded later tonight." I stand up quickly, putting a safe distance between the two of us. Roman smirks because he knows exactly where my mind just went.

"The longer you make me wait, the worse it's going to get." Roman's grin is menacing as his eyes bore into me.

"Looking forward to it." I wink at him, and then turn to wave at Ty. "Bye, Ty! Thanks for lunch! See you later."

"Bye, Maddie!" He waves wildly, tossing some rocks into the water.

"Goodbye, Dr. Taylor." The smoldering smirk Roman gives me hits me right in my core, and it's enough to make me consider heading home with him right now.

"Goodbye, Mr. Molanari."

Chapter Twenty

It was painful enough to drag myself back into the hospital for the rest of my shift, but when I glance back over my shoulder and see Roman and Ty as they run through the field together, my heart nearly combusts.

Somehow, Roman gets even hotter in dad mode. Playful, but protective, as he slings Ty over his shoulder and jogs up the hill. I almost hate how effortless he makes it look, but it's no surprise from a guy who is fit and muscular that he makes most professional athletes look scrawny. Thinking about his muscles sends me right back to last night, and my thighs almost clench in protest. God, I'm hopeless.

Ty giggles and pounds at his dad's back as they make the trek towards the parking lot. I know just how tight that grip of Roman's is from personal experience, and Ty's attempt to free himself is in vain.

Good luck, kid.

By the time they get to the truck, Ty has settled and swivels himself around so that he and Roman are face-to-face. Ty wraps his arms around his dad's neck and gives him a big squeeze. I've never seen a sweeter smile than the one on Roman's face as he sets Ty down and kisses the top of his head. They're so damn adorable together, and I can't stop watching.

That is, until I hear someone clear their throat behind me. I thought I was alone, so the noise startles me and I spin around.

Dr. Bauer is just outside the entrance of the hospital, arms crossed with a very pointed stare.

"Oh, hi, Dr. Bauer." I breathe a sigh of relief. "I was just heading up to see you."

"No worries. It was getting late, so I thought I would come and find you. Do you have a second to talk?"

"Absolutely." I swallow.

I don't know why I feel uncomfortable around him. We've been close for a while, but the way Roman reacted to him and the vagueness in his reply when I asked made me uneasy. Roman associates with a certain type of...personality, and Dr. Bauer certainly doesn't fit that. I can't imagine what might've transpired between the two for Dr. Bauer to be indebted to Roman to the point where Roman can pull the strings that he just offered, but something big must have happened.

"How do you know Roman Molanari?" He's not the type of man to beat around the bush, and he gets right to it.

"Uh, we're...friends."

He's instantly suspicious of the way I stutter through the words.

"Friends? Or more?"

My chest tightens. This isn't exactly an appropriate conversation to have with my boss, especially because I really don't even know what to call this thing between me and Roman yet. Are we friends? Are we more?

We'd gone from hating each other to falling into bed together so quickly that I can't keep track. Roman has been clear about wanting more eventually, but I don't know where that leaves us right now, and I don't know what to tell Dr. Bauer.

"Madison, I only ask out of concern. Roman Molanari is a dangerous man, and I would hate to see you mixed up in whatever he has going on."

I don't give an answer, but it doesn't seem like Dr. Bauer needs one because he continues.

"You've got a bright future ahead of you, Madison. I don't want to see anything impede that."

"I appreciate you looking out for me, Dr. Bauer." I force a smile. There's no need for my personal life to be on trial here, and I shut the conversation down.

He opens his mouth like there's more he wants to say, but just nods. "Anyway, the reason that I wanted to talk with you today is because one of my trauma residents is going to be gone for the next month. I was hoping you might want to fill his space while he's out."

"Wow! Really?"

"Yes. It's only temporary, but you'll get some good experience and it'll be good for your fast-track application next year," Dr. Bauer says.

"That's great. I would love to. Thank you so much!"

"No need to thank me, Madison. You're a great doctor, and we're lucky to have you on our team. As long as distractions don't get in your way. I'm heading into a surgery, so let's iron out the details later."

A flicker of hesitation rolls through me. Somehow, he made a compliment sound like a warning. I shove the feeling down, though, because Dr. Bauer gave me exactly what I've been waiting for.

I'm finally going to have my chance here, and I'm almost giddy. I can't wait to get home and tell Roman.

ROMAN

Today could not get any better.

Waking up with Maddie in my bed, kissing her goodbye on her way to work, time with Ty, and then a lunch date with both of them that was so damn wholesome that it feels like it's right off a storybook page.

So when Joe calls to tell me they picked up one of the Chavos members, it's just the cherry on top. Maybe the sex last night rocked my world right back into orbit, and my luck is changing.

This isn't just any gangbanger, either. He's the guy who pulled the trigger at the park, and according to Joe, potentially one of the men who attacked Talia. This is like a fucking dream.

Since Maddie is working all afternoon, I drop Ty off with Sarah and head to the warehouse to meet Joe and Dante. I'm buzzing with adrenaline by the time I get there. For the past few months, my sole focus has been on seeking justice for Ty and Talia, and now it's so close I can taste it.

"Where is he?" I ask, stealing through the front doors.

Joe nods to the back with a wicked smile. "Already in a cell. We were having a little fun before you got here."

He and Joe follow behind me as I make my way there. The warehouse is quiet today, which is probably good. I don't like handling this type of thing with an audience, although it sends a pretty strong message to my guys that they shouldn't cross me.

Strung up in the first cell, the guy is stripped down to barely nothing. His hands are tied with a chain secured to the ceiling, and he's on a splintering wooden stool. He's so terrified it's pathetic.

"Not so tough without a gun in your hand, are you?"

With three hard strides, I'm in front of him.

"You've got this all wrong," he trembles. "I don't—"

Before he can finish, I knock the stool out from underneath him. The pull of the chain yanks his shoulders out of socket and snaps his wrists.

The pained wail he lets out doesn't even phase me as I watch him dangle from the ceiling. He wiggled around, trying to get in a position that doesn't hurt so badly, but he won't find one. "Keep flailing like that. It's only going to hurt more."

"Please," he begs. "I was just following orders."

"Which time? When you beat my wife and left her for dead? Or the time you shot a gun into a park crowded with families and put a bullet in my son?"

"Both." His voice is hoarse as he gasps for air.

I grab a set of brass knuckles off the nearby table, sliding them onto my fingers. "I know how these things work. I can appreciate the fact that you were following orders. And if you tell me where they came from, I might consider letting you go."

I won't, but I need to see how hard I'm going to have to push him for information. This guy is just a small piece of the puzzle.

"I don't know. I swear."

"Wrong answer." I chuckle. Rearing my fist back, my first punch lands squarely on his jaw. Blood and fragments of his teeth fly across the room.

The hit releases something inside of me. Almost comfort. Solace. Satisfaction. Seeing that bastard bleed feels every bit as good as I thought it would, so I do it again. And again. And again until he can't even muster a scream or a cry. Barely any reaction at all.

His head falls forward in defeat. I fist his hair, jerking it back up. "I want to know why."

"It was nothing personal," he squeaks out. "I'm sorry."

He sputters blood as he speaks. The guy is in bad shape and if I don't stop soon, he won't live for me to do this another day. Quick and easy isn't something I'm good at. Punishment and retribution is my specialty, and this is just a small dose of what this guy has coming over the next few weeks.

"Get him out of here." A jagged growl escapes me.

Dante and Joe cart him off to one of our nearby holding cells while I rinse off. I can't go home with his blood all over me, and a shower will clear my head. By the time I'm done, the two of them are waiting for me in my office.

"What now?" Dante asks, leaning against the edge of the table.

"He didn't give you anything?" I rake my fingers through my hair. As fun as that was, I still don't have the answers I'm looking for.

"We know the name of his boss, but from what I can gather, he's just a low-level banger himself. We have no idea who's calling it from above."

"Then let's get eyes on anyone associated with the gang. Maybe even put somebody inside."

Both nod in agreement.

"So, how are things with the naughty nurse?" Dante smirks, trying to lighten the mood.

"She's a doctor, Dante—a highly skilled trauma surgeon, to be exact. And the immature nicknames are gross and misogynistic, so don't let me hear you disrespect her that way again."

"Sorry man!" He holds his hands up. "I just thought—"

"No, Dante, that's exactly the problem. You didn't think." I roll my eyes. "Don't let it happen again."

Dante recoils away, afraid to even speak now, but Joe eyes me suspiciously. Pretty soon, he chuckles and shakes his head. "I knew this was gonna happen."

"What are you talking about?"

"You really like this girl, don't you?" he asks.

Dante's eyes widen as he catches on. "Wait, you're fooling around with the...Erm, sorry. You're fooling around with Maddie?"

Jesus Christ.

"We're just seeing how things go. Nothing official." I clench my jaw.

"But you slept with her." Joe chuckles. "Sarah said you were in an uncharacteristically chipper mood when you dropped Ty off, but I figured it just had to do with our prisoner."

"So what if I did? We're two consenting adults. I don't know why that's any of your business."

"Because you're my best friend. And I happen to like seeing you happy."

CHAPTER TWENTY-ONE

Happy.

I scoffed when Joe said it earlier, because fuck, how much more cliche can a guy get? One night with a girl and my entire outlook on life shifts? It sounds pathetic, but I don't even care at this point.

I'm *happy.*

Spending time with Maddie makes me *happy.* Getting to know Maddie makes me *happy.* Watching as Maddie's toe curl as she comes makes me really fucking *happy.*

In some miraculous way, she's pulled me out of the dark cloud that's loomed over me for months. I wouldn't say it's completely clear skies yet, but it's a start and I'm optimistic, which has never been a word used to describe me.

"What sounds good for dinner?" I ask Ty as we load into the truck. After showering at the warehouse, I picked him up from Sarah's and we headed home. Maddie should be there soon, too.

"Isn't Maddie going to cook something?" he asks.

"She cooks for us a lot. Maybe it would be nice if you and I handled dinner for a change."

Ty seems less than confident about my cooking abilities, and honestly, so am I. So when he suggests we order pizza, I'm all over it.

"Now that sounds right up my alley."

Maddie's car is already in the driveway when we get home, and Ty skips in front of me to get inside.

"We're home!" he calls, throwing the front door open as I trail behind him.

"There's my favorite Molanari man." Maddie grins, coming around the corner and as he leaps into her arms.

"Hey!" I frown, trying to draw some sympathy. It's hard to compete for attention with an impossibly adorable six-year-old.

Maddie slips her arms around my neck, standing on her tiptoes to brush a kiss across my cheek. "And there's my second favorite Molanari man."

"You haven't met uncle Emmett yet. Dad might move down the list," Ty snickers.

"That's enough out of you." I chuckle, ruffling his hair as he lunges out of the way and disappears into the living room.

"Who's this 'uncle Emmett'?" Maddie smirks as she backs up.

Snaking my arm around her waist, I pull Maddie back into me. I'm not ready to let go of her just yet. "Emmett is my older brother, and Ty's right. He is much cooler than me. Now you never get to meet him."

"Well, if he's anything like you, then that's fine with me. I've got all the arrogance and charm I can handle right here."

"I don't know...I think you can handle a lot more. Maybe we should put that theory to the test tonight."

Maddie drops her head to the side as I lift her off her toes and nuzzle her neck. A gentle, sultry moan escapes her lips as mine brush across the sensitive spot. Palming her ass, my fingers dig into her muscle and pull her even closer.

"Roman..." Her whisper spreads across my skin like wildfire and, for a second, I forget that we're standing in my kitchen.

"Dad said we could order pizza!" Ty blurts out, charging back into the room.

Maddie and I frantically break apart, squashing the moment that was building between us.

"That sounds good to me! As long as we don't get anything with pineapples!" Maddie grins as she walks around the island, as if putting a physical barrier between us.

I can't help but laugh. She avoids my gaze, focusing on anything but me,, but when I finally catch her gaze, a pink flush hits her cheeks. I like the look of her on edge, especially knowing that I'll be the one to finish the job tonight.

The pizza is delivered relatively quickly for a Friday night, and we all eat together. Ty insists on showing Maddie his Lego set and the three of us spread out on the living room floor, assembling the entire thing. It's way past his bedtime by the time we finish, but when he crawls into my arms and thanks me for such a fun day, I almost melt.

While I put Ty to sleep, Maddie cleans up downstairs, leaving the kitchen sparkling by the time I return. For some bizarre reason, the sight of it makes me emotional. Tonight was perfect. For the first time in months, Ty got to have a glimpse of a normal childhood, and that's all I ever wanted for him.

When Talia died, I never once considered remarrying, let alone finding a mother figure for Ty. I just accepted that we were on our own, but Maddie has me considering all of it. It's crazy how quickly she's become so ingrained into our lives and I almost can't remember what life was like before. Introducing someone new into Ty's life is dangerous territory; the thought of him losing another person scares me, but hopefully it never comes to that.

"How was the rest of your day?" I ask her as I grab a couple of glasses and a bottle of wine.

"Great, actually." She smiles, tossing the rag into the sink. "One of the trauma residents is going to be gone for a month, and Dr. Bauer asked me if I want to fill in for him."

My throat tightens. "Wow. That's great."

I want to be happy for Maddie because I know it's what she wants and I know how hard she's worked for it, but I don't trust Bauer. Especially now that he knows we're seeing each other.

"You don't look excited."

"I am." I bite my lip. "I just...Be careful with Bauer, okay? I know you can handle yourself, but the guy is dangerous."

Maddie laughs, pressing the glass of wine to her lips. There's a smudge of her rosy gloss on the rim when she sets it down. "You know, he told me the same thing about you. Almost word for word. What's the deal there, Roman?"

I don't look up, drawing in a long breath as I figure out how to broach this topic with her. I had grand plans for tonight, and this is a downer I definitely don't need. Out of respect for her job, I initially kept the extent of my history with both Dr. Bauer and St. Luke's from Maddie,, but she needs to know.

"When Talia died...I told you I was out of town. Her mom is the one who found her, and she called an ambulance," I start. "Talia was taken to St. Luke's and treated for her injuries, but something happened during surgery. It was supposed to be routine, and she could have survived, but she never made it off the table."

Maddie's face falls, and she reaches out. "Oh, Roman."

"Dr. Bauer was head of Trauma Surgery back then, too. There was a mistake made, and he knew who did it, and he wouldn't tell me. All I wanted was a name."

I don't really even know what I would have done if he did tell me. It was a mistake, after all. I knew that. But still, I needed to know. I needed the information like I needed to breathe and the fact that it's so many months later and we're still coming up short wrecks me.

She bites her lip. "That's why you didn't want to take Ty to the hospital."

I nod. "I couldn't take him to the place where his mother died. I know what happened to Talia isn't common, but I couldn't chance it again. I guess Dr. Bauer has become my scapegoat. I don't know who was really responsible, but he's the closest target I can get. We spent months in litigation, but it got nowhere. Eventually, the hospital settled, sealed her records, and I never got the information."

"Roman, I'm so sorry." Maddie rubs my forearm gently, her arm draped over my back. "I don't even know what to say..."

"You don't have to say anything. I'm sorry I didn't tell you to begin with. I just want you to be careful with him. He ended up in some hot water over it and he's not my biggest fan. I don't want to make things harder on you at work, so maybe Ty and I shouldn't do any more impromptu visits."

She shakes her head. "You know, seeing you two was the highlight of my day. Even more so than getting the news that I get to fill in on trauma."

"Really?" I can't even help the dopey smile that spreads across my face.

"Yeah." She nods. "I love getting to spend time with you, so come whenever you want. And please, don't worry anymore about me and Dr. Bauer. I can handle it."

"I know you can." I chew on the inside of my cheek.

Just because I know she can handle herself doesn't mean I don't want to do it for her.

With the mood sufficiently killed, Maddie and I finish our wine and then head upstairs. We're both exhausted, yet convincing her to stay in my room again tonight is easy.

The irony of me begging her to stay isn't lost on me. I've never shared my bed with a woman. Never with any of my hookups. Never even with Talia. She had her own room and space here, to even further solidify that what we had was a business deal and not a romantic relationship.

But having Maddie curled up next to me, her perfume on my pillows, her hair caught in the sheets–something about that feels so fucking right.

CHAPTER TWENTY-TWO

Madison

"So you *are* alive..." Peyton slides into the empty chair next to me at the nurse's station. She's got her dark hair pulled back in a claw clip, and she tips her glasses as if she's staring down her nose at me.

Peyton is one of the overnight charge nurses in the Emergency Department. My job consumes so much of my time that I haven't made a lot of friends here, but Peyton is the exception. We quickly bonded over our shared love of cheesy Vegas hypnotist shows and the trauma of having older brothers. We swapped stories, recipes, and relationship advice, and we never missed a Friday night happy hour. Well, until recently.

Between our conflicting schedules and my hectic life outside of work, I haven't seen much of Peyton. In fact, I haven't seen her at all since I met Roman.

"Hey!" I grin, pulling her into a hug.

"Don't hey me." She smirks, pushing away. "You disappear for weeks and then show up a couple of days ago with a brand new boyfriend who has the entire hospital talking? Talk fast because my shift is over in fifteen minutes and not even your dating life can keep me here after the night I've had."

I laugh, turning my tablet off. My charting can wait, because a little venting session with Peyton is just what I need. "I don't know if I'd call him my boyfriend."

"Then let's call him Julius Caesar because, based on the pictures, the man is built like an Italian Warrior."

"Pictures?" I wince. Where in the world did she see a picture of Roman?

"Grace from Radiology snapped one. Don't worry, I told her how incredibly inappropriate that was and made her delete it right away. After I stole a look, of course. So spill. Who is he?"

"Well, his name is Roman, so you're not all that far off with the Italian warrior thing..."

"Roman..." The pitch of her voice gets higher as she says his name. "Love it. Where did you meet him?"

"In the park." Not entirely a lie.

"How long have you been seeing him?" she presses, resting her chin on the counter, and leaning forward.

Jesus, why did it have to be so hard to answer these questions? I'm going to have to get a better story because it's not like I can spout the truth to anyone who asks.

"A few weeks." Technically, that's not a lie either. We've been "together" in the sense that I've been working for him and living there for almost two months now.

"God, Maddie, that's so exciting. What's he like?"

Now there is a question I can actually answer.

"He's really cool," I gush. "Passionate about what he does. Driven. A great father. And we have a lot of fun together. He makes me laugh. And actually listens when I talk about work. He's interested in it."

"And you forgot to mention the very obvious fact that he's drop dead gorgeous."

"And there's that." I smile. Roman is the type of handsome that you never get used to. No matter how many times I see him, it always takes my breath away.

"Well, that's great. I'm really happy for you." She squeezes my hand.

"Thanks Peyton. Maybe we can all go out in the next few weeks and you can meet him."

I'm so immersed in Roman's world that it would be nice to have him in mine sometimes. I hope he'll be up for the idea.

"Done. You tell me when, and Mark and I will be there."

Peyton's shift ends, and she leaves me alone to work on my charting. I can't get my conversation with Roman from last night out of my head. The idea that Talia could have been saved must eat him alive, and I can't imagine how hard it is not knowing what happened.

He mentioned the records were sealed, but that isn't always the case and I might be able to access at least a portion of it. Maybe I can give him a bit of closure.

Records is down the hallway, and I take advantage of the lull in patients to go check. I provide the tech with some basic information, and she gets started.

"Let me just check..." She types furiously on her keyboard, staring at the screen. "Hmm. Are you sure this is the name? There's nothing coming up."

I nod. "That's strange. I'm sure it's Talia Molanari. It would've been about six months ago."

"Nothing." She shakes her head. "I can't see anything at all in the system, which is odd if she was ever a patient here. Even if the record was redacted, it should still at least show up that we treated her."

"How about Roman Molanari?" I frown. I really thought this would turn up something, but maybe it really is nothing.

The tech reenters the information, but shakes her head again. "Sorry Maddie, nothing is coming up under either of those names."

"Okay. Thanks for checking."

Roman is busy this afternoon, so after my shift, I head home to hang out with Ty.

I was never much of a babysitter growing up, but I really enjoy the alone time Ty and I get to spend together. He can be different with Roman around, and I recognized that desire to please his father right from the start. He looks up to his dad so much and doesn't want to disappoint him, so Ty puts on a brave face more than any kid should ever have to. I don't think it's pressure from Roman, but more that he wants to be just like him, so he's adopted the same independent, tough-as-nails front.

It's sweet, but when it's just the two of us, I see glimpses of that innocent, unsure little kid who just wants someone to tell him everything is going to be okay. He's come out of his shell little by little with me, and I think he really trusts me, which isn't something I take lightly. He's already been through so much, and the last thing I want to do is add to that.

Roman had to go in before I could get off, so he took Ty's to Joe and Sarah's. I head there and pick him up as soon as I'm off.

"So, what do you want to do tonight?" I ask him as we make the short drive toward the house.

Ty shrugs. "Video games?"

"Mmm, I was thinking maybe something a little more...active?" Ty has gotten used to a lot of TV and video games during his recovery, but some fresh air will be good for him.

"What about the park?" I watch him in the rearview as his little face tenses up.

"No, maybe something else." He fidgets with the sleeve of his shirt and stares out the window.

"Are you sure? There's one just down the street. We don't have to play on the playground. They have a little pond where we could watch the ducks."

Ty is quiet for a second, but then nods. "Yeah, sounds fun."

I smile at the small victory. Roman said that Ty has been avoiding the park since what happened, and I don't blame him in the slightest. I kind of have been, too, and when Roman said he was having trouble processing through everything, I thought maybe it was something we could work on together.

I pull into the lot of a park down the street from the house. Ty is slow to get out and drags his feet as we walk towards the water, I see his eyes on the park, a mix of fear and longing flashing in his eyes. I can tell he really wants to go play, but he just can't bring himself to yet.

Instead, we find a bench and I pull out some bread I had left over from my lunch and hand it to Ty. He picks off pieces and throws them to the ducks, who start to swarm, expectant for more.

"Wow!" Ty giggles. "Those guys look really strange."

"Yeah, they do." I grin, watching as he lights up. "I like that funny tuft of hair they have on the top of their heads."

"Me too," he giggles, continuing to throw food their way.

There isn't much and, once it's gone, the ducks meander back to the water and ignore Ty and I for the most part. He glances over at the playground a few times, and my heart breaks. He wants to go give it a try so badly, but I can see the confliction in his eyes.

"Do you want to go swing?" I ask him. "It looks like there are two of them open."

"I don't think so." He shakes his head.

"We could climb if you'd rather do that. That jungle gym looks kind of big, but I think we could probably do it, don't you?"

He hesitates, and then shakes his head again. "I don't think so today. I'm ready to go home."

Ty stands up and heeds for the car before I can convince him otherwise. Honestly, just getting him here feels like a success and maybe after a few more baby steps, he'll be confident enough to play again.

"So, where are you taking Maddie tonight?" Joe asks, casually leaning back in my office chair. He's got his feet propped up on the desk, and Dante is in an almost identical pose beside him.

"I'm not sure yet." I rub my temples. "But before you two dickheads even start, I don't want any help."

Truthfully, I haven't had much time to plan my date with Maddie tonight. She's not the type of girl who expects something big and flashy, which is one of the things I like about her. We have a good time no matter what we're doing, and I just figured I'd iron it all out on the run.

"Yeah, you do," Joe snorts. "It's been years since you've been on a proper date. Are you sure you even know how this kind of thing works anymore?"

That's rich coming from him. Joe's been locked down with Sarah since they graduated high school, so if either of us is out of practice, it'd be him.

Although, there's a little truth to what he says. Talia and I had an agreement—we could date whoever we wanted, as long as it was never out in the open where Ty could catch on. We wanted him to grow up in a normal family and understand the importance of respecting women, and to know I was faithful to Talia.

"It's dinner, you morons. How hard can it be?"

Joe and Dante share a concerned look, and I already know I'm going to regret asking.

"Look, you want to impress this girl, right?" Dante leans forward as if he's about to say something really profound. To be fair, he probably has the most experience out of all of us. He's always got a new girl he's trying to wine and dine.

"Pretty sure that's the point of taking her on a date, Dante." I roll my eyes.

"Then let us help you. Do you know what kind of food she likes?" Joe chimes in.

I shrug. "Ty said something about sushi."

Joe lets out a thunderous laugh, but the joke dies on me. I don't know what's so funny about that. "Yeah, you definitely need us. Your son has more game than you do."

"You should take her to the top of the Stratosphere," Dante suggests, putting his hands on his hips. "You can see the stars and the moon. Women love that romantic shit."

"What if she's afraid of heights?" Joe's forehead creases with doubt. "How about Mandalay Bay? I hear they have a restaurant where you can pick your lobster out of the tank. If she likes sushi, I bet she'd love that."

I've had about all of this I can take. "Thank you both for your suggestions, but I've got it covered. I realize it's been a while, but I think I still know how to treat a woman. If you want to help, you can watch Ty."

"Say no more." Dante chuckles. "I'd love to hang out with the little man."

"Great. Come over about seven. I'll see you guys later." I stand, grabbing my jacket. They might be idiots, but our conversation got me thinking. Maddie might not need all the fancy, extravagant stuff, but I know she'll appreciate the effort. And I've got something in mind that I think she's going to love.

Chapter Twenty-Three

ROMAN

"THAT'S WHAT YOU'RE WEARING?" Ty scrunches his nose at me as if I've just walked out in a clown suit. Dante and Joe arrived forty-five minutes earlier than I told them to, and now all three of them are lounging on my bed for my first date with Madison. The last thing I want is an audience, especially such a critical one, but it's hard to say no to Ty.

"What's wrong with this one?" I ask. He's already nixed two outfits I tried on, and at this rate, I'm going to run out of options. It's not like I have a shortage. I have a designer friend who's always bringing me suit samples and display pieces she's switched out, so it's not that hard to piece something presentable together.

"You look like the guy from Home Depot," Ty quips. Leave it to my son to diss Armani.

Joe slants his head at my jeans and gray v-neck tee. "He's not wrong."

"I think it's perfect." I check in the mirror one last time, reaching for my shoes. Maddie and I aren't going on a traditional first date tonight. We both agree that that ship has sailed, so instead, I'm taking her on a bit of an excursion.

Ty lets out a long, heavy sigh and shrugs his shoulders. "Well, we tried to help."

"Get out of here." I chuckle, tossing a pillow at him.

Joe grin, batting it away. "Alright, alright. Come on, Ty. Let's give your dad a little peace."

With a few minutes to myself, I spray on some cologne and grab a leather jacket out of the closet. I doubt it meets my son's fashion standards, but I like it.

When I reach the living room, Maddie's already waiting for me. The rest of the house is quiet, and I don't know where Dante, Joe, and Ty have run off to, but it's fine because I've had enough unsolicited opinions for one night.

Maddie looks like a goddamn smoke show. The dress she's wearing reveals a dangerous amount of skin, showcasing her body in all the right places. The loose fit sways at her hips as she walks, her heels accentuating every toned muscle of those long, tanned legs. Wild blonde curls spill down her shoulders, and her painted red lips purse as she stares at her phone. The floral fabric hits high enough on her thigh that all I can think about is how easy it would be to lift her onto the edge of that piano, inch it up, and take her right here.

Mmm. My god.

And just like that, I'm having second thoughts about this whole thing. How am I supposed to sit across from her all night and have a normal conversation when she looks the way she does and all I can think about is getting her home?

I can't kiss her the way I want in public. Can't touch her the way I want. Our chaotic schedules the last few days have made it almost impossible to see each other, and I'm shamelessly desperate to taste her again. Maybe we should order something in and stay home.

I'm just about to pose the question to her when she looks up and notices that I'm standing here.

"Hi!" She smiles, an excitement sparkling in her I like I haven't seen before. And as bad as I want to cart her back up the stairs and lay her over my bed, I want to satisfy all parts of Maddie. Mind, body, and soul. And tonight, that means taking her out for a little unadulterated fun.

The kiss she brushes across my lips leaves a question mark at the end of that thought, but I quickly force it away. This is the part of a relationship that might take some getting used to. The fluffy stuff girls love so much.

"Does this look okay? You didn't tell me what we were doing, so I wasn't sure what to wear..."

I give Maddie a quick glance, but I don't dare look at her for too long. I've already noticed every delicious detail about her appearance tonight, and if I indulge any longer, I'll be suffering through dinner with a hard on.

My cock definitely didn't get the memo that we're shooting for more than just instant shallow gratification with this one.

"It's absolutely perfect, Maddie. You look incredible," I say. "Did you pack a bag like I told you to?"

"I did...Are we staying somewhere tonight?"

"Nope." I grab my keys and the small backpack she's got by the door.

"So, why do I need a change of clothes?" She crinkles her nose at me, skeptical of what I've got planned.

"Guess you'll just have to wait to find out." I smirk, grabbing her hand.

I pretend not to notice when she pouts those full lips at me, because that look might just do me in.

We say a quick goodbye to Ty and the guys, and then I lead her to the truck and she climbs in.

"Would this be a bad time to tell you I'm allergic to coconuts?"

"Not at all." I rev the engine and pull out of the garage. "I already knew that, so we're having a coconut-free evening."

"How did you..." Maddie's eyes narrow as she connects the dots "Oh right. The background check."

"To be fair, I ran a background check on you because I was about to hire you as an employee, not because I was interested in you. I had to know you were a good person."

"Wow," Maddie quips. "You say that with such a straight face, it's almost like you believe it."

I can't exactly argue with that. There wasn't anything that scan would have flagged that would have deterred me from her. She could be an FBI informant and I probably still would have been interested.

"Okay, fine." I chuckle. "Tonight, I promise to answer all of your questions with a hundred percent honesty."

"Really?"

"Yeah. Anything you want to ask?" I might regret the offer, but Maddie deserves full transparency. There's a lot about me and the life I live that is dangerous, and if this is going to go any farther, she needs to be aware of it.

She turns to me, leaning her head against the back of the seat with a gentle smile. "I'll keep that in mind."

It's a bit of a drive out to the winery, but the conversation comes easily with Maddie. We commiserate about being the youngest siblings and what it was like growing up with older brothers, although our experiences were a bit different. Just as I expected, Maddie was the perfect child, following every rule and never getting into much trouble. I, on the other hand, spent the better part of my elementary career in the principal's office or suspended.

When I passed the exit to the strip, confusion flickers in Maddie's eyes. "We're not going to the Strip?"

"Nope." I shake my head. "I hate the Strip, actually. It feels overdone. I hope you don't mind that I picked something a little different for us tonight."

"Now I'm even more intrigued."

We drive for a bit longer before I pull into the parking lot at the Vineyard. Right away, Maddie's eyes light up as I help her out of the truck.

"Oh, wow!" she marvels, looking out over the valley. We arrive at sunset, and there aren't many things as beautiful as seeing the sun sink down over the mountains and rolling hills of grapevines. The only thing I can think of that's more beautiful is watching Maddie take in the pinks and oranges of the sky reflecting in her eyes.

Fuck. I am down bad for this girl.

"This is amazing." She beams, a megawatt smile on her face. "What is this place?"

"It's called Abbiocco. It's one of the oldest wineries in all of Nevada," I boast, slipping the keys into my pocket and taking her hand.

"It's hard to believe that something like this even exists in Nevada. It's so dry."

"Actually, this is the perfect climate for grapes. We're just far enough out of the desert area and close to the mountains. The grapes can't handle harsh winters, and if they're in too high of humidity, that can kill them off, too. This area is actually the perfect balance."

Madison smiles, clearly impressed. "You sure know a lot about grapes."

"I should." I laugh, leading her up the winding path to the entrance. "This is my vineyard."

"Y-your vineyard?"

"Come on, there's something I want to show you."

I NEED TO STOP trying to figure Roman out. Just when I think I have a bit of a handle on him, he does something like whisk me off to a vineyard and winery...*that he owns.*

What?

"Roman, wait up." I walk quickly to catch up to him as he climbs the stairs. "You really own this place?"

He nods. "It's kind of a side project."

I almost laugh out loud. A side project? For most people, a side project involves rebuilding a car engine or sewing a quilt. Not sustaining an entire vineyard that, according to the sign out front, is over a hundred years old.

Following Roman inside, I can hardly believe my eyes. It's not *just* a vineyard. Cobblestone walls house a full restaurant, a teaching kitchen, a tasting area, and a store. It feels like I've been transported to Italy with its delicious smells, upbeat music, and extravagant decor.

We wind through the main area to a door towards the back, out of the commotion where it's a little quieter.

"How do you feel about getting a little dirty?" Roman winks.

"Uh..." His question catches me completely off guard. "I guess it depends what you mean by that."

Roman gestures to the sign next to his head.

Grape Stomping.

"What?" I can't help but laugh. "We're really going to do that?"

"If you want to!" Roman nods. "It's an Italian rite of passage. Everyone has to try out at least once."

He tosses our bags into a nearby locker and starts to untie his sneakers. "What do you think?"

"I love it. This is so cool."

This is about the very last thing I expected Roman to choose for our date tonight, but he continues to surprise me.

"Mr. Molanari." A man approaches and introduces himself as one of the stomping room attendants. "Everything is all set up for you guys. And Jen is waiting for you in the barrel room once you finish up here."

"Thank you Stephen." Roman shakes his hand. "This is Madison. It's her first time here."

Stephen smiles. "Welcome! Ever been grape stomping before?"

"Never."

"Well, you're in great hands with Mr. Molanari. Let me know if you guys need anything else."

Following suit with Roman, I take my shoes off and put them in our locker.

There are two sets of stairs leading to a big wooden platform. Flanking the structure are two large holes, each positioned over a plastic-lined wine barrel.

"So we really just stomp on them?" I ask as he leads me up the steps.

"Yep." He nods, rolling my pants up a bit. The grin on his face is adorable. "Get your feet all up in there."

"Isn't that a little unsanitary?"

"Dr. Taylor, the germaphobe," he teases with a smirk. "Stomping is more about the experience. Although when it ferments, all the bacteria gets killed off, anyway. The juice we use for our wine comes from a mechanical crushing system, and it has to sit for a few weeks, so the process takes more time than we've got tonight."

"I see," I say. "Well, what are we waiting for, then?"

Chapter Twenty-Four

ROMAN

"Oh!" Maddie cries out, clinging to my arm and as she steps into the grapes. "That's kind of cold."

I chuckle, steadying her against me. "The colder they stay, the juicier they are."

"I'm seriously impressed." She looks up at me through those thick, dark lashes. "I had no idea you knew so much about this."

"Well, that's the point of tonight, right? Really getting to know each other?" I slant my mouth forward, capturing hers in a quick kiss. "Now get to stomping."

Maddie grins and gets to work, crushing the grape beneath her feet. She throws her head back, laughing as I join her; it's a sound I could listen to for the rest of my life. We spend an hour stomping across the bin of grapes until we're both nearly covered in juice and pulp, thoroughly stained and filthy.

Unlike most of the women I've been with, Maddie isn't afraid to have fun. A lot of women would have been too caught up in their appearance or messing up their make-up to really take part, but not Maddie. That adventurous spirit might just be my favorite thing about her yet.

"Okay, I had my doubts," Maddie says as I help her down from the platform. "But that was incredible. By far, the funnest date I've been on."

I'll take her praise all day, but we're nowhere near done.

"Good. And now you see why I told you to bring a change of clothes." I smirk, wiping a bit of grape juice from her cheek. "There's a shower in there. Why don't you get cleaned up and we can move on?"

"There's more?"

"Plenty more. They're expecting us in the barrel room to make our own wine, and then we've got reservations for dinner. Just put your dirty clothes in the basket. We've got a cleaning service that will take care of them while we're eating."

"You've really thought of everything, haven't you?"

"I wanted this to be special." I wrap my arm around her waist, bracketing her against my body. Even as a purple tinted mess, Maddie is the most beautiful woman I've ever seen.

Her smile makes me want to give her the entire world. Every planet, every moon, every star in the atmosphere.

I can't get enough of how she looks tonight—so happy, so content, so relaxed. Even though this is something we both wanted, she's been a little hesitant to fully let herself go, and I don't blame her. I've given her about every reason in the book not to trust me, and she's been slow to. At least, until tonight. Tonight, it feels like she's letting her guard down. Dropping her defenses. Letting me in.

Twenty minutes later and we're all cleaned up. If I thought the dress was bad, Maddie's second outfit might do me in completely. She tucks her tauntingly low cut tank top into ripped denim jeans that mercilessly hug her hips, and her blonde hair spills over her shoulder in a beautiful mess of curls. The look is more relaxed, but it hits in all the right places for me.

"Well, I can definitely say that showering and changing clothes mid date is something I've never done before." Maddie smiles, coming out of the dressing room.

"I'm all about providing unique experiences."

She lets out a sharp laugh, draping her purse over her shoulder. "That's for sure."

Down in the barrel room, Maddie listens to the sommelier detail every step of the wine-making process, and she's absolutely enthralled. We sample some of the new mixtures and I can't help but smile as I watch her swish and smell the wine, fully invested. Once we finish, we stroll among the vines. It's dark, but the moon and stars light the pathways as we walk.

Finally, we make our way to the patio for dinner, sitting on a private terrace overlooking the entire property. I'm here all the time, but the view never gets old. Especially not tonight.

"Ty told me you like seafood, and the chef makes an incredible cioppino. How does that sound?" I ask, scanning the menu.

"Whatever you recommend. Should I be concerned that you're taking dating tips from your son?"

"I'm just using my resources. The kid likes you almost as much as I do."

Maddie grins over the rim of her wine glass. "Well, what a coincidence. I like you almost as much as I like him, too." She eyes me playfully.

"Ouch!" I chuckle, resting my hand over my heart. "Cut me a little slack. I don't have the advantage of being a seriously adorable first grader."

"True. He is *really* adorable. You do have some other advantages going for you though..."

"Yeah?"

"Irresistible charm, annoyingly handsome. You came to my rescue when I was being attacked by the spider..."

"*Attacked* is a strong word. It was totally harmless."

Maddie shrugs. "We can agree to disagree on that one."

The server takes our order, and the food comes out quickly.

"So, how did you get into the wine business?" Maddie asks.

"This place has been in my family for years. My grandmother started it and passed it down to my mother, who eventually passed it down to me and my brother. Emmett isn't as interested in it as I am. He's more of a Wall Street guy, so he signed everything over to me a few years ago."

When I say everything, I mean absolutely *everything* to do with our family business. The winery, the shipping company, and even the house that my dad bought for him. Despite being the younger brother, it all belongs to me now.

"Do you get to see him very often?" she asks.

I shake my head. "Not as often as I'd like. He's just a year older than me and we've always been close. He's really busy, though. I said he was a Wall Street guy, but that's being modest. He's one of the most successful stockbrokers in the world. He travels quite a bit and splits his time between London and New York."

"He was never interested in what you do?"

"No. My dad was pretty tough on us growing up, and Emmett took the brunt of it. Probably because Dad was grooming him to take over. It should have been him in my spot since he's older, but Emmett sort of wiped his hands clean of the whole thing as soon as he could, as a way to stick it to my dad."

Maddie doesn't say anything, and to fill the silence, I continue.

"I guess I was kind of the fallback plan." I chuckle awkwardly, taking a drink of my wine. In the last thirty seconds, I've shared more about myself with Madison than I ever have with anyone else. She's so easy to talk to that it almost feels natural.

"Well, it seems like you've certainly proved yourself. I don't know much about the other side of things, but this place is incredible. Have you ever thought about making it more than just a side project? Getting away from the...other stuff like your brother did?"

Maddie is careful about how she asks, avoiding the Mafia label entirely.

"There really is no *getting away from it*." I swallow, chewing on the inside of my cheek. "Emmett only did because I stepped in. This is the kind of thing you're in for life, and like I told you before, I like it."

"What you said before is that you were good at it. And there's a difference between being good at something and liking it."

"Damn, you've got a good memory." There isn't much that gets past her, and it's refreshing that she cares enough to ask. Most people assume this is all I ever wanted to do and I'm having the time of my life in the position. "I guess what

I was trying to say is that it doesn't really matter how I feel about it. It's not something I can walk away from. And if things between us...you need to know what you're getting into here. I don't want you to have any illusion that you can change me or get me to quit or 'fix' me. This is who I am, and it always will be, for better or worse."

"Lucky for you, I happen to like who you are." She reaches across the table, setting her hand on mine. "I didn't ask because I want to change you or what you do, Roman. I just want to understand."

The discussion puts a bit of a damper on my mood. I wanted to keep things light tonight, but we've already gone for a deep dive.

"I want you to understand, too," I say, grazing the back of her hand with my thumb. "Because I'm falling for you, and it would wreck me if you walked away later because I tried to sugarcoat this and you didn't fully know what you were getting into. I've seen it happen before."

Her brows cinch together.

"Talia thought she could handle it, too. We spent the last years of her life constantly at each other's throats about trying to get out, and she knew this life better than anyone." Dark memories swarm through me as I think about the fights we had. Knock down, drag-out fights that always ended with her in tears and me avoiding the house for a few days. I wish I could have given her what she wanted, but it was impossible, and that was something she'd never understand.

"Look, I don't know how I'm going to feel in a few months about all of this, but I don't think you do either. The only thing I can promise is that I'm never going to try to change you. I mean, Jesus Roman, you put a gun to my head and threw me into the back seat of your car within five minutes of meeting, and I'm still sitting here."

I burst out laughing. "Yeah, I think that says more about you than it does about me. Maybe you should explore that a little. Do you have a good therapist?"

"Very funny." Maddie rolls those beautiful eyes at me. "I'm just saying I know who you are. I know what you're capable of. And that's the person I agreed to date. Trust me, I'm not into projects. I don't have the time to 'fix' somebody.

I don't want any other version of you, because I like this one plenty. However broody or arrogant or unstable you are."

"Was that supposed to be a compliment?" I raise an eyebrow at her.

Her lips slant into a smile. "I'm falling for you, too, Roman. Exactly as you are."

CHAPTER TWENTY-FIVE

"Okay, well now that I've aired all my dirty laundry, why don't you tell me about your family? I already know your dad is a prick. What about everybody else?"

A small laugh escapes my lips. "He's not that bad. You caught me on a bad day."

Roman narrows his eyes at me. "He passed you over for a spot you desperately wanted and gave it to your brothers, even though you were more qualified just because you're a woman."

"My brothers are qualified too..."

It's not even worth defending, because Roman is exactly right. Not only do I want it more than either of my brothers, I *am* much more qualified. I had better grades, scored higher on every test, and went out of my way to take internships and classes solely for how the experience would help me as a trauma surgeon. I even spent a couple of summers riding around in ambulances and observing EMTs. Everything I ever did was to position myself better, but that never mattered.

"I'm sure they are, but I've never met anyone as passionate about what they do as you. And I've seen you work. Not only are you an incredible doctor, but you're calm under pressure and you make your patients feel comfortable. A lot of doctors can't do that."

"Thank you." His compliment makes me blush.

Roman takes my hand and presses a kiss to the back of it. "Don't sell yourself short just because your family does. And don't expect me to bite my tongue about it when I meet them, either."

"*When* you meet them?" I raise an eyebrow at him. As hard as he tries, Roman really only knows one speed, and he's all in on this. It should worry me, but for some reason I don't mind. After not knowing where we stood for so long, there isn't any doubt in my mind now.

"Yes, *when* I meet your family, they better be nothing but respectful to you. No one gets a pass. Especially not blood." There's just enough of a menacing look in his eye that I can't tell if he's kidding with me.

After getting heavy so quickly, the mood lightens for the rest of dinner. Talk of childhood memories and hobbies fill our conversation until dessert arrives, but we're both so full that we can hardly take a bite. It's hard to resist a slice of chocolate cheesecake that's bigger than my head, though, and we get a box so we can have it at home.

"Thank you for tonight," I say, as Roman signs the check. "Everything has been so incredible."

"I'm glad you've had a good time." His knee brushes against mine underneath the table, but he's not in any rush to move it. "I'm a little out of practice with this whole dating thing, so I was nervous."

"Somehow, I find that hard to believe. You have every woman in this building fawning over you, and you expect me to believe planning a date made you nervous?"

Roman could have his pick of the women here—any of the women in the entire city—and he is irresistibly charming when he lets himself be. And he knocks this date out of the park. There is no way he's as out of practice as he claims to be.

He chuckles, finishing the rest of his wine before pouring each of us a little more. I should have put a limit on myself tonight because the more we drink, the more I feel myself falling for him hook, line, and sinker. "I'm serious. I haven't been on a proper date in...God, I don't even know how long. Maybe ever."

"Okay, now I know you're lying." I click my tongue.

"I'm not," he says. "I honestly can't remember a single time that I went on a real date with a woman."

"Well, you must have taken Talia out."

He shakes his head. "Talia and I...Our relationship wasn't...traditional."

"What do you mean?"

He shifts uncomfortably in his chair, scratching his chin as if he's searching for the right words. "We...were arranged."

"You had an arranged marriage?" My eyes nearly bulge out of my head.

"Yeah, it's kind of common in the Mafia." Roman talks about it so nonchalantly that I almost think he's kidding, but then he continues. "I was seventeen when my parents told me I had to marry Talia. Her dad was a powerful businessman before he passed, and our parents thought a union would strengthen everybody. She and I went out on some dates, but at that point, we already knew we were getting married, so it kind of lost its effect."

"And you went along with it?" Nobody makes him do anything he doesn't want to do, so this part surprises me most of all.

He shrugs. "If it wasn't Talia, it would've been someone else, and in the scheme of things, it could've been a lot worse. Talia and I grew up together; she was one of my best friends. I really cared about her."

"Did you love her?" My stomach twists. In my mind, I painted a picture of Roman as a grieving widow who lost his soulmate, but this changes things a bit.

"As the mother of my son, I did." He nods. "But I was never in love with Talia. Everything between us served a bigger purpose. A *business* purpose."

I've got so many questions, and with Roman's vow to be completely honest, I barely know where to start.

"Does Ty know that?"

"Definitely not. I always treated Talia well, and neither one of us ever brought anyone else we were seeing to the house."

My face must give my confusion away because Roman quickly explains. "Like I said, Talia and I were about business, and we both knew that. We were never romantically involved at all. In fact, I think I can count on one hand the number of times we slept together, and that was only when we were trying to get pregnant. So we had an arrangement, and we both saw other people."

"Wow, it seems like that would make it kind of difficult to date."

"Date is a strong word. At least for what I did." Roman shakes his head, reaching for his water. "It was more about a way to get off than an emotional connection."

I let out a sharp laugh. "I had no idea that arranged marriage existed in real life."

"That's right. I forget that you openly admitted all your knowledge about the Mafia came from the Godfather. I guess they omitted that part."

"They definitely did." I smile, pressing my lips together. "So you've really given up everything for this job. Your life. Your happiness."

He chuckles. "Sounds familiar?"

In a way, it does. I've given up so much of myself to become a trauma surgeon that I almost don't even know who I am without it anymore, and that's a scary thought. What if it's not all I've built it up to be once I get the shot? What if I want something different?

I've never even considered that before, but lately, I have. Roman and I have been playing house these last few weeks, and I'm surprised by how much I like it. And I don't know if that's something I can have if I make it as a trauma surgeon. Plus, from my experience, a lot of trauma surgeons are pretty shitty parents. My dad was rarely around while I was growing up. He missed games and recitals and spelling bees and holidays. And even when he was there, he was always distracted and focused on something else.

To be fair, the job takes so much time and dedication that he didn't really have a choice if he wanted to be as successful as he is. I guess you don't become a renowned surgeon who oversees an entire network of hospitals by being a dedicated family man.

The gravity of my relationship with Roman isn't lost on me. Ty is the most important thing we have to consider in all of this. It's heavy on its own, but considering the amount of loss and trauma he's already had, it almost feels suffocating.

I don't know if I can have both, but I don't think I'm ready to choose.

"You okay?" Roman squeezes my hand. "It feels like you went somewhere else for a second..."

"I'm good." I force the thought away for now, because nothing has to happen immediately. We've got a good thing going, and there's no sense in ruining that for a bunch of what ifs. A smile pulls across my face. "Are you ready to head home, or do you have something else up your sleeve?"

"Oh, I have plenty left up my sleeve for tonight, but it can all happen at home." He grabs my hand and I follow him out to the truck. We've been here talking for so long that we're nearly the last car in the lot.

"You mean like the cheesecake?" I tease.

"Mmm, I have something else entirely planned for dessert."

Good thing we're both on the same page there.

CHAPTER TWENTY-SIX

ROMAN

BY THE TIME MONDAY rolls around, I'm in a state of bliss like I've never experienced before. This weekend felt like I was living someone else's life, one I never believed I could have for myself.

Taking Maddie to the vineyard was only the tip of the iceberg. I woke up Saturday morning with her in my arms and we meandered down to the kitchen where she made us coffee wearing only my t-shirt. Every time she'd reach for something, that stupid hem would ride up her thigh and graze the curve of her bare ass like it was baiting me. And when she turned around with that playful look in her eye, I knew she was. After a few too many mishaps, we ended up right back upstairs, picking up where we left off the night before.

She came with me to get Ty from Joe and Sarah's and, somehow, I let the two of them convince me to spend the afternoon at the zoo. Ty was on top of the world, spouting off every fact he knew about the animals, and Maddie listened like she was hearing it all for the very first time. By the time we left, he was so exhausted that not even the cotton candy sugar rush could keep him awake on the way home. We spent the evening making pizzas from scratch and relaxing on the couch while watching the new *Despicable Me* movie. The day was like something conjured straight from Ty's dreams, but oddly enough, it felt like a dream of mine, too.

When Talia was alive, we spent a lot of time together as a family, but it always felt performative. It was all to provide Ty with as normal a childhood as we could. It's completely different with Maddie, though. It doesn't feel forced or like a part I'm playing. It feels natural.

Sunday was just as great. We had a lazy day just hanging out around the house and getting Ty ready to go back to school full time. It's been several weeks since the shooting, and he needed the time to recover as much as I needed it to feel comfortable sending him. I don't like the idea of him being too far away until I have all of this resolved, but we've got a solid plan and I know he needs it. As much as he claims he's content being home with us, he misses his friends.

Plus, I feel like we're on the right track with the Chavos member we've been working on and I'm confident he'll give me the shot caller soon.

Monday morning meant back to reality for all of us—Ty to school, Maddie to the hospital, and me knocking a man's teeth out one by one until he spills his secrets. None of us were all that excited.

Dropping Ty off was rougher than I expected, and I'm second guessing the decision I made to send him back to school. Is it too soon? Will he do okay? I make life altering choices every single day, but somehow being the sole person to make them for my son feels impossible. I don't know how you ever know what's right.

For now, I put it out of my mind, but switch my phone on just in case the teachers need to call. Until then, I've got plenty to occupy my time and I'm so close to retribution I can almost taste it.

Madison

MY SHIFT AT THE hospital is short today, and I told Roman I'd pick Ty up from school. He was in the middle of something and was worried about being late on Ty's very first day back, so I offered to step in.

I'm anxious to hear how his day went following the trouble he had this morning. Ty is so mature for his age, and sometimes it's hard to remember that he's still so young and the poor kid has been through a lot. This morning perfectly illustrated that, but hopefully, his day improved.

His school isn't far from the hospital, and I head straight there. I follow Roman's directions about where to park and which door is Ty's and find my way pretty easily. There is a big group of parents waiting to pick their kids up as well, but I stand back from the crowd a bit.

When the bell rings, a line of children comes out of the door and I search the faces for Ty. When he sees me, his face lights up and he runs toward me.

"Maddie!"

A few pointed, jealous glares from the group of moms greet me when they realize I'm here for Roman Molanari's son.

"Hey! How was your day? As bad as you thought?" I smile, reaching down and giving him a big hug.

Ty rolls his eyes as I take his backpack from him. "Worse. The only good thing was that my teacher and my friends were happy to see me."

"I bet they were. You're like a real-life superhero."

"I know." His grin fades. "But Dad said I can't tell them what happened so everybody just thinks I had the chickenpox. It's not fair."

"I'm sure it's hard not to tell them, but your dad is right. He just wants to keep you safe." I give him a sympathetic smile. "Did they like your new shirt?"

"Yeah." He nods. "Can we get ice cream on the way home?"

"Mmm, I think we could manage that."

"Hi Ty." A woman waves at us, a superficial smile on her face as she walks towards us with her little boy in tow. "We're so glad you're back. Elliott really missed you. What happened?"

Ty glances up at me before responding as if considering telling her the real story, but thankfully, he decides better of it. "I had the chickenpox," he mumbles.

"I'm sorry to hear that. I'm sure your dad is so busy taking care of you."

Ty shrugs.

"Maybe I'll drop off a pot of my famous chicken noodle soup and take some of that work off of his plate. It's got to be so difficult."

I bite back my laughter at the woman who hasn't even acknowledged that I'm standing here yet. It's clear she's interested in Roman and using Ty as a gateway. If it wasn't so repulsive, I might admire the creativity.

"That's okay. Maddie has been cooking for my daddy." He grins up at me. Apparently, Ty could see right through the woman, too.

"Oh, Maddie." The woman turns her attention to me for the first time, sizing me up. "You must be the new nanny."

I open my mouth to speak, but I'm cut off by the sound of Roman's voice behind me.

"Actually, Jill, this is my girlfriend, Madison." He presses a kiss to my lips, effectively silencing her. Ty beams up at us, thoroughly enjoying the moment as well.

I don't know if it's the kiss or the word girlfriend that makes my stomach flutter like it does, but either way, my knees feel weak. Roman's hand settles on my waist, drawing me in and positioning me against him.

"Oh." She stares at Roman in disbelief.

"Thanks for your offer for the soup, but like Ty said, she's been taking great care of us." His face is flat, but I see the satisfaction in his eyes. He loves that he has both Jill and I flustered—her, because he just shut down her very overt attempt to get to him, and me, because his hand keeps inching lower and lower as he holds onto me.

"Glad to hear that." Jill gives us a tight-lipped smile. "Come on Elliot. We'll set up a playdate soon."

Jill turns on her heels, dragging poor Elliot behind her.

"Jesus, these women are like sharks," Roman snickers as he plants another pointed kiss on my lips.

"Tell me about it." I roll my eyes. "I had no idea I was going to have so much competition from the carpool posse."

Roman lets out a sharp laugh, his hand sliding around my neck as he locks eyes with me. "Trust me, Maddie. There is absolutely no competition. In fact, when you're around, it's like everyone else disappears completely."

A furious heat courses through my body, and I have to catch my breath.

"Hello? Ice cream?" Ty throws his hands up, just to the side of us.

Chuckling, Roman backs away, lacing his fingers with mine as we walk. "You got it, buddy."

"Can we take our ice cream to the park? I want to show dad the weird ducks."

"Sure, we can!" I grin, taking Ty's hand as we walk to the car.

Roman arches an eyebrow at me. I haven't told him about the little trips Ty and I have been making to the park because I wanted Ty to be able to ease into it, and I can tell he's leery.

"The park?"

I nod. "We've gone a couple of times while you were at work. I hope that's okay."

"Of course, that's okay. I couldn't even get him to drive by it a few weeks ago." He smiles, slinging his arm around my shoulder as we walk to the car.

"He doesn't ever want to play, but he likes the ducks there."

"Hey, any progress is good progress. I'm just glad to see him excited about something like that again." Roman opens the door to the car for me before going around helping Ty into the back.

It's a short drive from Ty's school to the park, and we take turns picking music on the way. Surprisingly, Roman and I have similar tastes and all three of us sing along with the windows rolled down.

The mood shifts a little when we pull into the lot, like it does the other times I brought Ty here. Even being in the vicinity of the playground makes him nervous. We aren't even at the same park where the shooting happened, but it's the idea of it that has him so hung up.

Ty unbuckles his booster seat as soon as we're parked. "Did you bring some bread?"

"Oh shoot," My brow creases. "We forgot to stop for some on our way."

Ty frowns, dragging his feet as we walk down to the lake.

"There's a grocery store right up the street," Roman suggests. "Why don't I go get some?"

"Yeah! Maddie and I can wait here," he says, lighting up.

Roman ruffles Ty's hair and then gives me a quick kiss. "I'll be right back."

He jogs back up the hill and climbs into the car, driving out of the lot. I see Ty's set on the playground like they usually are when we come, and I have an idea.

"So, what do you want to do while we wait for your dad?" I ask him.

Ty shrugs. "I don't care"

"Actually, I was wondering if you could help me with something."

"Sure! What is it?" he says excitedly.

"Well, truth is, ever since that day in the park, I've been kind of scared to play on the playground."

Ty looks up with a funny expression. "You like to play on the playground?"

"Of course, I do. I love to climb. But lately, I feel weird. My chest gets tight and I get shaky and I don't feel like I can do it."

"Oh." Ty chews on his lip, staring over at all the intricate climbing equipment. If any park is going to entice a kid, it would be this one. The possibilities are endless. He wants to so bad, but that trauma lingers.

"Do you have any ideas what might help me? I really want to climb, but I don't want to feel so nervous about it."

His eyes are still set on the park as his mind swirls, but eventually he responds.

"Maybe we could do it together." His voice cracks, barely above a whisper and he doesn't even look at me.

"Yeah, that's a great idea," I say. "Let's try it."

I offer my hand out to him, and he takes it hesitantly. Ty likes to be brave, just like his dad, so maybe if he thinks he's helping me, it'll be the thing to get him back on the playground. Step by step, we make our way to the equipment until we're standing right in front of it. A big climbing dome with built in tunnels and monkey bars and a few other cool contraptions stares right back at us.

"Where should I start?" I ask him.

Ty reaches out, touching one of the bars. First, it's just with a finger, then the palm of his hand, and soon, he grips the whole thing. A smile pulls at his lips as he holds onto it, and then slowly he lifts his foot up.

"Like this," he says. "Put your foot up here."

"Okay." I follow his direction and then wait for another, giving him time to process through. Once he gets the hand of it, he needs no encouragement.

"And then this one!" he shouts. "Come on, Maddie!"

"I'm coming, buddy," I laugh, climbing up after him.

"Higher! Put your hand here. You can do it."

The encouragement is almost more than I can take. He's so sweet and adorable and the light on his face is contagious. I can't stop smiling as I watch him scale the giant dome, and as I teetering on the railing behind him, I actually do start to feel a little nervous. Just as we get to the top, I see Roman's car pulling back into the lot.

Even from here I can see the shock on his face, although I'm not sure if he's more surprised to see me or Ty up here.

"Daddy! Look!" Ty beams, waving as Roman walks down the hill toward us. "We're up here!"

"I can see that." Roman chuckles. "That's awesome, buddy. Great job!"

As I make my way down the structure, Ty basks in the praise and continues to climb all over it. It's like nothing can stop him now.

At the bottom, Roman helps me off, sweeping me into a giant hug. "You're pure magic, you know that?" He kisses me, and when he sets me back down on the ground, I notice a few tears in his eyes. "How did you manage this?"

"Well, I think I finally have you Molanari men figured out." I smirk, lacing our fingers together as we walk to a nearby bench where we sit and watch Ty.

"Is that so?" He laughs, arching an eyebrow.

I nod. "You like to fix things. I just had to make Ty think I was the one who was scared."

"That's brilliant," he says. "He looks so happy up there."

"He does." I agree. Ty hasn't missed a beat in the last few weeks and it's incredible to see.

There's an unfamiliar tug in my heart, and I can feel how attached I'm getting to Ty-to both of them—but the weight doesn't feel as daunting as before. It feels right.

CHAPTER TWENTY-SEVEN

ROMAN

As the week goes on, things get easier with Ty. He's far less anxious in the mornings, and when he comes home in the afternoons, he's excited to regale Maddie and I with all the new first grade drama. It's good to see him back in his element; a way I haven't really seen him since before his mom died.

He's slowly coming out of his shell again, and I'm painfully aware that we have Maddie to thank for that. She's so goddamn good with him that it's almost irritating. I've been at this parent thing much longer than she has, but she makes it look easy. She has a very special way about it, and it's why she's such a great doctor, too. People trust her. They believe her when she says it's going to be okay. They feel safe with her.

Safe isn't something I thought I'd ever feel. With a list of enemies a mile long, we never truly are, but it isn't physical safety that Maddie provides. She makes my heart and soul feel safe, and that's something completely new to me.

And she does the same for Ty. He's carried that little marble around with him all week, and regardless of whether or not her story was true, it's gospel to him now. I even found him clutching it in his fingers while he slept the other night.

"Ready to go, Bud?" I call, grabbing his backpack off of the table.

Maddie went to work early, so I was a little apprehensive about how this morning might go. I have a meeting I absolutely can't be late for and a full day of work, so I'm happy to see Ty bouncing down the stairs dressed and ready.

"Yep!" He grins. He takes his backpack from me and slings it over his shoulder.

He follows me to the truck and we're off. He's in control of the music on our way, and it wrecks me in the best way to look in my rear-view mirror and see him dancing along to each song.

"Did you remember to put money in my backpack? Thursdays are school store days."

Shit. "No, I didn't." I reach into my pocket, fishing for my wallet. Pulling out a couple of bills, I hand it to him, and he unzips his backpack to put it in.

"Thanks Daddy! See you after school!"

Ty opens the door and jumps out, backpack still halfway unzipped. When he takes off, a piece of paper falls out.

"Hey, Ty! Wait!" I call, but it's too late. I pick the paper up and take a look at it, expecting it to be some newsletter or permission slip.

But it's not, and suddenly my heart stops.

It's a picture. One of me, Ty, and Maddie from the zoo last weekend. There are two big red x's drawn across Maddie and Ty, and scrawled across the top are the words, "I'm coming for you."

A furious rage blind me as I throw my truck into gear and head toward the office. If this fell out of Ty's backpack, it means this bastard was in our house. This is pointed and brazen, and he's getting too cocky for his own good. He needs to be stopped.

"ALRIGHT, MY TURN," JOE says, taking a spot at the end of the table. He and Dante are playing some form of table football and it only infuriates me more.

What the hell are these two morons thinking when this guy is still out there and tormenting my family?

"We've got a problem." I slam the picture down on the table between them.

"Good morning to you, too." Dante chuckles.

Sweeping my arm across the table and knocking everything off, I leave no question as to how serious I am. "This motherfucker was in my house. Someone dropped the ball. I found this in Ty's backpack this morning."

Now I've got their attention. Joe's face folds and he picks up the picture.

"I'm coming for you." He repeats what is written on the picture, color draining from his face. "Did Ty see this?"

"I don't think so. It fell out in the truck this morning." I suck in a loaded breath, steadying myself against the rim of the table. "This has to end. I don't want Ty to live in fear."

"How do you know he got into the house? We've had security doubled the last few weeks." Joe hands the picture to Dante. "It could have happened while Ty was at school or even when he and Maddie were at the park or something."

"And that makes it better?" I growl.

"Of course not. I'm just saying we should keep some perspective here. Everything has been on lock down since the shooting and it doesn't mean we've got a hole somewhere." He's right, but blaming my own guys feels safer. I know them. I can control them. This guy is a wild card, and knowing he was close enough to Ty to slip this into his backpack has me feeling reckless.

I see the apprehensive exchange between Dante and Joe and know I'm going to hate whatever it is they're about to say. "Look, Roman, don't take this the wrong way, but the only person who has been in and out of your house a lot who isn't usually there...is Maddie. Are you sure this isn't something to do with her?"

"Of course it's not," I snap, nearly lunging across the table at him. I know how unhinged I'm acting, but I'm tired of this guy getting the better of us, while my team floats around theories that Maddie might be involved.

"Easy," Joe cautions. "I'm just saying we need to cover all our bases. How do you know she isn't involved?"

"Because I was with her all weekend and whoever did this threatened her, too." I toss the picture at him. "This started way before Maddie even came around. This came from whoever ordered the hits, and we need to figure out who."

Joe nods. "Okay, what do you want to do?"

"Dante, get this to analytics and see what they can pull from it. Prints, ink type, anything."

He takes the picture and disappears.

"I want someone at Ty's school, right outside his classroom. Eyes on him at all times."

"I'll send someone right away," Joe agrees. "And Maddie? You want protection for her, too?"

"Yes." I run my fingers through my hair. She'll probably fight me on it, but this isn't something I'm willing to risk. Not when I know what's at stake. "I don't care what you have to do. Make sure she doesn't know anything is off until I can talk to her about it tonight. Send Ernie and have him pose as a janitor or something."

"Got it." Joe is immediately on the phone to put our guys in place.

With Joe and Dante handling the administration stuff, that leaves me free to spend some time with the Chavos member I've got in lock up. As much as I want to drag this out, I can't wait on answers any longer.

CHAPTER TWENTY-EIGHT

I LOVE COMING TO work.

Even though the job isn't exactly what I pictured, I still look forward to it, but these past few weeks filling in with the trauma team have been even better. I feel like I'm in my element, finally getting a chance to prove myself and earn my spot here. That, coupled with how great things are going with Roman and Ty, and I'm happier than I've been in a long time.

There isn't much that can dampen my mood, but when I sit down for a quick break and my phone rings, the high is spoiled.

My dad.

I let it ring for a second, trying to decide if I'm going to answer. I could ignore it, but I'll have to call him back eventually. At least if I'm at work, I have an excuse to cut the conversation short if I need to. Reluctantly, I hit the accept button and press the phone to my ear.

"Hi dad!"

"Hi Mads." He sounds oddly chipper today. "Hope I didn't catch you in the middle of anything."

I roll my eyes, sliding the mountain of paperwork in front of me to the side. "Not at all. How are you?"

"Good! Busy with the awards ceremony and party this weekend. You're still coming, right?"

Oh shit. I slap my hand across my forehead. After Jake mentioned it, I put it to the back of my mind, and I forgot all about it. I usually need months to prepare myself to make a trip home, and I've left myself with about twenty-four hours before I need to be on a plane if I have any hope of getting there. As excruciating as flying home this weekend sounds, I know I'll never hear the end of it if I miss it.

"Of course I am," I answer, pulling up flights on the computer in front of me. "Wouldn't miss it."

"Fantastic!" he says. "Jake was telling us a bit about your new job. I'm interested to hear more about that. I can't imagine you have much time for a second job with how busy St. Joe's is."

Technically, I don't really even have a job anymore, but I'm not going to get into specifics with him. "Well, it's not really traditional hours, so it all works out."

"You know, if you needed more money, you could've asked your mom and I."

I bite back a laugh. Of course, I could have, but that would've meant accepting defeat, and it more than likely would've come with about a billion stipulations requiring me to move home and drop the trauma track entirely.

That's what I *want* to tell him, but I don't. There's no point in starting an argument that I never have a chance at winning. Sometimes it feels like my dad wants me to fail, so it proves that he made the right decision and gave the spots in St. Louis to my brothers.

And I don't dare mention that I'm having doubts about the whole thing because that would only be more proof for him that I'm not cut out for this.

"It's not about the money, Dad. I'm learning a lot and any experience is good experience, right?" I hope he doesn't hear the bitterness in my voice.

"That's right," he says. "Well, anyway, we're looking forward to seeing you this weekend. Mom and I have dinner on Friday night. You'll be okay taking a taxi from the airport, right?"

"Yes, I'll figure it out. Bye Dad."

"Bye Maddie."

Ending the call, I let my phone fall onto the desk and rub my temples. I don't know why I let him get to me that way, but it happens every time. Like I expect more from him, just to be disappointed. It's stupid of me to keep setting myself up that way. I'm dreading this weekend; celebrating another of my father's achievements sounds worse than walking across hot coals. But like the dutiful daughter I am, I'll go.

Too bad I can't bring Roman with me as any sort of distraction. The only thing they'll hate more than me not coming is me showing up with a boyfriend they've heard nothing about. Especially a single father with tattoos and a pre-existing axe to grind with them.

"Oh, Madison, I'm so glad I caught you. Do you have a second?"

I glance up to see Dr. Bauer in front of me. Yeah, so much for my good mood.

"Hi Dr. Bauer. Sure, what's up?"

"I have some good news. I got a call from one of my colleagues at our sister hospital in LA. You know, the one that runs the fast track program?" He sits down next to me.

"Of course."

"He let me know that they're opening up two additional slots in their program, and he wanted to know if I had any surgeons here who might be good candidates. I gave him your name as my recommendation."

"Y-you did?"

Bauer nods. "I sent him your résumé, and he was thrilled. Offered you the job on the spot."

I suck in a sharp breath, surprised. Three weeks ago, I had to beg him to let me work on any traumas at all, and now he's recommending me for one of the top programs in the entire world? I should be over the moon about this. It's exactly what I wanted, but something feels off and I can't shake it.

"Wow! That's...great! Why are they opening more spots?" I ask. That isn't usually how these things work. You have to apply years in advance, and programs don't just open up more spots without a lot of funding and resources. It doesn't just magically happen.

Not to mention I've been more cautious of Bauer ever since I found out what happened with Roman. It's a big coincidence that all this falls into place so soon after Dr. Bauer found out about Roman and I.

"I'm not sure exactly, but it doesn't matter. This is an incredible opportunity. I'll draft up the transfer paperwork for you."

"How long do I have to decide?"

The rush also makes me feel skeptical. They're in the middle of a cycle right now. Why would they be introducing new people?

Dr. Bauer gives me a strange look. "Decide? What do you mean?"

"How long do I have to decide if I'm going to take the position or not?"

His eyes widen, like he's completely baffled. I would even suggest such a thing. "Madison, this isn't the kind of thing you pass up. And I certainly hope you're considering declining because of your relationship with Mr. Molanari."

"That's not—"

"This is an incredible opportunity, Madison. It could set your entire career back if you don't take it." His expression is hard, not leaving any room for protest. I wonder why he's so adamant about this, and where his sudden change of heart came from. He's right, it is an incredible opportunity, and I hate that it's tainted by these doubts. Hopefully, I'm making something out of nothing.

Regardless, Bauer and my father are cut from the same cloth, and I know this is another argument I won't win today. "You're right. Thank you for putting my name in."

He nods. "I'll get the paperwork for you as soon as I can. In the meantime, I have a few first-years who need observation time in the emergency department and I just don't have the time. They're going to follow you around today."

I press my lips into a firm line. "Great."

He waves a group of students over; all three of them look like they have no idea what they've gotten themselves into. They're wide eyed and timid, and I can already tell this is going to be a long day.

Dr. Bauer says goodbye, and I head toward the emergency room with my new entourage.

We are immediately hit with three patients. A suture job, a little girl who fell and potentially broke her wrist on the monkey bars, and a man with alcohol poisoning from the night before.

Two of the students watch eagerly, paying attention, and taking notes while I work, but the other one hangs back. I don't notice at first because I'm distracted by the LA news, but it doesn't take me long to realize that he's not like the others. He doesn't even know the basics of medicine, and he hesitates when I ask him to hand me a scalpel and gives me forceps instead. Something seems odd about him, and my suspicions are confirmed when I notice a tattoo on his forearm. It matches one that I've seen on Roman's chest.

Unbelievable. He's one of Roman's men.

He mentioned sending someone to watch over me at work a while ago, but it never came up again, and I didn't think he'd do it without at least talking to me first.

The last thing I want is one of his men playing bodyguard and following me around the hospital. It's already nerve-racking enough, and the guy isn't even a decent actor. It's a matter of time before someone else realizes he isn't a medical student. I can handle myself, and this is a hospital emergency room for crying out loud. It's crawling with the police and security. What exactly does he think will happen while I'm at work?

When the other two students are out of the room for a minute, I take my opportunity. "How long is Roman making you follow me around for?" I ask, snapping my gloves off and tossing them into the trash.

"I don't know what you're talking about, ma'am." He's stone faced, not making eye contact with me at all.

"You can tell Roman that I don't need to be babysat. This is ridiculous."

A small smile pulls at the corner of his lips. "Pretty sure you are the only one who can get away with talking to Boss like that, ma'am. And this isn't about someone babysitting you. It's a precaution. There was a security breach earlier today."

His words turn my stomach. A security breach? What does that even mean? Am I in some kind of danger? Is Ty? Roman? "What happened?"

"I just do what I'm told." He shrugs. "Everybody is fine. We're just amping up security for a while, so you're going to have to get used to it, because I'll probably be here more often. I'm sure the Boss will have more information for you once you get home."

Either this guy really doesn't know what happened, or he takes his loyalty to Roman very seriously. Regardless, he's just following orders.

"Will you at least tell me your name? I should probably know that if we're going to be friends."

"Oh, I don't want to be friends with you." He chuckles. "I saw what Roman did to Russ for barely breathing in your direction that night at the warehouse, and I want no part of that. But my name is Ernie."

A few seconds later, the other students come back in. I do my best to act natural the rest of the day, but it's hard knowing that Ernie is watching my every move, and I have no idea what happened this morning.

The thought of Ty or Roman being in danger paralyzes me, and I'm a little irritated he hasn't called me himself. Then, my anxiety gets the best of me and my mind wanders. What if he's not calling me because he's hurt? Ernie's been here for hours. What if something happened in that amount of time that he doesn't know about?

I check my phone incessantly, but nothing comes from Roman.

This shift can't be over soon enough.

CHAPTER TWENTY-NINE

It isn't until I walk into the house and hear Ty and Roman laughing together that I feel like I can finally breathe. I've been on edge the entire afternoon, but that sound is like music to my ears and relief floods me. No matter what we're up against, they're okay.

"Hi guys." I give them an exhausted smile as I come into the kitchen. Everything seems business as usual around here; Roman even has dinner started.

"Maddie!" Ty leaps out of his chair and throws his arms around my legs. "Dad said we can go to see the sharks at the aquarium this weekend!"

"Wow! That sounds like fun!"

Roman laughs. "Only if you get all of your school work done, though, right?"

He walks over to me and presses a hungry kiss to my lips. "How was your day?"

"Interesting." I click my tongue. "Did you send one of your men to the hospital to babysit me today?"

Roman grits his teeth, completely ignoring me and the question. "Ty, let's get the plates out so we can set the table for dinner."

"Roman." Frustration drips from my voice.

He catches my stare and then nods toward Ty. "We'll talk about it later."

Whatever happened, he doesn't want Ty to know about it, and I can understand that. Although, by now, the anticipation is killing me.

Roman is tense. He's distracted and quiet while we eat dinner, and when he does answer, he's short and irritated. I do my best to keep up with Ty so he doesn't know anything is off, but it's a relief when Roman finally takes him upstairs to bed.

I get dinner cleaned up and change my clothes, and then wait for Roman in the kitchen. When he finally comes back down, he leans onto the kitchen counter, bracing himself against the granite. He won't look at me, but I can see the darkness in his eyes from here, and every breath he takes is shallow and tempered. I haven't seen him worked up this way since the day that Ty was hurt, and I hate it.

"You've got to talk to me, Roman. What's going on?"

He lets out a heavy sigh and finally looks up. He shoves his sleeves up, exposing his decorated forearms and folding them across his broad chest.

"I should have told you Ernie was going to be at the hospital, and I'm sorry I didn't, but he wasn't there to babysit you. Something happened this morning, and I needed someone there to keep you safe until I could talk to you about what's going on."

I chew on my cheek. The urgency in his voice sends a chill through me. It takes a lot to rattle Roman, and something clearly has.

"This morning, when I dropped Ty off at school, I found a picture in his backpack. It was of the three of us, taken the day we went to the zoo. It was a threat to both you and to Ty, and whoever did it was close enough to us to put it into his backpack."

I suck in the short breath, blindsided, and unsure how to even respond. Luckily, I don't have to. Roman hands me the picture, and I look it over.

I'm coming for you.

It's ominous and creepy and a very brazen invasion of our privacy. My hands shake as I hold it. I worried about a lot of different things when I thought about what it would mean to date Roman, but this wasn't one of them. It should have been, but I was too wrapped up in the other stuff, and now the danger he's tried to warn me about stares me right in the face.

"I'm not going to let anything happen to you or to Ty, Maddie, okay? Nothing. I worked all day trying to find this guy and I'm close."

When he reaches for me and rests his palm on my cheek, I notice the blood on his wrist and my mouth gets dry. *Worked all day.*

He tracks my eyes to his wrist and snatches it back. Raking his fingers through his hair, his desperate eyes met mine. "I'm sorry. I thought I cleaned up better. Do you want to know about it?"

"No, I don't think I do." I shake my head, pressing my lips together. I don't pretend to know the details, but it doesn't take a genius to figure out that 'worked all day' is code for 'beat the living hell out of someone to get information'.

But somehow, his offer to explain makes me feel at least a tiny bit better.

"What happens now?" I swallow, a heaviness settling into my chest.

"We're just going to tighten things up until everything is handled. More security around the house, Ty's school...And Ernie will be with you anytime you need to leave the house."

"Roman," I sigh. "Don't you think that's a little overkill? It's weird to have someone following me around all the time, and Ernie doesn't exactly blend in."

"Good. I want them to know that I have eyes on you, so maybe they won't be as quick to try anything." He clenches his jaw, he's so angry that his body shakes. "Someone was in this house, Maddie. They managed to get past my security, close enough to my son and to you, and left this picture somewhere that he knew we'd find it. It's a direct threat, and I've lost too fucking much to be worried about you being uncomfortable that someone is following you all day."

His words suck all the air out of my lungs. He's right. This isn't my area of expertise, and I didn't even consider how triggering this might be for Roman with all he's gone through in the last few months.

I reach for his hand, regretting any fuss I put about the whole thing. "I understand. And I'll do whatever you think is necessary. I'm sorry."

"It's okay." He shakes his head. "I know you're not used to this kind of thing, and I know it's hard to get used to. Hopefully, we'll get the guy soon and things can go back to normal, but for now, I need you to trust me. I swear I won't let anything happen to either of you."

"And what about you?" I ask as he wraps me in his arms. "Who's going to keep you safe?"

Roman grins, leaning forward and pressing a gentle kiss to my forehead. "Don't worry about me. I can take care of myself."

"Why don't we make a deal?" I suggest, circling my arms around his neck. "I'll let you take care of things when we're out and about, but when we're inside of these walls, I get to take care of you."

His brow creases, trapping me against the counter with his hips. "Just inside these walls? You're really going to limit the places that we can have sex that way?"

Roman is trying to make light of the situation, but I can't help but worry. He carries so much guilt that I can't imagine it's not eating at him. He took my comment at face value and turned it into something sexual, but I want to take care of him on *every* level. I want to be there for him and listen to him and support him. And I want him to *want* me to. When he drags his lips across my neck, I know I'm not going to get anywhere tonight.

"I have to go out of town this weekend."

"What? To where?" He pulls back, turning his attention.

"St. Louis. To see my family." The timing couldn't be worse. And I can see the mix of emotion on his face—worried about me traveling and annoyed that I interrupted his advance for this.

"Since when? I don't remember you mentioning it."

"Well, since a few weeks ago, but I only just remembered after talking to my dad today. He's getting some stupid award and they're having a big party."

"I'll come with you," he says without question.

"Roman, you can't." I sigh. "I need to do this myself and I'll only be gone a few days."

"I don't like the idea of being away from you. Especially with everything going on."

"I'll be gone forty-eight hours. I just feel like I need to talk to my parents before I show up and have to explain a boyfriend I haven't mentioned to them."

He snickers, his tongue grazing my ear. "I like it when you call me your boyfriend."

"Me too." I smile, melting into his touch. "I'll call you every day and I promise, I won't say a word if you want to send Ernie."

"You want to explain a bodyguard to your parents over a boyfriend?" He chuckles, scratching his chin.

"I won't have to explain it to them at all. I don't think they'll even know he's there. Ernie keeps a good eye on things, but you've got the poor kid terrified to even look at me."

"As he should be." Roman smirks. "But I could keep my distance, too."

I laugh out loud. "No, you couldn't. There's no chance we could be together all weekend and you could keep your hands to yourself."

"You're right. Keeping my hands to myself sounds like fucking torture."

"And besides, I feel like with everything going on, you should be with Ty."

"Yeah, I should. Hopefully, we'll have some answers soon and things won't have to be so tight." His arm slides underneath me and he lifts me into his arms. "I guess if we're going to be apart all weekend, I better send you off with a *bang*, then, huh?"

MADDIE SNUGGLES INTO MY chest, still trying to catch her breath after the little cardio workout I just put her through. Something about the thought of not seeing her for a few days made me even more desperate for her than normal.

As she settles in, she looks up at me with a sleepy smile on her face. "Would you be surprised to find out that having my life threatened by an assassin wasn't even the craziest thing to happen to me today?"

I can't help but laugh. "Do I even want to know?"

"Well..." Her fingers trail up my chest. If she wants any semblance of a serious conversation right now, she's going to have to stop touching me like that. "Dr. Bauer came to talk to me. I guess the fast-track trauma program in LA has an opening and they're offering it to me."

It takes a second for her words to register. Her dream program is offering her a position. In LA. I don't say anything. I don't trust what might come out of my mouth. What the fuck? Things have been going so well with us and now she might be leaving. It's selfish of me to even think, because I know how much this means to her, but I hate every second.

"Wow. That's...So you'd move to LA?"

Maddie bites her lip and nods. "I'd have to, yeah. But maybe you and Ty could come with—"

I cut her off with a low, exasperated groan and slide out from underneath her. "Maddie, this is what I was talking about. You said you understood that you couldn't change me."

"Roman." She lets out a nervous laugh. "I'm not trying to *change* you. All I did was suggest that potentially we go to LA for a while. Sorry, I thought things were going well enough between us that I could."

"Yeah, so did I," I growl. The way her face falls guts me, but, true to self, I can't stop the bleeding, I just make it worse. "Look, I'm happy for you. And if that's what you want, then you should do it. But I need to know sooner rather than later because Ty is really attached to you and it would really hurt him if you left."

Maddie arches her eyebrow. "Just Ty?"

I know what she's doing. She wants me to reassure her. To tell her how much it would fucking wreck me for her to leave. To do something besides shoot my walls up and block her out.

"How long have you known about this?"

"I found out this afternoon. It's not like I was planning this behind your back, Roman. Honestly, I don't know why you're so upset. I don't even know if I'm going to take it or not. You haven't—"

"Of course you are." I shake my head. "It's your dream. It always has been, right?"

"It has, but that doesn't mean—"

"Then I don't see what the holdup is. Congratulations, I guess."

Maddie's face twists into a ferocious glare. "Jesus, Roman. If you'd stop interrupting me and actually let me talk, then you might know what the holdup is. It's *you*. You and Ty." She huffs, throwing herself out of bed and dragging my sheet with her to keep her body covered. "I'm in love with you and I actually picture a life together. At least I was. I think I'll sleep in my own room tonight so I can pack. See you in a few days."

"Maddie, wait—"

She doesn't wait, though. She storms out of my room, slamming the door behind her. I hear her heavy, furious steps down the hall until she reaches her room.

Fuck! I feel like an absolute asshole. Even more than usual. I know I'm being selfish and unfair to her. There's no way in hell that I'd ever ask her to give up her dream, no matter how badly I want to.

Love. That stirs up a storm of emotions in my heart, and I wish more than anything I would have told her I felt the same. Admitting it feels unbearably hard when I know she's leaving, though.

The thought of her moving to LA kills me, so why couldn't I just say that? Why did I have to revert to my old bastardly ways? Drive her away? Push her buttons until she was angry and upset?

I tried to make her hate me once, and it didn't work then, but maybe it has now.

CHAPTER THIRTY

I THOUGHT ABOUT NOT answering the phone when Roman's name popped up. I thought about sending it to voicemail or just ignoring, or smashing my phone into a thousand tiny pieces just so I didn't have to talk to him.

After our argument last night, I can't face him—for several reasons. Not only was Roman a complete asshole about the whole thing, for some reason, I decided that was the best time to profess my love to him.

I didn't mean to tell Roman that I'm in love with him. I was angry and emotional and it slipped out of my mouth before I knew what I was saying.

That doesn't mean it isn't true, though.

I am in love with Roman, and I know he feels it, too. It's the only way I can make sense of his reaction. He's in love with me, too, and he's worried about me leaving. If he'd have let me get a word in edgewise, we could have had a civilized conversation about the whole thing. Instead, we both went to bed angry and alone hours before I had to hop a plane to St. Louis.

He wasn't up when I left for the airport this morning, and aside from a few short logistical texts, we haven't spoken. I hate fighting with him, especially with the pressure that he's under, so I swallow my frustration and I answer when he calls.

But when the screen flashes on, it's Ty's face I see instead of Roman's, which is kind of a relief.

"Wow!" He's spent the last few minutes telling me all about the adventure he and his dad went on this afternoon. "That sounds like so much fun. I'm sorry I missed it."

"That's okay." Ty grins. "Dad said we can go back again, and this time I might actually get in the tank!"

My eyes widen. "Really?"

"They have a program where you can snorkel in one of the tanks with nurse sharks. I told Ty we might be able to do that for his birthday," Roman says from somewhere offscreen, the sound of his voice making the hair on the back of my neck stand up, because I'm both nervous and desperate to see him.

"Except my birthday isn't until January," Ty groans, dropping his head back.

"Well, maybe I want to go for my birthday." I shrug.

His face lights up. "Yeah, see Dad? We have to go sooner."

"Now you're ganging up on me?" I still can't see Roman, but when he laughs, it makes me weak.

"We can't disappoint Maddie, Dad." Ty smirks, glancing off to the side. Roman's hand reaches over, ruffling Ty's hair, and then a few seconds later, he comes on screen.

"No, we certainly cannot." He gives me a smile, eyes dark and tired. "Ty, why don't you tell Madison goodnight? It's time for bed."

"What? It's not even a school night!"

Roman answers Ty's protests with a harsh look, and Ty concedes. "Fine. Goodnight, Maddie. See you in a few days."

"Goodnight, Ty!"

"I'll be up in a few minutes, okay? Make sure you brush your teeth," Roman calls after him.

Then he turns to me and we're all alone.

"Everything going okay there?" he asks.

I nod. "Pretty uneventful so far."

"And Ernie is still there?"

I roll my eyes. "He's got his van parked just down the street."

"Good. Thanks for humoring me." He runs his fingers through his hair. I hate how forced the conversation between us feels. "Look, Maddie, I...I have to go put Ty to bed, but can I call you after? Just so we can talk."

"Tonight's not really good, Roman." I suck in a sharp breath. "My brother is hosting a celebration dinner for my dad and I'm already late."

"After?" he says hopefully.

"I have to be up early." I don't know why I'm avoiding this like I am, but I'm not ready to rehash everything with Roman yet. And I feel like it's a conversation we should have in person, not on a tiny little screen with spotty reception.

"Okay." He bites his lip, nodding. "When you come back then."

"Yeah." My voice breaks, tears welling up in my eyes. *Damn it*. I didn't want to cry. He's the one who made this mess and I shouldn't feel as terrible as I do.

My tears break his resolve. "Babe—"

"I've got to go, Roman. I'll text you later." I swallow, cutting him off. "Bye."

"Bye Maddie."

Ending the call, I toss my phone onto the bed and swipe my finger under my eye to fix my mascara. I have exactly two minutes to compose myself and get downstairs for this stupid dinner, and if history is any indication, my night is only going to get worse.

I ALMOST THOUGHT Ty forgot about my promise to call Maddie tonight.

He mentioned it offhandedly while we were at the aquarium, but I distracted him with pizza and ice cream and a night swim out in the pool. But just as we were climbing the stairs to bed, he asked me to call her and I couldn't resist.

It went about as well as I expected. I hate seeing her upset, each of those tears in her eyes like a tiny stab to my heart. Especially knowing I'm the reason behind them.

Maddie declared she was in love with me and then told me she was moving away all in one short conversation, and I've been trying to sort through that ever since. It's not like I gave her any chance to explain, and that was a mistake, but the thought of losing her this way is a sucker punch.

She's a part of us now. I can't stomach the idea of Ty and I starting over from scratch again if she leaves. If. I have to keep reminding myself that she said she hasn't even decided yet. But I can't be the reason she gives up her dreams. That isn't fair either.

This is exactly why this thing between us scares me. I've never put myself in a position to be hurt like this, and it fucking sucks. But I also know I'm not ready to give up on us, so something's got to give.

I'll be the first to admit I jumped the gun. I should have let her talk instead of assuming she was trying to get me to quit. Any suggestion like a move or change is a trigger to me, caused by years of Talia's subtle attempts to drag me away from the Mafia, and I completely shut down after that. Madison isn't Talia, though, and at the very least, I should have let her explain.

And now it looks like it'll be awhile before I get the chance again. Maddie's busy, and she doesn't want to talk, and I have two more days to power through until she's home.

"Ready for bed, bud?" I push Ty's door open.

He's already laying in bed with a stack of books for me to read, but a big yawn stretches at his mouth. We get through two of them before he can hardly keep his eyes open, and I helped him under the covers.

"Daddy, are you going to marry Maddie?"

Jesus, kid. Timing could not be worse on that one.

"I-I don't know, Ty." I stumble over the words, thinking how much easier that question would have been to answer twenty-four hours ago.

"Can you?" He gives me an innocent smile, but he knows exactly what he is doing. "I really like her, and she makes you happy."

"What makes you say that?" A little, sharp laugh, amazed by how perceptive he is. Nothing gets past him, and the connection between Maddie and me is no exception.

"You smile more, and your eyes don't look sad."

"You're too smart for your own good. You know that?" I grin, tickling him and sending him into a fit of squirming.

He giggles wildly until I stop, and then he settles again, clutching his stuffed dog to his chest.

"She's not going to go away like Mommy did, is she?" The pain in his eyes shatters me as I sit on the bed next to him.

"Buddy..." I swallow, emotion catching in my throat. "Your mom didn't just go away. She never would have left you if she had a choice. You know that, right?"

Ty nods timidly. "It's because she got really hurt, right? By a bad man?"

"Yes." I chew on my lip, treading lightly. He understands so much, but he is still just a kid, so I'm careful with what I share. "A very bad man. Like the one who hurt you. And I promise, I'm going to do everything I can to keep both you and Maddie safe."

"And you?"

I hate that he even has to question that. Ty has seen and lived through more in his short life than anyone should have to, and it guts me that I haven't been able to shield him from it. I'm quick to take action, because it's what I'm good at, but I'm increasingly aware that Ty needs emotional reassurance just as much as anything. He's already lost one parent and the fear of losing another one seems to be heavy on his mind.

"Yes, buddy. No one is going to get hurt."

I rub my forehead, hoping I can make good on that promise.

Fortunately, he doesn't pick up on the uncertainty in my voice. Right now, I can't really guarantee anything. Not that we're completely safe. Not that Maddie isn't going to go away. Nothing.

My answer is enough for Ty, and he gives me a sleepy smile. "I love you, Daddy."

"I love you, too, Ty. Sweet dreams." I kiss his forehead one more time before turning at the light and going downstairs.

It's dark and quiet and lonely in the house tonight. I let out a heavy sigh, rattled both by my conversation with Ty and my lack thereof with Maddie.

Ty surprised me tonight. I've been so desperate to move us past this that I haven't even considered how deeply it's been affecting him. Clearly, he wants to talk it through, and I've tried to sweep everything under the rug, thinking he just needed to forget. I guess that's just another thing that I wasn't equipped for when Talia passed away.

The sharp creak coming from the kitchen catches my attention, and I whirl around, just in time to see a flash of black rush past me. Someone's in my house. Reaching quickly for my gun, I realize it isn't on my hip. I put it away right before Ty and I called Maddie.

An excruciating pain sears through my abdomen as I stumble back. Blood seeps through my fingers as I press the wound, watching as the intruder disappears out the front door. I lean against the wall for support, stumbling into the kitchen to get my phone as a trail of blood follows behind me. I slump into the chair, grunting in pain and grabbing a towel to absorb some of the blood. The bastard sliced me clean through, deep and long enough that I'm probably going to need stitches.

The blood loss is already making me dizzy, and I clumsily punch Joe's number into my phone.

"Hey man. I was just about to call you," he answers.

"Someone was here," I grunt, applying pressure to the wound, although it doesn't seem to do much to stop the bleeding. "Broke into the house while I was upstairs with Ty. He stabbed me."

My words come with labored, uneven breaths, and I wince.

"What? Are you okay? Is he still there?"

"He went out the front door after he stabbed me."

"Just stay there, man. I'm on my way. How bad is it?" I can hear rustling in the background as he grabs his keys and goes out the door.

"I'm okay." I clench. "It's deep, but I'll survive."

"Where's Maddie? Can she help?" Joe asks.

"She's in St. Louis."

"Fuck. That's right." He groans. "Okay, just relax. I'll be right there."

After I hang up, I try to take a few deep breaths to take my mind off the pain, but it isn't working. It feels like the world is closing around me as I try to keep myself upright.

Why can't I stop this guy? Why is he always one step ahead?

CHAPTER THIRTY-ONE

ABSOLUTELY NOTHING ABOUT THIS party is fun to me. Not the hordes of people I have to put on a happy face for. Not the overpriced and underwhelming catering. Certainly not my father's acceptance speech, where he referred to the trauma program as his baby, and failed to even mention that he had real human children. Well, at least until he had to brag about my brothers and all the success they're both experiencing.

The only thing remotely entertaining is watching Ernie pose as one of the hired event servers. I can't help but laugh as I watch him struggle to balance plates, but when he looks my way, he's clearly not amused.

I don't want to be here in the first place, and I especially don't want to be here after fighting with my boyfriend.

I guess we didn't really fight, though. That would require us to talk, and that didn't happen either. Instead, we both skirted around any real conversation, and then I hung up as quickly as I could. After a few tears and a mirror pep talk, I got myself together enough to join my family at the party.

But now I'm counting down the minutes until I can sneak away.

"It's so good to have you home, Mads," my brother Lucas says as we all sit down at the head table for dinner. "I can't wait until you're home for good and we can see you more often."

"Well, it might happen sooner than we think." My dad winks. "I have it on good authority that Madison was offered a spot in the fast track program in LA."

Oh god. Not only did I not know my dad knew about the offer, I wanted to avoid the topic entirely this weekend. At least until I knew more about it and had made my decision.

"What? Maddie, that's incredible! Congratulations!" Jake hugs me.

"Oh, sweetheart, that's wonderful! We're so proud of you!" My mom reaches over and squeezes my hand.

"Thank you." I force a smile on the pride, while inside, I'm about to have a panic attack. "I just barely found out about it before my trip."

"How soon will you have to be there? Jake and I can come help with the move if you want!" Lucas offers.

"That's really sweet of you, but I don't know yet. I'm going to talk to the surgeon in charge next week and then make my decision, so it's probably—"

"Make your decision?" My dad snorts, cutting me off. "What decision is there to make?"

Here we go.

"Whether or not I'm going to take it." I press my lips together.

"Why wouldn't you?" Jake looks at me in confusion, but he's the closest I've got to an ally at this table, so there's a hint of sympathy in his eyes. Mostly because he knows the wrath I'm about to receive.

"Don't be ridiculous, Madison. Of course you're going to take it." My dad recoils. "I had to pull a lot of strings to make that happen and—"

"You did what?"

It feels like someone punched me in the chest. Did I hear him right? *He* made a call? *He* pulled the strings?

His face flushes as he realizes he slipped up. "I called a friend of mine in LA and asked him to open up a spot for you on his team."

My stomach drops, like I might throw up right here. This can't be happening. It can't be true. I asked him for months to help me get in somewhere, and he always told me he couldn't do it. All this time, my spot was just a phone call away. It wasn't that he couldn't do it, he just wouldn't.

I swallow, carefully considering the next thing I say.

"Well, thanks Dad. If I decide to take it, I'll really owe you."

"There is no *if*, Madison. It's a once in a lifetime opportunity and if you turn it down, you'll tarnish your career. Your name."

"*Your* name." I bit my lip.

Don't do this. Just get through dinner and go home.

It's too late, though. The words are already out of my mouth.

"Excuse me?" My dad's face twists.

"If I turn the spot down, it will damage your name, which is really all you care about, anyway. You never thought I had what it takes. I'd think you'd be happy that I proved you right."

Jesus, Maddie. Talk about full send.

My dad chuckles, shaking his head. "That's because this has never been about you becoming a trauma surgeon, Madison. It's always been some stupid crusade to stick it to me. You were upset that I actually wanted you to put in the work and not have the whole thing handed to you, so you uprooted your entire life and spent thousands of dollars to prove some kind of idiotic point to me. Now, you don't even have the dedication to follow through with that. I knew you weren't cut out for this, but I humored you anyway. But here we are. Exactly where I thought we'd be."

His words prickle across my skin like thorns, and for a minute, I'm frozen. His words sting worse than I want to admit. I feel a burning hole in my heart, staring back at him and realizing this was all I'm ever going to get from him. Nothing will ever be enough and I have to accept it. He's never given me any indication that he'll change, and I have to quit hoping because it only makes me more disappointed.

I've never stood up to my father before, but I've had about all of his self-righteous act that I can stand and I'm crumbling.

"Maddie, your dad just means…" My mom reaches for my hand, trying to smooth things over.

"Do you want the truth? The real reason I'm considering turning down the spot?" I stand up. We are on the attention of some of the other guests now, but it doesn't stop me. "It's because I don't want to turn out like *you*. I don't want to have a family that's a decoration piece. I don't want to sacrifice time and care for my patients to chase down another stupid award or accolade. I don't want to be a doctor who only cares about the titles and records I hold—like you. And no, staying in Las Vegas isn't the fastest way. And it's not the most prestigious way, but I like it there. I have friends and I've built a life for myself and that's important to me, too. I know that's something you'll never understand. You think I'm the one playing games? You've always known how badly I wanted this, and then you passed me over and swore up-and-down you couldn't call anybody to get me placed. And then, what? On a whim you just decide to and it's all taken care of? This was all a game to you. It was never about my actual abilities. You wanted to drive my career because you knew you could."

My dad's face hardens, and I expect him to blow up at any second, but I continue before he can.

"And maybe you're right. Maybe I did move to Las Vegas and do all of this because I was emotional. It wasn't because I was angry at you or trying to stick it to you, though. It was because I wanted you to be proud of me. For once. But you know what? I don't care about that anymore. It's a pointless fight, anyway." Hot, angry tears pool in my eyes.

I grab my things and push out my chair.

"Maddie, don't go." Jake stands.

"Let her," my father says harshly. "Running away only proves how childish she is."

Every part of me wants to turn around and unleash my rage on my dad, but I know it's not worth it. I look around the room for Ernie, but he's right next to me, and I realize he heard the whole thing. A furious blush fills my cheeks, but I ignore it and quickly say goodbye to my mother and brothers.

Part of me hoped that coming back might rejuvenate some of the passion I had for medicine a few years ago, but it's actually done the opposite. The only thing that it rejuvenated is my bitterness toward my father and the job that monopolized him my entire life.

Even when I'm angry with Roman, I can admit what an incredible father he is. He's got plenty of faults, but I can see day in and day out that he does his very best for Ty, and that he puts him first in every situation.

That was never the case with my dad. To be honest, I only have one childhood memory that includes him. The day that I almost drowned in our backyard swimming pool. My dad was supposed to be watching me, but one of his trainees called and needed his help with something, so he stepped away for a minute. I don't know how long he was actually gone, but it was long enough for me to wander down to the deep end of the pool, jump in, and sink to the bottom. He got me out just in time, but I never told a soul what really happened that day. He got to be the hero who saved me, and I got to be the only one who knew it was his fault to begin with.

Dedication is a trait he passed down proudly. Jake missed the birth of his first child because he was on call at another hospital. And the love of Lucas's life walked away because she didn't want to come second to his work, and he couldn't make any compromises. This job has robbed my family of so much over the years, and the more I think about it, the less I like it.

But maybe I never really did at all. Maybe it's always been about proving myself to my dad. Making him proud. Being the best. Maybe I never wanted to give this career my entire life the way the rest of my family did.

There's never been any doubt that I love being a surgeon. And at its very core, it's about helping people. It's not about prestige or awards or fancy titles. And maybe it's time to give up my crusade to be the best. It clearly hasn't worked so far. Staying in Las Vegas will eventually make me a trauma surgeon, just not as quickly, but there's nothing wrong with that. With trusting the process. With taking my time.

I'm not chasing my father's footsteps anymore, so maybe it's time I make some of my own. I honestly don't know what the best choice is, but for the first time, I feel confident that I'll be making that choice based on what's best for me—not for my dad.

It's late, but Ernie comes to the rescue and finds us a flight home. As we're boarding, I try to call Roman a few times, but it just goes to voicemail, so he must still be mad at me.

The house is dark when Ernie and I pull up, and I know Ty and Roman are probably both sleeping. I don't care, though. I'm going to wake them up and tell them how much I missed and love them, and end this stupid argument with Roman. The people in my life will never have to wonder how I feel about them.

I use my key and open the door quietly.

"Do you want me to take your bag upstairs?" Ernie offers.

"You don't need to do that. You've already done enough. Thank you for everything." I give him a hug. "Head home. I'll see you tomorrow."

"See you tomorrow." Ernie gives me a tight squeeze. "And Maddie, for the record, I think your father is a sack of shit for saying the things he did."

I bit my lip to stifle my laughter. "Thank you."

Ernie smiles one more time before closing the door behind him. I let out a heavy sigh, happy to be home and excited to see Roman.

There's a creak on the stairs, and I turn towards it.

"Roman?" I ask, moving towards the noise cautiously.

Silence. Another creak.

"Hello?"

CHAPTER THIRTY-TWO

"H-HELLO?" MY VOICE BREAKS as I stand in the darkness, realizing how stupid of me it was to send Ernie away. At least until Roman knew I was home.

I gasp as a dark figure moves toward me. The man who left the picture threatening us is back to finish the job, I'm sure of it.

"Maddie? Is that you?" Right as the figure steps into the light, I recognize Joe's voice.

"God, Joe." I let out a heavy, shaky breath. "You scared me to death."

"Sorry!" He chuckles. He opens the fridge and grabs a beer as if this is his house and it isn't three in the morning. "I didn't expect you home. Aren't you supposed to be in St. Louis until tomorrow night?"

I fidget, not in the mood to get into everything with Joe right now. "My plans changed."

"You should have called. Roman likes to know when plans change."

"I did call. It keeps going to voicemail. He's upset with me, so he isn't answering." I fold my arms over my chest. If I'm going to be reprimanded for something like that, Joe should know the truth.

"Uh, I don't think that's why he isn't answering, Maddie," he deadpans, then lifts the bottle to his lips and drinks deeply.

"What do you mean?"

"Roman is at the hospital," he says flatly, crumpling up a wad of paper towels left on the counter. No detail. No explanation. Just drops a bomb like that.

"Why? What happened?" My chest tightens as I notice the blood soaking the paper towels in Joe's hand.

"He's okay," Joe says quickly, following my gaze. "An intruder got into the house. There was an altercation and he stabbed Roman. But he's completely fine, Maddie. Really."

"Then why is he at the hospital?" If he wouldn't even take Ty there, then I know there isn't a chance in hell Roman would go himself unless absolutely necessary.

"Because he wasn't conscious enough to fight me on it when I got here."

"Joe!" I burst. "He passed out? Where did he get stabbed? Why didn't anyone call me?"

"Easy, Maddie. He lost a good amount of blood, but we got him there and everything is fine. They've already treated him and they're only keeping him overnight as a precaution."

"I want to go see him," I say, my lips quivering. I can't believe this happened.

"Yeah, of course." Joe grabs a bag off of the kitchen table in front of us. "I just came to get a few things for him. Ty is at my house with my wife."

I nod, having trouble forming words. It's already been an exceptionally emotional day for me and now Roman's hurt. We haven't had a good conversation in days, and now, someone attacked him in his own house while his son slept upstairs.

Joe and I drive in silence, my mind swirling in a million different directions. It's a relief that Roman is going to be okay, but he should have told me what happened. Even if he was angry.

I shouldn't have to find out like this. Everything is fine this time, but it's a harsh reminder of the present danger in our lives. Nowhere is safe.

Joe parks in front of the hospital and we both hurry inside. He shows me down the hall to Roman's room and I burst inside with Joe close at my heels.

Roman sits in the bed, tapping away at his laptop, and looks up at me wildly when I rush toward him. "Madison?"

Without a word, I throw my arms around his neck, draping myself across his body as I bury my face in his chest. He holds me tight against his body, pressing a kiss to the top of my head as he rubs my back. Tears stream down my face, every emotion of today converging on me at once. Defeat. Sadness. Fear. Relief deeper than I've ever felt.

"I'm okay, baby," he whispers gently. "Everything is okay."

No matter what's happening between him and me, the moment I'm in his arms, he's my lifeline and everything settles.

Breaking for air, I pull back from Roman and sit on the edge of the bed. He reaches out, brushing the tears off of my cheek, and I put my hand on top of his, just holding it there. His touch is already calming my aching heart.

"I found something I thought you might like back at the house." Joe grins, slinging Roman's bag onto the bed. "I also smuggled a couple of beers into your bag in case you need something to take the edge off."

"Thanks, Joe." Roman gives him a halfhearted grin. "You should get home. Text me and let me know how Ty is, okay?"

"Absolutely, man." Joe nods. "Get some rest. Looks like you're in good hands here."

He gives me a quick hug and then leaves, latching the door behind him.

"You're supposed to be in St. Louis." Roman pulls me against him again, making some room on the bed so I can lie next to him in his arms. It's small and cramped, but right now, it's the most comfortable place in the world.

"My plans changed. I could have been here a lot sooner if you would have called me, though. I didn't find out until I ran into Joe back at the house."

Roman's eyebrows cinch together. "Wait, you were flying home in the middle of the night for some other reason? I told Joe not to call you, but when you walked in, I figured he must have, but it was something else?"

"That's not important right now." I suck in a sharp breath. "Tell me what happened."

Roman looks like he wants to press me for more, but he doesn't. At least for now.

"It's not a big deal, Maddie. I'm fine, I told you. It's barely a flesh wound." As tough as he wants to seem, his face is pale and his eyes are sunken in. He looks completely worn out.

"Not a big deal?" I laugh sharply. "Roman, you were stabbed in your house while your son slept upstairs. By a man who has been hunting you down for months. And you lost so much blood you lost consciousness."

He rolls his eyes, raking his fingers through his hair. "Lost consciousness is kind of dramatic. I was just dizzy and a little out of it."

"Why didn't you call me?" I bite my lip.

"Because I figured I'd tell you when you got home tomorrow. I knew you were busy, and you didn't really want to talk to me."

"Jesus, Roman!" Part of me wants to reach out and slap him, and if he wasn't lying in a hospital bed, I might have. "Even if we're fighting, it doesn't mean that I wouldn't want to know that you got hurt—attacked! Do you have any idea how scared I was when Joe told me? Imagine if that was me and I didn't tell you. You wouldn't take that well."

"You're right." He swallows. "I wouldn't. I'd be fucking pissed."

"Yeah, well, the feeling is mutual." I glare, folding my arms over my chest. "Sometimes you can be so impossible. It's stupid and immature to not tell me about your near death experience because we had a little argument."

"Hey..." Roman props himself up, brushing a strand of hair off of my cheek. "You're a hundred percent right. It was dumb. And I'm sorry. I won't let it happen again. Next time, you're my first call. I promise."

Next time. Two words have never felt heavier.

Tears threaten to fall again. "I don't want you to say that just to placate me. I want you to say it because you mean it."

"I do mean it, baby. I swear." His hand slips to the back of my neck and he pulls me forward. His kiss is different. It's emotional and raw and passionate in the softest of ways. When he rests his forehead against mine, our noses brush. "I'm sorry, Maddie. I should have called. But you know what? This might have been a blessing in disguise. Dante was able to pull a clear picture of the guy off of my security camera and they're going after him now. We're that much closer to catching him."

"But at what expense?" I appreciate the way Roman can find the silver lining, because I just can't see it right now.

"Maddie, baby, you've got to relax." A small smile is on his lips. "It barely even hurts. I got a couple stitches, and the only reason I'm still here is for observation to be sure there's no infection."

"Can I see it?"

"Of course." Roman lifts his shirt, exposing a long wound on his abdomen. I gently run my fingers along it, counting each individual stitch. Twenty-five, which is way more than a couple like he tried to convince me of.

"Does that hurt?" I ask.

"Not at all." He grins. "In fact, the way you're rubbing my chest...that's the best I've felt in days."

"Very funny. You know, three centimeters to the right and he would have nicked your abdominal aorta, and we'd be in a much different situation." It's actually amazing he didn't. That artery goes directly to the heart. Roman would have bled out before he could have even made a phone call to get help.

"God, you are so sexy when you use medical words like that." Roman certainly hasn't lost any of his spitfire and that's a comfort. His banter is starting to calm me down a little, too, and I can almost feel my heart rate slowing. "Now, can we talk about something else? Like, why you came home early?"

"No, we can't talk about that," I say definitively. I'm still processing everything, and I'm not ready to tell the story.

Roman gives me a sympathetic smile. "That bad, huh?"

"I said, I don't want to talk about it, Roman." I try to stand, but he catches my wrist and pulls me back.

"Fine. You don't have to talk at all, because I have plenty I want to say." His face falls a bit. "Starting with congratulations."

"Congratulations?"

"Yes. Congratulations on the offer to join the program in LA. It's incredible, and I know how hard you've worked for it, and I am so fucking proud of you. I should have told you that the other night."

I don't even know what to say as Roman talks. No one has ever said anything like that to me before, and my emotions are just fraught enough that I might cry again.

"I'm sorry about how I reacted when you told me. I know you weren't asking me to quit or anything like that, but it reminded me of so many conversations that I had with Talia where she tried to get me to leave. It's not an excuse, but I was scared, because I'm in love with you, too. And the thought of you leaving fucking destroyed me, so I panicked and went back to pushing you away to protect myself."

"Don't you know by now that you can't scare me off so easily?" I smile.

"I do." Roman nods. "And you know what else I know? None of that other stuff matters, because even if you decide to go, we'll find a way to work this out."

"Really?" I'm not usually such a crier, but today has completely taken it out of me and I start again. It's almost pitiful at this point.

"Absolutely. Los Angeles is only like four and a half hours from here. Probably three and a half with the way I drive." He chuckles. "But if you decide it's the best thing for you, then we'll make it work. Obviously, I don't want to go a day without seeing you, but it's better than losing you for good. And I'd never ask you to give up something like that for us. If it's important to you, it's important to me and Ty."

"Roman, I…" Words completely fail me. No one has ever supported me the way he is, and it is as beautiful as it is heartbreaking.

"I love you, Maddie. I know it's soon and that we have so much left to learn about each other, but I've never felt like this before."

"Neither have I." I shake my head. "I love you, too."

"Good." He smiles. "Because I'm not going anywhere. We're going to be right here to support whatever you decide. Whether it's here or LA or the moon."

I burst out laughing, wiping the rest of my tears off of my cheek. "Roman, I really appreciate you saying all of that. I needed it after today." He eyes me carefully. "But I really don't know if LA is the right thing for me."

"What are you talking about? Isn't that your dream program?"

"It was. But I found out while I was home that I only got offered the position because my dad called in a favor. Which means he could have done it at any point. He just didn't want to help me."

"What?" Roman clenches his jaw. "Jesus, Maddie. I'm so sorry."

"I don't want to get into it all right now. I'm not giving up on it completely. I just think I need to slow down and really think it over. I can't rush into something like that without being sure it's the right choice."

Everything about my career path has been go, go, go from the beginning and maybe a step back is exactly what I need to find a little clarity.

"Whatever you need, baby. I'm here for it."

I lay back down next to him, my head on his shoulder, and he sweeps a kiss across my forehead. I know with every fiber of my being that coming home tonight was the right decision. Lying here next to him is the perfect ending to an otherwise terrible day, and nestled in Roman's arms, safe and supported, is exactly where I'm supposed to be.

And thank God, so is he.

Chapter Thirty-Three

ROMAN

"I'm not so sure about this." Maddie frowns, pushing her plate of barely touched tacos towards the center of the table.

We met for a quick lunch before I had to head into work, and she's been distracted the entire time. In fact, she's been a little aloof since she came back from St. Louis, but I haven't pressed her on it. I know how raw and personal family issues can be, and I know she'll come to me on her own time. It doesn't mean I'm happy about it, or that it isn't irritating the fuck out of me that I can't figure out what is on her mind. But I'm trying a new thing where I am respectful of people's boundaries, so instead of prying it out of her, I focus on the issue that she *is* talking to me about—the hospital fundraiser gala this weekend.

"What exactly aren't you sure about, babe?" I reach across the table and take her hand in mine. "Going to the gala or going with me as your date?"

Maddie looks at me like I'm crazy, but it's a valid question. I've been to this gala before, among others, but this is Maddie's first time and she doesn't know what to expect. That uncertainty, plus all the stress she's been under, has her completely strung out.

It's been that way since she got back, but she hasn't elaborated much more than what she told me in the hospital that night. That little snippet was enough to make me detest her father, and her whole family, for that matter. What kind of father wouldn't help his child if he could? Especially when she's worked so hard for it and he so readily did it for her brothers. While Maddie didn't tell me directly, Ernie's colorful account of how the conversation went down made me want to hop on a plane right then and confront the bastard in person. I could kill him for speaking to her the way he did, but I've managed to bite my tongue and not interfere out of sheer respect for her.

"Trust me, you aren't the issue. If you didn't agree to go with me, I wouldn't even consider going at all."

"Then what's the problem?"

She lets out a heavy sigh. "I hate this kind of thing. It's so over the top and excessive when all I really want to do is to be at home with you and Ty."

"As much as I like the sound of that, I'm looking forward to showing you off as my girlfriend. And think of how much fun you and I will have sitting in the shadows and making fun of all the pretentious people there." I've been to these kinds of parties a thousand times before, and if nothing else, the people watching is good. It usually is when you mix a bunch of Las Vegas elites with free alcohol and a chance to flaunt their wealth. At the silent auction last year, a signed Vegas Vipers jersey went for half a million dollars, and the whole damn team isn't even worth that. One thing about old rich men, though, is that they rarely pass up an opportunity to throw their money around and that certainly benefits the hospital.

"Do we have to?" Maddie's glossy lips pull into a pout.

"Yes." I let out a sharp laugh. "It's not like this is some sort of torture. Most girls would love a night out like this. A fancy dress, four course dinner, open bar...And besides, aren't you required to be there for work?"

"Yeah," she grumbles, twisting a golden curl between her fingers. Her shoulders slump as she stares off toward the busy street beside us. "I'm just nervous about seeing Bauer. I haven't run into him since I've been home and I know he's going to push me for my answer about LA."

Maddie's been over this LA thing backwards and forwards and a thousand times over, and she still isn't any closer to making a choice. Now that she knows her dad got her the spot, the whole thing has been tainted, but she's not quite ready to give up on everything she's worked for. That program has been her dream, and it's right in front of her now, but her bastard father ruined it. Obviously, I'd rather she stay here, but I won't be the holdup. She deserves to live out her dream, however she sees fit, and if that's LA, then that's LA.

I've gotten used to the idea of commuting if that's what needs to happen, and I'll support her, regardless. The fact that her father hasn't makes me want to snap his spine—not that he has one to begin with. God help the man if we ever meet in person.

"You leave Bauer to me, Maddie. He won't bother you about LA."

She's skeptical, but doesn't fight me on it and comes back with yet another excuse of why we shouldn't go. "I don't even own a fancy dress. What am I supposed to wear?"

"You can leave that to me, too." I reach for my wallet and slide out a business card. "A friend of mine owns this shop. Stop by there this afternoon and she'll take care of you. Put it on my account."

Maddie clicks her tongue. "You're not buying me a dress, Roman."

"Relax." I chuckle, taking a drink of my water. "I'll figure out some way for you to repay me."

She narrows her eyes, not appreciating my innuendo as much as I thought she might.

"Just humor me, okay? I want to do something special for you. I'm sure you'll find something you like."

"If you're so set on this, why don't you come with me and we can find something for me to wear that *you* like?" She flutters her eyelashes at me as she leans forward onto her elbows. The view I get of her cleavage is almost enough to make me cancel my afternoon plans. We haven't even been together all that long, and yet Maddie knows how to push every button I've got. Some I didn't even know I had.

"I'd love to come with you, but I have to work this afternoon. But feel free to send me some sneak peeks from the dressing room." I wink at her.

"God, you're impossible sometimes." She rolls her eyes, laughing at me. "Speaking of work...aren't you supposed to be there at one?"

"Damn," I growl, glancing down at my watch. "I am. But I can always rearrange things for you."

"I appreciate it, but I promise I'm fine." She smiles, squeezing my hand gently. "I'll see you for dinner?"

"I'll be counting down the seconds." I nearly vomit as the words came out of my mouth. What the hell is happening to me?

A taunting smile tugs at Maddie's lips. "You know, for such a big, tough mafia leader, you're kind of a big sap."

There's that sass I love so much.

"Don't you dare ever repeat that to my men, or I'll have to show you just how scary of a mafia man I can be."

"I'm not scared of you." She purses her lips confidently, almost begging for me to kiss them.

I happily oblige, giving her a hungry kiss and pulling away at the exact moment I feel her relax into it. "You should be."

"I love you."

"I love you too." I brush my lips against her forehead quickly so as not to fall even deeper under her spell. I have to get some work done today, and if she keeps looking at me like that, I won't ever leave. "Even if you are a tease."

She giggles, waving innocently at me. I don't even look back because it's already taking so much restraint to walk away from her. The sooner I can get this over with, the sooner I can go home and thoroughly enjoy her.

Dr. Taylor's been holding out on me since my injury, claiming sex was too much activity and I might bust my stitches. She cleared me this morning when I all but threatened her life, and I was planning on taking full advantage of it tonight. The girl needs a good fuck to relax just as much as I do.

The warehouse is a quick ten-minute drive from the restaurant. Joe and Dante located a Chavos leader, and we're right on the cusp of breaking this entire thing wide open. I can't wait to put this shit behind me and finally move on with Maddie and Ty. They both deserve that more than anything, and I've never craved something so much in all of my life. Right now, it's all I can think about.

I want this to be over as soon as possible, and all distractions have to be on the back burner until I get what I need from him. And that's a name. The name of the guy who's been behind all of this.

I find my way to the back room where Joe and Dante are waiting for me.

"It's about time you got here." Joe chuckles. "Maddie let you off the leash for the afternoon?" He and Dante share a smirk.

"I have a lot of pent-up aggression saved up this afternoon, boys. I'm sure our prisoner would be glad if I took some of it out on you two morons." I'm wound just tight enough that their banter rubs me the wrong way today. It's gone on long enough, and it's time to get serious.

"Alright, alright." Joe grins, walking over to the chair in the center of the room. The prisoner is tied to it, a bag pulled over his head. Joe removes it roughly, and the guy looks around like a deer in headlights. He's already bloody, bruised and worn down. Dante and Joe obviously made good use of the time they were waiting for me. "Roman, meet Ryker. He's a lieutenant in La Eme and was the one who killed Talia, went after Ty, and his fingerprints were found all over your house."

Sounds like game over to me.

"That's not true. I had nothing to do with that shit. I swear!" He shakes his head wildly, trying to backtrack.

Dante rears his fist back, landing a powerful punch on Ryker's jaw and sending blood sputtering across the room. His brass knuckles clamor to the floor.

I bend so I'm at his level, meeting his glare. "Ryker, I think you'd say just about anything right now to save your own skin. I think it was all you. You killed my wife, and you tried to kill both me and my son. You have thirty seconds to convince me otherwise."

Quiet at first, he seems to be questioning how serious I am about the time limit, yet as I pull out a jagged, six-inch hunting knife, he changes his tune. "Okay, okay. It was me. But I was just following orders, I swear! I'll tell you whatever you want to know, just don't kill me." It's amazing how many men like this preach loyalty, but sing like songbirds once they're faced with death.

"How about you talk and then I'll decide whether you live or die?"

He jerks against his restraints. "I've never met the guy. I don't even know anybody who has. All I know is he is some rich white guy. Doesn't even live in Vegas. They call him Doc and he calls the shots now."

"Doc?" Joe repeats.

Ryker nods. "He never shows his face, but everything runs through him. He sends his jobs through a Chinese restaurant. A brown takeout bag showed up on my doorstep with all the details and that's all. I swear."

I stare at him intently, trying to decide if he's telling the truth. He has no reason to lie to us when we're his only hope of staying alive. Either we kill him, or we let him go with a target on his back. Whether or not he tells us anything won't matter, it'll look like he did to his group.

"What do you think?" Joe sneers, the same thoughts running through his mind.

"I think we aren't in a position to overlook any leads." I grit my teeth. If Ryker is telling the truth, we're closer. I hate the thought of this dragging on even longer, but I want to be sure. I *have* to be sure.

Joe nods to Dante, and he leaves the room, ready to chase down the lead.

"Look, you've got to protect me. I can get you to Doc, but I need some assurances first," Ryker pleads, well aware of his fate the second he walks out of my door.

Joe lets out a sharp laugh. "Protect you? You're lucky you're still breathing right now."

I rub my jaw, contemplating my options. Unfortunately, he's right. He has the closest ties to whoever this guy is, and he's our best chance of ending it swiftly.

"You have three days," I concede.

"It's going to take longer than that. I told you, this guy doesn't do face to face."

Joe shoots me a curious look. Bargaining isn't a method that I use often.

"Three days. If you don't deliver him by then, La Eme can have you." I turn to Joe. "I want eyes on him at all times. And taps on the phone."

Joe grunts, hauling Ryker off.

The last thing I want is a war with La Eme. It's too unpredictable, and I've got too much to lose if something breaks out. This is all I've got right now, and I have to make it work.

CHAPTER THIRTY-FOUR

ROMAN

As I pace at the bottom of the stairs waiting for Maddie, I'm actually antsy. Pre-date jitters are a new thing for me in general, but tonight is next level.

Maddie and I have been out dozens of times, but something feels different about going to an event like this together. Like truly going public with our relationship. Many of my own associates are donors to the hospital and will be there tonight, not to mention all of Maddie's coworkers. The event draws national attention, and it will for sure be heavily photographed. First impressions are everything in my world, and I love the idea of having Maddie on my arm.

It feels like a big step.

She took me up on my offer to buy her a dress, but I don't know anything about what she picked. She and Lucinda have dodged my questions about it all week, only telling me it's black so I could dress accordingly. After learning from my last experience, I dropped Ty off with Joe and Sarah earlier in the afternoon so Maddie and I could get ready in peace. He was less than thrilled, but when Maddie offered to send him a picture of us in our outfits, he mellowed out.

I glance at my watch and groan. I hate being late for these types of things, because all the tables in the back are usually taken by then.

"Maddie?" I call up the stairs.

When she doesn't answer, I head up the stairs. I hear her music playing from down the hall and edge her door open when I get there. "Maddie, are you—"

The second I see her, I lose all train of thought. *Holy shit.*

Maddie stands in front of her floor-length mirror, angled just enough that she can't see me. It gives me a few seconds to drink her in before she notices that I'm here. My heart thunders in my chest as I trace her curves, thinly veiled with the fabric of the black, floor length dress she and Lucinda chose. The slit in it is so high that I love it as much as I hate it—love, because it gives me easy access and hate, because I know it'll have the imagination of every man at the party running wild. Her golden curls are pinned back on one side, spilling over her bare shoulder on the other as she fastens a sparkling diamond drop earring. She bows those candy color lips as she gives herself one more look in the mirror and then turns around.

I don't know how she manages to get even more beautiful than she already is, but somehow she does. She'll be the envy of every woman there tonight, and the best part about Maddie is that she'll have no idea.

She flinches a bit when she finally sees me. "Hey! I didn't realize you were up here."

"I came to see if you were ready to go, but when I saw you..." I sweep my arm around her waist and take her hand in the other, spinning her back and laying her onto the bed. "I completely forgot why we were leaving." I nuzzle into her neck.

"Oh, no..." Maddie smirks, playfully pushing me off of her. "You're the one who said we had to do this. You can't back out now."

Groaning, I roll over and lift myself off the bed, and Maddie follows. "That was before I knew you were going to pick a dress that purposely tortures me all night."

"Mmm." Maddie presses her lips together. "I distinctly remember asking you to come with me so you could pick it out."

"You did." I let out a heavy, dramatic sigh. "This is my fault. I deserve it."

Maddie giggles, rolling her eyes at me.

"All joking aside, you look like an absolute dream, Maddie. So fucking gorgeous."

"Thank you." She blushes, straightening my bowtie. "So do you. I like the all black look."

When Lucinda dropped off Maddie's dress, she left a couple options for me as well, and I settled on the black on black on black tuxedo.

"Well, with the way you reacted, it felt like we were going to a funeral, so I decided to dress accordingly." My hand slides across her ass as I lead her out of the bedroom. There's a spice to her perfume that fills my lungs, so sweet that I could get drunk off it.

"Very funny," she quips. "To be fair, I haven't exactly been in the celebrating mood, but I am tonight."

I raise my eyebrow. "Really?"

She nods. "You're right. It is kind of fun to get dressed up and go to a fancy party. Plus, I'm excited to meet some of your friends."

"I'm excited for you to meet them, too." I grin, squeezing her hand as we walk to the truck.

The gala is at the Bellagio, and by the time we get there, it's already crawling with elitists. Maddie seems hesitant, as if she thinks she doesn't belong here, but I give her hand a reassuring squeeze and lead her inside.

"I'm nervous," she whispers as we pick up our name plates and head into the dining room.

"You have no reason to be." I put a rough finger to her chin, forcing her to meet my eyes. "You are the most beautiful person in this entire room. Hell, you're the most beautiful person I've ever seen in my entire life. Compassionate, brilliant, and you're going to make an incredible trauma surgeon one day. You belong here, more than about seventy-five percent of these morons. So stop doubting yourself."

Maddie blushes, but before she can respond, we're being rushed by another woman.

"Maddie! I'm so glad to see you! When your name wasn't listed on our table, I was worried you decided not to come." The woman throws her arms around Maddie, and I step back.

"Hi Peyton." Maddie smiles, relaxing and regaining her composure a bit. "It's good to see you."

"So what's the deal? Does Dr. Bauer have you sitting with your dad tonight?"

Her dad? A haunting chill settles in my bones. Maybe I'm going to get that face-to-face meeting sooner than I thought.

"My dad is here?" Clearly, Maddie had no idea about this either and her face turns sheet white.

"Well, I haven't actually seen him yet, but his name was listed in the program." Peyton frowns.

"Maddie is sitting with me tonight. I'm sorry to steal her away from you guys." I put on my most charming smile and step in because Maddie looks like she's about to be sick. "I don't think we've met. I'm Roman Molanari."

"Of course!" Peyton turns her peppy attention towards me. "It's so nice to finally meet you. I've heard a lot about you. Maddie and I have been friends for a long time. I guess if I have to give her up tonight, you're a good enough reason."

"I appreciate that." I chuckle, snaking my arm around Maddie's waist.

"Well, come find me later." Peyton gives her one last squeeze. "And it was lovely to meet you, Roman."

She flits away before either of us can respond.

"Are all of your friends so bubbly?" I grin, turning to Maddie.

She bites her lip, letting out a small laugh. "No. That's just Peyton's personality, and she's even more upbeat tonight because she loves this kind of thing."

"A rare breed."

"That she is." Maddie's voice is tight.

"You're worried about running into your dad, aren't you?"

"Yeah," she breathes. "I didn't even know he was coming. We haven't spoken since I left St. Louis. I mean, he's always invited, but he's never made it out before. I didn't think this year would be any different, but..." she trails off. "I guess it is."

"Babe, if he's here, we'll deal with it. Okay?" I press a kiss to her cheek. "Peyton said she hasn't seen him yet, so there's no reason to get stressed about something that we don't even know is true."

She swallows, nodding. "I could certainly use a drink. How about you?"

"Yeah, definitely."

I follow Maddie to the bar, and after we get our drinks, we wander around for a bit until it's time to find our seats. We're at a table with a few friends of mine, which is perfect. It'll take a bit of the work pressure off of Maddie.

Even though the gala is for the hospital, most of the people are unassociated donors. Because these events focus on attracting money, the guest list is filled with some of Las Vegas's most affluent people. Most of them I do business with and know very well. I probably know more people here than she does.

When we take our seats, I make introductions, and can see her start to relax as she chats with a few of the wives. I watch her for most of dinner, amazed by the way she fits into any crowd. She has them all on the edge of their seats as she tells them about the things she's seen pass through the ER, and I feel so fucking lucky to be the one she's with.

"How did you guys meet?" Craig, one of the men, asks.

"Uh..." I scramble for an explanation because, while most of them know what I do, I can't exactly admit the truth about how all of this started between us.

Luckily, Maddie jumps in. "I treated his son a few months ago. We just kind of clicked."

I lean forward, one arm around her shoulders and the other hand resting on her bare thigh, right where that slit pulls. "I knew right then there was no way I could let her get away."

"I'm surprised he didn't kidnap me," she taunts, shooting me a wink.

"I am, too!" Craig chuckles. "Roman certainly has a way of getting what he wants."

"I'm going to get another drink while you all harass me." I stand and grab our empty glasses. "Another champagne, babe?"

"Sure, thanks." She smiles, cheeks already turning a soft shade of red from the buzz.

"Whiskey on the rocks and a champagne, please." I set our glasses on the bar as I order.

A man comes up next to me and at first, I don't realize who it is. When I turn to see Dr. Bauer, I look away in disgust before I do something I'll regret.

"Roman." He slaps me on the back as if we're old friends. "Enjoying the night?"

"Yep," I answer shortly. Conversing with him isn't high on my priority list. I can play nice because he's Maddie's boss, but that's about it.

"I'm glad I caught you alone. I've been wanting to speak with you ever since you brought lunch to Madison."

I shoot him a harsh glare. "Well, here I am."

"What exactly are you trying to pull by dating Madison? Is this some kind of way to get back at me for not telling who made the mistake with Talia?"

"What?" I let out a sharp laugh. Of course, this pompous bastard thinks my relationship with Maddie is about him. "You're out of your mind. I love Maddie and I haven't given a fleeting thought to you in months."

"Roman, let's be real here. What are the chances you wind up with one of my most promising surgeons after everything you and I have been through?"

"I don't know what to tell you, Bauer. This has zero to do with you. Now if you'll excuse me..." I turn, but he catches my arm.

"Roman, before you go, there's someone I want to introduce you to." He waves another man over. "This is a friend of mine. Dr. Mark Taylor. He's a trauma surgeon in St. Louis, and his daughter works with me at St. Luke's. Madison. I believe you've met her."

I clench my jaw, hand cinching around the drinks in my hands. This son of a bitch. He's really going to do this right now? "I do know Madison. She treated my son earlier this year, and she's a wonderful doctor. It's nice to meet you, Dr. Taylor."

Fortunately, the words come out sounding less bitter than I mean them, a skill that I've perfected.

"That's good to hear." He gives me a stiff smile, but from what I can tell, he has no idea about Maddie and me. "But she won't be working at St. Luke's much longer, right Dr. Bauer?"

"Not if we can help it." He snickers. "Mark and I need to go chat with another donor, Roman, but I'm glad that the two of you got to meet."

"So am I."

I watch until the two men join another group and get engulfed in conversation. I don't know what they're up to, but it can't be good, and I need to find Maddie and warn her before either of them do.

CHAPTER THIRTY-FIVE

As much as it pains me to admit, Roman was right.

The gala has been more bearable than I expected, maybe even enjoyable. Somehow, I've managed to avoid Dr. Bauer and his judgmental opinions for most of the evening, and if my dad's here, he hasn't shown his face. I love getting to see Roman with some of his friends. It's like a whole different side to him, even than when he's with Joe and Dante, and I feel oddly proud that he's choosing to include me in it.

I don't know why it never occurred to me that Roman had friends outside of the Mafia, but it surprised me just how well connected he is. A lot of people here tonight are actively involved at the hospital and trying to make positive changes. Some of them are even engineers who designed the very technology I use daily.

It's fun getting to know his friends, but Roman's been gone for a while, and I glance around the room to find him. He went to get drinks, but the bar is empty now. Maybe he stepped outside for a few minutes. I excuse myself to go look for him to try to convince him to join me on the dance floor. We're here, after all, might as well fully immerse ourselves.

I step out onto the balcony and into a cloud of smoke. Several men are outside enjoying cigars, but Roman isn't among them. Thinking I might catch him by the bathrooms, I start that way, but I'm quickly stopped.

"Madison." Dr. Bauer stands in front of me. "I'm glad I caught you. I need an answer about LA. Have you thought anymore about it?"

"I have, actually." I press my lips together. "I don't think that job is the right thing for me. I really appreciate your recommendation, but I'm happy here."

"You realize that you're throwing away your entire career with this move, don't you?" He sneers.

"I don't think I am. I'm just not rushing through my training. There are plenty of places I can learn to be a trauma surgeon on a regular timeline. The fast track is—"

"A once in a lifetime opportunity," he interrupts. "The doctors there are world class and if you turn this down, you can say goodbye to any future opportunity with them." His sharp eyes sear into me as he speaks. "And for what? Roman Molanari? That man will ruin you, Madison. He'll use you just long enough to crush every bit of spirit inside of you and then throw you out with the trash. I've seen it happen before."

I can't get away from this conversation fast enough. "Dr. Bauer, you have no idea what you're talking about. This has nothing to do with Roman, and even if it did—"

"It got his wife killed, you know. Roman and his bogus business dealings. Did he tell you that?" His face reddens as he speaks, clenching his fists at his sides. "You remember Talia?"

"Of course I do. She was murdered by someone Roman works with, and he tried to blame it on my staff. I'm telling you, Madison, take the job and get out of here before you meet the same fate."

I swallow the lump in my throat. I know nothing he says is true, but it doesn't make it any easier to hear.

"We're not done here, Madison," Dr. Bauer growls, catching my wrist and jerking me back as I try to walk away.

Before I know what's happening, somebody moves between us. It's Roman.

"You most certainly are." His words spew like venom. "If you ever lay a hand on her again, I'll bury you so deep in a sexual harassment suit that you'll never touch a scalpel again."

Bauer chuckles. "Oh, you're picking the politically correct route now."

"How about this? You so much as look in her direction again and I'll slice you up and throw you into the shark tank at Mandalay Bay and let the tourists watch you get eaten alive."

"Take care of this one, Roman. I'd hate to see Madison end up like the first Mrs. Molanari, wouldn't you?"

Roman cocks his arm back and then punches Bauer with a resounding pop that echoes off the walls. It knocks him backwards, hitting the ground; I cover my mouth, watching blood spew from Dr. Bauer's nose.

"Let's go." Roman interlaces his trembling fingers in mine and pulls me to the door.

Oh my God. I can hardly believe what just happened. My fight with Bauer. Roman punching him. It all seems like a nightmare as I follow Roman out of the event hall and toward the business of the casino.

I'm so distracted that I don't even notice anyone is following us until I hear my father's voice.

"Madison."

It stops me in my tracks, and I whirl around, all the air sucked right out of my lungs. "Dad."

"So this is why you're turning the position down? Because you're dating this guy?" He stalks toward us with a familiar, condescending look on his face.

"*This guy* has a name." Roman glares. "Roman Molanari, and I suggest you think very hard about the way you're about to speak to your daughter."

I can feel every muscle in Roman's body tighten through his hold on my hand, and he looks at my dad, like he might tear his head off right here.

My dad laughs. "Why? Because you'll hit me, too?"

"Dad, please," I beg, stepping in before things get out of control. "I'm not turning it down because of Roman. I've thought a lot about it and—"

"Don't expect me to believe that, Madison. You're doing this to spite me, aren't you? I had to beg them to take you on short notice. You never would have got in without me."

My stomach drops, tears stinging my eyes. Tensions are always high and this is going down quickly.

Roman takes a step toward my dad with a heinous look on his face, and I pull him back. "Don't, Roman. Please."

He catches my gaze and pauses. I can see the confliction flash across his face, but eventually he backs down.

"I didn't do it to hurt you, Dad, and I'm sorry you feel that way."

"You've never been cut out for this, Madison. At least now you realize it."

I bite back my tears and turn toward the front door. I pull Roman's hand, but he doesn't move.

Oh, no. Please don't do this.

"You're wrong, you know." Roman stares at him, so harshly that it gives me chills. "Madison is an incredible doctor. She's kind and steady and she has more compassion in the tip of her finger than you do in your entire body. And she actually cares about her patients, not just what her stats are. I feel sorry for you that you can't see that side of her because..." He glances back at me. "Your daughter is literal perfection, and she's so fucking good at what she does, and someday, she's going to make an incredible trauma surgeon."

Roman's words obliterate any hope I had of keeping it together. Heavy tears stream down my cheeks as realization sets in. I can't even be mad at Roman, because no one has ever defended me the way he did tonight. No one has ever cared enough to. And the feeling is overwhelming.

ROMAN

Maddie doesn't say much on the way home and neither do I. I don't really know what's appropriate at this point. I knocked her boss out, made a stellar first impression on her dad, and we had to leave the gala right as she was starting to enjoy herself. Tonight will forever go down as one of my biggest fuckups.

Usually, when Maddie is angry, it's easy to see. She'll fight and yell and argue, so it's this silence that scares me. When I pull the truck into the drive, I'm prepared to get down on my knees and grovel.

I lock the door behind us and head into the kitchen with Maddie a few steps in front of me. I reach for her hand and spin her back around, sweeping her into my arms.

"I'm sorry. I shouldn't have hit your boss and I shouldn't have mouthed off to your dad. I'm sorry I fucked up our night."

Maddie's brow creases. "You're sorry? Roman, you have nothing to be sorry for. No one has ever defended me that way, and you took on my boss and my dad on the same night."

I let out a sharp laugh, her reaction the polar opposite from what I was prepared for. "And I'd do it again every time. No one should talk to you that way, Maddie. Especially not a man who claims to love you. Both he and Bauer are pricks."

She nods, more like she's trying to appease me than like she actually believes it. I lift her chin. "I'm serious, Maddie. You deserve to be in that program as much as anybody. Maybe even more so because your dad has been battling against you the whole time. Whatever you choose, please do not let the opinions of those bastards affect it."

"Roman, there's something I want to tell you." Maddie presses her lips together. "I'm not going to go to LA."

What? LA sounds like a dream come true for her and despite our initial argument, I thought we'd come to a compromise about the whole thing. Her sudden change of heart takes me by surprise.

"Are you sure? If it's because—"

Maddie holds her hand up. "Before you say anything, my choice has nothing to do with you and Ty. Or I guess in a way it does, but only because you showed me that there's more to life than just chasing after titles and records and trying to be the best. We could break up tomorrow and I'd still be happy with my choice. I was in a hurry to fast track everything because I wanted to prove myself to my dad, but that's not important to me anymore. What's important is being great at what I decide to do, and a few years here in general surgery will help me do that. I'm a good doctor, but like you said, part of that is because I take the time to get to know my patients and to make them comfortable. I think for a while I forgot that medicine is about helping people. It's not about checking off boxes and hitting the numbers rushing through things to make a name for myself."

Once done, she lets out a long breath, as if she'd been holding it the entire time she was talking. She bites her lip as she looks at me, waiting for my reaction.

An unabating grin spreads across my face, so wide that my cheeks ache as I wrap her into a hug. "I'm so goddamn proud of you, you know that? I know how hard it is to shift your dreams, but I think you're right. What's important is that you're happy and that you're doing something you love. And that it's for you. No one else."

"And that I get to see you and Ty every day is a nice plus." She smiles.

"You know I would have done whatever I needed to in order to make LA work."

"I do." She nods. "But that made my decision even easier. I've never had someone believe in me the way you do, Roman. Someone willing to inconvenience themselves to make my dreams come true, and I just...I can't tell you how much that means to me."

Cupping her chin, I slant her face up so I can capture her mouth in a kiss. Maddie melts into me, her tongue sliding through my lips for a quick taste before pulling away with a sweet moan.

"You're not the only one getting something out of this relationship, Maddie. You've completely changed Ty's and my life for the better, and I'll never be able to thank you enough. I can't imagine a life without you in it."

On her tiptoes, Maddie kisses me again, her hands slipping into the back pockets of my pants. "Me too."

Chapter Thirty-Six

THE NEED FOR MADDIE hits me like a freight train. It's blinding. It's consuming. And I know there is no chance in hell that I can wait long enough to get up the stairs.

Instead, I slide my arm underneath her, lifting her up onto the kitchen counter.

"Roman..." she whines, draping her neck back as I leave a scorching trail of kisses along her bare skin. "We should go upstairs."

"No one is home. I want you right here." I grunt, my hands covering every inch of lace covering her body. It's the fight of my life not to rip it to shreds. Instead, my fingers fumble with the zipper, slowly inching it down until the dress loosens and her full, perfect tits come spilling out. Jesus fucking Christ. She hasn't had a bra on this whole time?

Maddie must read my mind, because she blushes, inching forward with her hands holding onto the counter in a way that pushes her breasts up. "Then get to it."

Her encouragement is nice, but I don't need it, because I'm about to fucking explode with anticipation. There will be nothing gentle about tonight. Nothing soft. Nothing slow. And as I lay Maddie against the cool granite, she knows it.

Her teeth sink into her lower lip and she lets her arms fall to the side, laying in front of me like a fucking masterpiece. Like a painting that belongs in the Louvre. A piece of art sculpted by God himself.

Those gorgeous tits bounce in front of me as she arches her back, every bit as desperate as I am as she tilts into me. My lips drag down her jawline to her neck and across her collarbone. When my tongue swipes against the smooth, creamy skin of her breast, Maddie trembles, parting her lips.

"That feels good?" I ask.

She gives me a gentle whimper and I take that as my answer. Catching her nipple with my mouth, I flick my tongue against her as I massage her other breast in my hand. The peak hardens, and Maddie wriggles beneath me. I grab her hips, bracing her against the counter so she stays in place. With every suck, her moans grow louder and more intense, while her nails dig deeper into my back.

"Oh god, Roman," she whines as I switch sides.

I peel the rest of Maddie's dress off, piling it on the floor. The only thing that shields her naked body from my gaze is a pair of gauzy panties that rip with one swift tug.

"Roman!" she squeals, playfully squirming in my hold as I work the fabric off of her. Ignoring her half-hearted protests, I throw my jacket to the side, buttons popping off of my shirt as she tears it away.

There's a familiar thirst in her eyes as she runs her fingernails down my bare chest. "God, you're so hot, Roman."

She says my name like it's a dirty word and I love the sound of it.

Maddie's legs wrap around my waist, pulling me into her. With nothing between us, our hips grind against each other, her skin like silk on mine. The friction between us makes my cock throb, prickly desire winding through my body like wildfire until it reaches every inch of me. I've never felt anything so intense and unrelenting in all my life.

I drag my fingers along her thigh, brushing the pad of my thumb against her clit. She's soaking wet and the sensation makes her shiver. Goosebumps scatter across her skin as she moans.

"Mmm." Her eyes flutter shut.

"Jesus, Maddie. I'm sorry, but I can't wait. I have to fucking have you."

Maddie presses against my chest, shoving me away from her and for a second I'm confused. That is until she hops off the counter and drops to her knees in front of me. She looks up at me through those thick lashes with the most seductive look in her eye and I know exactly what she's about to do.

Fuck.

"We'll get there." A devilish smirk plays at her lips as she kisses down my chest, unfastening my belt buckle and sliding it through the loops. She unbuttons my pants and slides them off, then does the same with my boxer briefs. "But I want to do something for you first. You were so good to me tonight, and I want to return the favor," she purrs.

Jesus Christ. How am I supposed to resist that?

Her fingers wrap around my already pulsing erection, and with every stroke, I feel the rest of the world slipping away. Her touch is pure magic. After a few minutes, I feel the warm rush of her breath as her lips wrap around me.

"God, Maddie," I groan, wrapping those curls around my fist as she bobs her head in a steady rhythm. "Holy shit."

With every move, she takes more and more of me in, my tip reaching the back of her throat and still she goes deeper. She flicks and sucks and laps at me with the perfect combination and rhythm, so damn harmonious that I don't even know which way is up right now. When a moan escapes those sexy lips, I almost come undone right then.

"Maddie, fuck. This feels so good."

With the way she's sucking me off, I'm not going to last long, and there's so much more I want to do to her. Part of me wants to move slowly and make her feel every bit as cherished and worshipped as she is, but there's another part of me that's fucking destitute without her, and I can't wait another second.

Fast. Hard. Pure sin.

Something tells me she might enjoy that just as much.

When she takes a breath, I yank her hand up and flip her around. She gasps as I press her chest into the cool granite countertop, hiking her hips up until she's on her toes. "Is this what you want, Maddie? Is my girl ready for me?"

I grab her hips and spread her legs apart. My fingers swipe against her swollen, glistening clit and she whimpers. "Yes. Please, Roman. Please."

That damn begging. It's like an electric shock to my system, and I lose all control.

"You sure? Because it seems you like this plenty?" I rub firmly against her folds, and she cries out, reaching for the edge of the island to brace herself.

"Please, Roman!"

"You want to feel me inside of you, Maddie? Or should I make you come with my fingers?" I plunge two inside of her, and she arches again.

"Come for me, baby. Show me how bad you need me." My tongue grazes her ear.

"Ahhhh!" Maddie cries out, writhing with orgasm as she twists and trembles beneath me.

Her cries only make me harder, and I edge her knees a little further apart before pushing in. Still not fully recovered from her first orgasm, Maddie's body tightens around me as I start to thrust. Slow at first, and then I settle into a scorching pace.

"Oh god, Roman!"

"How does that feel, baby? Too much?"

Maddie shakes her head wildly. "It's perfect. Please don't stop."

Please. I don't think she knows what that word does to me.

I buck against her, pushing her forward, and I drive inside of her over and over. Each thrust takes her breath away and she gasps for air; for a little reprieve.

Never in my life had anything felt so good. So fulfilling. So satisfying. Maddie's everything to me, and holding her in my hand feels like a dream. One I hope I never wake up from.

It doesn't take long for the pressure inside of me to become too much, and it explodes like a fucking gun. I brace myself against Maddie's hips, pinning her to the counter as I ride out my climax. It hits me so hard that I barely remember my own name as we both fall against the granite. It takes a minute for either of us to gather ourselves enough to speak, but finally, Maddie does.

"You know, the whole sex on the counter thing was hot, but do you think we can move the rest of this upstairs? Like to your bed?"

"I completely agree. This granite is going to murder my back." I chuckle, sliding off to the side and reaching my hand out to help her down.

"Now you sound like an old man. I just meant I'd like to continue this with a little more privacy."

"Old man?" I arch my eyebrow, reaching over and slapping her ass. "You're going to be sorry you said that."

Maddie grins and starts up the stairs, playfully gesturing for me to follow her. It doesn't seem like we're going to bed soon, but that's perfectly fine with me.

CHAPTER THIRTY-SEVEN

Madison

AFTER THE NIGHT WE had, the sound of my alarm feels like nails on a chalkboard. I've got an instant headache and I haven't even opened my eyes yet. I probably should have reconsidered one or two of those champagnes or maybe the third or fourth round of sex Roman and I had once we got home, because I'm hurting today and I have to be to the hospital in an hour.

I reach out for Roman, but his side of the bed is cold. The running water in the bathroom tells me he's been up for a while. When we went to bed last night, he didn't elaborate on what exactly he had to do, just that he would be occupied for most of the day. I had a hunch that both of us would be looking forward to a quiet night at home after last night.

The gala was a rush of emotions, and I'm just as exhausted mentally as I am physically. Bits and pieces of the evening run through my mind, including Roman knocking Dr. Bauer out on the cold marble floor of the banquet hall. I could still vividly see Dr. Bauer's head snapping back with the force of the blow and hear the sound of Roman's fist connecting with his jaw. Although Dr. Bauer deserved it, it still makes me cringe. I know that that side of Roman exists, but

I didn't like seeing it firsthand. I doubt Dr. Bauer and I will be on good terms after that.

Then there was the confrontation that Roman had with my dad. The sting of my dad's words is still fresh, but Roman swiftly came to my defense in a way that I wasn't used to. He defended me; he supported me; he loved me like I've never been in all my life and that's what sticks out to me most of all.

When my alarm reaches the end of the snooze cycle, I reluctantly pull myself out of bed. Reaching for a robe, I slip it over my body. It's not surprising that I didn't even end up in pajamas last night, but the morning light makes me slightly more modest.

The bathroom door is cracked open, and as I get closer, I can see Roman leaning against the counter shaving his face. He's shirtless, in only a pair of jeans, as he hums along to a song playing from his phone. Pushing the door open a little more, I lean against the frame and soak in every detail of his broad, muscled back.

No matter how many times I see it, just the sight of him makes my knees weak. I've traced the lines of every single tattoo on his body at least a dozen times, but I feel like I always find something new in his artwork. This morning, it's a pair of songbirds right at the base of his neck. I've never noticed it before, probably because they're entwined in a larger picture, but they're stunning. Inside one are the initials RM, and inside the other, NC.

My brow furrows in confusion. The RM is pretty self-explanatory, but the other one is baffling. NC? What does that stand for?

"Are you just going to stand there staring all morning?" Roman smirks at me through the mirror.

I smile, joining him in the bathroom. "I was just admiring how handsome you are."

"Oh, well, in that case..." Roman sets his razor on the counter and turns toward me. "You are in luck. This is a hands-on, interactive exhibit. In fact"—he reaches for my hand and tugs me forward, trapping me between his knees—"touching is encouraged."

"Mmm, I *do* like the sound of that. But you know that if we start this, neither one of us will make it to work today." I smile, reaching up and wiping a bit of shaving cream off his nose with my thumb. Roman lurches to the side, pretending to bite me. He hungrily kisses my neck, dragging his teeth along the skin and smearing shaving cream all over me.

"Roman, stop!" I try to squirm out of his grasp, but the more I move, the tighter he clenches his legs around me.

"Fine. You win. We've both got work to do. But I plan on picking this back up tonight."

"You better. It'll be the only thing getting me through the day." I sigh, breaking out of his grasp and picking up a wet washcloth to clean his shaving cream from my neck.

"You know, you don't have to go back. You could just quit," he suggests, grabbing his razor and resuming his shave.

"No, I can't. I turned down the LA position last night, and if I quit this job, I'll be completely out of work." I shake my curls out gently. The mascara underneath my eyes and rat's nest in my hair makes me fully regret just falling into bed last night.

"You can always have your job here back." He winks. Before leaving, he gives me one last deep kiss. "See you tonight?"

I nod.

"Ernie is going to be at the hospital with you today."

"Does he have to be? It's weird having someone hanging around me all the time. I can't work in those conditions." I like Ernie, but it's getting a little old, and it seems like the threats have died down.

"Nice try." Roman chuckles, playfully slapping my butt. "He's coming. End of discussion."

I let out a heavy, petulant sigh and fold my arms over my chest. It's not really that big of a deal, but with the mood I'm in, everything is going to irritate me today.

Roman slips his shirt over his head, but even with it on, the wings of the songbirds peek out from the top, reminding me of the strange initials on his back. "Hey, I've never seen the tattoo of the birds on your back. It's really neat."

"Thanks. I got it for Talia. Birds symbolize immortality."

"What do the initials NC mean, then?"

"Natalia Castillo," he says. Why does that name sound so familiar to me? "That was Talia's real name. She didn't take my name when we got married. She wanted to keep some separation, so she wasn't a target."

That explains why I never found any records for in the hospital. All of a sudden, an idea hits me. I've been thinking about the perfect way to thank Roman for everything he did yesterday, and maybe now that I know Talia's real name, I can figure out what happened. Bringing him a bit of relief and closure could be the perfect thing.

"That's really beautiful, Roman."

"Thanks." He kisses me one more time. "I'll call you in a bit to check in. Please don't give Ernie a hard time."

"Yes, sir." I fake salute him.

Roman groans, dropping his head back. "Fuck, I love it when you call me that."

"I love you," I call after him.

"I love you, too, Maddie."

After Roman leaves, I quickly get myself ready. I'm anxious to get to work now that I know Talia's real name. I don't know what I'll do with the information once I find it, but I have to try. There's no doubt in my mind that Roman will seek revenge on whoever is responsible, but doesn't he deserve to? Talia is dead, and no one is being held accountable. It goes against everything I took an oath for, but I kind of understand it.

When I get to the hospital, I check on my patients. It's a relatively quiet morning in the emergency room, but I don't dare say that out loud. By ten o'clock, it's almost a ghost town, so I head upstairs to the Records department.

"Hey Juliana!" I greet the tech. "I'm looking for an old file a client is requesting. Could you take a look for me?"

"Absolutely." She smiles. "What's the name?"

"It's Natalia Castillo."

"Hmm." She frowns, sympathy filling her eyes. "I know exactly who you're talking about. Such a tragedy. Dr. Bauer was actually looking at this file this week, too."

Bauer was looking into this? Something about the timing of all of this feels off.

She grabs the file off the counter and hands it to me. "Here you go."

I thank her, and then I quickly turn toward the lounge.

The file feels like it's burning a hole in my hand, but I want to be alone when I look through it. I'm anxious about what I'm going to find, and even more anxious about what I'm going to do once I know. How could I ever keep something like this from Roman, knowing how it eats him up?

When I finally reach the lounge, I shut the door behind me and nearly fall back into my chair. I brace myself before opening it.

At first, it looks like a routine case. While critically injured when she arrived, she was at least stable. They rushed her into emergency surgery to stop the internal bleeding and the surgeon on-call was...Dr. Bauer.

That bastard. He wasn't protecting someone else; he was protecting himself.

I clench my jaw, digging further into the file. Talia's official cause of death was that she lost too much blood, which seems odd for someone who was declared stable. I turn to the medications page and when I do, my heart stops. Why is my signature on this page? Did I—Oh my God.

Things start to come back to me. I had just started my training at St. Luke's with Dr. Bauer as my mentor. It was so early on that I wasn't even cleared to participate in surgery yet, so when he was called into an emergency surgery that day, I had to wait outside. After a few minutes, he asked me to go to the meds station and get a dose of Warfarin. It's a common blood thinner and we use it a lot when we're worried about people getting clots post surgery, but it's the exact opposite of what someone would use when the patient is still actively bleeding. Since I was outside, I didn't know what was happening during the procedure, so I took his word for it. I got the Warfarin and brought it back for him. When

I got back, he swore he had asked me for a clotting medication instead, and said that I must have misheard in the commotion of things. He sent me off to get the right medication, but he kept the Warfarin, and I didn't even think twice about it because I was so embarrassed I messed it up to begin with. Except now, I don't think I messed up at all.

There was no mistake. No miscommunication. It was intentional. No wonder Bauer had tried so hard to hide this from Roman. Bauer meant to *kill* Talia, and I gave him the medication to do it.

I feel sick as I stare at my name on the medicine log. Tears well in my eyes as I realize what this means. I might not have been the one to kill Talia, but if I had paid more attention or taken the meds back myself, or something—*anything*—maybe I could've stopped it.

God, Roman is never going to forgive me.

Chapter Thirty-Eight

Life can be funny.

One minute the thought of getting married again makes you break out in hives, and the next, you meet a woman who has you believe in things like fate and true love.

One minute, work is your safe place, and the next, you're counting down the hours until you can get home to your family.

One minute, you're bashing a guy's skull in to force information out of him, and the next, you're thinking about buying a diamond ring for a girl you can't live without.

After the last couple of weeks, my morning is actually kind of boring. I need to finalize some existing accounts and check in on one of our shipping warehouses. It's the most I've been involved in the daily details for a while, because vengeance has been the only thing on my mind, but things feel different now.

I still want to get this guy. I want him to suffer. I want to watch the life drain from his eyes as he takes his last breath. I want my face to be the last thing he sees on this earth. But being with Maddie has opened my eyes a bit.

The best thing I can give Ty is my time and attention, and I guess witnessing Maddie's relationship with her dad really drove that point home. I want Ty to grow up and know how much I love and support him, and that might mean letting some things go. No amount of revenge will bring my son's mother back, and my obsession with it hasn't helped him at all.

It's time to move on; time to get back to normal. Or, at least, a new normal. One that includes Maddie.

"Damn it!" I hiss, pulling the flaming pan out of the oven. Twenty-seven minutes ago, this was a beautiful salmon filet, and now it's completely unrecognizable.

Fantastic.

I came home early intending to make a nice, romantic dinner for Maddie and I while Ty was at his playdate. Charred fish wasn't what I had in mind, so I guess we'll be settling for take-out again. I've given this cooking thing the whole college try, but it's pretty clear that Maddie is the chef around here.

By the time the front door opens, I've somewhat got the fish smell out and Chinese food on the way.

"Roman?" she calls.

"In the kitchen, babe."

When Maddie comes around the corner, I can't wipe the smile off of my face. Getting to come home to her at the end of the day will never get old.

"Wow! What is all this?" she asks, walking into the kitchen and setting her bag on the counter.

When Maddie won't meet my eyes, I know something is up. Her whole demeanor is off, even the tone of her voice. As she looks away, I can see that her eyes are red and swollen, like she's been crying, and a twinge of fear pulses through me.

"Ty is at a playdate. I thought you and I could have a romantic dinner before we have to go pick him up. I tried to cook, but that was a massive fail, so Chinese is on the way," I say, reaching for her hand. "Everything okay?"

"Yeah." She musters a convincing smile. "That sounds great. Let me just go change."

"Okay, babe."

Everything is clearly not okay, but she doesn't seem like she's ready to talk about it. I want tonight to be relaxing, a break from all the shit that we've been dealing with, so I won't press her on it. Instead, I'll distract her as best I can.

Security brings up the Chinese delivery, and I start to spread it out on the counter. When I move Maddie's bag, a file falls out of it. I bend to pick it up, sweeping the papers back in, but something catches my eye.

Natalia Castillo.

My heart sinks. Holy shit, is this...it can't be. There's no way that Maddie got Talia's file. I thought it was sealed. I thought it was impossible. Why didn't she mention it?

As I flip through it, though, I realize that must have just been more of Bauer's lies, because it's all here. Every last detail. As I read over Talia's injuries, I relive every emotion of that day and my heart nearly stops. Blunt force trauma to the head. Broken ribs. Broken jaw. Strangulation. Blunt force trauma to the abdomen. Each detail is listed off like a shopping list.

I knew all of this, but seeing it in black and white hits me like a fucking wrecking ball. She suffered so much.

Bauer's name is all over the place. The bastard was the one to operate on her, and he lied to me this whole time. He let me think it was someone else, when really, I was staring the monster right in the face every time we spoke.

I clench my jaw, already imagining all the ways I'm going to go after him.

In the back is a log of medications that she was given, and right there in the middle is Maddie's signature. What the hell?

Warfarin. Why did Maddie authorize blood thinners for Talia when she was on an operating table bleeding out? Why was Maddie working on her to begin with? And why the fuck is this the first time I'm learning about it?

"Roman, do you..." Maddie stops dead in her tracks when she sees what I'm looking at.

"What the hell is this, Maddie?" I stand up slowly, afraid of the rush I might get. "You worked on Talia and you didn't tell me?"

She sucks in a sharp breath. "I can explain, Roman."

"You better." I narrow my eyes at her.

Maddie flinches like she's scared of me. "Can we sit down?"

"I'd rather stand." I grit my teeth. "Tell me what the fuck is going on."

"Look, Roman, I...When we first met, I had no clue..."

"Get it out, Maddie. Now." I hate how harsh I sound, but fury and rage wind through me, gripping my mind and my heart like shackles.

"The day that Talia was attacked was my first day at the hospital." Her eyes fill with tears. "Bauer was my mentor, and he was pulled into surgery. I was still so new that I couldn't even be in the operating room, but I waited outside. Bauer asked me to grab some medication about halfway through the surgery."

"The Warfarin."

She nods. "We give Warfarin a lot if we're concerned about clotting, so I didn't think anything of it."

"But Talia wasn't having issues with clots. She was bleeding out." I can barely get the words out as the vice around my lungs tightens.

"Yes, she was. But I wasn't in the operating room, so I didn't know that. I should have double checked or talked to someone else or..." She bites her quivering lip.

"What happened, Madison?"

"I got him the medication, but when I came back, he swore he told me to get something different. Something to clot the blood instead of thin it like she should have had from the beginning. He was angry, acted like *I* messed up, so I rushed back to the pharmacy to get the right medication. I never knew what happened to the Warfarin. At least until I found Talia's file this morning. Bauer gave it to her and she...God, I'm so sorry Roman."

Heavy tears stream down her cheeks, burying her face in her hands.

I can't think. I can't breathe. I can't even fully comprehend what she just said. All I hear is that Bauer killed Talia *on purpose*, and Maddie was involved.

Not just involved, she basically gave him the loaded gun.

I know it's wrong, and I hate myself for feeling that way, but I just can't stop it. I've been killing myself the last several months, trying to find some kind of justice for Talia now...It's all for nothing.

"Please say something, Roman." Maddie sniffles.

I should go to her. I should comfort her. But I can't. I'm frozen in place as my conflicting emotions hold me hostage. This is Maddie—the woman I love and want to spend the rest of my life with. But she had a hand in killing Talia, the mother of my son, and someone I really cared about, too. My heart feels like it's been ripped out of my body and I don't know what to do. So, like usual, I turn to what I'm good at.

"I'm going to find Bauer."

I step towards the door, but she reaches for my wrist. "I know you're upset, but do you think that's a good idea?" she pleads.

I check my arm away from her and recoil. "Now you're defending him? The prick is a monster! He killed my wife, he terrorized my family, and now he's finally going to pay."

"Roman, stop. I'm not defending him, but this isn't..."

"This isn't what, Madison?" I bellow, sweeping my arm across the counter and sending the dishes I had laid out shattering to the ground. "This isn't a good idea? I'm pretty sure that shit went out the window long ago. He killed Talia with drugs that you gave to him. I've waited for this day since I buried my wife, and now that I know the truth..." I shake my head, fighting back my own tears. I'm so blinded by anger and confusion and hurt that I can't make sense of it.

"Please," Maddie begs, staring at me with the same big brown eyes I fell in love with. The lips that I let kiss every inch of me. The hair that has been sprayed across my pillowcase every morning for the last few months. God, how did this happen?

I'm such a fool. This is what I get for falling in love. For thinking I can have a normal life.

"Go to LA, Maddie. Take the job. I think we're done here."

Without another word, I turn and rush out of the house. If I stay in there one more minute, I have no idea what will happen and I can't take that chance right now.

I have to protect my family.

CHAPTER THIRTY-NINE

ROMAN

"YOU KICKED MADDIE OUT?" Joe stares at me like I'm speaking a completely different language as I explain everything to him. I know my anger is so intense that my words sound less like English and more like caveman grunts, but is that really all he got out of that?

"Did you listen to anything I just said? It's been Bauer all along. With medication that Maddie signed off on. I think he's Doc."

"You realize what you're saying here, Roman? You're going to accuse a decorated, respected surgeon of being a part of the criminal organization," Dante clarifies, as if I haven't thought any of this through. I didn't come here for their shitty opinions, just to let them know.

"I'm not just accusing him, Dante. I'm going to make it my life's mission to take that man down."

"Roman, you know none of this is Maddie's fault, right?" Joe rubs his forehead. "Especially if Bauer is the 'Doc' that Ryker was talking about."

Of course, I know that. I know that with every rational bone in my body. That she was played, just like we all were, but it still stings. Maddie didn't deserve my fury, but it was all I felt when I looked at her a few hours ago. It's wrong and misplaced, and I know that better than anyone, but I'm so fucked up that it doesn't even matter.

I've never felt like less of a man than I did when she was standing in the kitchen, clearly torn up about the whole thing, a complete wreck herself. All she needed was for me to tell her I didn't blame her. She wasn't at fault. That I do love her. Instead, I threw out the only person who's ever meant a damn thing to me besides my son.

Honestly, it's probably for the best. I tried to warn her—people around me get hurt. Maddie deserves more than me, and tonight is proof of that. All I did was show her I'm no better than all the shitbag men she's used to, and I pushed her away. Forced her away. Threw her away.

Of all the things I've done to Maddie, this might be the worst.

Joe slides a glass of whiskey my way and I throw it back, almost as quickly as it appeared. If I don't get something to take the edge off soon, I'm going to go out of my mind. "Here's the thing, Roman. Maddie is a good person. Did you ever stop to think why she even had that file in her bag to begin with? She probably went searching for it so she could help *you*. She could have easily hid it from you. She could have gone on like she never found out and, honestly, you probably would have been better off. But she didn't. She knew what it would look like for her, and how angry you'd be, and she told you anyway."

I clench my jaw. It's not fair how right he is. Joe's never been the friend to sugarcoat something to make me feel better. He gives it to me straight, and as painful as it is, that's exactly what I need right now.

"You're right."

"We're going to get Bauer, Roman. I promise you that. But you've got to find a way to fix this with Maddie. You've been a completely different person these last few months. Fun, sarcastic, adventurous...like the guy we used to know and the one your son deserves. Not this angry, impulsive guy who can't even see how badly his son needs him, or how much that woman loves him. She brings out the very best in you, and I know you love her, so why is she taking the brunt of all of this when this wasn't her fault?"

That's a great question. Maybe Maddie was an easy target. Maybe she was there, and I needed someone to lash out at. Or maybe this is something else entirely. Maybe I'm scared about how in love with her I am and maybe this was an easy out. Maybe I reverted to my old ways, and this was my conscience's way of pushing her away.

"She isn't going to want to talk to me after the way I acted tonight." I rub my forehead, replaying the things I said to her. Or more importantly, the things I didn't say.

I'm sorry. It's not your fault. I love you.

"I think that's a decision you should let her make herself." Dante shrugs.

They're right. None of this bullshit matters if Maddie isn't around. She's completely transformed my life, and Ty's life, and I'm a complete moron for casting her aside. Fuck Bauer. All that matters is making sure that Maddie knows this isn't her fault and I'm not upset with her. Obviously. I didn't communicate that the first time we talked and I have to clear the air before it's too late.

Leaving Joe and Dante to track down Bauer, I race back to the house as fast as I can.

"Maddie!" I burst through the front doors. My first stop is the kitchen, as if she'll be in the same place I left her. Instead, the mess has been completely cleaned up and there is no sign of her.

Still calling her name, I head up the stairs, taking them two at a time until I reach the top. "Maddie!"

I throw the door to my bedroom open, and my heart sinks the second I do. All of her stuff is gone. Everything off the nightstand. The clothes that hung over the back of the armchair just this morning. Even her scent is gone. The bathroom is the same way, her side of the counter cleared off.

God, I fucked up so badly this time. I ruined everything.

Just to be sure, I check her old bedroom, but it's dark and empty. *Okay, think, Roman. Where could she have gone?*

She canceled her old apartment lease, so she wouldn't have gone there, and I highly doubt she would run back to her parents. No, she was still in the city somewhere. She has to be. Maybe a hotel or a friend or a coworker from the hospital?

Determined to find her and make this right, I fly back down the stairs right as the doorbell rings.

I'm not expecting anyone, and it's pretty late at night. I get a small glimmer of hope when I think that maybe Maddie left her key, and she was coming back.

It's not Maddie, though. It's two police officers.

"Good evening, Mr. Molinari. Can we come in? There have been a few developments in your wife's case," one of them says with a sympathetic smile.

"Uh, sure." I swallow, moving aside so they can come in. Having police officers in my house is an entirely new concept for me. This will be interesting.

"We wanted to let you know that we have a suspect, and will be making an arrest. It seems the Doctor who treated her at the hospital made a mistake with her medication. We are arresting Greg Bauer for negligent homicide."

It feels like all the air has been sucked out of my lungs. They're actually arresting him. He's going to pay for what he did, and Talia will see some kind of justice. It isn't the justice I would've provided, but maybe that's a good thing. Maybe it's time to finally put all of this to rest and move on with the rest of my life. Just as soon as I find Maddie.

"Thank you so much. That's great news." I smile with relief. Who knew that the police could actually be good for something? "If you don't mind me asking, how did you find out?"

"A woman came to us this evening with the proof that we needed, but we can't give you much more information than that. As soon as we locate Dr. Bauer, he'll be taken into custody," he says politely. "Have a good evening, sir."

Maddie. She must've gone to the police station when she left. That means she's still here, and I have to find her.

CHAPTER FORTY

ROMAN

"HAMBURGERS AGAIN?" TY GLARES at me as if I just put a plate of yesterday's trash in front of him. He shoves it away, sending his tater tots toppling over the edge and onto the table.

I let out a heavy sigh, not having the strength to fight him on this tonight. It's been like this all week, every single thing turning into a fight or battle. When he gets up for school, what he wears, why he can't have candy for breakfast, how quickly he needs to move so we aren't late, who buckles his seat belt, where I drop him off for the day. This is all before nine o'clock in the morning, and it just continues all day until we both collapse into bed at night.

"Bud, please just eat it. I promise tomorrow we'll get pizza or something, but for tonight..." I'm so desperate for him to eat something of value that I bribe him. We can't live like this any longer.

"Maddie says pizza isn't healthy and you should only eat it for special occasions."

"Well, Maddie isn't here, so eat your damn burger." The second it's out of my mouth, I regret it, my frustrations getting the best of me. I rub my forehead. "Ty, I'm sorry, I—"

"I wish you had gone away and not her," he growls, knocking his glass of milk over and tearing out of the room.

"Fuck," I hiss, tossing my plate into the sink and slumping into the chair. I expected it to be rough without Maddie, but this is an absolute disaster. We're way worse off than we were before, and I don't have a lot of fight left in me.

It's been a week since Maddie left. Seven days. One hundred and sixty-eight hours. I guess technically she didn't leave—I kicked her out in what could go down as the most asshole-ish move of my life. Even if I can somehow find her and convince her to talk to me, I'll regret the way I treated her for the rest of my life. I've spent every one of those ten thousand four hundred and sixteen seconds trying to track her down, and so far I have nothing. I have less than nothing.

Maddie turned off her cell phone, closed every account in Nevada she had, and if she's still in the city, she isn't using her real name to stay at any hotels. She evaporated into thin air and it's really starting to piss me off.

And apparently Ty feels the same.

I told him that she took the job in LA, but he's a smart kid. He knows something happened between us and he blames me. He should, of course, but it's still hard to stomach. My son hates me, the girl I'm in love with is gone, and the one mission that has defined me the last few months is over. I'm about to throw myself the world's biggest pity party when I hear Ty shrieking from his bedroom.

Bolting from my seat, I rush to him and find him curled up on his bed in the fetal position. He's clutching his stomach, rocking back and forth, moaning in pain.

"What is it? What's wrong, Ty?" I kneel on the floor next to him.

"My stomach hurts." He sobs.

When I reach for him, he recoils away. "Can you show me where, buddy?"

Ty points to his stomach in no specific area, just writhing around on the bed.

A thousand possibilities run through me. An appendicitis? Complication from his wounds? All the junk food I've bribed him with the last few days? It could be many things. Fuck, I wish Maddie was here. I don't want to overreact, but he's in so much pain that I can't ignore it. It's after hours at his pediatrician, so now I'm left with only one option—St. Luke's.

"Okay, come on, bud." I scoop him up into my arms and carry him to the truck. He groans, still holding his stomach the entire way there, and even as we go inside.

There is a check-in desk at the front of the Emergency Room and I start there.

"Good evening, sir. How can I help you?" the bright-eyed receptionist asks.

"My son is having severe stomach pain, and he needs to be checked out," I say. Ty lays his head on my shoulder, a little calmer, but still whimpering softly.

"Absolutely," she says. "I just need you to fill out a bit of paperwork and we'll get someone to see him right away."

I take the clipboard from her and fill the forms out quickly. Within just a few minutes, she leads us back to a room, and I lay him on the bed to rest. His stomach doesn't seem to bother him as much now that we're here, which is strange considering how severe his pain was just minutes ago.

"Good evening, I'm—Oh, Roman. Hi." Maddie's friend Peyton comes into the room and washes her hands.

"Hi Peyton," I stumble. "This is my son, Ty. He's having some stomach pain."

"I see." She smiles at me, and then sits next to Ty. "Hey there, little man. My name is Peyton and I'm a nurse here. I'm going to do a quick exam if that's okay with you, and hopefully we can figure out what's going on with your tummy."

When she reaches for him, Ty jerks away.

"Actually..." Ty's eyes fill with guilt, and he looks at me like he's about to cry. What the hell? "Daddy, I'm sorry. My tummy doesn't hurt. I just thought Maddie would be here and..."

He dissolves into tears, burying his face in my chest.

Peyton raises her eyebrows as we glance at each other, a small smile on her lips. "Oh."

"What?" I can hardly believe what I'm hearing. I just got thoroughly played by my six-year-old, and if I wasn't so embarrassed, this might be funny. *Might.*

Jesus Christ.

"Ty, this is serious. There are people here who really need help, and you know you're not supposed to lie."

"I know, Daddy," he pouts, eyes cast down as I scold him.

"Peyton, I am so sorry. We'll definitely be having a discussion about this at home." I rub my forehead. "I'm sorry we wasted your time."

She gives me a warm, understanding smile. "It's really okay, Roman. I get it. Change is tough."

Yeah, no kidding. Ty is still in trouble, but now that the urgency has passed, I won't let an opportunity pass without asking her about Maddie.

"Do you think we could talk in the hallway for a minute?"

"Of course." She nods. "I'm glad you're feeling better, Ty. It was nice to meet you."

Peyton and I head out of the room, and I latch the door behind me. I don't expect Ty to cause any more mischief, but I didn't expect him to try to set me up, either.

"I know what you're going to ask me, Roman." Peyton puts her hands on her hips.

"I just want to talk to her, Peyton. Is she in tonight?"

She shakes her head. "No, she isn't with the hospital anymore. When she found out the truth about Dr. Bauer, she went straight to the authorities. There were no charges filed against her, because she was just a trainee, but the board asked her to leave the hospital."

Fuck. I run my fingers through my hair in frustration. She threw herself under the bus to make sure I got the justice I was looking for. Rejecting the opportunity in LA meant that she'd have nowhere to turn, and yet she went to the police, anyway.

"Do you know where she's staying? I've been trying to find her all week."

"I wish I could help you, Roman, but I can't."

"Look, Peyton, I know you're just looking out for your friend and that you want to protect her. I get it. But you have to trust me. All I want to do is apologize. I fucked up the best thing in my entire life and I'm willing to do anything I have to do to get her back. *Anything.* And I know if she could just hear me out, she would feel the same. Please. I'm begging you, please just give me an address."

Peyton studies me carefully, trying to determine whether or not she's gonna give me what I want. "She'll kill me if she knows I did this for you."

"I'm not trying to hurt her, Peyton," I plead. "And if she doesn't want to see me, I'll let it go. But I at least have to try."

"Fine." She lets out a heavy breath. "All I know is that she's going to be here tomorrow around lunchtime to clean out her locker. I don't know where she's staying, so that's your only opportunity."

I can't wipe the smile off of my face. I'm not too late. I still have a chance to make this right. "Thank you so much, Peyton. You have no idea how much I appreciate..."

"Yeah, yeah. Just don't make me regret it." She smirks. "And don't give your son a hard time about lying. I think it's pretty sweet that he's so determined to get the two of you back together."

"I'll see you tomorrow." I chuckle.

It is pretty sweet how much Ty loves her. I just hope I don't screw this up again.

CHAPTER FORTY-ONE

Madison

"ARE YOU SURE YOU have to go?" Peyton squeezes my shoulders tightly, locking me into a hug and refusing to let go of me.

"It's not like I'm leaving forever. You can come visit me whenever you want!" I insist, trying to ease her mind a bit. Peyton's become somewhat of a mother hen towards me, and I know she's worried about me moving to San Francisco. She's been constantly trying to change my mind since I told her, but at this point I'm set.

The last few days have been rough. When I told Roman about my part in Talia's death, I was a little disappointed in his reaction. It's not like I was expecting his gratitude or even his acceptance, but I also wasn't expecting him to be so harsh either. Regardless, I knew I needed to make it right, so when Roman kicked me out, I went straight to the police and gave them everything I had. By the end of our conversation, they said they had enough to put Bauer away for murder and a host of other charges. It's a small consolation, but it's the only thing I have left to give Roman and Ty.

Coming clean to the police also meant that the hospital board was made aware of what happened, and they politely asked me to leave. Even without a plan, I was happy to, because so much about this hospital—medicine in general—has been ruined for me. I wanted to help people, and instead, I was part of a murder. One that I knew about, at least. God only knew what else Bauer did. In my heart, I know it isn't my fault, but I still feel partly responsible and I know I'll never be able to completely shake that feeling.

My first call was to the doctor who runs the LA program, but they'd already filled the fast track position. Instead, he gave me the number of a friend of his who runs a trauma center in San Francisco. It won't be as fast-paced, but I can start right away and the best part is, it has nothing to do with my dad or with Bauer. Putting some distance between me and Roman sounds pretty good, too.

I love him, more than I even want to admit, and cutting him and Ty out of my life will be torturous, but in the long run, it's for the best. I'll just be a painful reminder to them.

"I know," Peyton whines, finally pulling away. "I'm just going to miss you."

"I'm going to miss you, too." I sigh, letting my new reality sink in.

It's going to be tough starting over. I have friends here in Vegas, I have a life here, and now I'm picking up and moving to another state, without much of a plan. The girl I was a few months ago wouldn't even recognize me now. I showed up in Vegas with my life completely planned out—my job, my career path. I thought I had it all together. And now, I'm leaving with no idea what the rest of my life will look like. It was a little exciting, but mostly terrifying. "I just think it's best for me to get out of here for a while."

"Because of Roman?" She arches her eyebrow at me.

"No, not because of Roman," I lie. "Just because, okay?"

"He was here looking for you last night."

My heart nearly stopped. He was looking for me? "He was here? At the hospital?"

She nods. "Well, actually, Ty faked a stomach sickness to get Roman to bring him here so he could ask about you. He really wants to talk to you, Maddie. I think you're making a mistake by not doing that before you go."

I can't help but laugh at Ty's attempt to take matters into his own hands. I didn't get to say goodbye, and the poor kid was probably confused and hurt.

It's so sweet that it almost makes me cry, but I take a deep breath and push the thought away.

Of course I want to talk to Roman. I want him to forgive me and tell me he doesn't blame me and that nothing has changed between us. But hearing those words will only make leaving harder. "Peyton, I think it's best if I just go at this point. It's too complicated right now and I don't want to hurt him or Ty worse than I already have."

"But Maddie, you haven't hurt them. I got the impression that he just wants to make things right with you. He loves you, Mads, and you leaving isn't going to help things, it's going to make things harder on you both," she persists.

"I appreciate the thought, but I don't think—"

All of a sudden, an alarm blares over the loudspeaker. "Attention all staff, we have a Code Black. Please adhere to department evacuation plans immediately."

"Stupid kids." Peyton rolls her eyes. "Do you know this is the third time this month we've had a fake bomb threat? Every time I take all my patients out, then back in, just to find out it's a bunch of dumb high school kids that think they're funny."

"Attention all staff, we have a Code Black. Please adhere to department evacuation plans immediately," the speaker repeats.

"How about I help you get your patients out for old time's sake?" I offer with a smile. I know how irritating things like this are. It happens a lot in Las Vegas because the city is a breeding ground for crazies. It never amounts to anything more than an annoyance for hospital staff and a fun trip outside for the patients.

"You're an angel. I'm supposed to clear the third floor. Why don't you take that one and I'll get the rest?"

"You got it."

"I owe you!" she yells over her shoulder and heads down the hall.

Many of the patients can walk out on their own, and our job is just to assist and direct them to the evacuation route. I take the stairs to the third floor and start scanning rooms. The third floor is post-op recovery, so it'll be pretty empty at this time of day. I check each room, but quicken my pace when I hear a little girl crying down the hall.

I get to the last room on the right and open the door. "Is everything—"

My eyes widen as I process the scene before me. A little girl, about ten, sits next to the window, tears dripping down her cheeks. Bauer stands behind her, holding onto a ticking backpack. A timer on the front reads 15:48 and it's continuously counting down.

"Well, if this isn't just divine intervention." His face curls into a sickening smile. "I had no idea you were going to be here today, but it just makes it all that much sweeter."

"Dr. Bauer, what are you doing?" I ask, taking cautious steps into the room with my hands up.

"Don't come any closer, Madison. One push of this button and the three of us and this entire building go out with a bang."

The little girl starts to wail, his words terrifying her.

"It's okay, sweetie." I reach out, trying to soothe her. "That's not going to happen. He's going to let you out of here, aren't you, Bauer?"

My heart thunders in my chest, but I try as hard as I possibly can to remain calm.

"Now, why would I do that?" he snickers.

"Because this isn't about her. It's about you and me and this hospital. It has nothing to do with her."

"Shut up," he hisses. "It's your fault we're in this mess to begin with. If you had just let things play out as they should have, none of this would have ever happened. You would be on your way to LA and I would be well on my way to tenure. But you had to go and open your big mouth."

"Bauer, you need to let her go, and then you and I can have this conversation," I say quietly, careful not to escalate him even further.

"You chose a criminal over your career, your family. Everything!" he continues, ignoring anything that I have to say.

"I did what was right, Dr. Bauer. Talia's death was—"

"An unfortunate side effect," he interjects. "But it was a piece of something much bigger than you could ever imagine."

"What are you talking about?"

He throws his head back and cackles; the sound making me sick to my stomach. I use the opportunity to move a bit closer to the little girl, who's staring wide-eyed at me in complete terror. "Oh Madison, I really appreciate your naivety, but it's getting old. Roman started this war a long time ago, and it's time I finish it. I thought I had shut him down with Talia, but then I found out that he was dating you...derailing everything I had worked so hard for."

"I don't understand."

"Of course you don't." He rolls his eyes. "Well, let me spell it out for you. Before your boyfriend moved into town, I ran the top drug ring in the region. Not that hard to do when you're a respected doctor." He chuckles to himself. "I had the entire area cornered, and then came Roman Molanari, Mr. Holier-than-thou, and his crusade to take the drugs off the streets. He thinks he's better than me because his group doesn't deal drugs, but he's just as much at fault. What does he think his clients do with the guns they buy from him? Target shooting? Roman came in here and my business plummeted. Everyone was too scared to cross him with his Italian Mafia ties. I thought if I could just force him out, we'd be back on track. I nearly did it too, when his kid got shot. But then Roman met you and, of course, the stone-cold mafia leader gets heart eyes for a resident in my program. It's almost laughable."

"It was you all along," I say breathlessly. Everything begins to click. Bauer was after us all along in his attempt to force Roman out.

He narrows his eyes at me. "My last ditch effort was to get you to go to LA. I saw him with you that day, and I knew he was falling for you. That this was my chance and he might follow you out there. So I called your dad and raved about how amazing you were doing. I couldn't tell him the truth, of course, but it got the job done, and he made some calls. You can imagine how surprised I was to hear you turn down the job."

"You're disgusting." I glare, tears stinging my eyes. "You're going to rot in jail for all of this."

"I'd have to be alive in order for them to throw me in jail, Madison." He smirks. "And neither of us are walking out of here alive."

CHAPTER FORTY-TWO

ROMAN

I WATCH TY CAREFULLY as he takes a bite of his waffle. The kid has a killer poker face, but he hasn't stopped eating since I set them in front of him and that's more than he's done the last few mornings.

Determined to win back both my son and my girl, I got up early this morning. I worked out, showered, shaved, and whipped out a cookbook to teach myself how to make waffles. This is the only chance I've got, so I'm pulling out all the stops.

I don't have much of a plan, except to sit there until she agrees to hear me out. I want to make sure she knows how much I love her and that I'll do absolutely anything for her to stay. I want her to know that I don't blame her, and that nothing about what happened changed my feelings for her. If she still wants to leave after that, at least I know I did what I could to get her to stay.

Right now, I'm not sure if Maddie or Ty will be harder to win over.

"So?"

Ty finishes chewing and shrugs his shoulders. "They're alright. Not like Maddie's, but you're making progress."

"I'll take it." I chuckle, ruffling Ty's hair. "Are you going to be okay with Joe and Sarah today?"

Ty nods, wiggling out of my reach. "Are you going to make up with Maddie?"

"I'm sure going to try, bud."

"Don't be an ass to her again." He narrows his eyes on me.

I bit my lip to keep my laughter in. "Hey, watch your mouth."

"You say it all the time."

"Well, I'm a grownup, and that's a grownup word. Don't let me hear you say that again," I warn.

Ty rolled his eyes, reaching for another waffle.

"Who's ready for some paintball?" Joe calls from the foyer.

"Paintball?" Ty's face lights up, abandoning his breakfast.

"Hell yeah! Dante is going to meet us with his nephew so your dad can get some work done today." He winks at me.

"So you're the one teaching him all the curse words?" I toss Ty's plate into the sink. "Why don't you go get your shoes on, buddy?"

"First of all, I don't want to be blamed for Ty's language. You've got a filthy mouth." Joe chuckles, handing me a piece of paper. "Second of all, I have some information you might find interesting."

I read it then glance up at him. "Maddie's job offer?"

He nods. "I did a little digging. Bauer called in a favor to get her transferred out of here and away from you."

"I thought her dad was responsible?"

"Technically, he's the one who called in the favor, but Bauer called him to make it happen." Joe scratches his chin. "What do you want to do about it?"

I think for a second, and an idea hits me. "Russ has done enough time in the cage. I think I have a better idea for him now."

"Yeah?"

"Let's get him picked up for something so that he can take care of Bauer in jail."

Joe chuckles. "I'm guessing you know Russ already has two felonies and they throw the book at him if he gets a third."

"That's too bad." I shrug. Honestly, the guy is lucky to be alive after trying to steal from us. Although he might not feel the same way when he's serving a life sentence.

"Creative. I love it."

Joe's gaze darts over my shoulder at the TV and his face turns white.

"What?" I ask, turning and seeing a picture of the hospital on the news. "What is that?"

I point the remote at the TV and turn the volume up.

"Breaking news, out of Las Vegas now. A bomb threat has been called in to the local hospital and staff and patients are being evacuated. Police are asking the public to avoid the area and proceed to the evacuation site to reunite with their loved ones who are at the hospital."

"Is that..."

"Maddie's there," I say flatly, staring at the screen. It takes me a few seconds to gain my bearings, but when I do, I grab my keys and take off towards the door, not even bothering to tell Joe what I'm doing. All I can think about is getting to her. I won't be able to breathe until I do.

I get there in record time, throwing my truck into park and racing toward the building. Everything is blocked off with police tape, but I run full steam ahead, with no regard to where police are trying to direct me.

"Sir, you can't go in there." An officer tries to block me.

I jerk away from him. "My girlfriend is in there!"

"Sir, I understand, but we're working on getting everyone out of the building right now. You can meet your girlfriend over at the reunification site."

I glance where she points, but there's no sight of Maddie. I know if there are still patients inside, that's where she'll be. I make a split-second decision to go in after her, brushing past the officer and entering the hospital. I've got to find Maddie and get her out of here.

"You can't just go in there! Sir!"

By the time I get inside, most of the first floor is empty, but I run into Peyton, who's wheeling a bed outside.

"Peyton!" I jog towards her. "Have you seen Maddie?"

"She's helping me evacuate patients on the third floor." Peyton's tone is tight. "Roman, I think there might really be a bomb. This isn't like the other times that we had threats. Maddie thinks it's a prank."

"I'll find her, I promise," I say, squeezing Peyton's shoulder and heading towards the stairwell. I take them three at a time until I get to the third floor.

"Maddie?" I call down the empty hallway. There's no response, so I make my way from room to room as quickly as possible.

"Maddie, are you up here?"

Still no response.

"Come on, Maddie." I'm almost to the last room, and at this point I have no idea what I'll do if I don't find her. I start to panic a little. If this really is a bomb...

My heart lurches as I look into the last room. Maddie stands in the center of the room, between a little girl and Dr. Bauer. There's a backpack with wires poking out of it at his feet, and I see a digital clock ticking down with each passing second.

Son of a bitch.

"Well, it looks like the gang's all here." Bauer gets a sinister grin on his face. "This just keeps getting better."

Maddie gives me a desperate look as we lock eyes.

"Are you okay?" I ask, stepping into the room.

She nods, biting her lip with tears in her eyes. All I want is to reach out for her and hold her in my arms, to comfort her and to protect her, but Bauer has all the power here and he knows it. The little girl behind Maddie is bawling, terrified of what is about to happen.

"Look, I'm sure we can work all of this out." I turn back towards Bauer cautiously.

"We're not working anything out, Roman. I was just explaining to your sweet little girlfriend here that no one is walking out of here alive. We're way past that. But if it makes you feel any better, you'll both die here together."

"Dr. Bauer, please," Maddie begs. The look in her eyes shatters my heart. "This is between us. You and me and Roman. Please let her go."

"I'll stay in her place, Bauer," I offer myself up. "There's no sense in hurting an innocent little girl. I'll stay here and do whatever you want."

Bauer chuckles to himself. "I'm not a completely unreasonable man. If you stay, she can go."

"Okay." Maddie sucks in a sharp breath of relief, kneeling in front of the little girl. "Okay, sweetie. Do you think you can get outside by yourself?" Maddie's maternal instinct kicks in and she wipes away at the girl's tears.

"Not without you." The girl continues to cry, clutching Maddie's hand.

"I can't go with you right now, but I promise, when all this is over, I'll come meet you outside and everything will be okay."

"Don't make promises you can't keep," Bauer growls. "Get her out of here before I change my mind."

Quickly, I assess Bauer and try to figure out what exactly I'm dealing with. I can see the bomb, and if I don't move soon, he's right—no one will be leaving here alive. I inch my way toward him while he's distracted by Maddie and the girl.

His hand is on a trigger, and if I tackle him, it will come off. More than likely, that will blow the entire place up. I have to avoid that at all costs, but I have no idea how.

"The elevator is right down the hallway," Maddie tells the little girl. "Do you know how to get it open?"

She nods. "I always press it when I come here with Mommy."

"That's so fun," Maddie chokes, biting back her tears. "You get inside that elevator, just like you do with your mommy, and you press the L button. Can you remember that?"

"I think so."

"I know you can," Maddie assures her, squeezing the girl's shoulders and forcing a brave smile. "Now go. Run as fast as you can, okay?"

The little girl takes one last look at Maddie and disappears out the door. We're all silent until we hear the doors of the elevator close. It's just the three of us now.

"Bauer, I'm the one you really want, right? It's my fault you lost business. My fault Maddie didn't follow your plan. This whole thing is on me. Let Maddie go, then you and I can settle this like men."

Bauer eyes me carefully. "What you said is true Roman—this is about you. But I know I can cause you the greatest pain in your life by taking Maddie's right in front of you, knowing there is nothing you can do about it."

Bauer is out of his mind, and there is no reasoning with him right now. I'm going to have to take this by force if we have any hope of making it out alive. And just in case it goes badly, I turn to Maddie, ready to bear my soul.

"Maddie," I say softly. "I'm sorry, baby."

Tears spring to her eyes again.

"I don't blame you for what happened. I was angry, and I said some things I shouldn't have, but I love you. I love you more than anything, and I came here today to tell you that." My voice breaks with emotion. "You're all that matters to me, Maddie. You and Ty."

She nods, a gentle smile on her face. "I love you, too, Roman. So much."

"This is all very touching, but you're running out of time." Bauer rolls his eyes.

He's right. With only three minutes left on the timer, it's now or never.

"Run, Maddie."

"What?" Her brow furrows.

"Now, Maddie. Run!"

She glances at me for a second, debating what to do. I give her a pleading look, and seconds later, she takes off out of the room.

"Shouldn't have done that..." Bauer is halfway through his sentence when I lunge at him.

Gripping his shoulders, I wrestle with him violently for a few seconds before shoving him backwards. It seems like everything moves in slow motion and then it all happens at once. I'm not even sure which comes first, but as I shove Bauer backwards, his finger comes off the trigger remote and the two of us crash through the window.

Glass shatters all around us as we collapse on the rooftop below, both reeling from the fall.

I look up at the window we'd just fallen out of, helpless as the entire hospital goes up in a cloud of smoke.

Chapter Forty-Three

ROMAN

I'VE EXPERIENCED PAIN IN my life.

There was the time Emmett dared me to jump off a swing in our backyard when I was seven, and I splintered the bone in my leg so badly that shards of it were poking through the skin. I've been captured by an enemy, and for twenty-eight hours, I was beaten with a pillowcase full of bars of soap until I was absolutely senseless. And once when I was a teenager, my dad took me ice fishing in Northern Canada. I fell through the ice and the brutal frigidity of the water felt like one thousand knives stabbing every inch of my skin.

Those were all painful experiences, but nothing compares to the feeling of watching someone you love and care about hurting and not being able to do a damn thing about it.

The influx of displaced patients and doctors overwhelmed area hospitals, forcing the transport of serious cases to better-equipped cities. Maddie was flown to Denver, and as soon as I was cleared, I came to her. I've sat next to her bedside for the last three days, listening to the hum of the machines she's connected to and praying that today is the day she wakes up.

After she left the room, Maddie must have known she wasn't going to make it down from the third floor in time, so instead of heading for the stairwell, she ran in the opposite direction and ducked under the desk at the nurses' station. No one expected the explosion to be as big and destructive as it was, so she probably thought she could shield herself from some of the debris there. Thankfully, she had the peace of mind to think of that, because the stairwell completely collapsed. Her quick thinking saved her life. I can't even bring myself to think about what might have happened if she was in the stairwell when it came down or trapped on the elevator when it happened.

Everything seemed to happen in slow motion once Bauer and I crashed through the window. There are parts I remember so vividly it's like I'm playing back a movie, but other parts are so hazy I'm not even sure they happened at all. I don't know how I got to the triage area, but after the explosion, the first thing I could remember was sitting in the tent being checked out by one of the nurses. I remember asking for Maddie about a dozen times, but no one would tell me what was going on. I wasn't sure how much time passed, but eventually, Peyton came to find me. She told me they found Maddie, but they were taking her to a different hospital, which made no sense to me at the time. All I wanted was to see her, but I didn't have the chance before they loaded her into the medicopter and headed for Denver.

When they made me stay for observation, I was irritated, but soon found out it was more about clearing me in the investigation into Bauer. Once they were satisfied I wasn't working with him and he'd done this on his own, I was cleared. I was optimistic about Maddie, but it all faded once I got to Denver. She was in bad shape and hadn't improved much at all in the thirty-six hours since the bombing.

I had to lie to the nurses and tell them she was my fiancé to get any kind of information about her, but I didn't think twice about it. They wouldn't release medical information to me because we weren't technically family, so I didn't have a choice.

Maddie has several fractured ribs, a collapsed lung, internal bleeding, and her left leg is broken in three places. The worst of her injuries though, and why she is still unconscious, is the small bleed in her brain. Right now, they can't tell how extensive it was because of the swelling, but from their imaging and tests, it looks like it's at least been contained—it's not getting any worse, but it's also not getting any better. I guess that's as good as anything right now. It means that her body is trying to heal, and we will hopefully know more soon.

Her doctor warned me about all the possibilities. That she might not remember anything when she wakes up. That she might need months of rehab and therapy to regain simple skills and movements. That she might not wake up at all.

I can't let myself consider that possibility, though. I know in my heart that she's going to wake up, and she's going to be okay. That I'll see her beautiful eyes again and hear her sweet voice. I have faith that soon I'll be taking her back to Las Vegas, where she and Ty and I will be a family.

Ty didn't know the details of the explosion, which is a minor miracle considering how much the news channels have covered it. My brother flew in to stay with him for a few days and Ty's been thoroughly distracted by his excitement to see his uncle. It temporarily took his mind off of things, but it's just a matter of time before he starts asking questions and hopefully when he does, I'll have some answers.

Bauer survived the explosion, but was taken into custody immediately. I would have preferred him to have been blown to bits, but I know that he'll get exactly what's coming to him. There's a moral code in prison, and people like Bauer don't stand a chance.

I rub my forehead, leaning back into the recliner and settling in for another long night in the ICU. Maddie's hooked up to so many machines that every twenty minutes or so, an alarm goes off and a nurse has to come in and check it. Most of the time, it's just faulty tape or a disconnection, which makes the interruption pointless. I've barely left this chair for longer than it takes to get a cup of coffee or use the restroom, so I've gotten to know the nurses pretty well.

"Mr. Molanari?" One of them peeks her head in the door. This one is here a lot, but I can't remember her name. All I know her by is her rainbow stethoscope.

I give her a polite wave, but don't say anything.

"I just wanted to let you know that someone delivered breakfast burritos this morning, and there are a few left over at the nurses' station. They're cold and possibly stale by now, but if you'd like one, you're welcome to them."

I run my fingers through my hair, shaking my head. "Thank you, but I'm okay. I'll go get something from the cafeteria in a little while."

She lets out a small laugh. "You said that last night, but I have it on good authority that you didn't leave the floor." She smiles, letting herself inside the room. "You know, you sitting here is not going to make her wake up any faster. She needs time. Let her body work its magic."

"I know," I assure her, not really in the mood for company. "But I want to be here when she wakes up. She'll be confused, and I want to be the one to explain it to her."

"That's very sweet of you. But you should take care of yourself as well," she insists. I humor her only because I need her help.

"I am taking care of myself, but I appreciate the concern. If you want to be helpful, you could find out for me if anyone has contacted her parents."

She clicks her tongue. "You know I'm not supposed to give you that information, but I'll see what I can do."

"Thank you." I smile. I know she can't tell me. They'd been telling me that since I got here, but at least it'll keep her busy for a while.

I've been anxious about Maddie's family showing up since the moment I arrived. I'd assume the hospital has been in contact with them or they've seen it on the news, but as time goes on and they don't show up, I start to second guess that.

Obviously, her dad is an irredeemable asshole, but I'd expect at least her mom and brothers. I don't pretend to understand family dynamics, but there's nothing in the world that could keep me away if my brother was in the hospital.

As I stand to stretch my legs, Maddie's heart monitor starts to beep faster. I snap my neck in her direction, watching for any sign of movement. Is that...No, it's just wishful thinking.

Wait. Slowly, her fingers wiggle and I race to the side of the bed, taking her hand in mine. The nurses hear the beeping as well and the room gets crowded.

"Is everything..." Rainbow stethoscope starts.

The words aren't even out of her mouth when Maddie's eyelids flutter. After a few seconds, she opens them and blinks several times. Her lips part and she moans gently.

I put my hand to her cheek, tears pooling in my eyes. "Hi baby," I whisper, completely overcome with relief. She's awake. After all the unknown and worry, she's awake, and whatever comes next, we'll deal with it together.

Maddie moans again, unable to speak with the tube in her throat.

"Sir, I am going to need you to step outside for a second," one of her doctors says, stepping in front of me and adjusting something on Maddie.

"Can't I just—"

"Mr. Molanari, the doctor is going to take the breathing tube out and then you can come right back in." Rainbow Stethoscope smiles.

Unsure, I step back and let them do their jobs as Maddie locks eyes on me. All the other possibilities the doctor told me flood my mind. Does she even recognize me? Is she trying to figure out who I am?

"Madison, my name is Dr. Talbert. Can you hear me?"

Maddie nods her head, watching as I walk outside.

It's torturous to stand out here and not know what is going on inside her room. I want to be there with her. I want to know if she's okay.

After about fifteen agonizing minutes, they let me back in. The doctor is standing next to the bed talking to Maddie.

"I need water," she says softly, a flicker of relief in her eyes when I come back into the room.

"I'll get it," I jump in, desperate to take care of her.

Dr. Talbert nods. "Do you know why you're here, Madison?"

"I...I think..." She glances at me as if looking for reassurance. "There was an explosion."

With all the awful outcomes the doctor prepared me for, even those words out of her mouth are like music to my ears. She remembers.

"That's right." He smiles. "There was an explosion at your hospital in Las Vegas. We brought you here to recover in Denver, and that's where you've been the last few days."

Maddie is quiet, letting everything sink in as he talks.

"You've got some pretty extensive injuries and we're going to have to talk about recovery, but I'm sure you two are anxious to catch up, so I'm going to let you rest for a bit and then I'll be back. Sound okay?"

"Thank you." She nods with a small smile on her lips.

Dr. Talbert and the nurses leave, and then Maddie and I are alone.

There are ten thousand things I want to say, but when I open my mouth to speak, nothing comes out. Instead, Maddie speaks first.

"You're okay." She shifts, adjusting her weight in the bed.

I let out a sharp laugh. "I'm okay? You're the one in a hospital bed right now."

"When I left the room, I didn't think I was ever going to see you again."

"I'm right here, baby." I walk over and sit next to her on the bed, pressing a kiss to the back of her hand. "You're not going to get rid of me that easily."

"I'm not sure I'd call a psychopath with a bomb easy..." Maddie smirks, and then her face softens. "Roman, I never really got to tell you how sorry I am for what..."

I shake my head before she can continue. "I don't want to talk about it. You have nothing to be sorry for. I am the one who should be sorry. I acted like a complete fool and I almost lost you because of it. I'm the one that fucked up, and I hope you'll forgive me and give me another chance."

"Of course I will."

"I swear to God I'll spend the rest of my life making it up to you if you'll let me." I grin, kissing her forehead. It's like I can't stop touching her, like I'm trying to convince myself she's real and this isn't all a dream.

"I think I'll enjoy watching you try." Even lying in a hospital bed, she's still got her feisty spirit. "Where is Ty?"

"He's back in Las Vegas with Emmett. They airlifted you to Denver after the explosion and I came as soon as I could." I put my arm behind her and pull her toward me so that her head rests on my chest, careful not to jostle her too much. If all the movement hurts her, she doesn't let on, snuggling into me.

"Your brother?"

I nod. "He came when he got word of the explosion. He's looking forward to meeting you."

"And Bauer?" She stiffens.

"He survived the blast, but he was arrested immediately. You don't need to worry about him anymore."

"I just can't believe he would do something like that. He dedicated his entire career to that hospital." She shakes her head in disbelief.

Well, half of his career. The other half was as a drug dealer.

"He's a sick man, Maddie. Nothing he did makes sense," I assure her. "This has been going on for years, and there's no way you could have known."

"How many people were killed?"

I hesitate before telling her, knowing it certainly won't make her feel any better. She'll find out eventually, though, and it's better that it comes from me. "Ten. A doctor, two nurses, and seven patients."

Maddie closes her eyes tightly, biting her lip.

I press a kiss to the top of her head. "Maddie, I want you to put Bauer out of your mind. He's not going to be a problem for us anymore, I swear."

"I'll do my best." She sighs. "You know what would help?"

"I like where your head's at, but I don't think we can get away with having sex in here. Trust me, the nurses are in here all the time." I give her a cheesy wink.

"Hmm, that sounds good, but I was actually thinking something more along the lines of ice cream. Cookies and cream, to be exact." She tilts her head up and catches my gaze.

"I'll tell you what," I say with a chuckle. "I'll go down to the cafeteria and try to sneak some up if you promise to stop thinking about Bauer."

"Deal."

"I'll be back in a few minutes. Do you need anything else while I'm gone?" I ask, prying myself away from her. I really don't want to leave, but I'd do just about anything she asked of me.

"Nope. Just the ice cream."

"Easy enough." I give her one last kiss. "I love you, Maddie."

"I love you, too."

I slip out the door, shutting it behind me and nearly running into someone as I do.

"Oh, I'm so sorry. I didn't—"

He stops when he sees me, and a wicked chill winds through me when I realize who it is.

Maddie's dad is here.

Chapter Forty-Four

FEW THINGS ARE AS deflating as seeing the man who hurt the woman you love outside her hospital room.

The timing really could not be worse.

"Roman. Hi." He trips over the words, just as startled to see me as I am to see him.

"Hello." I clench my jaw. For Maddie's sake, I try to keep it civil. A scene will only stress her out more, and she needs to relax in peace and quiet.

At the moment, I'm not sure which thing I hate him for most—working with Bauer to fabricate a position for Maddie, showing up three days late to see his ailing daughter, or just the all around shitty way he treats her.

"Uh, I came by to see—"

"Mr. Molanari?" The nurse from earlier comes toward us. "Someone will be down to take your fiancé in about thirty minutes. Dr. Talbert wants to do a scan just to be sure everything looks okay."

Fuck.

"Oh...Okay. I'll let her know." I nod, noticing how Mark perks up at the word *fiancé*.

The nurse smiles, turning on her heels and heading back towards the nurses' station.

"Fiancé?" He raises his eyebrow at me. "You and Maddie are engaged?"

Now what the hell am I supposed to do? I told the nurses, so they'd give me information, and at this point, I just have to go with it.

"Yeah. We are."

"Wow." He lets out a labored breath, sliding down into one of the chairs in the hallway. "I didn't even...she didn't tell me."

I let out a sharp laugh. "I don't blame her. It's not like you're the most supportive person in her life."

Jesus, Roman. I grit my teeth before I can dig myself into an even deeper hole.

"You're right," he says as I sit down. "I haven't been a good father to Maddie for a long time. Maybe not ever."

"Why did it take you three days to get here?"

He swallows, gripping the arm of the chair. "It took me a while to find out where they took her after the explosion, but I got here yesterday. I've been trying to work up the nerve to come speak to her after the way I've been acting."

I remain silent. If he's fishing for sympathy, he won't find it with me. He acts how he does and then doesn't even have the balls to face her? If it was up to me, I'd send the bastard back to St. Louis right this second.

"Is she..."

"She's awake," I say. "But she's in rough shape. Fractured ribs, collapsed lung, broken leg...She just barely regained consciousness this evening."

"Jesus." He runs his fingers through his hair, lip quivering. "Roman, you and I have a lot to talk about, but I'd like to go see my daughter if that's okay."

"It's not okay with me, but fortunately for you, it's up to Maddie. And just to be clear, if she doesn't want you here, you're gone. No questions asked."

"Thank you. I won't be long."

We stand, and I gently knock on the door. "Maddie?"

"You're back with ice cream already? You're my hero!" She smiles, looking over towards the door.

"Uh, actually. I ran into someone in the hallway. You have a visitor." I move to the side, revealing her father standing behind me.

Maddie's eyes widen and she glances between the two of us.

"Dad." Her voice breaks.

"Hi sweetheart." Mark smiles sheepishly. Good. He should feel fucking ashamed. It isn't enough to be an asshole, but he has to be a coward, too.

I put my hand on her shoulder protectively. "He wants to talk to you for a few minutes. Are you okay with that?" I ask, hoping she'll tell me to kick him out. That's something I'll gladly take pleasure in.

"Sure."

"You're sure?" I ask.

"Yeah. I'll be fine, Roman. I promise."

"Okay." I bend to kiss her. "I'll be right outside if you need me."

"Thank you."

Maddie could handle herself, but I'm reluctant to leave her alone when she isn't at full strength. To distract myself, I use the time to check in with Emmett and Ty and see how things are going. Hopefully, it will take my mind off of the asshole at her bedside.

WHEN ROMAN WALKS OUT, I halfway consider calling him back into the room. I'm not in the frame of mind to fight with my father right now, and despite the concern on his face, I have my suspicions about him being here at all. I want to think he's here because he's concerned, and deep down in my heart, I'm actually glad to see him. It's amazing what a near death experience can do to a person.

We haven't spoken since the gala, and as angry as I am, something inside of me still wants his approval. Or maybe it's more love than approval. Maybe that's all I ever really wanted. To know my dad cares about me, that I'm important to him, and that's something I battled with my entire life.

"How are you feeling, sweetheart?" he asks, approaching me cautiously. He sits on the edge of the chair next to me, looking as uncomfortable as I am.

"Better than ever."

He starts chuckling. "You're right, that's a stupid question. I spent the entire time on the airplane trying to decide what I wanted to say."

"And that's the best that you came up with? Asking me how I'm feeling days after I was nearly blown up?"

"Believe it or not, that *was* the best out of all the opening lines I was considering...But I agree, it sucks. So why don't I just say this?"

He pauses, composing himself.

"Maddie, I am so sorry," he blurts out, tears pooling in his eyes. "Before you say anything, you need to know that. I am so sorry for the way I have treated you lately. I only ever wanted what was best for you and now I've caused us to spend the last several years at each other's throats instead of connecting. And it was entirely my fault. I'm sorry, and I will never be able to tell you just how much."

I open my mouth to speak, but I'm too shell-shocked to form words. I didn't expect much from my dad, let alone an apology. Maybe my nearly dying had an effect on him as well.

"Dad, I—"

"No." He holds up his hand, shaking his head. "Please don't say anything. All of this is my fault. If I hadn't sent you to work with Dr. Bauer...Maddie, you should know that the only reason I called and asked my friend to give you the spot in LA was because I wanted to get you away from Bauer. He called me, and he was frantic about getting you out of Las Vegas. He wouldn't tell me why, but he told me it was for your safety. None of it made sense but, I wanted to get you away from him as fast as I could, so I called about the position. It had nothing to do with playing games with you, and I should have come right out and told you that. But when you were home, and you said those things to me..."

I press my lips together, the memory of the fight still fresh in my mind.

"I got defensive because it was true. I've never been a good father to you or your brothers. I pushed you too hard, and I set a terrible example of putting notoriety above all else. I wish I could go back and change things, but I can't. I wish I had something more to say to you besides I'm sorry, but that's all that seems to matter to me right now. I'm sorry about everything. For not believing in you, or supporting your dreams, and for putting you in this position, and for not being the parent you deserved all these years. If you give me another chance, I swear, I will do whatever it takes to make things right with you. All I want is to fix our relationship."

I've never seen my dad cry before, but a few errant tears drip down his cheeks, and I can see how genuine he is about all of this. It's such a welcome change that I nearly burst into tears myself. It doesn't change the past between us, but it's a start and it gives me hope for our future relationship.

"I appreciate that, Dad, but it's going to take some time. Maybe we could start with dinner? I'd like to come see everyone when I get out of here."

He smiles widely. "I would love that. And you know, if you'd like to come back home to recover for a few weeks, your mom and I would love to have you."

"I know you would. But I think I'm going to go back to Las Vegas with Roman as soon as they release me. I promise I'll visit as soon as I'm feeling up to it, though."

"Ah yes. Despite our rocky start, your fiancé seems like a wonderful guy. I'm looking forward to getting to know him. Why don't you bring him with you when you come to visit?"

Fiancé? What? Did Roman tell him we're engaged? Or did I seriously hit my head so hard that I don't remember him proposing? Either way, I don't correct my dad.

"Yes, he is. I think you guys will love him once you get to know him."

My dad stands and kisses my cheek. "I won't keep you much longer. Your mom and brothers will be here tomorrow. I asked them to wait until you and I had time to talk. We'll be by tomorrow if that's okay?"

"Sure, that would be great."

"Good. We'll see you tomorrow then."

"Bye Dad."

After a few minutes, a nurse comes in and checks my vitals, making all kinds of notes in my file before rushing out. She lets me know that they'll be in to take me for more testing in a few minutes. I start to get restless and am about to stand upright as Roman comes back into the room.

"Hey!" he scolds, rushing towards my side. "You're not supposed to get up without someone to support you."

"I just wanted to stand up," I pout, hoping my frown would make him cave.

"No way. Your leg is broken. You're not going anywhere until the doctor says it's okay."

"Does it matter that I'm a doctor and *I* say it's okay?" I raise an eyebrow at him.

He rolls his eyes. "How about a doctor that isn't concussed? Now, climb back into bed like a good little girl and I'll give you your ice cream."

"I'm fine, Roman. It will probably do my body some good to get up and move around. I'm sure we can find some crutches." I prop myself up, not willing to accept staying put just yet.

Roman shakes his head. "The doctor said to stay put. You better keep your cute little ass in this bed until I say otherwise, or there will be serious consequences."

I settle back into the bed, sulking.

"I can already tell you're going to be a terrible patient." He sits on the bed next to me. "Seriously Maddie, I know you're feeling better, but you're not out of the woods. You're always preaching to me that I need to take care of myself, and now it's your turn."

"Thank goodness I have a fiancé to take care of me."

Roman freezes. "I panicked. I told the nurses I was your fiancé so that they would give me information on you, and then one of them called me that in front of your dad," he rambles, anxious. "Don't be mad at me. I was just worried about you and I..."

I lean forward and brush a kiss across his lips. "Would you relax? It's okay. I kind of like being called your fiancé."

Roman breaks out into a smile. "You do?"

I nod. "Someday, anyway. I think we've had plenty of excitement over the last few days."

He climbs in next to me and wraps his arm over my shoulder and the two of us lay there enjoying our ice cream in perfect silence.

"For the record, I like the sound of it, too," Roman says. "And I fully intend on making an honest woman out of you very, very soon."

His words send a giddy rush through me. The last few weeks have been such an emotional rollercoaster and now here we are. There is nothing in the world that would make me happier than the idea of spending the rest of my life with Ty and Roman, my own perfect little family. I hate to think about everything we had to go through to get to this point, but at the end of the day, our love was the only thing that matters.

I can't wait to get home to Ty, but right now, all I want to do is enjoy my time with Roman, and relish in this moment. We may be cooped up in a stuffy hospital room, but right now, I am on top of the world.

CHAPTER FORTY-FIVE

"Okay, easy does it," Roman coaches, holding tightly to my arm and guiding me into the house. It has been a few weeks since the explosion and I was finally cleared to fly home.

Despite weeks of rehab and most of my wounds healing up, Roman insists on treating me like I'm made of glass. At first, I was annoyed, but it's kind of cute and I know there's no arguing with him. He didn't leave my side the entire time we were in Denver, refusing to even get a hotel and staying in that tiny hospital room on an awful pullout couch every single night. I think we're both looking forward to an actual mattress.

Roman fumbles with the keypad and lets us both into the house. I hobble in on my crutches, still not able to put much weight on my leg.

"Let me just get the lights..." Roman flips the switch and, as the foyer lights up, I see a group of people with balloons and posters and flowers and all kinds of things staring back at me. Ty, Peyton, Dante, Joe, and even some people I don't recognize.

"Surprise!" they all yell.

"Welcome home Maddie!" Ty grins ear to ear, bouncing towards me. He wraps his arms around my waist as tightly as he can.

"Not so hard, buddy," Roman cautions, ruffling his hair. "She's still recovering."

"I missed you!" I kiss the top of his head and give him a tight squeeze back. "Did you plan all of this?"

"For weeks." Joe smiles. "It's been all he could talk about. How are you feeling?"

"Not too bad, actually. It's been a long day of traveling, but I'm happy to be home."

"And we're so happy to have you." Peyton gives me a big hug. "You look great! No one would even know you were nearly blown apart a few weeks ago." She winks.

"Okay, not in front of the kid." Roman lets out a sharp laugh.

"Ah, come on Dad." Ty rolls his eyes. "All the kids at school are talking about it. My teacher thinks it's so adorable how you saved Maddie."

"The kid's right. The phones have been ringing off the hook here." Dante laughs. "You guys are celebrities."

My cheeks flush with embarrassment. In preparation for Dr. Bauer's trial, small details of the incident have leaked out. One of the biggest stories the media is focusing on is Roman and how his heroics saved so many lives that day. And what's a good story without a romantic twist?

Somehow they found out that the only reason he was even there was to win me back, and they've eaten it up. Mostly, we've been able to ignore them, but even driving through the security gate was tricky today because of all the reporters and cameras.

"Maddie, you and I haven't met yet." A man comes forward who looks just like Roman but with a tinge more gray in his beard, and hands me a bouquet. "I'm Emmett, Roman's older and better-looking brother."

"You wish!" Roman chuckles, slinging his arm around his brother's neck. "Good to see you, man. I thought you'd have to be back by now."

"Well, sometimes it takes an explosion to remind you how much your family matters to you." He smiles. "Turns out I can do a lot of the day-to-day stuff I need to from just about anywhere."

I feel a small pang of frustration that my own family isn't here, but that's something we're working on. My mom and dad and brothers all spent time with me and Roman while I was in the hospital, and things were definitely getting better. It'll take time, and in the meantime, I have a lot of people who love and support me. "I hope that means you'll be around more often."

"Absolutely. I'm looking forward to getting to know my new sister-in-law."

"Woah, woah," Roman says. "No one is talking about marriage yet. We're taking things slow." He glances over, flashing me a funny grin.

That reminder is as much for him as it is for anyone else. Ever since the idea of marriage was brought up, Roman's been dropping it into normal conversation as often as possible. He's waiting for my cue, but I can tell he wants to make it happen soon. Luckily, we're on the same page with that.

"Well, we live in a city where there are about four hundred places you could do it at any second if you change your mind," Peyton suggests.

"She's right, you can even have Elvis do it in a drive-through!" Joe adds.

"I think the only thing we're thinking of doing right now is getting Maddie laid down so she can rest." Roman guides me toward the stairs.

"Good point. We'll get out of your hair and let you guys settle in," Emmett says. "Who's up for some pizza? I'm buying." The group heads out the front door and we're finally left alone.

"I'm sorry." Roman kisses me softly. "I had no idea they were all going to be here."

"It's okay, that was really sweet. It was good to see everyone."

"Why don't we get you settled in our room, then I'll come clean up down here and bring you something to eat?" he suggests.

"Are you sure you want me back in your room? I'm happy to sleep down the hall while I'm recovering. I'll be up a lot and it's kind of noisy—"

"Not a shot," Roman cuts me off, scooping me into his arms and starting up the stairs. "Let's get you comfortable right where you belong."

Once I'm upstairs, I change into some sweats before climbing on top of the bed. It feels like absolute heaven after the last few weeks of sleeping on the hospital cot and I know Roman will feel the same. It's nice to just have a few minutes to myself, something that's hard to come by lately.

Everything has been a whirlwind, and it's hard to process all of it. So much changed in such a short amount of time, but I feel more settled than I have in a long time. Dr. Bauer is behind bars where he can't hurt anyone anymore, things are moving in the right direction with my family, and most importantly, my life here with Ty and Roman feels like a dream. My position in San Francisco is ready whenever I feel up to it, and until then, I'm happy right where I'm at.

"Okay." Roman comes into the room carrying an array of food, setting it next to me on the bed. "Does anything look good to you? Otherwise I can order takeout."

"This is perfect." I smile, eyeing the grilled cheese he made. "Your chef skills are getting better."

"I wish I could say I made this, but Joe's wife left enough food to feed a small army. This is just a small sample."

"That was really sweet of her. And for them to take Ty for a few days while we get settled again."

Roman nods. "We're lucky to have friends like them. Even if you haven't officially met her yet."

"I'm sure I'll love her. Anyone who puts up with Joe has got to be a saint."

"Very true. Although the same could be said for me."

"You're not so bad." I grin, propping myself up in bed. "Just a little hot tempered."

"More like hot and bothered." He chuckles. "How many weeks did the doctor want you to wait before we could have sex again?" Roman's been patient, but both of us are desperately waiting for an opportunity to properly make up.

"He said three more weeks for rigorous activity…but if you could be gentle…"

Roman's eyes get big and a temptatious smile tugs at his lips. "Oh, I can be gentle. In fact, I don't think I've ever shown you just how gentle I can be. Why don't you lie back and let me take care of you like you deserve?"

"How can I refuse an offer like that?" Roman brushes his lips softly against mine and I set my sandwich to the side. Food could wait. I'm hungry for something else.

SIX WEEKS LATER

Roman holds my hand tightly as we walk out of the courtroom. It's a blazing hot day in Las Vegas, but it doesn't stop the crowds of reporters gathering at the sentencing for Dr. Bauer.

"Mr. Molanari, do you think the sentence was fair?"

"How are you feeling, Madison?"

They shout questions, but Roman leads us through the crowd confidently until we get to the truck. Once we're inside, I feel like I can finally breathe. Moments ago, Bauer was sentenced to life in prison without the possibility of parole. It's the highest-level sentence he could receive, and it feels like a weight has been lifted off of my chest. He really is going away forever and will never be able to hurt anyone ever again.

It was tough to stomach at first. The man had been my mentor. I'd looked up to him and learned nearly everything I knew about being a doctor from him. Little did I know what was happening behind the scenes. It makes me nauseous that I was a part of it, but I know there's no way I could have known what he was really up to, and Roman reminds me of that all the time.

Things between us are better and stronger than ever before. We've settled into a routine and life with Ty that feels so right and so seamless that I hardly remember what my life was like before. My parents have been out to visit a few times, which was really nice. While our relationship will never be quite what I imagined, they're fully embracing being grandparents to Ty. Maybe this is some sort of second chance, but they dote on him and he loves them just as much.

Roman sets his hand on my knee as we drive away, swerving through the mass of people. "You doing okay?"

I nod. "I finally feel a sense of closure with him. He's really not going to hurt us anymore."

"That's right, babe. And I'm pretty confident that he'll get exactly what's coming to him in prison."

"How are you so sure of that?" I eye him suspiciously. Roman's done an incredible job of trying to stay out of everything to do with Dr. Bauer, but I know he has his limits. Bauer went after nearly everyone that Roman loved, all because he was jealous of his success, and if I'm being honest, I can understand where Roman's coming from. Sometimes I crave a little retribution of my own.

Roman chuckles, refusing to look at me. "On the record, just a feeling. But off the record, I have friends in some pretty low places with nothing to lose. Bauer won't last long on the inside."

"Is it wrong that I'm glad to hear that?"

"Not at all." He shakes his head.

"Where are we going?" I notice Roman turned off the highway and we aren't headed toward home anymore.

"I just wanted a second to clear our minds after court this morning. And I've got a surprise for you."

"What kind of surprise?" I ask as he whips into a gravel parking lot.

"Relax. Come on." He helps me out of the truck. I got my cast off a few weeks ago, but I still have some pain after I've been on my feet for a while.

I follow him down a pathway and into the park to where a small bench sits. When we get close, I can see it's a bench put there in memory of Talia.

"This city holds a lot of memories for my family, and most of them are bad. I lost my wife, I almost lost my son, and I almost lost the love of my life," Roman starts. "I used to love Las Vegas, especially when we first moved here, but now it just kind of feels suffocating, you know?" He keeps his eyes on the bench as he speaks. I grab his hand, stroking the back of it, and Roman lets out a heavy breath. He reaches into his pocket, and at first I think he's about to pull out an engagement ring, but then I see a piece of paper. "I've been doing a lot of thinking, and with me taking a back seat with the organization for a while, I think it might be time for a move."

I arch my eyebrows at him in shock. This is the very last thing I expected. "A move?"

Roman nods, handing me a piece of paper. There are three one-way tickets to San Francisco printed on it. One for me, one for him, and one for Ty. "I know they said your position was safe for next year, but I think we should go now."

"You're serious?" I ask, trying to process all of it. "I thought you couldn't leave Vegas. What about your work?"

"Well, San Francisco has some of the biggest ports in the world. I've been limited to land shipping mostly, but with access to ports..." He raises an eyebrow and then chuckles. "Let's just say the move will be good for all of us."

I let out a sharp laugh. It's tough to wrap my mind around, but honestly, he's right. The timing couldn't be better with Ty about to be out of school for the summer. We'd have plenty of time to find a place to live and settle in before he had to go back. I'm also anxious about getting back to work. The break was nice for a bit, but I'm not really one to sit around; all the rest and relaxation has made me stir crazy.

"You're sure about this?"

"I'm positive." He takes my hand. "Like I said, I'm ready to move on from some of these memories and start making new ones with you. And our own family. So what do you say? How about it?"

I can't help but smile. "I think it sounds incredible."

"I was hoping you'd say that." Roman's smile is a mile wide. He sweeps me off of my feet, spinning me around as he kisses me.

A new start sounds incredible, and a new start for all three of us sounds even better.

A fresh start. A place where we can build our lives together, where we can raise our kids. A place that is full of adventure and opportunity and so many new things for us. It feels like we are closing the door on a really rough chapter in both of our lives and moving on together towards something much greater.

There is something kind of fun about the future being unknown. Neither of us have any idea what's to come, but we know we have each other and we have Ty. And we're ready for our next big adventure.

ACKNOWLEDGEMENTS

This book was made possible by gallons of coffee, a husband who shapeshifts into Mr. Mom as soon as my laptop comes out, and a wild imagination that comes with being an only child :)

But seriously—a massive thank you to everyone who made this story possible!

To Jessica, my editor extraordinaire, Alyssa, who fields all my medical questions both real and fictional, and Anna, who jumped right in to help with all things marketing and promotion!

To my friends and family, who have supported me and my dreams since I was a little girl.

And last but not least, my incredible fans. Thank you for the endless support and encouragement. I love bringing my stories to life for you, and hope that you enjoy them as much as I do!

ABOUT THE AUTHOR

Nicole Knight is an award-winning contemporary romance writer from Denver, Colorado. With nearly twenty-million reads online, her books include feisty female leads and brooding bad-boy types that will have you loving and hating them all at once. If you like relatable characters, steamy connections, and a side of comedy with your dark romance, her books are for you!

When she's not writing, she can be found traveling, listening to a true crime podcast, or spending time with her husband, kids, and giant furry friend, Finn

Also by Nicole Knight:
Ties That Bind Us

For the most up to date information and links, scan the QR code!

SCAN ME